FIRE AND MORNING

FRANCIS LEARY

FIRE AND MORNING

G. P. PUTNAM'S SONS NEW YORK

© 1957, BY FRANCIS LEARY

Library of Congress Catalog Card
Number: 57-6730

ACKNOWLEDGMENTS

The author wishes to express gratitude to trustees and staff of the British Museum, for generous grant of facilities; to the authorities of the Public Record Office in London; to Mr. R. P. Howgrave-Graham of Westminster Abbey; to M. Armand Grunzweig of the Royal Archives in Brussels; to M. René Henry-Gréard of the University of Paris, for advice in consulting French sources; and especially to his friend, Miss Isolde Wigram, of the Fellowship of the Whyte Boar, who has been most extremely kind in supplying information concerning English sources.

CONTENTS

But Man is a noble animal, splendid in ashes and pompous in the grave, solemnizing Nativities and Deaths with equal luster, nor omitting ceremonies of bravery in the infamy of his Nature.

—Sir Thomas Browne

HISTORICAL NOTE

*I*N the year 1471 in England, the long agony of the Roses concludes with the triumph of the House of York. The Lancastrian Henry the Sixth is murdered in the Tower; his son Edward is slain at Tewkesbury; Queen Margaret of Anjou is a grief-crazed prisoner. The last male descendant of John of Gaunt, first Duke of Lancaster, is Edmund Beaufort, fourth Duke of Somerset. Beaufort, commander of Lancaster's forlorn hope at Tewkesbury, is beheaded following the battle. The remnant of the Red Rose has scattered far and wide: to Brittany; to France; to Burgundy. Their property confiscated, the Lancastrian emigrés are reduced to beggary.

Edward the Fourth is seated firmly upon England's throne. For the victory of York, tens of thousands of ordinary men have perished; while scarce stands a noble House that does not reckon bitter losses. For sixteen years the land has echoed to the clash of steel and flare of trumpets. Now—arms are stacked; the grave pits closed.

The survivors of the House of York can count themselves lucky. A struggle that has annihilated Lancaster has left York with three elder princes of the blood and numerous noble adherents. York may look forward to long years of tranquillity, generations of kingship. The English are tired of war; willingly, they accept the rule of York's White Rose. The green secluded island returns to everyday life after passionate adventure in royal tragedy.

But apparent tranquillity masks smouldering fires. The King and his brothers, George, Duke of Clarence, and Richard, Duke of Gloucester, are hostages to the past. What they would like to do—to establish York brilliantly and for centuries upon the throne—is denied them by their legacy of violence and treachery.

A curious thing happens. In the warring of the Roses —the mortal feud between two branches of England's Royal House—Lancaster took on a guise of exalted doom, an ancient and prophetic destiny of blood to the last male descendant. York was the practical side, remembering trade and taxes. But in this fierce anguish, pitched forever upon flaming battlements of tragedy, the role of the blood-crowned alternated. A century before, the gleaming Richard the Second, son of the Black Prince, had opposed his anointed arrogance to the craft of Henry, Duke of Lancaster and son of John of Gaunt. Richard had fallen. But the heirs of this Lancastrian monarchy had gone down in ruin.

Now the tragic roles shift once more. In York appear stigmata of doom. What remains of Lancaster, shrivelled into bald meagre Henry Tudor, is full of plots and guile, forswearing gallantry for success. In York, the change does not show immediately. Only as the years pass in the glorious summer of kingship does discontent harden into hatred and hatred lead to blood.

Elizabeth Woodeville, the Queen of the White Rose, is a woman of insatiable ambition and greed. Not for herself— her splendours are not notable—but for the Woodeville family. Already the Queen's lust for power and riches has almost caused the ruin of York. In the crucial year of 1470, the uxorious Edward the Fourth is abandoned by his chief pillar, Richard Neville, Earl of Warwick, and by his own brother Clarence—in protest against the rapacious regiment of Woodevilles who infest the court. Warwick and Clarence come to terms with the exiled Queen Marguerite d'Anjou; Henry the Sixth is briefly restored; and Edward forced to flee England. Only a military miracle enables Edward to regain the crown in 1471.

Elizabeth's enormous family of five brothers and six sisters has the pick of the marriage mart. Dowries, freehold manors, religious livings, and titles of nobility rain upon the Woodeville clan. The Queen acquires a stranglehold on the disposition of any desirable property. Yet this cold, grasping woman is not invulnerable. Her marriage is tainted at its source. A widow with two sons, she has enticed—some persons say "bewitched"—Edward into a secret marriage, a marriage invalid by law and custom, as the King is already betrothed to a lady named Eleanor Talbot, the daughter of the Earl of Shrewsbury.

This frantic urge of Elizabeth for bulwarked secure marriages among her kin arises in part from terrible uneasiness at her own position. All her married life this haughty Elizabeth, who sold her blonde body for the title of Queen, must walk on glass. For her secret is known to several: to Edward's mother, Duchess Cecily of York; to the royal Dukes, Gloucester and Clarence; to the jilted noblewoman, Lady Eleanor; to at least one Reverend Father in God, Robert Stillington, Bishop of Bath and Wells.

Elizabeth Woodeville is not a violent spirit. If she commits murder, she will do so coldly and for profit, as she does everything. She endures the taunts and schemes of Clarence over a period of years before she determines to act. Then the threat to denounce her publicly as an adulteress and the mother of bastards brings Clarence to the Tower. A secret warrant for execution—again the woman acts under colour of law—is obtained from an Edward steeped in drink.

There remains Richard, the King's last brother. Loyal, indispensable Richard. He is too shrewd to risk his own neck defending Clarence. He looks on warily, speaks smoothly to the Queen. No one knows what Richard really thinks.

Suddenly Edward dies. He has been out on the Thames in a little boat, catches a chill and comes home in a fever. The roistering giant—he is six feet four—has wrecked his magnificent body with drink and whoring. It is April ninth, 1483. York's tragic apotheosis begins.

Time accelerates. Edward the Fifth is proclaimed, the fourteen-year-old son of Edward the Fourth and Elizabeth Woodeville. The little King's uncle, Richard of Gloucester, becomes Lord Protector by the testament of Edward the Fourth. At once a mortal rivalry takes shape, the Woodevilles seizing the royal treasure and the royal ships and taking possession of the new King's person—and Richard shoved aside. But not for long. Richard is not a George of Clarence to let himself be mewed up in the Tower and quietly disposed of. He is England's greatest captain, the lightning of Barnet and Tewkesbury.

Richard strikes. Anthony Lord Rivers and Sir Richard Grey, brother and son of Elizabeth Woodeville, are arrested and hustled to Pontefract for execution. Sir Edward Woodeville and Thomas Grey, Marquess of Dorset, another brother and another son of Elizabeth, flee abroad to Henry Tudor in Brittany. Elizabeth herself goes into sanctuary with her five daughters: Elizabeth; Cecily; Anne; Katherine; Bridget.

The tenacious Woodeville woman is driven to earth. Her royal second son, ten-year-old Richard, Duke of York, is cajoled from her and sent to join his brother in the Tower. Richard prepares the coronation of Edward the Fifth, but this is so much flummery; at Crosby Hall, in Bishopsgate, the Protector's London house, the real work goes forward of deposing young Edward and transferring the crown to Richard.

Now comes Stillington's brief but crucial moment on the stage. He suddenly avows the secret of Eleanor Talbot's betrothal to Edward the Fourth, barring that King's subsequent marriage to Queen Elizabeth Woodeville. How came the Bishop of Bath by this knowledge? From Lady Eleanor herself before—convent-caged—she died of a ruined heart. But it is a secret known already to Richard. This "revelation" —so opportune for the Protector's plans—is in the nature of a stage-managed effect, the stage manager being the twenty-nine-year-old Henry Stafford, Duke of Buckingham, and principal coadjutor of Richard Plantagenet. Elizabeth Woodeville's invalid marriage and the bastardy of her children by Edward are solemnly proclaimed. Twenty years are wiped out. Queen Elizabeth becomes plain Lady Grey, aging widow of a long-dead Lancastrian knight.

Richard the Third, only lawful heir of York, ascends the Leopard throne. . . .

The golden summer is gone. York is now an autumnal monarchy, a blood and russet monarchy. Hardly have the gorgeous coronation robes been put away than alarms shake the land. Richard's friend and High Constable, Buckingham, betrays the King. The plot fails; and "that most untrue creature living," the Duke of Buckingham, joins Rivers and Grey in the shadows. John Morton, Bishop of Ely, once a priestly confidant of Queen Margaret of Anjou and now Tudor's master conspirator, weaves a net about the King. Not all Richard's brilliant talent for kingship, not all his falcon reputation in war, not all his careful cultivation of his people's hearts may offset the dread rumours about him. Perjury—incest—murder. His name stirs the night. The most damaging of all: the disappearance of those young Princes locked in the Tower, the King's own blood and given to his guardianship by his dying brother Edward. Morton charges Richard with the murder of the boys.

Like a man besieged, Richard rushes from one critical salient of his monarchy to another. He prepares to resist Tudor's invasion with all the strength at his command. He should be confident, for Tudor is no soldier and Richard is unbeaten on the field of battle. Yet—he cannot sleep; he has an air of fatality.

He is a man cursed, and cursed with the curse of a dead woman—his great enemy, Margaret of Anjou. Hatred burning bright beyond the grave. Her slain Edward; her murdered Harry; her butchered cavaliers; the spoliation of

Edward's tender bride, Anne of Warwick—such was flaming Margaret's score with Richard. She writhed upon the iron rack of her life, and died in darkness. But if ever a soul may return to hunt down vengeance, it is the ravaged soul of Margaret. Inspiring her faithful Morton, driving him with whips of hatred to destroy York's kingship, and haunting with her raven curse the last King, to the outermost reaches of memory. . . .

Happiness fades; but the souls of the tragic shine like heralds in time's dark pavilions. . . .

CAST OF CHARACTERS

RICHARD THE THIRD, King of England

ANNE OF WARWICK, Queen of England

ELIZABETH PLANTAGENET, Princess of York and daughter of
Edward the Fourth

LADY ELIZABETH GREY, widow of Edward the Fourth

CECILY DUCHESS OF YORK, mother of King Richard

FRANCIS VISCOUNT LOVELL, Chamberlain of King Richard

JOHN HOWARD, DUKE OF NORFOLK, Earl Marshal and ranking
peer of England

SIR JAMES TYRELL, Master of the King's Henchmen

WILLIAM CATESBY, Speaker of Parliament and councillor of
Richard

JOHN KENDALL, Principal Secretary to King Richard

LORD THOMAS STANLEY, High Steward to King Richard

LORD STRANGE, son to Stanley

JOHN MORTON, BISHOP OF ELY, Chancellor to Henry Tudor

CHRISTOPHER URSWICKE, Chaplain to Lady Margaret Beaufort

JOHN DIGHTON, a priest

NICHOLAS LATIMER and JOHN WINGFIELD, Tudor squires

JOHN FLORY, soldier and Old Lancastrian

PERRETTE, ward of Flory

IN THE TIME OF THE BOAR ...

OH they say that in the year of grace, 1485, England groaned under the fang of a monstrous Boar. Ferocious and maddened by blood, the Boar harried the land. The centuries cowered at the tale. Unblessed were they that shivered beneath the rule of the White Boar; and lacked an Edward or a Harry to defend them. Oh in the time of the Boar, the ripe killing time when children shrank from the hunched shadows on the wall, grandmothers prohesied an owlish twilight and kirtle maids crept past the north corner of the churchyard. Oh the time of the Boar, in the mirk and midnight hour, when even princes knelt to hooded captains and the stones shrieked. The time of the Boar, when God quickened the heart of a noble grey-eyed Earl over the gate of the Narrow Sea; vows were taken, pledges exchanged, the warrior's earnest of valour—this monster must be hunted, this ravaging Boar taken and slain.

Yet—a moment, sir! The tale is not done; not even well begun. Other times, other deaths—and to each time its own death. A tale of firelight and winking brass; a tale of midnight. What Kingdoms of the Air come invading! Memory, that haunted child, plays laggard tricks. And the greatness that once we knew . . .

But the very stones cry out for vengeance . . . the souls of Edward's little sons . . . the gallant ghost of the Prince of Lancaster . . . Hastings, Anthony Lord Rivers, Richard Grey . . . the lost and lampless Margaret . . .

Who, then? If not the Boar, how may these be avenged? What rest for these poor spirits that must wander? The ghostly fathers have warned of it. And there be evidence aplenty. The bloodprint beside the door; the hand that held the key to the locked dungeon.

Murder will out. . . .

Even if the dagger be that of an anointed king, even if murder comes arrayed in purple, yet must vengeance be acquitted. Kings have been called to account ere this. Fetch him from that obscure and ruined tomb. All crownless, with the gaping wound in his thigh and the smashed and hated skull that took the blows of a score of maces, the broken body that dangled naked behind the Pursuivant of Arms called Blaunche Senglier. Fetch forth the King. . . .

In secret ways, brambled and cruel, the Boar roots. In lost kingdoms of time, where once hearts broke like hearts of glass. In arching vaults, cold, cold, as the body of the sea, where last torches flare and nakedly sounds the grate of iron on stone . . .

Now this was the legend of Richard, third of that name to reign in England. A legend consecrated by the shrewd grey-eyed Earl in whose bowels ambition had nourished. But —this midnight reign had begun long before. The blood-anointed second Richard—the murdered Golden Rose—had cried out for living souls. The third Richard was the last of the Leopard line. Between him and that second Richard stretched a waste of terror. Out of a hundred years of hatred, of treachery, of killing, he had leaped into his kingship. Betrayal had armed him; vengeance was his right hand. He had lost a father and a brother. Aye, more. He had lost childhood, youth, pity. He had lost love.

This dark final monarchy was prepared. To answer for the anguish; to fulfill the prophecies. Truth was a shattered skull, a piece of twisted iron. The King was shaped in the image of his House—the Lyon-gleaming Princes of Plantagenet.

Richard, men clamoured, had burst his tomb! Richard flared again through England. In grave pits everywhere the slain stirred. At Wakefield and Towton; at St. Albans; at

Barnet and Tewkesbury. Death fell on thriving days. It was not the living disturbed the land. It was the dead. The restless dead of a ruined Rose. Richard: the flaring court, torchbright faces and a sound of dancing. Richard: the whispered legend. Richard: the melodious voice, the long lank hair, the haggard cheek and piercing eye. Richard: the shadow greater than the man.

Yet—no pity anywhere?

I liked never the condition of any Prince so much as his, *vowed the Bishop of St. David's.* He doth content the hearts of the people.

And others acclaimed him: his loyal Northerners and Yorkshiremen. The great cities of the White Rose—London, Gloucester, York—offered him grants of money. Benevolences which he refused, saying he would rather possess the hearts of his subjects than their purses.

Greatness—splendour—pride. But if he come by night or by day, if he come in russet or in tissue of gold, if he smile and strew sugar or if he snarl—look to the colour of his knife.

But the Boar was also a Falcon, unfettered. And who might know the fierce and solitary Falcon? A woman that died of him, another woman that loved him—and a soldier that hunted him. These knew the Falcon.

Gentle sir, attend. The first day of spring, 1485. And all this, purple glory and anointed ruin, sorcery and evil fame —now caught in that shining instant. The river, the ancient stones, the immortal light of time and burnished afternoon —and a queen alone, in velvet-curtained silence. A queen who withered. A queen who had lost the power to weep.

Beneath the glinting spring, the river surging on forever past the Norman stones and great drawbridges of the soul . . . Her heart might break. All at once, like a heart of glass. Shiver into bright fragments. But she would never cry . . . she would never cry . . .

Oh Richard! Oh the King!

FIRE AND MORNING

I. THE GOLDEN DOVE

The silver is white, red is the gold;
The robes they lay in fold.
  The bailey beareth the bell away
  The lily, the rose, the rose I lay.

And through the glass window shines the sun.
How should I love, and I so young?

—Fifteenth-century ballad

*H*ER life was tragic and strange. She seemed to have been cast by mistake in a part intended for another. She was, or so she appeared, a fragile brown-eyed girl never meant for intense passion. She should have been the mistress of a country house, surrounded and protected by servants. The bride of a Master of the Staple with gilt-edged revenues abroad and a grand London manor like John Crosby's in Bishopsgate. Or one of those young women who occupied an unconsecrated but dignified post in a large convent, since no proper husband had been found. Any one of such roles would have suited her. She would have known a quiet orderly life, in harmony with her nature.

If there be any Intention in this world, surely a cruel jest was played on this gentle young woman. She became a queen. A being on a vast and pitiless stage, illumined by the glow of pearls and rubies. Aye, more. She became Queen of the White Rose of York; the White Queen of a mortal chess board upon which a ferocious contest of Red against White had flourished for thirty years. . . .

She knew of no good reason why she should suffer. Had she been deeply religious, she might have explained what

3

had happened to her in terms of the Will of God. But this simple outlet was denied her. She had no strong conviction on the subject of religion or anything else—except that people ought to be kind and decent with one another. Kindness, she thought, was more important than glory. But few about her agreed. Such views as she possessed had been given to her, completely fashioned, by the fierce blue-burning spirits in her life; by her great father Richard Neville, Earl of Warwick; by Queen Marguerite d'Anjou; by her husband King Richard.

All her life she had been doing what others had wanted her to do. This sad obedience had concluded in the greatest agony of soul and crucifixion of hope possible to imagine. For it was a gross error to suppose with her, as with others of a like nature, that because this young woman was not made or intended for suffering that therefore she could not really suffer.

She suffered horribly. Her life was a wound that bled continually. Had she been of a poetic mind, she might have exclaimed with that gracious lovely Margaret Stuart who was tormented to death at twenty by a fiend in human form— her husband—*Fie upon this life! Speak to me no more of it! I wish to know it no more!*

But she, Anne Neville, had not even command of the appropriate words for her tragedy. She would be conversing of gowns or the latest in steeple headdresses and all the time her soul would be screaming and shivering in the dark; all the time standing regally, a smile frozen on her lips, her body cased in stiff brocade, and choking inside, gasping for breath, drowning in a sea mist of agony.

On this afternoon in early March, she was tucked upon a cushioned window seat, her ivory fingers teasing a little flame-coloured cat. Though it was bright day without, the heavy green and gold curtains were drawn and all the candles lit in the Queen's presence chamber. The air was close and stale.

Anne was waiting for her cousin Elizabeth Plantagenet, whom King Richard for reasons of his own had forced on her as a maid-in-waiting. Anne and Elizabeth were cousins in the second degree, since Anne's grandfather Richard Neville had been brother to Elizabeth's grandmother Cecily Neville, the Duchess of York. This blood tie did not prevent the two girls from being as different as it is possible for two gently-bred young women to be.

Anne had never hated in her life. Yet with Elizabeth she knew the strongest impulses toward both hate and love she had ever felt. It was not merely that Elizabeth glowed with health and beauty beside the ailing Queen. Nor was it the girl's lively, managing spirit that tried to organize the sick woman, when she preferred to be left alone. It was rather a difference of soul that offered a constant challenge to the Queen and drove her into confessional states of self-pity and despair.

Elizabeth was ambitious; she lusted for the sun. She overwhelmed Anne by her assaults upon life. The Queen, who had never acted but complied, was astounded by this disinherited daughter of a mighty race who insisted on kicking the door that life had crashed in her face. She was moved to envy and revulsion, alternatively, as if appalled by the younger girl's smashing of all rules—yet having secretly to admit that smashing the rules might be the only way to win satisfaction from life.

Elizabeth was coming at the Queen's bidding and when Anne considered the reason and what she must do, she felt a rare thrust of anger. She would have put the girl at once in a cloister had she the power—which she had not.

She possessed only weapons of moral persuasion. She could warn, she could cry out—but she could not do anything. She braced herself, summoning what strength she had. The bright paws of the little cat danced before her. "Toison," she whispered. "Toison d'Or!"

And here came the tap of slippers on the stone flags of old

Westminster, click-clack, click-clack, a military beat for a military heart—the girl that Anne feared and envied and could never understand. A knock upon the door of the presence chamber.

"Is it you, Elizabeth?" Anne said.

Dressed in yellow, she flared through the door. Anne stared. Yellow? This holiday colour? A blazon of defiance flaunted at the sick Queen. Anne was wearing a loose dark robe furred with ermine. Her complexion was dead white, her sunken eyes looked out from heavy shadows. The delicate bones of her face were outlined.

The girl before Anne was radiant with vigour. She was tall, with full breasts tight-laced; her fresh beauty was crowned by lustrous red-gold hair coiffed in black velvet. Her voice proclaimed a decisive mind. "I've come, Anne!"

Their cousinship permitted first-name intimacy between the Queen and her maid-in-waiting. Anne was not a girl to insist on rigid ceremony. She was startled nonetheless at the nineteen-year-old Elizabeth's tone, as if the York Princess knew what Anne intended and were daring the Queen to do her worst.

Rallying, Anne turned to the window seat. "Come and see Toison d'Or," she said.

"Toison d'Or?" Elizabeth laughed. "A brave name for a cat!" She stooped, offering a finger to tiny pink jaws. "Where did you get him, Anne?"

"Richard gave him to me," Anne replied. "Isn't he pretty and quick?"

The girl in yellow smiled. She made a mental note to ask the King for a cat of her own. "Very pretty little beast," she remarked, sitting down with Anne on the crimson velvet. She folded her hands, gave the Queen a direct look. "How do you feel today, Anne?"

The haggard young woman sighed. "I am tired continually," she said. "I have headaches and a fever that comes and goes." She paused, putting a hand to her forehead. Her breathing rasped in the shuttered room.

Elizabeth's face took on a commiserating expression. "What do the physicians say?" she asked.

Anne shrugged. "You know how they are. Never tell you the truth. Rest, rest. Avoid excitement. Keep warm. Eat." She made a grimace. "At least they do not advise me to wear a silken bag of spiders about my neck, as did the astrologer from Knightriders' Street."

Elizabeth was immediately interested. "Who was that, Anne?"

The Queen shook her head. "I don't know the man's name. He came to me one day in a peaked cap and a blue robe with signs of the stars in silver. What did he want? I never knew. He was no man of physick, that was plain. Talked of the Dog and the Hunter, he did—and Scorpio in the House of Mars."

"He wanted money," Elizabeth suggested.

"Perhaps," Anne agreed. "You never know with such people. He told me he feared for me in the month of March. A great darkness, he said, would cover the earth."

Elizabeth held her breath. She seemed to be thinking of that which she would never willingly share with anyone. Her glance wandered over the crimson velvet cushions braided in gold with the Arms of Warwick. She noted six crosslets in the first quarter, a diagonal cross in the second quarter, a griffin in the third quarter, and three chevrons and a checky field in the fourth quarter.

This assemblage of quarterings reflected Anne's descent from the noble families of Beauchamp, Neville, Montagu, Clare and Despenser. It also indicated that in addition to possessing the bluest blood in the kingdom, the wasted girl on the gold and crimson cushion was the richest heiress in England.

Elizabeth looked up at her mistress and cousin. "What

would you like to do today, Anne?" she inquired. "Shall we have the cards?"

Seventy-five years before, the barber of King Charles the Mad, in despair at inventing harmless diversion for his master, had introduced the game of playing cards to the Court of France. In the English deck, it was claimed that the face of the Queen of Wands was that of Queen Elizabeth Woodeville, while the face of the Queen of Swords was that of Queen Marguerite d'Anjou.

Anne coughed and averted her head. Two patches of evil brightness appeared in her cheeks. She struggled for breath. "No," she said. "No cards today."

"Music, then?" Elizabeth pursued. "We may have lutes and old French airs."

Anne said shortly, "No, Elizabeth."

The girl looked curiously at the Queen. Anne withdrew into herself, feeling Elizabeth's keen glance exploring her cousin's hollow cheeks and wasted body. Silence once more. A green and gold silence. When I am gone, Anne was thinking. When I am gone . . .

Elizabeth gazed about the royal presence chamber. Her blue eyes admired the gold-backed brushes and mirrors of the Queen; the carved chest of sandalwood filled with precious tissues; the chaplet of diamonds and rubies that rested upon a black velvet cushion. York's Princess sighed.

Anne knew what that sigh meant. If only I were Queen! If only I possessed this treasure and this glory! I would know how to enjoy my diadem. . . .

Anne leaned forward, her lips parted as she breathed with an effort. "Listen to me, Elizabeth," she said. "I am not like to live."

"Oh, Anne, Anne—of course you will!" the girl exclaimed, her face troubled. "Spring is coming. You will surely be better."

Anne breathed, a ripping sound. She shook her head. "I know, Elizabeth," she said. "You need not cry out. I don't

want a vain show, cousin. Life is not precious to me. For
months I have waited in this room, with the curtains drawn
and the candles lit, evening always about me—waited for
him."

Elizabeth wrinkled her brow. "Waited for whom, Anne?"

"For Death. . . ." the Queen replied.

Elizabeth looked down at her hands, folded in her lap.
"You are young, Anne," she remarked.

The Queen made a gesture of denial. "I am old," she said.
"You will never know how old, Elizabeth. It's not years that
make one old. It's memory, Elizabeth. It's Tewkesbury:
blood . . . and screams that never fade. It's hiding as a
kitchenmaid, being found by Richard, made Duchess and
then Queen . . . diamonds and trumpets for Anne Neville.
Ah, she never longed for such!" Anne paused, said in a
haunted voice, "And paid for, cousin. Paid for. Edward, my
son Edward that had years ten—dead this twelfthmonth.
Died without me, in an April night. He cried out for pity,
they said. . . ."

Anne broke off. She had not meant to go on like that, to
lay bare her soul before this girl. Grief, the vision of death,
and her memories rushing in together had given the Queen
a strange eloquence; had torn words from her heart. She
turned, to stay the tears. That she might still weep! She had
not known she had any tears left.

"You have suffered much," Elizabeth said softly. "A queen
—oh, a queen is not like other mortals."

Anne lifted her head, remembering what she must do.
"You would like to be a queen, would you not, Elizabeth?"

The girl in yellow grew tense. Was this a trap? She looked
blankly at the Queen. "I never thought of it," she replied.

Liar! Anne cried, to herself. Liar, liar! Think of it day
and night, you do. She coughed, tasted blood. She fumbled
in her sleeve for a "handcouvrechef"—or handkerchief, that
useful little square of silk introduced by the resplendent
second Richard. After a moment she said: "I know, Eliza-

beth. I know. It's no use to pretend with me. A woman in my state has no use for pretense."

The girl frowned, drawing together bright brows. She really had a regal air, in her youthful imperiousness. "What do you mean, my cousin?" she said.

Anne gazed at her. The Queen, often so shy and tentative, had on occasion a surprisingly direct glance from those limpid brown eyes. "I mean, Elizabeth, that you think Richard might remarry. And he might marry you."

"Nothing of the kind!" Elizabeth blazed. "How can you say such a thing, Anne? Richard is next of kin to me, after my mother. Marriage between us? It could not be dreamed of!"

Anne had foreseen that Elizabeth would flash out in denial. Impossible for the girl to admit that she wished to marry her uncle. Elizabeth Plantagenet was a marriage prize for both White Rose and Red. The last obscure Lancastrian, Henry Tudor, pursued the Yorkist Princess with urgent offers. As for that uncle, Anne's husband—he was frantic for his throne. If King Richard should marry his niece, that would kill Tudor's hope.

"You are blood royal of the House of York," Anne remarked. "You have ambition."

Elizabeth checked another flaring. She replied coldly, "I have nothing to tell you, Anne."

Anne saw that she was hard. Hard and with an ambition that gleamed. She was waiting for the Queen to die, waiting to step into this gold and green presence chamber as mistress; waiting to inscribe her name in letters of fire among the roll of England's queens.

"Have you considered everything, Elizabeth?" Anne inquired. "Do you realize what such a marriage would mean?"

"Nay, I have no need to consider what can never be," the girl replied. "You will not accept my plain word."

Anne marvelled at the facility of young Elizabeth. She had

the shrewd dissembling quality of Lady Grey, her mother. The Queen coughed, turning and hiding her mouth in the handkerchief. She did not want the girl to see the rain-light of blood.

Elizabeth watched with knowing eyes. "You are ill, Anne," she said. "You are shut in this room, hour after hour. You conjure fancies of the King and me. In your loneliness, you deceive yourself. You need distraction. Music; cards."

"Cards—music—" Anne gasped, straining for breath. "Why not dancing as well? Why not a masque, cousin? You may play the Queen."

Elizabeth flushed. Anne alluded to that boldness of last Twelfth Night when the disinherited Plantagenet Princess had appeared at a Court masque in a gown exactly similar to that worn by the Queen. An over-daring thrust that had caused an explosion of rumour and embarrassed the King.

Anne hesitated. She felt the moment had come. "Answer me one question, Elizabeth," she said.

"What question, Anne?"

Anne gathered herself. Oh, she was not strong enough for this! Her head hurt unbearably and she seemed to go from one coughing fit into another. If only they could have been friends, she and her handsome cousin! "You wish Richard to take off the bar from you," Anne said. "To make you legitimate. But if the bar is taken off you, it is taken off your two brothers as well. Think you Richard will uncrown himself for your sake?"

Elizabeth had become pale and taut. The room was beginning to seem insecure; there were shadows deep and strange beneath the golden flicker of the candles, the small bright flames like souls, the burning moment of life between darkness and darkness. . . .

"Edward, your brother," Anne went on feverishly, "lost the throne because of his bastardy. The bar lay equally on you, as on him. If you are legitimate, then is your brother Edward the Fifth of England!"

"It will be all right with Edward," Elizabeth said. "I am not concerned about him."

Anne stared at Elizabeth, not sure she had heard aright. The girl was not worried about her brother! "What are you saying?" the Queen exclaimed.

"Edward is all right," Elizabeth said, as if repeating something she had heard in a dream.

"I do not understand you, Elizabeth," Anne said.

"Yes, he is safe," the girl whispered, looking fixedly at the small bright flames, at the shadows crouching below. "He and little Richard . . ."

Anne had a sense of horror in the green and gold stillness, in the velvet light. They had slipped out of afternoon; they had entered night. Oh God, what if there were no grace anywhere? What if all life were really a quivering on the edge of terror? No, no! She could not endure that this be so. Decency and kindness. Richard, her husband, was an honourable man. A man of duty. *Loyaultie lie me.* "Loyalty binds me!" That was his watchword of the Belted Knight.

"We have had word from Sir Robert Brackenbury," Elizabeth said, with that absorbed look. "He bade us be of good cheer. My brothers are well. They sent messages of love by Sir Robert."

The Queen swallowed. Her throat was closed and dry. Sir Robert Brackenbury was Lieutenant of the Tower. The brothers of this girl, Edward and Richard, had been locked up in the Tower by King Richard, their uncle. That was in July, 1483—twenty months ago. Since September of that year, or eighteen months previous, no one save Sir Robert Brackenbury had been given access to the boys. Dread rumours circulated. The one certain way of allaying suspicion—to display his nephews publicly—had not been taken by the King.

Why?

"Do you believe in God?" Anne asked. It was clearly a

question that had never occurred to Elizabeth. She went to Mass. She made her confession. But as for God present in this room, listening to every word—why, she could not say. . . .

God may—or may not—have been there. But something else certainly was. Anne froze; she was sure that Elizabeth also was aware of it. The sound of a child crying . . . *do you hear a child crying?* Wordless, Anne gazed at her cousin. Her son, Edward? Elizabeth's brother, Edward? Or another?

Do you hear a child crying?

The Queen put out a blue-veined hand. "Go away," she said. "Go away from this life. Hurry!"

Elizabeth looked at her in wonder. In the stillness, in the green and gold silence—and God—was it God in the sound of a child's voice? God crying in the shuttered room, in the golden terror of the candlelight? "I don't hear anything!" she said. "I don't hear anything!"

Denying God . . .

"Go away," the Queen implored. "Now. Before it is too late. You are young. You will find your heart."

"You are jealous, Anne," Elizabeth said.

Jealous! Anne felt the room narrowing about her, the shadows approaching; once more, she heard the sound of weeping. The Queen closed her eyes. When she opened them, Elizabeth was staring at her from a cowl of light as if she suspected that Anne had become mad. "When I am gone—" the Queen began and broke off. She perceived that the girl was unmoved. She had the icy February feeling, the most terrible feeling of all, that the persons she loved were waiting for her to die.

Anne coughed; the stain on her handkerchief was bright. Her glance wandered over the luxurious hangings, the arras woven of cloth of gold, the crimson velvet with the proud Arms of Warwick. And this was the magnificence of death; these were the gorgeous tissues of the tomb. Oh God, she was afraid! She was only twenty-nine and she was afraid.

"Believe me, cousin, I have never willingly done anything against you," Elizabeth said. "I swear—"

"Don't swear to me!" Anne cried. "Don't take an oath, Elizabeth." She pressed a hand to her throbbing temples. "There have been too many oaths," she murmured.

The girl shone with her secret glory, her cold and gleaming pride. She triumphed over the sick woman. She could even afford to be generous. A little kindness; it did not cost much. Soon, so soon. He whom the Queen awaited, he would come.

"I shall pray for you every day, dear cousin," Elizabeth said.

Anne turned away. She could no longer trust herself to speak. She understood Elizabeth's kindness. She was dying; they both knew it. Only—she did not know the hour, the moment, the instant of the candle's quenching. *When I lay me down to sleep*—but it might be this night or another. It might be next week or next month. But she was dying. And suddenly, with agony, she knew that nothing of what she was really mattered. Love was what mattered. And love had passed her by, with a muffled flourish of drums.

Was it love or ambition that drove Elizabeth? Despite the nearness of blood; despite the silence of the Tower. Oh, Grace of Heaven, who might follow the ruthless and infinite heart?

Not Anne Neville. . . .

❀✢✳✤❀✢✳✤❀✢✳✤❀

IN the bright Kingdom of the Sword he had lived for fifteen years. It was life and death; and home and country. The landscape of his mind stormed with violent memories; with torn comrades, bleeding fields. He might tell over his battles, like a monk telling over his beads. He had glimpsed Death's iron mouth, smelled his stinking breath. Known, too, the fire and the wound.

He was not happy; but then, he was not unhappy either. His usual condition was that of desperate acquiescence. Not that he was in any sense passive or immobilized. He led, in fact, the most active life imaginable, wandering from place to place, serving in free companies, wearing indifferently the Golden Lilies, the Lyon, or the Greyhound.

He had been at Granson in Seventy-six, the rockwalled Swiss Jura; when ironhatted Helvetians had cut to pieces the finest cavalry in Christendom: the Household of Burgundy. He had weathered the terrible final hours at Nancy, in Lorraine, when the Great Duke of the West had been left naked and bloody in a frozen marsh, to be devoured by wolves—as the Great Duke had devoured other men. He remembered blazing sea fights in the Channel, ships under the Norman free-captain Piers de Brezé slashing at the red George of England—while King Lewis and King Edward dwelt in formal peace, collecting the booty of their privateers.

But none of these battles, or all of them together, had left on him the imprint of his first field. For this first death had been a moment of faith; of love, even. Then it had seemed to him truly that war had a meaning; like a radiant loinwringing mistress to whom he might give himself utterly.

But Tewkesbury, in 1471, down in green Gloucester, had been a fearful end to this ardent vision. More than an army had been destroyed. Joy and faith had been slain. Never would a man who had survived Tewkesbury look the same upon life. Never would a man believe, as he and the young horsemen of the Rose had believed, in life's shining May, when the world was green and white and red. . . .

And with the terror and loneliness that crippled his spirit came an overwhelming knowledge that love had failed. Love was not enough, had never been enough. Love of youth; of the Rose; of the bright companions. He was left alone; and he turned to other things.

So between him and the ailing curtained Queen in her

velvet chamber was not such a difference as might appear. He knew her sorrow; for he had known her in the time of May, in the golden weather; his own time. The time that would never come back. . . .

Sometimes, now, sentried in Westminster's dusk, in his black and tawny livery with the great badge of the White Boar upon his breast, the soldier John Flory saw men passing like ghosts in the yellow flicker of torches: other men, liveried like himself in the Company of King Richard the Third. A grin and a halloo, signalled from some shadow that bore the likeness of a man.

He had to remember, then, who he was. A recruit from the North, from Yorkshire—for King Richard ever liked Northern men about him. A recruit named Martin of the Sea, from Holderness. Joining Richard's Company had been easy. The White Boar desperately needed men. A flick of the pen to enroll Martin of the Sea on Sir James Tyrell's muster sheet; drawing livery and weapons from the Tower stores; an assignment to guard duty at Westminster.

Flory would have liked duty at the Tower, for reasons of his own. But one didn't argue duty assignments with Tyrell. Sir James was a knight and Master of the King's Henchmen. He too had fought at Tewkesbury, but on the winning side. He had won his spurs in Lancastrian blood. Flory had measured Tyrell at once: a keen cruel blade to serve unbridled ambition.

But there was something about Tyrell, some hard blue shutter in his gaze that concealed the workings of his spirit. Flory did not know what it was that Tyrell concealed; but he much longed to find out.

And he wondered, too, what Tyrell might say if he knew that which Flory himself kept dark: the oath of fealty to Richard sworn in Westminster's red flare was a lie; the soldier's White Boar badge a mere deceit; his duty assignment a means to help destroy the King.

Things for which Flory felt a little ashamed. . . .

For, as he had often reflected, a spy, no matter how just his cause, was a kind of scavenger, preying on the good faith of those whose bones he plucked. It might well be that in time a spy's soul gave off an odour, from the nature of the spiritual nourishment, just as the black-winged scavengers eating carrion of the streets stank like the plague sickness.

He had known men in his line of work whose souls did seem to smell.

But his masters, those whom he served, were not knightly, valourous champions. They knew better than to hazard themselves on the same battlefield with Richard. They laboured in shadows, backstairs, by means of rumour and treachery. They intended to rot the fabric of Richard's monarchy. And difficult as it was for a man of his ilk to accept, Flory had to admit they were right; their methods got results. And results were all that his masters in France cared about.

"Let me have but thirty true knights, such as served my great sire, lion-bearded Edward, against the pick of France," Richard had vowed, "and I will hazard my body against Tudor and five score traitorous mongrels!"

This kind of chivalrous trumpeting was laughed to scorn. Flory's masters schemed to unhorse King Richard before ever he rode on the field of war. Times had changed since Poitiers; since Sir John Throckmorton and the Combat of the Thirty. Winning a kingdom was a business enterprise, financed by French loans and served by shrewd anonymous agents all over England.

So now, having for the moment laid aside black Boar jacket and fanged Head, Flory was on his way in February dusk through the lanes of outer London, beyond Ludgate, to see a man whom he disliked but whose business skill he respected.

The soldier walked briskly. Chill February cut through his cloak; the chill, he thought, that pierced Westminster and even that stifling chamber where the Queen lay. He had heard her coughing once or twice, an agonized strangling cough that gripped his soul with pity. It was common brut that the King no longer slept with her and that the royal physicians gave her little time.

Hurrying beneath a rusty crow-haunted sky, Flory crossed Fleet Bridge and went along Fleet Street toward Temple Bar. He was in the ward of Faringdon Extra. At Fetter Lane, he turned in and came to a house near St. Dunstan's in the West. The small frame house with white gables and a red-tiled roof was like hundreds of other London dwellings. It was for the moment "safe"; that is, the nightly comings and goings had not as yet aroused the attention of the Watch or the neighbours.

Flory gave the signalling knock: two hard raps, a pause, and then a soft rap. He waited; presently the door swung inward. The room was lit by a rush flare; rushes strewed the floor and there were several sticks of bleak furniture. In imagination, Flory saw upon the bare wall a large portrait of the pinched, avaricious face of that Mighty Highness, Prince Henry Tudor, Earl of Richmond—as he styled himself.

A man in black clerical gown greeted Flory with a nod. "Late," he said dolefully. "I've tarried an hour and more. Time, Master Flory; time is precious. Lady Beaufort awaits my presence."

Lady Beaufort! One day Flory might have the inestimable privilege of kissing the wrinkled hand of that dry, pious lady, the last of her race and so different from the hot-blooded Gascons, her cousins, who had died for Margaret and the Rose. She was now wife to Lord Thomas Stanley, High Steward of King Richard.

"I'm just off duty," Flory replied. "I came directly, Master Urswicke."

Christopher Urswicke, chaplain to Lady Margaret Beaufort, regarded Flory from deep-set eyes in a hollow face. "You must arrange your duty. This comes first!"

Flory shrugged. "Tell that to Tyrell. He arranges the duty."

Urswicke frowned and continued to regard Flory. "Well," he said at last, "have you found out anything?"

The soldier shook his head. "Nothing further. The Queen is the same. The King visits her daily, as does the Princess Elizabeth."

Urswicke stroked his jaw. "This rumour of marriage," he said. "This monstrous incest between the Usurper and Elizabeth. Have you heard anything concerning that?"

Flory hesitated. "Well, you know, Master Urswicke, the King's Company is close-mouthed on such dangerous matters. The King is with Princess Elizabeth much. A lackey in the Palace saw them kissing."

"Saw them kissing!" Urswicke's gaunt face writhed in disgust. "Abominable! Lusting for his own niece, forsooth. God will punish him."

Flory walked to the chill black hearth, the February hearth. "Can't we have a fire, Master Urswicke?"

"Costs money," Urswicke snapped. "Besides, people will notice the smoke from the chimney. They will talk."

"Ah, God's Blood!" Flory said.

"Don't use that language with me, John Flory."

Flory shrugged. After a wintry silence, he said: "After all, the wight didn't say what kind of kissing. A cousinly kiss, mayhap. An uncle and niece kiss."

Urswicke glowered. "You know what kind of kiss it was, Flory. The lecherous crouchback!"

"He's not a crouchback," Flory said mildly. "And I have heard it said the lass loves him."

"Love!" Urswicke exclaimed. "What does a young girl like Elizabeth know of love? She's under a devil's spell. Bewitched! God send we may not be too late to save her."

"Amen to that," said Flory. His face was in shadow and Urswicke could not see the expression.

Master Urswicke walked morosely up and down, his black gown flapping about his shanks. Flory thought how he resembled one of those scrawny scavengers of the streets.

"If only we had specific evidence," Urswicke muttered. "Something on which to hang a case." He swung around to Flory. "There are men close to the Usurper that would take alarm, if they knew. Men like Catesby, Ratcliffe, and Lovell. Do you think they want this girl as their Queen? Ratcliffe murdered her uncle Rivers and her brother Grey at Pontefract. And Lovell is well known to be a friend to Anne, that poor lost creature."

"You are right," Flory agreed.

"Then get me that evidence," Urswicke rasped. "And make haste! Anne may die at any time. The fiend will poison her, if need be, to work his will upon Elizabeth."

"Oh come now, Master Urswicke," Flory protested. "You don't credit that painted rumour, surely. Why, men have seen him come from Anne's chamber with tears on his face."

Urswicke lifted a skinny claw. "All deceit. Nothing but deceit. He cozens where he is most like to kill. Take care, Master Flory. He is like to cozen you."

"I don't think so," Flory said. "I know his record. But there are some things—"

"There is nothing!" Urswicke cried. "Nothing he will stop at. Remember that, Flory."

They were silent in the iron February, the creeping dusk, the last quick boots of Londoners homeward hurrying. . . .

Urswicke looked up. "And this other matter, Flory? This dread murder. What do the men say?"

Flory wrinkled his brow. "You mean the Princes that were mewed up in the Tower? There again, a perilous subject for the guardroom. Officially, the lads are always in the Tower. Alive and well cared for."

"How can men believe such a lie?" Urswicke demanded.

"I didn't say they believed it," Flory replied. "I said that's the official story and it's not openly questioned. If in that case, too, we had evidence—"

"What do you mean evidence?" Urswicke said quickly. "The bodies?"

"I hardly think we shall find the bodies," Flory said. "I mean men who were in the Tower at the time of the deed. Men who might be willing to talk—for a price."

Urswicke nodded; seemed to go into some gaunt reverie. Time, dark time, fell in cold quiet drops like bitter rain.

"You know," Flory resumed, "this must certainly have involved several men. Even supposing it were done by night and by someone who had the authority of the Tower keys. I have heard mention of a priest that was in the Tower and who disappeared afterward."

Urswicke said nothing.

"What if that priest were found?" Flory urged. "I should like to try."

Urswicke gave Flory a piercing look. "No, Flory," he said imperiously. "Don't waste our master's time with such fancies. If there had been such a man, he is certainly dead. The murderer left no talebearers."

"I'm not sure," was all Flory said.

Urswicke walked to him, his hollow face beneath the raven hood close to Flory's. His breath *was* bad, Flory discovered.

"Let the matter rest, Flory. Do our master's bidding. Despatch! We must prevent this diabolic marriage of the Usurper and young Elizabeth."

Flory gave him a quizzical glance. "I'm not sure that Richard intends to wed her, Master Urswicke."

Urswicke gripped Flory's shoulder. "I know; Bishop Morton knows. Crouchback's purpose is to forestall the union of our Henry with York's Elizabeth—the union of the Roses. We have one chance. Evidence, sure and damning before Crouchback can act. Evidence to rouse England and his own captains against this hideous incest. Now go!"

Flory turned. As he went out, it seemed to him that the bright calculating eyes and knifelike smile of Henry Tudor followed him. . . .

❂↷✱↝❂↷✱↝❂↷✱↝❂

KING RICHARD dismounted in Westminster Court, about him the mighty stone surging like grey billows. With the King were Francis Viscount Lovell, Lord Chamberlain, and Master Will Catesby, Speaker of Parliament. The triumvirs of York, come saddle-weary at the fell of day, the horizon veined crimson and purple and from the clock tower the stroke of Evensong.

England's King—the Anointed, the Red Cross Knight. In a murrey cloak lined with satin, on his head a black velvet chaperon with a ruby glowing on the turned-up brim. A slight, richly clad figure, he gazed about the broad forecourt, with stairs leading down to the landing stage and the river. Yeomen of the Crown in jackets of blue and murrey—York's Household colours—patrolled Westminster, while here and there was glimpsed the black jacket of the new special corps raised to act as personal bodyguard of Richard the Third. From the spire of the Clock Tower flaunted the Royal Banner of the lilies and the leopards, the white lilies of France and the golden leopards of Normandy and the Plantagenet Kings.

All this was reassuring. Yet Richard was haunted by the vision of another kind of welcome, of riding one day into the iron greeting, the Dragon Standard of a sly grey-eyed Welshman. Henry Tudor, calling himself Earl of Richmond, pretender to the throne of England.

Richard had often dreamed of such a man. Lean, going bald at twenty-eight, meanly dressed. Not enough money. Not enough courage. Not enough royal right. Not enough of anything, but the best bare ruined Lancaster might do. Henry Tudor, son of Edmund Tudor and the pious vixen Margaret Beaufort. Who was Edmund Tudor? He was the eldest son of a landless ambitious Welshman named Owen Tudor and of Katherine Valois, of the Royal House of France, widow of the Hero-King, Henry the Fifth. Margaret Beaufort was the daughter of John, Duke of Somerset. The Beauforts were royal bastards, descending from Katherine Rovet, the French mistress of John of Gaunt. On one side— Welsh crossed with Valois; on the other side—the bastard blood of a French girl, mistress of an aged and adulterous Prince.

Such was the claim of Henry Tudor to the Crown of St. Edward. . . .

Richard heard the voice of Catesby. Lancastrian shadows and that shrill tribunal, Master Will Catesby—shrewd pleader of the royal cause. "What shall we do with the rogues, Your Highness?"

It was a question of a few rascals flushed by the cliff watch along the Kentish coast. Caught with forbidden flares, they had protested their innocence of traitorous intent. Smugglers, they claimed to be—and threw themselves on the royal mercy. Richard shrugged. "Fine and discharge the knaves, Catesby."

"Tudor spies," Catesby suggested. "Make certain of them, sire. In these times—" He made a gesture as if cupping a candle.

Blood—there had been enough blood. Why were lawyers always the cruellest? It was in just such times that mercy had most meaning. He knew now he must rule by mercy. "Thieves, only thieves," Richard said. "Let them go."

Catesby bowed. He wore a black riding mantle and black hood. He was only just taller than the King. Beside them loomed the tall Lord Lovell, in open helmet and gold-studded brigandine. Grooms came to lead away the horses, taking with loving admiration Richard's cream stallion, noble White Surrey.

From a palace casement flashed a yellow sleeve. Richard glanced up. It was Princess Elizabeth, his niece. He was ever happening on her, in an evening gallery, down a lonely stair. Quick family kisses. Nothing more. They could not blame him for affection to his own blood. Not even Lovell. He was Elizabeth's uncle, her lawful protector. Blood of her blood. They were York-sealed.

Sweet Bess, sweet lass . . .

Behind him, Richard heard a footstep. He whirled, saw no one. He sheathed his dagger. Catesby and Lovell were staring at him. Richard gave them a narrow look. Their gaze was hooded. "Echoes . . ." the King said.

Lord Lovell put out a hand. Dearest friend; heart's companion. Richard and Francis and Anne had all been together in that child's green hunting land of Warwick, so long ago. "You are tired, Richard," he said. "You must rest more. Anne is waiting for you."

Richard walked with chained step toward the Palace portal. At his back he heard Lovell and Catesby whispering. Probably deploring the royal nerves. His anxiety had been growing worse. Night and day phantoms were at his back. He found peace only in dashes over the countryside, hunting the ferrets of Tudor.

Rest . . . rest . . . how little they knew what he needed! How might a king rest when traitors prowled? He was thirty-three and he looked fifty. Old and twisted with cares. He had never forgot the treachery of Buckingham. In October, 1483, Henry Stafford, Duke of Buckingham and High Constable, had led a revolt against his benefactor Richard. A revolt that might well have succeeded had not Buckingham's forces been scattered by a storm and flood at the crucial moment. By that betrayal some glow was lost forever from Richard's monarchy. Now his councillors wished to forbid him the comfort of his niece, Elizabeth Plantagenet. Lovell, especially. Elizabeth was causing talk, the Lord Chamberlain fretted. Hear him but now: "Anne is waiting for you. . . ."

Yes, she was always waiting. He had a little touch of horror at the thought of her, sweating, coughing; ice-cold hands and a body drenched in fever. How came he to be burdened with such a woman? When he remembered her clammy hands and wasted body—that body from which he had long since ceased to obtain even the meagrest delight—the King momentarily forgot how much he owed to Anne Neville. Yet but momentarily—for he was after all a scrupulous man, and it was not too much to say that he would not have become King without the tremendous backing of his position as heir of the great Earl of Warwick.

But a man did not live by castles alone; or even by kingdoms. By St. Edmund! a man was a man and needed the comfort of a healthy, loving woman. A girl like Elizabeth Plantagenet. Yet this was wrong. In his conscience, the King knew he ought not to desire his own niece, the daughter of his brother Edward. He could have put aside Elizabeth, had it been only a question of desire. But she was pursued by his mortal rival Tudor. Not for love's sake. Impossible to imagine stirrings of love in lean Welsh loins. No, for ambition and a crown. The Welshman wanted Elizabeth of York to solidify his own feeble claim.

And for that very reason the King must keep Elizabeth safely pledged to himself. And the Queen? The Queen must die. . . .

Oh, there was no thought of anything so desperate as poison or a silken pillow suddenly pressed over a gasping mouth. Suffocation, they say, is a very quiet death. The King was not a murderer . . . yet in his soul he knew that he was killing Anne Neville, he was killing his wife—but in a way for which he could never be openly blamed. He was killing her simply by wanting her to die.

At first he had struggled against this feeling. Oddly, perhaps, this Richard Plantagenet considered himself a good man. There was a universe of difference in what many people thought about the King and what the King thought about himself. And after all, there was much to be said for the King's view. His government was strong and just. And if some persons had lost their heads, they would have done so under any wise ruler who valued his crown. He kept the peace; he upheld the Church; his judges were incorruptible —oh, the catalogue of his virtues was long! He was more than a good King; he was a competent King. From boyhood he had trained himself as a leader, a doer, a man of foresight, skill and craft.

And yet—men conspired against him. In his own capital of London dread rumours circulated about him. His councillors thought he was not aware of what the people were saying. He was well aware. With all his skill and uprightness, with all his lawful descent from the blood royal of Plantagenet, he faced a formidable threat from a poor creature like Henry Tudor, a man who had not and never would have one tenth of the royal attributes of King Richard the Third.

He had to defend himself. The sick woman who was his wife had become a liability, to him, to his crown, to the monarchy of England. He abstained from her bed. He listened to the gloomy reports of her physicians with barely suppressed eagerness. So necessary had her death become to him that he thought of her as already dead; and when they conversed it was often as if he were speaking to a ghost. He no longer asked himself if Anne Neville deserved death, if she had not burnt her life upon the altar of her husband's ambition. He could not afford such sentiment. In his mind he had even set an approximate date, based on what the medical reports stated. The middle of March, he had remarked to one or two of his advisers.

Richard passed along a dim gallery hung with tapestries given to the Lord Edward by Philip of Ravenstein. Lovely Flemish works, Bruges and Ghent. And high up the light fell dying through the casements, about the limping King, and he thought of Edward his brother. Did Edward know? Was he gazing at Richard? Edward that had been so splendid and life-loving, so careless. . . .

There was always Richard, loyal dependable Richard to repair the mistakes, to safeguard the throne for Edward's boy, young Edward.

The King heard footsteps in the gallery, his brother's favourite walk. Footsteps! Nay, not Edward. Oh, he was proud, cold and proud in Windsor's vault with his golden armour and his sword of victory glittering above his tomb. A stone-wrapped certain sleep . . .

Richard moved alone through the echoing gallery. Time, his soul cried, and light! And it seemed to the King that he must hurry, that the gallery was growing dimmer moment by moment and he could barely see upon the walls the stately lords and ladies of Ravenstein.

Why was there no light for him?

He came to an archway and a staircase winding into shadow. He leaned into the archway. "Halloo!" he called.

An echo drifted down. Richard peered. About him fell the Norman dusk, the granite light of fading day . . . and from above sounded a step. He started. Was that Will Slaughter, jailor of the Tower, standing there? Black Will?

"Will!" Richard cried.

But it was a man the King had never seen. He floated down the dusk with a winking light, a single candle. He wore a black doublet and black hose, a close-fitting black cap. On his breast was the royal cognizance of the White Boar. He was a member of the King's special corps of black jackets.

The King knew most of his guardsmen by sight. The new corps had been enrolled following the betrayals and defections among the traditional Yeomen of the Crown at the time of the Buckingham Rebellion. But this fellow Richard did not recognize. "Who are you?" he demanded.

Lifting the candle, the man pointed to his breast. "I am of your Company of the Boar, sire."

Richard nodded. He felt wary, not quite at ease with this strange soldier of the guard. He plucked his dagger up and down in the gold-embossed sheath. "Your name?" he said. "Your shire?"

"Martin of the Sea," the fellow replied. "From Holderness." His face was lean and swart, with piercing eyes. He held the light before the King.

Richard was not happy with this reply. He liked to be exact. "Martin of the Sea?" he repeated. "What do you mean by that name? What is your deed-poll name, your name in the registers?"

"An orphan, sire," the man said. "I was raised by the good Fathers. I never knew who my folk were."

Richard stared at him for some moments without speaking. The man bore the scrutiny well. His name haunted the King like the rag of an old memory. "Holderness, in Yorkshire," he finally said. "We like Northern men here."

"I was at Ravenspur, sire," the guardsman said.

That was it! The Landing at Ravenspur, fourteen years ago—almost to the day. The great adventure of Edward and Richard to break Warwick's grip on England. "Are you really that Martin of the Sea?" Richard wondered, groping in the past. Martin had been a man of ripe years fourteen winters ago.

"I am, sire," the fellow said.

He had an ageless face, the flesh drawn tight over the bones. A shrewd midnight face. Only the thrusting glance— "You came with a priest named John Westerdale," Richard recalled, "and about four thousand Yorkshire lads to challenge us. Edward my brother took an oath that he had returned to claim his Duchy of York. Then you gave us ale and good refreshing."

"You laid claim to England after," the guardsman remarked.

Richard gave him a pale smile. "First, York; then, England," he commented. "You cautious fellows of the North. You wanted to be able to swear to Warwick that you welcomed my brother as Duke of York only—just in case our heads ended on London Bridge. Wasn't that the way of it?"

"That is right, sire," Martin agreed.

"Well, you did not fail us," Richard said, a little more warmth in his tone. "Despite your caution. How came you here, Martin?"

"Your Highness wrote to York for men," Martin replied.

Richard plucked the dagger up and down. He was still uncertain about this newcomer with no family. He liked to know where his men came from, the essential facts about them. "Can I trust you?" the King mused.

Martin knelt. His lips touched the small jewelled hand. Whom might the King trust, if not the men of his devoted North? Aye, they came to him at his beck. In the trysting time of danger. In the golden-shining spring. . . .

"I shall have work for you, Martin," Richard said.

The guardsman stood up. "I am ready, sire. The North is ready. At your call, ten thousand will leap to arms. We want no hell-spawn of the French for King!"

This was the kind of talk the King savoured. The hearty uncomplicated comradeship of the North. The more secret and inward-looking he became, the more he valued the old English virtues of bluff loyalty, of unquestioning soldiership. The black jackets, his lifeguards, were sworn to defend the King's person to the death.

"Always the French," Richard said, picking up the reference to the hereditary foe. "It's young Charles now, son of Louis the Spider. Louis poisoned his gentle wife Margaret. There is murder and madness both in the House of France. Both grandfathers of this boy were mad. He is ruled by the Regent Anne, his sister. She was instructed in guile and treachery by the Spider himself. Oh, it's from France come all our English woes!"

"Honest Englishmen give no heed to these lying French tongues," Martin vowed.

Richard drew the soldier's black sleeve. His voice taut, he asked: "What are they saying of me, Martin? What are they saying in my old country of the North?" Almost against his will, he had to seek the view of this stranger, this guardsman without a name. If the North remained true, Richard might scorn Tudor. He had to know what they felt in the North.

Martin pronounced vigourously, "They say, sire, that never King was better liked nor deserved to be so than England's Richard the Third!"

The King lifted a gleaming hand. "I knew their love!" he exulted. "They are English. English of the old way."

About them the twilight increased. Richard's hand fell to his breast. For an instant, in the glow of this simple fellow's faith, he had felt the grandeur and joy of his kingship, the consecration to his people—as if, by some starborn magic, he had become the king of his imaginings, that knightly, stainless and oath-keeping monarch who was the old old promise of the English dream. . . .

But he was not that king. That king was lost or had never been. Richard turned; whispers like screams far off came to him from the Bruges Gallery. And footsteps . . . footsteps . . . *this my brother that was lost is found again!*

"They are bringing torches, sire," Martin said.

Richard heard them on the stairway, but these were not the footsteps that rang and echoed in his mind. He recalled suddenly that he had mistook this soldier for Black Will Slaughter. Black Will looking down a twilight stair; a hushed timeless moment, a moment of terrible wonder.

Torches cut red flares in the gloom, the dusk leaped up bright-tongued. The King glanced at Martin, now seeing him plain; lean, weathered, a rugged loyalty. My old country of the North! He was strangely moved and held out his hand. "Welcome to our Company," Richard said. "I'll speak of you to Sir James Tyrell."

Martin clasped the King's hand. "Thanks to Your Highness." He bowed.

King and soldier they hovered in the red evening, beneath the flaring banners of light. Richard turned to the torchbearers, pages and grooms of the chamber in dark blue tunics. "You were long enough coming," he said. "Look you, keep a torch burning in the Bruges Gallery. I want light continually in the Gallery."

He went in to his wife. . . .

***

ANNE caught the bedcurtains, red satin with white tassels. She sat up, staring into the dark. She did not know where she was. She had been dreaming. Warwick again, and spring. She saw once more the immense Hall of her girlhood, the red and white Warwick livery, and high up through an oriel window the haunting glow of May. In the castle courtyard men whistled and she heard bridles ring.

Oh heart, this was the light of childhood! This was the sun of yesterday, the time of fourteen. She had fled through lost bright lanes to the beginning of the world, to that first morning she had heard the lutes. And young Francis Lovell came laughing, goshawk on his wrist. The ponies were saddled, the day was gold and wine—and they were going to the woodland. Did she not remember? Oh, did she not remember?

Morning, the dazzling leaves. What was it had stirred then, had passed winged and shining above their heads as they rode into the day? Toward the secret track and the green hunting land; toward the tender morning. . . .

Francis Lovell, oh how clearly she saw him then! The firm line of the taut jaw, the proud head, the dark intelligent eyes. He was tall for his age and sat his pony like a man. He tossed up his glove, a trick he had, and they sang the old air, "Alas, Departynge."

In the dream of Warwick, where yet she passed beneath the light of fourteen, the morning dimmed. Anne was alone.

She cast alarmed glances. The wood was quiet as a witch, the birds mute. Over the sun crept a shadow. The day hung pale and old. The pony whimpered.

Anne grew afraid.

Why was she alone? Where was Francis? The light was a lanthorn dwindling. The sun was going out, the world putting on a shroud. In the sick fading light, she heard a twig snap. The sound of a step, stealthy, fettered. Terror pierced her soul. What was she doing in this wood?

Escaped . . .

Yes, that was it. They had been escaping, she and Francis Lovell. Giving the slip to duty and to Richard. How they had laughed together! A little crooked prince, trying to play the warrior. Did he think they were deceived? Strange that her father, the Great Earl, defended the boy, was gentle with him. She only wished to get away. Richard must never know; never discover them. He was happy with his hawks. Escaped! Out of time; out of duty. Out of life's gorgeous cruelty.

Why did you laugh? Why did you mock?

Who said that? Why, she had never hurt anyone in all her life. She was guilty only of kindness. She could not help loving Francis. So gallant, so tall and greenmantled. Who would not love him?

In this dream morning, this Warwick yesterday, the wood about Anne became ever more silent. There was a scampering in the brush that died away. Only the footsteps increased. Richard, it flashed upon her. His fettered step; his furtive, overlooking habit. He was coming with deadly anger. Betrayed! Betrayed! Blazing before her in letters of fire.

It was a moment of enchanted dread. Fear had neither shape nor a name, but was a strangling of the heart. Fear was the very texture of the twilight about her. The dream wood was stained by the sound of this soft mortal step.

"Richard!" she cried.

Anne was awake, her outcry splintering the dark. She huddled beside the red satin curtains, feverish, shaking with chill. She forced herself to peer about, to establish her room, to calm her agonized wits that seemed to run shrieking up and down in the black cave of her mind.

And now she knew: she had been prey to some monstrous deception! Some curious and subtle torment devised by the brooding Master of Sleep. This fear in her dream had no echo in her life. In her dream she had been fourteen, it was the golden May of 1470. But Richard—who as a boy had been tutored in arms at Warwick—had been departed for more than two years. The Great Earl was deep in plots against the House of York, and Richard, a lad of eighteen, was with his brother King Edward.

Anne sat rigidly on the edge of the bed. Guilt . . . whence came this guilt? From the anguish of today—not from the sunlight of yesterday. She had failed Richard; failed her husband. She had lost in the most irreparable way of all—as a woman. He could not bear to touch her now. Her wasted body disgusted him.

An echo of bitter laughter . . .

In the time of Warwick when she had been pretty and desirable, the lad's meagre twisted form had aroused pity in her—and a secret repulsion. Was this the guilt that lurked within her? Pitied him in his manhood, his immense strivings for man-achievement, the insistence on the biggest horses, the wearing of heavy exhausting armour. So that even the Great Earl, not the most tender of men, had to moderate the intensity of his pupil. And this feeling of pity and repulsion had increased when at fifteen—in November, 1470—she had been wedded to the handsome straight-limbed Edward of the Red Rose, son of Queen Marguerite d'Anjou.

First love, white love, and again the time of May—so long ago and stained by moonlight. The Prince of the Red Rose had been slain in the spring, a young god dragged to the old bloody altars of his people, a green renewal of life and fortune bought by this murder of innocence. Or so York promised the people. But she, the deprived bride of Lancaster, she could not avow that her heart had perished with the Prince. She had been too young; it was all like a shining vision, this lost marriage of the white, first years. Reality—she had gone on to reality afterward. Richard of the White Rose, Duke of Gloucester and High Constable of England, who had been that striving secret malformed boy of Warwick, now laureled with the carnage of Tewkesbury, claimed Anne for his own.

The proposal had at first seemed grotesque. She did not love him, she would have been glad not to have been aware of him. Only later did she begin to admire his hard undaunted spirit, his greatness that overcame not alone his own suffering but the suffering that he must inflict upon others in his rise. She even began to love him. She little thought that one day his mastery of human weakness would be turned on her.

And now—for she was not a proud person and she could imagine the world going on without Anne Neville—she was reduced to facing the last truth: that her husband was waiting for her to die.

But could this be true? Had she not misunderstood his coldness, his impatience, the feeling that when he was with her he always seemed to long to be elsewhere? A sick woman might exaggerate. Richard had many worries. She could do so little for him. She was not amusing. She could not comfort him with her body. She could not give him another child. What then could she give him? Faith. . . .

She got out of bed, groping toward the door. She must see him now, at once. She had to know how he felt about her. She went into the dim presence chamber where a nightlamp glimmered. Beside the outer door lay a young page upon a pallet. It was part of her strange queenship that almost all her ladies, save Margaret Howard and Elizabeth Plantage-

net, had left with the dimming of her star. Margaret Howard was a good decent woman, the kind Anne liked, but she
had many claims as Duchess of Norfolk and could spend but
little time with the Queen.

The page rose and bowed. "Go to the King," she directed.
"Tell him to come to me."

He was young, in his dark blue livery. Fifteen or sixteen.
In the small hooded light, she could barely make out his
features. She had an odd idea that he looked like Richard.
"Is Your Highness not well?" he inquired politely.

Not well! This boy would be living years after she was
cold, talking sometimes of the strange sick Queen that it
had been his honour to serve, how she would appear suddenly in the middle of the night, wild and pale. Anne
pulled the heavy woollen nightrobe about her limp breasts.
"I am the same," she replied. "Go quickly and fetch the
King!"

He sped off. . . .

By the half-open door, she glimpsed the red glow of torchlight. The King, in his passion for light, had posted torchbearers throughout the Palace. Anne knew that if she went
into the halls and galleries she would find these midnight
statues with their flaring torches at every threatening-place
of shadows. A precaution, Richard said; but she knew why.

She went back into the bedchamber and lit two candles for
Richard. Then she sat down. She tried to collect her
thoughts. She had acted impulsively and now that in a few
moments he would be with her she was not at all sure of
what she wished to say. It surely couldn't be possible that in
this world one might just die without saying anything. She
remembered how someone had told her, a Lancastrian
squire perhaps, that on the scaffold after Tewkesbury Edmund Beaufort had tried to make a speech—and failed. He
had stood in gleaming May with his death in his hands and
found no words; nothing before the overwhelming fact of
eternity.

If Edmund Beaufort, eloquent and courtly fourth Duke of Somerset, had lacked words, how might Anne Neville give voice to the terror and loneliness in her heart?

Presently she heard the King coming, that fettered evening step; the step of her dream. The page had been quick. She sat tensely, watching the arras before the doorway that blew ever so gently with the current of midnight. She glanced at the tall white candles, flickering at opposite sides of the chamber. Would there be enough light?

And suddenly he was standing before her, in a blue velvet robe sewn with golden rosettes. A robe that she had given him on his birthday, this last October second. What would she give him next October? Her life, perhaps? The gift he wanted. The only one. . . .

"Why did you send for me?" Richard demanded. "Do you know what time it is?"

"It is very late," she replied. She gazed about the chamber. "I had a bad dream."

"A bad dream!" He stared at her. "Everyone has bad dreams. You are a child, Anne."

She had feared it would be like this. Yet, she had summoned him. She must go on. "Sit down, Richard," she urged. He was walking up and down, plucking his dagger. He shot her a glance, his reddish brows drawn together. Saying nothing, he sat down upon a low three-legged stool.

"The doctors were here today," she said. "What did they tell you?"

He hesitated. "The usual report," he answered. "You must rest. Avoid draughts. Eat, and drink a little wine every day."

She nodded; she had expected to hear nothing else. After a moment she said: "Do you think I'll die, Richard?" She was asking her husband if there was a place for her in the house of life, asking if that last gift from her to him was to be her death.

"We must all die, Anne," he returned.

She looked at him with direct eyes. He avoided her glance. He was drawing a sapphire ring up and down his left pointing finger. "Will I die tomorrow, perhaps even tonight?" she said.

He frowned. "Did you call me from my work to ask me such a thing? Your fever is not worse, is it? What do you want me to say?"

"I thought you might tell me the truth," she said.

He made an impatient gesture. His face was pale and sunken. His cheek twitched. He was working too hard. Working and worrying—but not about her. "What of this dream?" he asked abruptly.

For an instant the dread of the wood rose up to engulf her. She trembled, felt drops of sweat upon her forehead. She could never tell him. "I was afraid," she said. "In the dream I was afraid. I wanted you, to see you. Is that strange?"

Richard got up, pressed a kiss upon his wife's cold cheek. "My poor Anne," he said. Her hands reached up, caught the blue fold of the robe across his shoulders. She felt the powerful muscle of his strong right shoulder, disciplined to the sword. Her cheek touched his, for a moment she trembled in his embrace. Then she sensed the involuntary tightening of his body, the withdrawal, the rejection. Her arms fell.

He moved away from her. "You must go to bed now," he said.

She was bothering him. She was swept by a kind of bewildered anger as she recalled all that she had done for him. His castles and lordships in the North; his connection with the proudest blood of the kingdom; his very crown; their son Edward, that had been Prince of Wales. And all this was nothing now. She was only a sick, wasted being who could have no more sons and had nothing left to give. He was moving on to other, more desirable possibilities.

"You don't love me, Richard," she said.

The accusation seemed to act as a catalyst on his mood.

He swung about, facing her. "What nonsense is this?" he exclaimed. "Of course I love you. I have many anxieties these days. You know well why. I cannot be with you as I would wish. But I am thinking of you daily. I am doing everything for your recovery. I have even sent for a physician from Italy!"

He was convincing himself, as much as her. Perhaps even trying out the speech he would give to his friends after she was gone. She knew him. But this was unfair. She was blinded by her resentment. He was not a man consciously to lie to himself. No doubt he had convinced himself that he was doing everything. And afterward, when she lay dead, and he was free to marry again, he would say that it had been the greatest grief of his life and that no one knew what he had suffered.

"Yes," she said. "You are doing what you can. But you don't love me, Richard. For some time I have known it."

Anne was silent while the tall candles cast their wavering shadows and the King, her husband, walked softly up and down. It was very late, how late she had no idea. They seemed to have passed into a glimmering suspended moment where the sand of time ran on forever and no door was found.

"What do you want?" he said, dagger-plucking again. "How may I persuade you?"

"Send away Elizabeth," she replied. It was out before she realized. Well, he had asked her. It was the one thing he could do for her.

He looked at her, astounded. "Why?" he wanted to know.

"For my sake. For your sake. For her sake," she said.

He shook his head. "What has she done? Has she offended in some way? She has a bold tongue and a temper to rush at things. She needs a checkrein. But she is loyal and worthy, I swear."

Anne perceived that he was truly perplexed. He was not pretending in order to shield Elizabeth. He had persuaded himself of the lawfulness of his interest in the girl. Especially since Elizabeth was sought by his enemy Tudor. Love flew in where ambition nested. The Queen said desperately, "It will be best for us all."

"I must know why," he insisted. "I can't punish the girl without a cause."

"Elizabeth fancies herself in love," Anne drove on. It was a dangerous thing to say. She had to take the risk. She had to be plain. "And you—you like her very much, Richard."

He turned rigid. "What do you mean, Anne?"

She was frightened again. She had been frightened in her dream—and after Tewkesbury, when *he* had come to fetch her and she was hiding as a kitchenmaid. In the firelight, in the golden rooms of evening . . . and York's young hero, the victor of Tewkesbury, talking, smiling, his net closing about her.

"I don't know," she fumbled. "I see the way Elizabeth looks at you. She has the lust of royalty in her eyes. Oh, yes! I know it, Richard. And you—you let her think—" She broke off as he came near her.

He sat down. His face had a remote stare. His lank brown hair fell over the gold-threaded blue collar of his robe. He was the King and he was the young hero in the firelight. "Mad fancies!" he exclaimed. "I didn't know how ill you were, Anne."

She listened to him, while crying out within that she wasn't mad. She wasn't mad! She had a bad cough; she had fever—but not madness. A kind of black whirling with flashes of crimson and the far-off screams of great birds.

Richard gazed at her. Leaning forward from his velvet cushion with the shrewd, knowing look he assumed when he sat with his judges on the Court of King's Bench in the Great Hall of Westminster. "You are sick," he said. "You must be careful, Anne. Very careful."

She put a hand to her burning face. Her head throbbed. She felt a coughing spell coming on. And through the flicker of the candles, the little glimmer between death and night, she saw him shrouded in the blue robe royaled with golden rosettes—her husband, his mouth stern, his eyes gleaming. And heard his voice, solemn, warning. . . .

"Very careful, my dear," he was saying. "Don't go out. See no one. I have sent for a doctor from Italy."

Had he really said this? Or was this throbbing in her head, this whirling and pain like little knives, was this the beginning of madness? Anne looked at her husband. She was wrenched into a frozen quiet. "You won't send away Elizabeth?" she whispered.

✿✱✦✿✱✦✿✱✦✿

WEDNESDAY, the ninth of March. The Council Chamber of the White Tower. Present: Our Most Dread Lord and Mighty Highness, King Richard the Third; Viscount Francis Lovell, Lord Chamberlain; John Howard, Duke of Norfolk and Earl Marshal; John Russell, Bishop of Lincoln and Lord Chancellor; Lord Thomas Stanley, High Steward; Sir John Touchet, Lord Audley and High Treasurer; John Gunthorpe, Dean of Wells and Lord Privy Seal; Sir Ralph Ashton, Vice-Constable of England; Master Will Catesby, Chancellor of the Exchequer and Speaker of the Commons.

So might run a chronicle entry of the future concerning this Privy Council of Wednesday, the ninth of March. . . .

The White Tower was the original Norman fortress of the King's Tower of London. Built upon a site of Roman fortifications by the Conqueror William, the White Tower had a massive square-looking Keep with turrets at the four corners and walls fifteen feet in thickness. The entrance was by means of an outer staircase on the south side, leading up to the first storey. Since Norman times, the Great Hall of the second storey, divided in half by a curtain wall, had been the scene of councils of state and of such momentous occasions as the abdication of Richard the Second in favour of his cousin Henry, Duke of Lancaster—the initial act that sparked the long ferocious rivalry between the Houses of York and Lancaster.

In the place where Richard, the Golden Rose and legator of York's title to the throne, had been wrongfully deprived of his birthright by Henry of Lancaster, sat another Richard with his loyal cohort of the robe and the sword about him.

The King enjoyed these occasions. His wit and brilliance flowered when he was in the midst of his royalty, wearing a doublet of crimson velvet figured in gold and over that a loose sleeveless cotehardie of white brocade, with a purple chaperon upon his head. Had the fashion not gone out with the Normans, he would have liked to wear his crown as well. For he was a sovereign who judged correctly how much his subjects were impressed by the trappings of kingship, rich brocades and velvets, golden armour, silver spurs, caparisoned horses. Besides, he liked to appear as the visible symbol of gorgeous monarchy, consecrated and set apart from ordinary men.

Yet on this Wednesday in early March, though his costume was as fine as any he had worn, Richard had not his customary alacrity and power of easy exchange with his councillors. Frowning, he listened to the remarks of Audley, the Treasurer, a small grey-haired man in a modest robe.

"An army is beyond our present means," Audley said. "We have renounced the 'benevolences' of King Edward. We have given up the tribute of fifty thousand crowns annually from the French. Our customs levies are down in these unsettled times. We have barely enough for the normal expenses of the government. Already we are paying the highest wage in Europe for soldiers, a shilling a day plus keep for each man. Where shall we get more money, milords?"

It was a report—and a gloomy one—on the state of Richard's finances. He had been generous with his friends, rewarding liberally the loyalty of his captains at the time of

Buckingham's rebellion. He had also played the open-handed lord with his subjects, lifting from them the heavy load of Edward's forced drafts for wars that were never undertaken. In addition, he had long been known for his refusal to take bribes from the French. As a result of all this generosity and honour, the royal treasury was in not much better case than it had been under poor old Henry the Sixth, of murdered memory, he who gave away what he did not lose.

"What about the Jews?" Catesby suggested.

"What Jews?" Audley queried. There had been no Jews in England since the time of Edward the First, two hundred years before. At the behest of English merchants and debt-haunted nobles, Edward had put out the sons of Abraham for their success in supplying this very need now threatening the present King of England.

"Jews in Germany. Jews in Lombardy. What about the Fuggers or the Florentines?" Catesby replied.

Audley shrugged. "We would have to give twelve per cent interest to them," he said.

Richard intervened, leaning forward and looking about the great oak table set in the middle of the hall. "It's not the Jews we need," the King said. "This is an English matter. We shall call upon English hearts and English money. Let the case be fairly presented to our people and the means of defense will be forthcoming."

Catesby raised his brows, but said nothing. Lord Stanley had a detached look. He was lean and wiry and wore a steel corselet beneath his ample robe. Audley nodded. "What does Your Majesty propose?" he asked.

Richard hesitated. It was unthinkable to return to the system of arbitrary taxation, the hated "fifteenth" exacted by his brother Edward. Richard had pledged his royal word against a renewal of direct taxes. Perhaps there was another way.

"We will borrow," he said. "Not from Jews in foreign

lands, but from our English lords and gentlemen and our burghers. We will give a promise to repay a loan to put our forces on a war footing. The business can be managed through the shire lieutenants. What do you think we require, Audley?"

The Treasurer stroked his chin. He was a career man of York and an able administrator. "For ten thousand men, fully equipped, to be maintained for ninety days—" He gazed at the lofty oak beams of the ceiling. "Sixty thousand pounds might do it."

"Sixty thousand pounds!" Norfolk, the representative of the landed nobility, was on his feet raging. "Are ye mad, Sir John? You will never get any such sum from the gentry, either by loans or otherwise."

"Well, perhaps we do not need ten thousand men," Audley said. "That is for the King to say."

Richard flashed a look at Norfolk. He had made him a duke, the first peer of England—and he could unmake him. "Sit down, milord," the King said gently. He turned to Audley. "Ten thousand is what we need, Sir John. At present we have only the royal guard of the Tower and of Westminster."

Lovell broke in: "We can furnish many of these fellows with pikes and bows from the Tower Armoury. But for jackets and boots and coat armour for the men-at-arms, we must purchase here or abroad. You know how the army wasted under Edward."

"But is all this necessary?" Norfolk grumbled. "I have come to these meetings as often as any of you and I have heard only reports of desertions and ruin in Henry Tudor's camp. Are our spies amiss? What reasons compel this array of soldiers?"

"Reasons, Norfolk? I'll give you reasons!" Richard's voice rose. "We need not only a field army; we need to defend our coast from invasion. Five hundred miles of coast! We need to reinforce the royal castles in Wales and the West. The re-

ports of Tydder are true. Only a handful of English turn-
coats have gone over to this Welsh renegade. But the French
are supplying him. The French are emptying the jails and
the galleys; they are levying Norman peasants; they are
preparing a fleet. Are we to sit by and do nothing, while our
ancient foes are readying to invade England?"

"I never said we should do nothing, sire," Norfolk protested. "But I submit that Sir John's estimate is impossible
to obtain."

"Milords, a word—" It was Stanley, "the Auld Eagle," as
he was fond of hearing himself called, after his personal
badge of an Eagle Displayed. "We need not burden the
King with all these forces. Surely the old English way of
forty days' service owed by every liege, from His Grace the
Duke here to a simple knight banneret, to his sovereign
lord the King—that is the proper way!"

"You mean the old livery and maintenance," Lovell commented. "A score of little forces that assemble when and
how it pleases them and take orders or not as it suits each
captain. We wanted a royal army, an army that would give
allegiance to the King first and last."

"Since it seems we cannot raise the money for such an
army," Stanley said smoothly, "at least the older practice
has the advantage, not to be gainsaid, of putting the burden
of maintenance onto the individual knight. He not only
maintains himself, but his men as well—all who fight beneath his banner."

"It has also the advantage for you, Milord Stanley,"
Lovell rejoined, his tone knife-edged, "that it would make
you the strongest captain in the army, since you and your
brother Sir William between you dispose of more men in
livery than any of us. A fact, I am sure, which has not escaped your notice."

"I put my sovereign's welfare above any such consideration," Lord Stanley proclaimed, his scarlet sleeves opening
and revealing a glint of steel underneath.

The councillors listened to Stanley with wonder. Tom Stanley was a strange figure at this council board; yesterday called back, the old corrupt and lavish summer of York. One of those hail-fellow greedy blusterers around the luxurious Edward, always posing as a simple hearty country squire— Norfolk and Hastings were two more of the same—but with an eye as cold and avid as the eye of a magpie and a heart stuffed with sawdust, such was bluff Tom o' Derbyshire. And there wasn't a man at the council table but saw plainly every time Stanley opened his mouth the vision of that other council of Friday, June the thirteenth, in 1483, when the present King had been Lord Protector for Edward the Fifth and the Council faction against Richard had been led by Will Hastings, John Morton and—Tom Stanley.

That Council had ended in an explosion with these ancient walls echoing to shouts of "Traitor!" and armed men rushing in under the Duke of Buckingham, seizing Hastings and Morton, and someone slashing Stanley with a battle-axe and "the Auld Eagle" plunging under the table with blood running about his ears. They had hustled Hastings down to Tower Green and stretched his neck upon a log and hacked off his head with two or three strokes of a dull sword. Buckingham had been all for giving the same treatment to Morton and Stanley, but Richard said no.

The greatest error of his career. . . .

Morton escaped to hatch the Tudor conspiracy and Stanley got off with his lordships intact and that diagonal scar on his bullet crop that shone white and ugly when he turned his head in the sunlight. But everyone wondered when Richard would weary of the bland lies of the man who had fought him once for power and lost—but who was not too old to try again.

None of this was lost on the King. He knew what the councillors were thinking; he knew why Stanley wore steel under his robe. But he knew also that he must pretend to believe in bluff Tom o' Derbyshire. Too strong and too dangerous to keep out of the Council. A day would come when Stanley would be forced to show his hand. Richard intended to make a clean sweep of the Stanley power, but let Stanley first expose himself for the traitor and schemer that he was.

"What can you do for us, milord?" the King asked.

"Three thousand stout fellows in red jackets," Stanley offered. "And my brother Sir William will bring another two thousand with the Silver Buck's Head on their breasts."

"Five thousand men!" Norfolk exulted. "There's your army, milords!"

"Yes?" Francis Lovell remarked dryly. "Whose army?"

Richard turned in the high-backed chair of state, with the carved griffin on either wing. His glance passed over the rigid blackjackets standing with steel-fanged glaives along the wall; and roved upward to the huge vaulted beams from which depended bright banners bearing the arms of Knights of the Garter, from their stallplates at Windsor. The King found his own banner, the white lilies upon azure quartered with the golden leopards upon crimson.

How rash to give up the benevolences! To weaken his military strength at a time when the French grew daily more powerful and arrogant—a nation of fourteen million against England's less than three million!

Lovell was right about the army. He wanted an army of his own, not the old feudal array that nobody commanded. Every King of England had the same problem: money and soldiers. Could he screw the price of an army out of the gentry? Richard's regal gaze went down the council board. "There's money in country strongboxes," he said. "And I mean to have it. I want your approval, milords."

The councillors looked at one another. Norfolk said judicially, "What do you think, Catesby? What will Commons say?"

Each estate of the realm always wanted to pass on the load, always eager to press financial schemes on the other estates. Catesby, as the Speaker of Parliament, represented the knights and townsfolk at the Council. He turned to the Duke. "The Commons will do their share," he said.

Norfolk glanced at Russell, the Chancellor. "What will the Church do, Milord of Lincoln?"

Lincoln's Bishop was a man of middle years, imposing in his purple episcopal robe and purple biretta. He was the type of churchman who went in for public administration. He lifted a slender hand. "A military matter, Your Grace. The Church does not make war."

Norfolk said irritably, "The Bishops gave Henry of Monmouth a fat purse for Agincourt. Why can't they give us something?"

"I agree with Norfolk," Stanley said. "When others of us are undertaking such sacrifices for duty, I think the Church should do its share."

Lovell gave a sardonic smile. The Chancellor had a quizzical look. He was a diplomatic man, disliking broils. "If his Majesty chooses to impose a tax—" he said.

Richard cut in. "No," he said firmly. And to Norfolk: "Don't bother the Church, milord. Churchmen will give as they please. Isn't that right, Your Reverence?"

"Quite right, sire."

But Norfolk had a final word. "We have Stanley's five thousand redjackets; we need but thirty thousand pounds from gentry and Commons. I think we can get that."

Five thousand men, they were giving him! Five thousand to defend the coast, garrison the castles, meet Tydder in pitched battle. If the Welshman had any luck recruiting among the unstable sons of Llewellyn in the approaching campaign, the King's forces would be insufficient. Then would Richard be prisoner of the Stanleys, hopelessly dependent upon Stanley good will for his crown. For an instant he longed to throw the offer in Norfolk's florid face.

But the last Plantagenet was a king. He had to take with good grace what was offered and survive, or go down in royalty. That was the Plantagenet way. Even so—damn Norfolk for a thickheaded grog drinker! He had persuaded the Council; look about the table; only Francis Lovell, aloof, despising . . . He knew!

"If there is nothing further, milords," Richard said, "our Treasurer Audley will send the requests for the loan to our shire lieutenants. Each note issued will bear the King's signed pledge to repay."

Lovell came forward. "I would like to put a matter before the Council," he said.

Richard shot him a questioning glance. The war loan had been the important business of the day. Or so the King had thought. "Very well, Lovell."

"This is personal to Your Majesty," the Chamberlain said. "It concerns Princess Elizabeth. May I have leave to speak?"

Everyone sat up. Richard was conscious of a sudden tension filtering among the councillors. He nodded to Lovell. "You have leave, milord."

"To put it plainly, milords," Lovell said, "a fellow called Henry Tudor, now in France, is offering himself as a bridegroom to the Princess. You know what he is after. An alliance with the Woodeville faction and perhaps others—" He paused and his eye rested briefly on Stanley. "This marriage scheme is deadly," Lovell continued. "But there is one easy way out. The girl can be married off at once to some loyal gentleman."

No one spoke. Silence weighed upon the Council; in the vast waste of the Hall an insect buzzed. Stanley cleared his throat. "Is this Council business?" he queried. "Elizabeth is ward of the King. It is for His Majesty to dispose of her in marriage."

"I am aware that she is a royal ward," Lovell said. "But this girl's marriage is crucial. I have the King's leave to speak. I am not asking for your leave, milord!"

Stanley flushed. The old scar on his bullet crop was ugly. He tapped the table. "I don't like your tone, sir," he said.

"Did I think you would?" Lovell retorted. "It is time to speak out. Henry Tudor is your stepson, Stanley. And your wife, Margaret Beaufort, mother to Tudor, has been equally mother to this marriage plot that threatens us all."

Stanley sprang up. "You touch my loyalty, Lovell!"

Richard must seem to avoid taking sides. Later they would clip the wings of "the Auld Eagle," he and Lovell. He rapped the board. "Save your warring for the French, milords," he said. "Here we are loyal English!"

Lovell turned scornfully from Stanley, who started to sit down. "Marry Elizabeth without delay," he affirmed to the Council. "Or send her to a nunnery."

Richard checked an impulse to flare out. Lovell was his ablest supporter. Yet the Chamberlain encroached dangerously on the royal prerogative by acting as if the Council could dispose of Elizabeth's future. "You can't marry off a girl like that, Lovell!" Richard snapped his fingers. "She must have a dowry, a proper husband, Lady Grey's consent obtained. I have pledged my royal word to it."

"Why must we be tender of Lady Grey?" Lovell rejoined. "She should be glad the girl is getting a husband."

"I am much of the opinion of Lovell," Norfolk said. Audley, Ashton, Catesby nodded. The Bishop preserved a judicious quiet.

The Devil take them! Richard could not brook interference in the family affairs of York. Was Lovell to be more Yorkist than the King? "I cannot pluck husbands from the clouds," he informed the Council.

Only Stanley sided with him. Stanley! Tudor's stepfather and the man who always wanted a double choice in everything. Elizabeth unmarried was that choice. The councillors stared at Richard in his gold and crimson. Stared and glanced away. Was this the young Mars who had blazed the triumph at Tewkesbury?

His sword arm was uplifted. "I shall decide. Elizabeth is —Plantagenet!" He had almost said: Elizabeth is mine! O rare Bess! He needed her now, more than ever. Her eyes, her smile, her cloak of yellow!

The councillors scraped their chairs. Stanley had a thin, knowing smile, as if he and Richard shared a secret. . . .

❀✛✿✛❀✛✿✛❀✛✿✛❀

RICHARD crouched on the high canvas-sheltered seat of the afterdeck, gazing into the rainswept dark. The river was lonely. London was a shadow on a far shore, with a bracelet of twinkling lights in the ducal palaces along the Strand. The King listened to the muffled wash of oars, the long wherry blades dipping deep, sending back the great ripple of the stroke. By the glow of the stern lamp, he saw the ripple glimmering and spreading.

"We shall make the turn soon," Richard said. His voice was dim, blown on the night's rushing wings.

The young man, sitting a little below the King and facing him, said softly, "In another few yards, sire. The boatmen know the river blindfolded. At any hour of the night."

"Our Chatelaine of Baynard doesn't mind the lateness of the hour," Richard remarked. He was silent a moment. "She never sleeps any more, she tells me. She is old." He gave a small laugh. "I can't sleep either, and I have half her years. What do you think? Is sleep fleeing my kingdom? That's something for you to put in your book."

"It will be a big book," the young man said.

"Yet not half big enough!" Richard exclaimed. "Not if you could set down everything. No man ever will. No man ever could. But what a book it would be, eh?"

"The most curious ever wrote," replied the young man.

"I'll tell you another thing, Kendall," Richard said. Books were one of his favourite subjects. This was the beginning of the lustrous Age of Books in England and the King gave his royal patronage to the making of them. "Knighthood is in fashion in books, as it goes out in practice. That's why everyone is reading Thomas Malory, King Arthur, Lancelot, and the Round Table. What do you think of Malory, by the way?"

"He's never seen a battle," Kendall commented.

Richard nodded. "He's pretty and fanciful, and folk like it that way. The knights in Malory have more rules about fighting than all the Courts of Love in Old Provence. I wonder what Malory would have said to Tewkesbury."

"According to Malory's rules, sire, you should challenge Henry Tudor to personal combat," Kendall said. "Remember how Harry of Monmouth challenged the old mad French King before Agincourt?"

"Ah, I'd give half my kingdom to slake my sword in Tudor's guts!" Richard cried, a tone ringing through the dark so that the shadowy boatmen seemed momentarily to pause in their stroke. "But Tudor never fights. He's a cowardly little mongrel. A Welsh mongrel."

"A challenge would put him out of countenance," Kendall said. "Publish his cowardice to the world."

"That is already well known," Richard said. "You know how Tudor ratted on Buckingham in the October Rebellion. Off the Dorset coast he was, with a mighty power of hired Frenchmen—and didn't dare to set foot on English soil."

"Will such a man have courage to try again?" Kendall wondered.

"This is Tudor's last throw," Richard answered. "He has no choice. He must enter the lists. If he does not, he is finished as a pretender. His supporters will put up someone else."

The barge turned sharply against the current, heading for the huge bulk of Baynard Castle. Richard had a moment of doubt. He was troubled by the thought of his mother, Duchess Cecily of York. Why had she summoned him to this evening appointment at her residence? He would have preferred to see her at Westminster. But never since he was a little boy had he contested her wishes.

Now the stroke was cut and the tillerman behind Richard gently manoeuvred the craft into the water gate. They rowed under a great arch into a passage of grim dark water. They bumped and an oarsman leaped out with the mooring line. Richard stood up. It was pitch gloom. He had to grope his way forward and was handed from the boat by the oarsman.

"No light here," Kendall said.

"The Duchess is sparing of her servants," Richard told him. "You have never met her, I think?"

"No, sire. I have not."

"A very proud lady," Richard said. "She should have been a queen."

They stepped along the stone ledge beside the water, passing beneath a raised portcullis to enter the Castle Keep. Richard gazed about. He knew this vaulted gloom as he knew his own boyhood. "There's a stairway opposite," he said.

They found the winding stone stairway, a part of the original Norman fortress, and began to climb. Richard looked anxiously for light. Suddenly he had to halt. It was like the moment when he had glimpsed the guardsman of the Boar standing in the Norman twilight. The moment of Will Slaughter. Only here was nothing but shadow and groping upward and a current of chill grey air that seeped down upon them. He was a man who needed light; he couldn't abide the ancient darkness of a stone stairway, a stairway that might conceal some horror. . . .

Kendall was just behind the King. "What is the matter, sire?" he asked.

"Why didn't we bring torches?" Richard fumed.

They went on and the darkness receded a little and presently they glimpsed a red faint light filtering through an open doorway. They emerged into the first hall of Baynard Castle. Richard spied a groom in York livery of blue and murrey. "Where is your mistress?" he demanded.

The man knew the King at once, despite the plain sombre mantle that Richard wore. "Come with me, sire," he replied.

After another stairway, but this one well lighted by flaring wall cressets in iron sockets, Richard and Kendall reached the presence chamber of the Duchess Cecily. They found her seated in a tall oak chair, the back scroll-tipped like a chair of state. With the Duchess was a young girl in a pale blue gown, a fillet of gold about her fair hair.

Duchess Cecily was a woman of seventy years, her noble face deeply lined, her grey eyes keen. She wore a flowing gown of black velvet lined with white miniver fur, a white widow's barb about her chin, and a close-fitting white hood. Upon her breast hung a large silver cross.

Richard limped forward. He bowed, kissing the hand of the Duchess. He beckoned Kendall. "John Kendall, madame. My Principal Secretary."

Duchess Cecily held out her hand. "Welcome to Baynard, Master Kendall," she said, her voice strong and clear. She turned to the girl. "Don't you know your uncle, Margaret?" she said. "Give him a kiss."

Margaret, the daughter of the attainted Duke of Clarence, advanced hesitantly. She pecked Richard on the cheek and retreated. The King smiled. "What—are you afraid of me, Margaret?"

"She is shy," the Duchess said. "But a good girl. She is a solace to her old grandmother." She turned to the groom. "Stir up the fire, Thomas." The man poked at the yew logs in the great hearth. Blue flames leaped up and bathed the room in a phosphorescent glow. "Now fetch wine and sweet almond cakes," she bade him.

The visitors gave their mantles to the groom. The King wore a hunting doublet of tawny leather flecked with silver studs. He had been out with falcons that day. Kendall was clad in salmon-coloured hose and a loose green jacket with wide sleeves.

"Master Kendall is writing a book about the House of

York," Richard said. "You can tell him much for his work, madame."

The Duchess had a shadowed smile. "There are things cannot be told in books, Richard. Things locked in secret cupboards of the heart. All this story of York begins long before." She paused, seemed to go into some blue-lit reverie of the past. The ghostly light flickered on her old hands.

"Books are important, madame," Richard said. "Master Will Caxton and his press of the Red Pale are but the beginning. Soon we will have a score and more of printers in this realm of England. Everyone will be reading books. We want to set down the marvellous history of York."

Duchess Cecily nodded. "I understand you, Richard. But you make me wonder. So many concerns, so many dreams. When last you were here, you talked of music. You would have the finest singers in Christendom for your Mass. And now, books. You have changed, Richard. Once you spoke only of battles and mighty deeds of war."

Richard smiled. "The world is different now," he said. "There is a new wind. A wind of learning blown out of old ruined Byzantium. A wind of discovery and adventure. We mean to sail with it. Oh, there is much to be done in England!"

He was riding one of his favourite horses. This new wind that he had felt seemed to carry him right out of the blood and terror of the past into splendid kingdoms. Morning, a new world—a city bannered in the sun!

He forgot that the past was a lifelong infection of the soul.

The Duchess leaned forward. "Master Kendall's book must wait," she said. "Tonight I shall talk privily with you, Richard." She glanced at the girl. "Margaret, go with Master Kendall to the outer room. Give him wine and good speech."

It was done before Richard could say yea or nay. Margaret took John Kendall away and he was left with his mother. Silence fell between them, while Thomas passed a silver tray of wine and almond cakes.

The Duchess took a cup of wine. It was malvoisie, or malmsey, the sweet white wine of Madeira. A wine of which the Duke of Clarence had been inordinately fond. She sipped and said: "Why have you been absent, Richard? For months Baynard has not seen you."

To please his mother, Richard took the malvoisie. The King preferred a dry wine. He drank a little. "I have many cares, madame," he replied. "I am sorry indeed. I had not thought it was so long since my last visit."

"What is this I hear of you and that young Elizabeth?" the old lady said abruptly. She bent upon Richard a sharp gaze.

He had tried to ward off such questions by including Kendall in the visit. Now that he was fairly trapped he could only shrug and say, "Rumours, empty rumours. London must have something to buzz about."

"Why do you keep this Elizabeth at Court?" the Duchess persisted. "She is one of those wretched Woodevilles. What does she have to do with us?"

Richard frowned. He didn't like being questioned as if he were a boy. His mother ought to remember that he was a king. "Elizabeth is also of the blood royal of York," he reminded the Duchess. "I keep her near because she is loyal and worthy. And to make sure she is out of reach of Henry Tudor."

Duchess Cecily breathed deeply. She looked at her son and then looked away. "You could marry off the girl," she remarked. "That would settle Henry Tudor."

Richard gave his mother the same answer he had given the Council. "I can't pluck husbands from the clouds. He must be a proper person."

"Are you looking very hard for this proper person, Richard?"

He had a flash of anger. With all his troubles, his mother had to add fresh irritation. She was seventy years old and ought to live quietly, without interfering. "Yes, I am looking," he said shortly.

"Well, I have heard, Richard," she declared in her proud voice, "that there is some understanding between you and Lady Grey, this girl's mother, concerning marriage. I have heard, forsooth, that if Anne dies, you may marry Elizabeth!"

Blood of Christ! where did his mother hear such things? From Francis Lovell? From Catesby? Richard pulled at his gold ring, got it up to the end of his left middle finger, and thrust it back again. "I have no such understanding," he said. It was the first time that he had lied to his mother.

"There's something I wish to tell you, Richard," she said. "Never have I related this before. I am Northern, of the North. My people are hard and shrewd, they reck little of visions. For that, you must go to the Cornish and the Welsh. Ah, but I could not forget this that happened to me one night. Did I wake or sleep? I cannot tell. In the moonlight that whitened my room stood a young man in a wonderful robe. Even you, my son, have never had a robe so fine. A blue robe shining all over with gold—and the head of some noble beast worked in gold. The young man was tall, his hair was long and bright—*but he always hid his face.*"

The Duchess paused, gazing into the fire. Her beautiful hands, like old delicate ivory, lay folded in her lap. She said: "Do you know why the young man hid his face?"

"No," replied Richard, fascinated.

"Well, I will tell you," she went on, her voice suddenly fearful, flickering across the evening's blue gleam. "His face was covered with blood! They had beaten and trampled him."

"How did you know this," Richard inquired, "since you could not see his face?"

"I knew it," the old lady said. "I don't know how I knew,

but I did. He had been horribly hurt about the face and head. I saw him—as plainly as I see you, Richard. The blue robe blazing with gold, the bright hair, the tall proud look of him. And that was—oh, let me say it now! That first time was a few nights before Wakefield, twenty-five years ago. Wakefield, that butchering ground of York! Your father, the Duke, and your brother, gentle Edmund—murdered and despoiled by the Wolf-bitch of Anjou. Wakefield! that was the first . . ."

Where was all this leading? Had his mother really summoned him to Baynard for this? Richard took another cup of wine. She was old, old. Rambling a little.

"And the next time? That was the night Clarence was murdered in the Tower by the doing of this Lady Grey. Oh, it was years afterward that she came to me. It was just after she had come out of sanctuary. She knelt here before me, crying, the tears pouring down her cold bitter face; knelt, I say, and me an old woman with naught but rags of memories left. She begged me to have her sons delivered from the Tower. I let her speak and when she was done, I said to her: 'Do you remember the night of the eighteenth of February, Lady Grey? The night you had my son, the Duke of Clarence, strangled in the Tower? You deliver my son, Lady Grey, and I will deliver yours.' "

The grim old Duchess rose to black majestic height; she stepped down from her chair as from a throne. She walked in the shadows, in the blue glimmer. She walked erectly, staring. The Chatelaine of York. Haunted . . . haunted . . . She heard voices of long ago, she saw the faces of the bright and unforgiving dead.

"The last time the young man came—" she turned to confront Richard—"it was two nights past. He hid his face, as before. But I knew his face was a mask of blood. Cruelly had they used him."

She hovered before the hearth, hands clasped below her silver cross. An old woman. "I've buried six sons," she said.

"Henry—William—John, they died young. Edmund, that was savaged at Wakefield. George of Clarence, that was murdered in the Tower. Edward, that perished in his monarchy's glorious noon."

Oh, now! Now! The sound of York time, the clock, the trickling sand, the lovely unbearable echoes of great bells. Six sons . . .

The Duchess stood before the hearth, hands clasped. The flames leaped up and she was painted in gold and black. Her face, her hands were old ivory. "Lady Grey brings death," she said.

❦➤✱➤❦➤✱➤❦➤✱➤❦

MASTER MARTIN, King's archer of the Boar, bent over a sheet of foolscap on which were traced a number of fine black lines. He studied the drawing. It was a plan, in part, of His Dread Majesty's Tower of London.

Within the archer, apprehension thickened. Apprehension that had been his since he had awakened that morning. Usually the early morning was the best part; the only time when he felt almost happy. It was waking to pure melodious light, the echoes of the Clock Tower bell fading in his mind, and then hearing the voices of birds. Martin never knew where the birds came from. Perhaps the Swan Park, beyond the Gatehouse. Voices of finches and thrushes, of starlings, the cooing of doves. And one ghostly call that was like the wood owl, the *chouette* of Brittany. And just at the first silver-blue light, lying on his pallet in the old West Gate, the first bird cries, oh small, tender, haunting!—the magical moment between night and morning, and then the song taken up and trilled from perch to perch and dawn breaking out.

This was the best part. Afterward the drum began to bluster, sharp commands pierced the tender morning, there was a rattle of steel harness and a sound of grunting and spitting. He was a soldier and this was a soldier's life. Indeed, conditions among King Richard's men were better than for common soldiers elsewhere—save perhaps in the famed Household of Burgundy that had been destroyed by hogs of Swiss peasants. Richard paid his men a shilling a day, plus their keep. In addition, most of them received excellent equipment from the Tower Armoury. It was said, and truly, that these soldiers of the Boar—had there only been more of them—were the equal of any company in Christendom.

Martin got up from the bench, peered from the doorway of the guardroom. Sun flooded the base court. A few guardsmen clanked about. From the Clock Tower whipped the Royal Arms. Richard, by the Grace of God King . . .

Waiting for the drum, the old vaunted raging of the drum.

He was startled by a blow on the back. "Taking your ease, master? A gentleman, by Saint Duncan!"

Martin swung about. He saw the bristling red face of Captain Jamie; no true captain he, but a Scottish raider of great daring that had followed his captor Richard to London, to take the King's colours.

"Off duty, Jamie?"

"Right, mun. Anything to drink?" He shambled into the guardroom. Martin handed him a leather bottle from the shelf. Red Bordeaux wine that was imported in great pipes or casks from the former capital of the English domain in France.

Jamie drank, a long pull. He lowered the bottle, wiping his lips with the back of one hand. He held out a new steel bow. "How d'ye like 'er, eh?"

Martin laid the bow over his knee, testing for balance. "It's a good enough bow, Jamie."

"Good enough, ye sheep wain! Ye'll never find a better. From the Tower Armoury, she be."

Martin stood the bow on end. The polished crosspiece glinted in a splash of sun. He gave the crank a turn. "Nothing like the longbow for reloading," he remarked.

"I'm with ye, laddie!" Jamie exclaimed. "Curse the day

the knights brought back a steel bow from the East!" He shook his head. "And now, hand-gonnes. That's the latest. Devil a mun knows what he'll be shooting next. The long-bow was the bow for Cressy."

He took another swig from the bottle. He gave a satisfied sigh and cocked an eyebrow at Martin. "I hear ye met him, ye friggin' swell!"

Martin said: "Met him?"

"Don't play innocent. Met old Dickon. The King."

Martin shrugged. "Aye, so I did."

"Be that all ye can say?" Jamie was indignant. "Meeting the Boar himself in his own lair, talking to him as if ye be the Lord Chamberlain! What in blazes did he say to the likes of you?"

"He asked me where I came from. I told him and he wanted to know what folk up North were saying about him."

"Did he now?" Jamie was attentive. "Fancy that, now. Old Dickon asking some sod of an archer what folk be sayin' about the King. Seems he's troubled for the opinion of the common sort. What did ye tell him, laddie?"

"I gave him the plain truth," Martin replied. "That the North is always for him."

"Not venturing any risks on other places, eh mun?"

Martin grinned. "He didn't ask me."

Jamie lifted the bottle. "I'll drink on that," he said. Martin watched his gullet work, while the soldier reflected on the sensitivity of the Westminster gossip chain. Already it was all over the guardroom that the Yorkshire recruit had obtained a private conversation with the King. Henceforth he would be a marked man.

He rose and walked toward the door. He was conscious of time passing, of the sun burning in a cloudless blue. God's teeth, if he had only reported sick today!

Jamie rocked gently, peering out of a haze of wine. "A

fine day," he remarked. "Lunnon will turn out. Every wight for Tower Hill!"

Martin said nothing. He was thinking of Sir Roger Clifford, knight and old Lancastrian. Clifford of the martial Northern family that had taken the Red Rose. Cousin to that Lord Clifford who had cut down Richard's brother Edmund at Wakefield, twenty-five years before. That pitiless act was the real reason for Tower Hill today. Not Roger Clifford's small part in the Tudor conspiracy. Richard had sworn blood vengeance on the whole family of Clifford.

"I thought he might get off," Jamie said. "Dickon's let off a fair number that he caught writing to Tudor."

"Not Roger Clifford," Martin said grimly.

Jamie nodded. "They're giving him the full punishment," he said. "Hanging, innards plucked out, beheading and quartering. Jesu, what a business!"

Martin's stomach tightened. The full punishment! What was Roger Clifford feeling at this moment? Lying in irons, shivering and burning. The prison keeper coming with a priest. The doomed man mumbling his confession into the green dungeon light. The last door grating open, the door into the bright horror of the Hill.

"Ye look doolie, laddie," Jamie said.

Martin wiped the sweat. "It's hot in here," he said.

Jamie squinted at him. "Ain't you ever seen an execution?"

"Aye," Martin said. "I have." He stood in a splash of sun at the door and he listened to the stillness of the court outside.

"Sit down and have a drink," Jamie suggested. "This ain't going to help, standing and thinking."

Martin took the bottle. He drank, trying to kill the vision of Clifford. The wine flowed into his knotted stomach. He knew an instant of spreading warmth, the old treacherous lie of well-being. For an instant. Suddenly he put down the bottle. "Do you hear it?" he demanded. "Listen!"

Through the radiant court, through the shining air of spring, came a flare of drums. The quick fierce red beat of drums. . . .

❀↷↯↬❀↷↯↬❀↷↯↬❀

TOWER HILL is not, of course, a real hill. It is a sloping rise that ascends from the northwest corner of the Tower moat to a point about fifteen hundred yards distant from the Lion Gate. At this time of year, in early spring, the Hill is covered with greensward and little white and gold flowers. It had always been a verdant, pleasant spot until the late King Edward had begun the practice of executions on the Hill. This innovation had much annoyed the city governors, for while the Tower itself was a royal fortress and the King might do as he liked within its precincts, the Hill belonged to the City. The burgesses considered Edward's Tower Hill slaughterings as an affront to London's jealously guarded boundaries.

Be that as it may, the bloody custom had taken hold. Executions continued to flourish on Tower Hill and to attract crowds. But these were no ordinary displays. The Hill was reserved for the carrying out of treason's dread law. Pirates and cutpurses might be stretched by the neck at Tyburn or hung in chains for the overflow of three tides at Wapping Old Stairs. To the Hill came gentlemen. Those of proud old lineage convicted of the ultimate crime—betrayal of their King. And as they were special violators, special punishments had been devised for them.

The executioner in black hood and black doublet was a man of skill, adept with rope, knife and axe. For his duties comprised all three. He was also well paid, receiving the usual professional fee of a gold noble, or eight shillings four pence, for each execution.

Master Martin stood in the guard detail about the scaffold. Below him lay London, gleaming like a bride—the red tiles aglitter and the gilded spires flashing. The sparkling morning had brought a horde of bright-cloaked citizens, massed all the way down the slope of the Hill. To the soldier, this crowd appeared like any crowd on holiday. A good deal of laughter and brisk talk eddied about the Hill. Boys chased one another. Women gossiped. Young men caught smiling girls about the waist. Nobody seemed to rue the moment.

Martin glanced at the men about him, the fellows of the guard. Easy, jesting—just another guard duty. Two of them were head-wrestling in the sun. The White Boar badges stood out on black tunics. On the scaffold above, the executioner and his two assistants went about their work. Martin was thinking: will Clifford be senseless when they cut him down? If he is, it won't be so bad. He won't know. Merciful Christ, make him senseless!

Jamie stared down the Hill, shading his eyes. "They're late, the losels. Where is Sheriff Dick Chester? Been here an hour by the clock, we have."

"Ye've not heard, man?" Red Hugh growled. "Chester was stoned in St. Martin's Lane, nigh the Sanctuary. Desperate a pack of 'prentices was to drag Clifford into the church."

"That garlick-seller Chester!" Jamie spat. "He's always in a mess and having to be pulled out. A sheriff! Why, he be no more Sheriff than a bitch mongrel."

"They oughter bring these traitors by river," Tom the Cat remarked.

"Canna draw a man by river," Jamie said. "The law lays down he's to be drawed through the streets o' Lunnon."

Martin considered the punishment meted out to those convicted of treason. First: to be bound to a hurdle and drawn head downward through the mocking streets. Second: to be hanged by the neck until almost dead. Third: to be cut down, stretched living upon a block, belly ripped open and vitals torn out. Fourth: to be headed and quartered and the four quarters of the body put up on various City gates, with the head on London Bridge.

Such was the law.

Martin remembered Will Collingbourn, sometime Sheriff of Dorset and Wilts, and how Collingbourn had written a doggerel which began: "The Cat, the Rat, and Lovell the Dog rule all England under the Hog." And other stuff about how "the crookback boar the way hath found to root our roses from the ground." He had posted this on the great door of Paul's Church. William Catesby, Richard Ratcliffe, and Lovell with his badge of the Wolf Dog, they ruled England under King Richard. And the crookback boar, that was Richard also—though everyone knew the limping King was no crookback. They had caught Collingbourn and torn out his entrails on Tower Hill.

"Here they come," someone said. "Just rounding Tower Street. Came by Cheapside and Gracious Street, they did."

Martin gazed at a glitter of helmets and lance tips. A party of horse escorted the hurdle up the Hill. He glimpsed the grotesque form of Clifford bound head downward to the hurdle, bloodying the path. Sir Roger de Clifford, of the fierce Northern Cliffords. Again Wakefield came back. Wakefield: the first exultant cruelty. The unstanched wound. . . .

"They'll break his rotten skull to bits," a voice said.

"Good job if they do," another voice replied. "Called Tyrell, did they not? The milk-tit knaves. I'll lay Tyrell gave it hot to Sheriff Chester!"

Aye, it was Sir James Tyrell, Knight Banneret and Master of the King's Henchmen, riding a fine roan and flashing a sword at the crowd. Tyrell came to execution day in a gold-studded Seville breastplate. He cleared a passage to the scaffold, the people muttering and falling back. Martin could hear him curse.

"When there's a bit of nasty work to be done, it's Tyrell they call on," Jack o' Ninepence said admiringly. "I heerd tell there ain't anything he won't do."

"Tyrell is Dickon's man!" Red Hugh said.

Dickon . . . Dickon . . . the twisted image of the King

seemed to brood over the scene. Martin's glance was caught by Richard's personal standard, the banner of the Boar, that flared from the Lion Gate. The Dread Lord was in his Tower of London.

Then Martin saw the ravens. They were Tower ravens, beef-fed, big black glossy birds with shiny beaks. There were three of them and they swooped above the moat in black, graceful arcs. He wondered what they were looking for.

The crowd saw the ravens too. The colour of the day, the merry Joseph-coated day, began to alter. It was like the sudden appearance of the crows before Cressy fight, flying very low and fast and bunched together. Fleeing the huge black thunderheads in the sky. That was Cressy, that was what you remembered. Not the plumed knights and the flaunting banners, but all those hundreds of crows coming out of a huge snarling sky. . . .

Martin heard the people go quiet, a distinct unmistakable moment as vivid as shouting and laughter. Talk dampening, fire smothered by ashes; faces freezing into that peculiar absorption of cruelty when a great company is about to banquet on blood. The soldiers as well. They stiffened in ranks as Captain Sir James Tyrell, Knight Banneret, Squire of the Body, rode gleaming past.

Then Martin saw Clifford. Saw him close up and framed in the hushed bright noon. He was a man of fifty years, his greying hair now streaked and matted with blood, deep wounds in his head. About him were the lances of the guard, Sheriffs in scarlet and buff, a Recorder in a violet hood. The party reached the scaffold.

Clifford was groaning and weeping. Martin looked up. In the sky the ravens wheeled.

They were dragging Clifford from the hurdle, dragging him to the steps that led upward to an unspeakable altar. The man staggered, blood pouring down his face, his grey tunic torn and stained. Ah, you would have imagined he could not have known anyone about him. They were dragging him to the altar, like any doomed beast, and the sound of their curses was like the music of prayers rising in the still blue air.

Martin was immediately beside the scaffold steps. And the moment happened, the moment he had feared from the first. For an instant the raw quivering bloody nerve that was Roger de Clifford confronted the soldier of the Boar. Clifford cried out, his hands wavering up—and the pale soldier turned away.

Sheriff Dick Chester, he that sold garlick and rancid butter in Friday Street, gave Clifford a great buffet that knocked him sideways into the scaffold and then they hauled him up the steps—to the black priest with his loving knife.

Martin watched, his soul icy. Terror blew out of a steel-bright glinting noon. He glanced up at the ravens.

Jamie nudged him. "That bugger acted like he knew you, laddie. Queer, ain't it?"

Martin turned, seeing old bloodshot Scottish eyes. "What d'ye mean?" he said. "You're drunk."

"What's got into ye, laddie?" Jamie asked, aggrieved. "Fair scunnered, you look."

"Shut up, damn you!" came through Martin's clenched teeth. Tyrell was approaching. He was a man of medium height, with jowls and mean eyes. A career man of York, he wore the White Boar badge over his heart.

"Keep this bloody swine back!" Tyrell barked to the archers. "Don't let them rush the scaffold." He turned to another officer. Martin recognized Sir Ralph Ashton, Vice-Constable of England, whose duty it was to carry out the execution. "We're ready, Sir Ralph," Tyrell said.

Ashton nodded. He glanced at the scaffold, where the executioner fitted the noose about Clifford's neck. The Vice-Constable drew his sword. The violet-hooded Recorder stepped forward, to read the ferocious death; Latin phrases that dropped like old rotten bones into a shining void. The crowd's gaze hung fascinated on the point of Ashton's sword, glittering in the sun. The recorder broke off; silence spread out, wave on radiant wave over two thousand staring faces. The executioner waited.

"Le Roy le veult!" Ashton cried. His sword whipped down.

Clifford's body kicked upward. A great "ah—ah—ah" like a sigh of orgasm burst from the frozen faces. This was what they had come for; this was their show.

Let him lose his senses, Martin pleaded. Let him not know!

But the executioner knew his trade. Could he not measure with his practised eye the exact moment when the crimson hue of choking was deepening to the purple-black of death; when the cords of the neck seemed like to burst; when the frantic legs fell limp? They wanted their man alive; nay, they wanted him aware!

Clifford was cut down. Now came the butchering. And you might have thought that of those cherry-lipped maids in popingay, of those matrons in gorgeous scarlet, of those holy clerks of God—that among those at any rate would gleam pity, a refusal to watch. No one stirred.

They stripped him naked and laid him upon a long flat block, like a butcher's block. Martin glimpsed the razor-keen blade pointing toward Clifford's belly. With the first incision, always made in the form of a cross, Clifford screamed. And went on screaming, while the executioner carved.

Sweat drenched Martin. Just like the bugger knew you, Master Martin! Treason—this was the way treason ended. He remembered that chance meeting with Clifford, more than a year ago. Clifford was already a marked man, but he had to go on. He was in too deep. Had Clifford remembered? Did he know Martin? Or was it a last cry for pity to a man he had never seen?

He went on screaming. . . .

The executioner drew on a tight black glove. Martin

stared at the gaping wound in Clifford's belly. Purple-dark blood fountained, staining the executioner. And screams that rang and echoed and would never cease. The soldier wanted to vomit. Would they never shut off that shrieking?

Proud regal birds; birds of darkness, cruel and splendid, out of the blazing noon. And rising with the ravens into the gunbarrelled blue waste a crescendo of shrieks and the ecstatic moaning of the crowd: "ah—ah—ah." Then radiant silence, immensity and terror. . . .

The executioner, blood-dappled, stood in the torrent of noon with black-gloved hand upraised and the stench of bowels and blood steaming on the spring.

Le Roy le veult!

❀✧✻✧❀✧✻✧❀✧✻✧❀

THE COMPANY of the Boar was nervous. Men would come off duty and crouch tensely in the guardroom, not speaking. Trivial happenings exploded into bitter disputes. On one occasion the kitchen blackguards upset a tureen of boiling soup. Another time a crossbow crank flew up and struck a fellow in the back. Men would leap about, cursing and threatening. One morning, after the Company had received a tongue-lashing from Sir James Tyrell, two brawny archers came to blows.

A lad fresh from Kent had joined the Boarsmen and the second day a blow-up had occurred. Someone had spoke of gossiping Londoners, so different from North Country folk. The lad from Kent suddenly piped: "There be but one tale abroad now. They say the boys in the Tower have been put to silence. 'Tis whispered the two babes were murdered in their beds and thrust into a deep hole."

The room froze. Everyone stared at Miles. He was a towheaded gangling nineteen. He began to stammer and wave his hands. "You know it's what they say. Whatever you pretend, you know they do."

Red Hugh O'Rourke, from the wilds of Connaught where

many talked only the old Irish, gripped the lad's arm. "It's new yez be, boyo," he said thickly. "Douse that gab."

Miles looked at their angry, shut faces. "I meant no harm," he muttered. "It's only what I hear on the outside."

"Shit," said Red Hugh O'Rourke. "Lunnon shit."

The Kentish lad rubbed his arm. After a moment he asked: "If the King's nephews be alive, why don't the King show them to the people?"

A question that every man had to answer for himself, since Richard gave no help. The great and terrible question that for a twelvemonth had been growing daily more urgent. But the soldiers of the Boar were not paid to ask questions.

Tom the Cat said: "Dickon knows his business, boy. D'ye think he cares to stir up Lunnon by walking those two bastard Princes about the streets? They be snug in the Tower—out of trouble."

They left the matter there.

Yet uneasiness grew. It was an infection in the air. The guards at the outer gates were doubled and those within the Palace had to stand watch around the clock. Westminster came to resemble a besieged fortress. King Richard would appear unexpectedly, sniffing at the defenses.

Martin stood duty at Westminster Stairs with young Miles. The two had struck up a friendship during their hours together. Miles persisted in speculating on the Princes. "How many gates in the Tower, Master Martin?" he said.

Martin felt the cool wind from the river. He replied thoughtfully, "Four armed gates and three bridges to pass. In the Outer Ward, three gates: the Lion Tower; the Middle Tower; the Byward Tower. In the Inner Ward, a fourth portcullis."

"No one could escape that way," Miles remarked. "What about getting over the wall?"

"Sir John Mortimer managed it sixty-odd years ago," Martin said. "The Tower was leanly watched, then. You must get over an inner wall forty feet high, cross a moat one hundred feet wide, and scale the outer barbican wall. Both walls patrolled in Richard's reign. To escape now by the wall would be nigh impossible."

Miles nodded. "How well you know the Tower, Master Martin!" he exclaimed. "Why, you might have laid out the stones."

Martin looked at him, the March wind whipping his jacket. The great badge of the White Boar stood out. "D'ye think so, lad?" he said.

Miles pursed his lips, rocked gently on the balls of his feet. Like everything else about him, his soldier's garb was a curious makeshift. He wore a pie-coloured jacket of lemon and blue with tawny breeches generously patched. Never a less military-seeming figure. "What of the river, Master Martin?"

"A bribe to the keeper of Traitors' Gate. A boat waiting . . ."

"And down the river by night to a ship anchored off Gravesend."

"Then to Burgundy! To Burgundy and Lady Margaret. York's rich magnificent Margaret . . ."

Martin knew better. He had been leading on young Miles of Kent. The lad was a catch-basin of gossip. To find out what people were thinking, that was a passion of the man called Martin.

Miles had a sudden furrowed look. He gazed up the river toward the nineteen arches of London Bridge. Beyond the bridge, in the silvery hood of the river sky, reared the Norman Tower. "Why does Lady Margaret hide the Princes?" he wondered.

"Perhaps she does not have them after all," Martin suggested.

Miles turned sharply. "But you just said—"

Martin smiled. "Guessing," he explained. "Like all of London. The Princes may be still in the Tower."

"No one thinks they be both alive and in the Tower," Miles commented. "Either the Princes are alive and out of the Tower. Or they be dead and resting in the Tower."

This interested the archer. It struck him as a sensible summary of the known evidence. "And what do you think?" he queried.

"I don't know," Miles admitted. "Sometime one way. Sometime another. Small marvel Old Dickon can't sleep. Either way, he's got the blame."

Martin was silent. Dickon had the blame and his foes the benefit. The disappearance of the King's nephews had given an enormous weapon to the King's enemies.

"But what if Dickon didn't do it, master?" the Kentish lad said excitedly. "What if the Princes were slain by another? What if—?" he broke off, gazing about a little wildly.

"Go on, boy," said Master Martin in a strange voice. "What were you about to say?"

Miles laughed and ran his large hands through his bright Saxon hair, a nervous habit of his. "I'm not sure what I mean," he answered. "It sounds crazy. But how could Dickon have done it? He's shrewd, Old Dickon. Someone else, someone free of the Tower . . ."

"A traitor?"

"Why, I think traitors and others," Miles said slowly. "It were not a thing to be managed by one man."

Martin pondered this. The odd boy in the pie-coloured suit was surprising, a little alarming. "A mystery," he sighed. "We might debate from now till breakfast."

Miles shot him a curious glance. "Excuse me, master," he said, "but you don't sound like Yorkshire in your speech. People up North, they say 'nowt' for nothing and 'breccus' for breakfast. Like Scots. I never heard you use such words."

Martin shrugged. He replied with achieved casualness, "Nothing strange about that. I've travelled much. Lost some North-Country flavour, more's the pity."

The lad had a foxy glint. "Master, if I were to guess—I'd hazard you came from Devon."

Martin laughed and turned away. "You're not good at guessing, lad," he said.

They were silent for a time, each absorbed in his own thoughts, in the grey-gold tender light, under the silvery hood of the river-sky, the English spring. . . .

Martin heard the tap of heels, tap-tapping along the broad esplanade of the forecourt. He stared into the white dazzle of morning and saw her, lovely in murrey and gold, walking on the esplanade. Miles nudged him. "Who is that girl passing there?"

Martin looked after her. "She is the Princess of York. She is Elizabeth," he said.

The lad expelled a breath. "The girl Dickon wants! She's number two when the sick Queen dies."

"Damned be that! She'll never—" Martin said, looking after the proud gleaming girl. And as he gazed a shadow came over the day, the glory faltered, grey drops of rain began to fall. And there were flashings in the sky. It happened quickly, without a warning, without a sound. And now the girl was gone.

And somewhere, oh beginning very softly, the echo of lutes long dead and the song rising: *Oh down, oh down in merry Lincoln* . . .

Miles was staring at the sky. "What day is this, Master Martin?"

"It is Wednesday. It is the sixteenth of March."

"I know an astrologer in Knightriders' Street. This day will be a day of darkness. A wondrous darkness over England."

Martin heard a cracking in the west; and a great portcullis seemed to clang. . . .

❂↷✳↶❂↷✳↶❂↷✳↶❂

SHE was very tired. Yet she had a sense of excitement, as

if something marvellous were about to happen. This life of hers, so narrow and curtained, might suddenly be illuminated, light blazing into all the dim corners. She was lying on a low couch, her body supported by cushions, one blue-veined hand across her forehead. The candles were burning in the afternoon, in the hot curtained room, and on the window seat sat Princess Elizabeth with a book.

All the promises they had made to her: her father; her husband; Queen Marguerite d'Anjou. If she would only do as they directed, her life would be glorious. And she had always done it and the promises had always failed. But perhaps the fulfillment had been delayed. Perhaps now, the thing that she felt, the strange excitement—perhaps this was what all her life she had been looking for. She had sent for Richard, but he had not come. This did not displease her. Finally, she understood that they were strangers to one another. Again that old uneasiness and need to escape she had known as a young girl. Her husband stared at her in a way that made her do odd, nervous things. She dropped a vessel, forgot a name, mislaid a death. For the persons in her past—in her various lives—were sometimes mixed up and didn't seem dead at all, and she would speak of her son, worrying whether he were warm and comfortable in his little bed.

Especially if she had fever. Then she might be listening to voices long vanished, but still echoing in the haunted nunnery of her mind. As sickness wasted her body, it gave her in return an enlargement of the spirit. Though at times she was racked like a creature in a barbed trap, she had hours with scarcely any pain during which her exhausted body lay drugged with shock and her mind groped into the sunlit gorgeous days of memory or drifted away from Richard and the bright eternal candles of her doom into some land that she had never known, where she acted a pleasant part among pleasant company. Oh the fountains and the voices! Oh the old soft colours of the twilight!

Anne became aware that the girl opposite, on the window seat, was watching her over the book. Staring in a manner that reminded the Queen of Richard. She had a horrible fear that those about her thought she was mad. Perhaps that was why so few came to see her any more; or why she seemed never to see anyone without Richard or Elizabeth in the room.

"Do you want me to read aloud, Anne?" Elizabeth asked. She was looking very beautiful in a gown of murrey velvet with dagged sleeves and a low-cut bodice. Over her lustrous hair was a coif of tissue of gold with tiny pearls. How splendidly Richard dressed her! Anne knew; but she had ceased to feel envy on that score.

"In the book—the book—" The Queen put a hand to her temple, frowning. They had been reading in it that day. Why could she not recall the name?

"The Book of Launcelot and Elaine," Elizabeth prompted.

"Of course—Launcelot and Elaine." The strange world of Sir Thomas Malory. Heroic quests; monsters; savage combats. A world of terror. Yet fascinating, as long as the dragons were safely inside the covers of a book and not roaming fierily about the world.

"You may read," she said—and sank into a coma of fatigue and aching. Dimly she heard the girl's melodious voice— the purity and the cruelty of the armed heart.

" 'And then Sir Bors was ware where came in an hideous lyon. Sir Bors dressed him to that lyon and anon the lyon bereft him his shield, and with his sword Sir Bors smote off the lyon's head. Right so forthwithal he saw a dragon in the court, a passage perilous and horrible, and there seemed to him letters of gold on the beast's forehead, and Sir Bors thought the letters signified: *King Arthur.* And right so there came a horrible leopard and there they fought long and did great battle together. And at the last the dragon spewed up as it had been a hundred dragons; and all the small dragons slew the old dragon and tore him all to pieces.' "

Anne moaned. She had a fever and a knife was scraping her breast and she didn't want to hear any more about the dragon that vomited small dragons and was torn to pieces by them. Elizabeth looked up, annoyed. She loved Malory.

"Shall I go on?" Elizabeth said.

"Give me a cup of water," Anne whispered. The girl in murrey got up. As she did so, she glanced between the curtains and abruptly drew back. She poured a cup of water from a silver jug.

Anne drank. Richard had been talking of a doctor from Bologna. But she no longer believed in his promises. The man would come too late. Elizabeth hovered beside the sick woman, a queer fright in her face. "What is the matter, Elizabeth?" Anne murmured.

The girl breathed rapidly. Her face was pale. "I looked into the court," she said, with horror.

Anne lifted herself on her cushions, her dull matted hair straggling about her neck. Pain slashed her breast; and she felt her own heartstroke, like the stroke of a broken bell. "What did you see?"

"Darkness . . ." the girl answered.

"Is it night?" Anne wondered. "How long have we been reading?"

"It is the fullness of afternoon," Elizabeth said. "And the sun is gone."

Anne was silent. She recalled the old astrologer who had come to see her. In his blue robe with the silver signs of the stars. He had warned of this; warned of the deadly wonder of the sun. She struggled to rise. Elizabeth took her arm. "Where are you going?"

She looked up at her cousin. "I want to see the darkness," she whispered. She staggered to the window, hair matted with sweat. The room was like an oven. In one corner a brazier glowed. The Queen pulled aside the heavy green and gold curtains.

Westminster was shrouded in gloom, broken here and there by the red ghostly flare of torches. Faintly came the cries of soldiers and a sound of hurrying feet. She wondered where Richard was. Would he come in time? And once again she had the sense of urgency, of excitement. All her life had been shaped toward this moment. A rush of cold dark air came through the casement.

He saw a dragon in the court. . . .

Elizabeth was trembling. "Come away," she said. "Let me shut the casement."

Anne glanced at her. "Are you frightened, Elizabeth?"

The girl swallowed. "Yes," she said.

"The first time—" Anne said, shivering. She began to cough, fighting for breath.

"You'll kill yourself!" Elizabeth cried.

The Queen put a handkerchief to her mouth. When she took it away, it was stained with blood. But she no longer bothered to hide the handkerchief.

"You're bleeding," Elizabeth whispered. "You're bleeding, Anne."

Anne had another coughing fit, her sharp wasted face flushed and wet. Her lungs were like torn rags. Outside, while she gasped for breath, the marvellous darkness muffled the Kingdom of the Sunne.

Elizabeth took the Queen's arm, urged her away from the casement. Anne saw the tall candles flickering, as if a wind passed over their flames. On the wall the shadows played, hunched and tall-hatted. And in a corner the little cat trembled. The room was printed on Anne's mind at that moment; printed for all time. What if she could never escape this room?

But such cruelty could not be true. . . .

And she was once more lying on her cushions and the

green and gold curtains were drawn, shutting out the night. It had all been foretold; it had all been known.

"Fetch me a clean handkerchief," she asked Elizabeth.

She lay back on the silk pillows, thinking of the old astrologer. That strange talk of Scorpio in the House of Mars. Richard, her husband Richard. His sign. She had found that out afterward. And this darkness, this dread smothering of the sun—would *he* understand? She could see Elizabeth pale and tense beside her with a new white handkerchief and the cat quivering in the corner, its fur upended, and the candle flames swaying. A cold dark wind stealing through the casement, as through chinks in a coffin.

"What are you staring at?" she said to Elizabeth.

The girl gazed at the couch, fingers fluttering to her mouth. "There's blood upon the cushions," she said.

Anne looked down. It was true. Dark splashes of blood upon the gold-tawny silk. She lay in her own blood.

"I'll bring fresh cushions," Elizabeth said, glancing about a little frantically.

"No—too late," Anne murmured. "Don't leave me, Elizabeth."

"What do you want me to do?" the girl asked. Thoughts of the doctor from Italy; of all that might have been done and had been left undone. Of this final hour shrinking to a small suffocating room set in the midst of tremendous night.

Anne had difficulty in speaking. How tired she was! If only she did not have to make the effort of breathing, the effort that seemed to tear her breast with each gasp. What had she done to deserve such torment? "Nothing to do," she managed to say.

Elizabeth sat down. "Richard is coming," she told the Queen.

Anne nodded. Richard was on his way to her. The King, her husband. But she had ceased to think of him. For now she knew that she was alone and outside the great hawk of darkness spread black wings over the Kingdom of the

Sunne. She could pity Richard, his ambition, his pride, his ruined glory. But no more would she turn to him. The broken joy; the lost wonder . . . Again the knife slashing. . . .

"I'll read to you," Elizabeth said nervously. Anne made no reply. The girl in murrey picked up the book. " 'And then Sir Bors saw four gentlewomen come by, plainly arrayed. And he entered a chamber where there was great light, as it were a summer light. And the women kneeled down before an altar of silver with four pillars. And as Sir Bors looked above his head, he saw a sword like silver, hovering over him, and the brightness thereof smote his eyes and was like to blind him. And then he heard a voice saying: *Go hence, Sir Bors, for as yet thou art not worthy to be in this place!* ' "

The girl paused. She glanced at the rigid Queen upon the blood-stained cushions. She leaned forward. "Anne . . ." she said. The room was flooded with silence; the candles fluttered; and through the stifling hush blew a midnight chill.

"Anne!" she cried.

Suddenly Elizabeth was frozen. The silence, the accusing silence, was worse than anything Anne might have said. She forced herself to rise, to go to her cousin. Elizabeth stooped over the couch. The Queen's eyes stared at the girl with the anguish and pity of the dead. The mouth sagged open and a thin froth of blood was on the lips.

Elizabeth was bending over the dead woman, shaking her, whispering to her; that shrunken body, the beautiful, lost and terrible dream that had been Anne of Warwick.

The girl straightened. In the stillness, in the dragon cave of darkness, she heard a step. A step, light and broken—a limping step. Elizabeth turned, her hands uplifted. With terror, she perceived blood upon her hands. She thrust them behind her.

Richard stood in the doorway. . . .

II. THE ROSE

*. . if the daughters of Elizabeth Grey, late calling
herself Queen of England, to wit, Elizabeth, Cecily,
Anne, Katherine, and Bridget, will come to me out of
the Sanctuary of Westminster, and be guided, ruled
and demeaned after me, then I shall see they be in
surety of their lives and suffer no manner of hurt, by
ravishing or defiling contrary to their wills, nor any
of them imprison in the Tower of London or other
prison; but I shall put them into honest places of good
fame and them honestly and courteously shall be
treated, and have all things necessary for their exhi-
bitions and findings as my kinswomen. . . .*

—Oath of King Richard

*A*T the sign of the White Lion in Southwark, the fire
blazed merrily, the oak benches were filled with men wearing the badge of the White Boar, and two serving maids
scurried back and forth with foaming ale. On the spit a car-
cass of boar slowly turned, dripping fat. The dark oak-pan-
elled walls were hung with faded banners from the French
wars: the standards of the Free Companies that once had
ruled whole provinces of France.

Master Martin and Miles of Kent sat a little apart, cutting
strips of glistening porc and drinking from half-gallon
leathern pottles. There was a noise in the broad low-ceil-
inged room as of feeding time at His Majesty's Lyon Tower:
a steady champing and grunting and gulping. It was possible
to talk undisturbed amid the mighty music of the table; no

one heeded the two guardsmen or considered their words anything more than the usual brut.

Miles leaned forward, his face shining with grease. "I've been watching you, master," he said in a strained voice. "I think I know what you are."

Martin wiped his knife carefully on the side of his trencher. He said nothing.

"What if I ask: do you have friends in France?" the lad inquired. "What then, Master Martin? What then?"

Martin shrugged. "Ask it. Just another of your fancies."

The lad smiled. Capless, his straw-coloured thatch stuck up like a wren's nest. "You can trust me, master," he said. "Listen, I'll tell you a tale. D'ye recall the rising of Tom of Falconbridge in Kent, fourteen years ago?" Martin nodded. "My father and my brother Rafe were out in that fray," Miles went on. "Came down to Lunnon, they did, with ten thousand men of Kent to take the city for Tom the Bastard, stout Falconbridge. Three days they hammered at the gates, while the two Woodevilles, Lord Rivers and Lord Dorset, were shut up in the Tower and frightened to stir. By night the fires of our Kentish freemen ringed Lunnon and every inn of Southwark was filled with the 'Hey trolly lolly!' of the boys from Kent. It was Jack Cade, the great Captain of Kent, come again."

He swigged the ale. "They brought York's army from Tewkesbury, on the double, young Dickon that's now King driving the soldiers night and day. He was a lad then, just turned nineteen, and hot from Tewkesbury field. Entered Lunnon on the twentieth of May, Dickon did, and rode through the streets with his banners of the Sunne and the Boar. The Army of Tewkesbury! Twelve thousand mounted knights, men-at-arms, archers and pikes. Dickon was in the city two days and two nights. On the night of the twenty-first, old King Harry, that was prisoner in the Tower and that brave Tom o' Falconbridge had sworn to deliver, was found dead in his blood. Perished, York said, of pure displeasure and melancholy!"

Miles shook his head. His boyish face stiffened in a look of hate. "Murdered an anointed king," he said. "They cursed themselves by that deed, did every Prince of York. Why, old Harry was a saint! Were not miracles done at his tomb in Chertsey?"

Martin glanced about. This talk was dangerous. But no one looked their way. "Soft, lad," he cautioned. "Keep your voice down."

Miles nodded. "I don't fancy my head grilling on the Bridge no more than you, master," he said. "Give heed! Dickon broke up Tom the Bastard and our poor yeomen of Kent. What chance had they with rusty bills and old harvest forks against the Army of Tewkesbury? Smashed the lads, Dickon did. Burned out whole villages. They took my brother—" He clenched a fist, staring into the yellow light streaming from rush lamps. "Took Rafe. Hanged him, they did. Left him for crows, for vultures. An example to the people, York said." He gave a fierce laugh. "Aye, an example in truth! So that for every lad of Kent hanging eyeless in the sun, there be a dozen hale fellows with love in their hearts for our Dickon!"

Martin took a thoughtful drink. He wiped his lips with the butt of his hand. After a moment he said: "Well, it was a long time back, was it not? Do they still remember in Kent?"

"Do they remember?" Miles exclaimed, so loudly that two Boarsmen at a nearby table looked up from their dice. "Do they remember?" he repeated, in an easier tone. "Mark it, master. If ever this Dickon calls on Kent for aid, he will find out what memories our people have. Let him send his Commissions of Array. Kent will not stir. More like folk are to see him damned and in Hell!"

Martin stroked his cheek. Through the tumult and the

dice, he heard the sound of April rain, soft and black and lonely in the evening street. He had been twenty at Tewkesbury, just Miles' age. Young and with that touch of sad glory to set apart the knightly company of Lancaster. How immortal they had been! Each day a day glowing with a terrible beauty. Those who went forth armoured and singing . . .

At his side the lad pleaded: "You can trust me, master. I can do good service."

Martin nodded. The boy's eyes were bright with longing; the cry of the fallow heart. It was more than vengeance that Miles wanted. "Why did you join King Richard?" Martin asked.

"I wanted to find out what Richard was really like. Some folk said one thing; some said another. No one knew. Oh, Kent hated him all right for the Falconbridge rising, but even Kent had to admit he'd done well as King. His judges and assessors were honest; the like had never been seen under Edward. And Dickon took no dirty money off the French."

Miles paused; added softly, "Done well . . . until this foulness of the boys in the Tower and that girl."

"Girl?" Martin wondered.

"Elizabeth," Miles said. "She's a witch! Like her mother, Lady Grey."

Martin drained the last of the strong brown ale. He signalled a serving maid. "What has Elizabeth ever done to you?" he inquired in a reproving tone.

"If her name wasn't Plantagenet, if she was plain Bess Bedtick—she'd be on the town ere now. Look at her, pushing the poor Lady Anne into her tomb so that she, Elizabeth, might leap into Dickon's bed."

"She did nothing of the kind," Martin said. "Anne was sick and like to die for months. You shouldn't talk that way, boy. What do you know of Elizabeth?"

Miles flushed. "I know more than you think, master."

"You have the secrets of a princess." Martin's tone was scornful. He was beginning to tire of the lad's cockiness. "Elizabeth of York has whispered to Miles of Kent."

"Mock," the lad said. "Mock. John Morton would pay dear to know what I know."

"What d'ye mean—John Morton?" Martin controlled himself with an effort.

"Your friends in France," Miles replied. "Isn't it John Morton does the thinking for Henry Tudor and the rest?"

Martin shrugged. "Does he? I should hazard Tudor thought for himself."

"A little begging Welshman!" Miles jeered. "You know better, Master Martin."

The serving wench came with a crock of ale. She was a plump small lass with whorls of bright hair—another Jane Shore, Martin thought. "What is your name?" he asked.

"Lucy." Her blue eyes smiled.

"Thanks to you, Lucy." He paid, adding a shilling tip.

"Thank you, master!" She glowed. "A fine gentleman—oh, it's too much."

"Take it," Martin said. She leaned over to wipe the rings of ale, giving Martin and the boy a view of her breasts. She was like Jane Shore, Martin perceived.

"What did you do that for?" Miles asked, when Lucy had gone. "Lord Jesus! You might have taken her upstairs for that money."

"I like the wench," Martin said. What he was thinking was that now he would have a friend and gossip in the White Lion, a favorite spot for the Company of the Boar.

Miles lifted his brows. "I didn't know you looked at that sort. Why didn't you tell me? I can get you anything you fancy, half-price, at the Cardinal's Hat. French and Lombard doxies."

"That's fine of you, boy," Martin said. "I'll remember it."

Miles missed the glint of humour in the soldier's tone. He hunched forward, looking serious. "When do we start?"

Start? Martin stared. He thought the boy proposed an immediate call at the Cardinal's Hat.

"When will you take me in your circle?" Miles explained. "Listen! Ask anyone around Hopkin's Corners about me, Miles Melton. My folk have lived at the Corners since King John's time. If any man says I'm a cheat, you turn me in to Tyrell. Fair enough, ain't it?"

Martin frowned, regretting he had encouraged Miles. Martin was no longer one of a plumed company; a band of immortals—and tomorrow dead. He was alone; silent and secret as the April rain, falling like tears in the little lost street. He laboured for a vision: Lancaster. But sometimes he suspected that Lancaster was a faith left in the blood and sun of Tewkesbury. Left forever in the ruined song of Margaret. Something new and monstrous had come out of the grief of the Rose; something shrewd and pitiless and aching for success. Did he serve York or Lancaster? He hardly knew.

"Stop guessing, boy," he said. "Let the matter be. Speak no more of it."

Miles drank. He put down his pottle, suddenly reproached: "You don't trust me. Thought I was lying about Elizabeth. I'll show you, Master Martin. I have proof!"

The lad began to attract attention. Martin eased along the bench. Miles clutched his arm. "Wait! This is worth gold, Master Martin."

Martin eyed the boy. "Friend of mine knows a steward of Norfolk," Miles said. "You know that big house in the Strand, by the old Savoy. A fortnight ago this steward had papers from the Jockey of Norfolk to put in the privy box. This steward was looking through the lot, curious—you never know what a duke may turn up—when it was just like a crossbolt hit him. He saw a letter writ in the hand of Princess Elizabeth." Miles glanced at Martin.

"What did the fellow do?" Martin asked.

"He read the letter, of course," Miles replied. "Do you know what it was? Have a guess."

"No idea in the world," Martin said.

"This jade, Elizabeth, begged the Jockey of Norfolk to intercede for her with Richard," Miles said. "She wanted Norfolk's aid in becoming wife to Richard, when poor Anne is dead."

Martin listened intently. This letter to John, Duke of Norfolk, that everyone called "Jockey" of Norfolk, might or might not be genuine. If it were a true letter, it meant matters had gone further between Richard and Elizabeth, his niece, than anyone had dared suppose. "What did Norfolk's steward do with the letter?" Martin inquired.

"Put it in the Duke's privy cabinet, like he was told," Miles replied. "But he made a copy."

"What use is a copy?" Martin said. He wondered if he should trust this lad.

"Wouldn't such a letter interest John Morton?" Miles gave a prod in the ribs to Martin. "Wouldn't it, eh?"

He decided to risk it. After all, the lad had offered proof of good faith. And his father and brother had been hanged by Richard. Master Martin said carefully, "Such a letter might interest a number of persons. But a copy is no good. A copy can be denied. Or this may be only a tale."

"It's no tale," Miles said. "I know the fellow. He's not inventing tales like that. Norfolk would have him quartered, if the Duke knew."

Martin gave the lad a speculative look. "How did Norfolk's steward come to tell you about the letter, Miles?"

"This steward is a Kentish man," Miles explained. "He comes from a village nearby. I went to him for work, when I came to London. He had none to give, but he said to me that King Richard was looking for likely lads."

Martin nodded. So far, the story fitted. But why should Norfolk's steward impart such an explosive secret to a mere boy from a neighbouring village in Kent?

"He needs money," Miles said. "He'll do anything to raise money. And he trusts me. He knows I won't give him away."

"Doesn't Norfolk pay the fellow?" Master Martin wondered.

"He needs more than what Norfolk gives him," Miles said. "He's been speculating in swans."

"Speculating in swans!"

"That's right. There's a heap of money in swans. Especially since King Richard's Parliament allowed ordinary folk to keep 'games of swans.' This steward thinks he will make a fortune."

Martin marvelled. Such an undreamed-of trading enterprise as swans had led, by a strange chain of circumstance, to a most valuable discovery for John Morton.

"What will Morton give for this letter?" Miles asked, suddenly practical.

Martin shrugged. "Morton is not rich."

"No, but the King of France is," Miles said. "Everyone knows where Morton gets his money."

Martin frowned. The statement was too uncomfortably true and made Morton's men seem like a gang of hired cutthroats. "You know nothing about that," he snapped. "The steward can have two gold nobles for the letter."

"Three gold nobles," the boy said.

Martin turned with a touch of irritation. "Swans!" he snorted. "All right. Three gold nobles. Not a farthing more."

"Don't tell anyone how you came by the letter," Miles requested. "The fellow is scared pissless of Norfolk."

"Tell Norfolk's man not to worry," Martin said. "I don't even know his name." He paused abruptly. Someone was sitting near him, listening. He twisted around on the bench, seeing a drunken grin and beady magpie eyes. It was the guardsman called Jack o' Ninepence.

"Who's not to worry?" Jack asked, rocking gently. He was very drunk. "What are you knaves up to?"

Martin stared at him. How much had the drunken fool heard? He went cold as Jack slobbered, "Norfolk; Norfolk. I heard the name Norfolk."

"You misheard, Jack," Martin said quietly.

"I heard Norfolk," the drunken Jack insisted. "You up to something with the Jockey of Norfolk?"

Martin glanced at Miles. The lad was gazing into the smoky rushlight. His face was hard and white. "It's a wench we're talking of, Jack," he said, still looking into the lamplight. "A wench at the Cardinal's Hat. They call her 'Norfolk.' She's a real low bitch. She'll do anything."

Jack leered. "Take me to her," he said.

"How would you like to go right now, Jack?" Miles asked softly.

A look of horrible lust came over the man's face. "Right now! By the Holy Martyr—" He lurched to his feet.

Martin glimpsed the young sweet smile of Lucy as they went out. In the black street, April rain fell.

❀✦❀✦❀✦❀✦❀✦❀

ELIZABETH, daughter and sister of kings, Princess Royal, Heiress of York, looked at her mother. This was Lady Grey, she who had made the tainted secret marriage; who had been a widow with sons, a Lancastrian widow, when she had captured York's young Edward. This was she whose sons by Edward had been taken from her by Edward's brother Richard; who had lost three sons and a brother to Richard's ambition; whose royal marriage had been publicly branded unlawful and the children thereof bastards. Queen no longer, ruined wife and mother, barely tolerated, doomed to rack out her days in silence and in grief—she was now simple Lady Grey, widow of Sir John Grey that had died for Margaret at Second St. Alban's field. Richard had erased twenty years from her life.

Yet, deprived as she was, she was far from nothing. Even Elizabeth, her daughter, who knew her so well, felt the uneasiness in Lady Grey's presence that the child Elizabeth had experienced. That ash-blonde cold queenliness; that gaze, pale and calculating. What will *you* give? What use can be made of *you?* How shall *your* heart, *your* riches of mind, *your* young body be put to work for the House of Woodeville?

York was nothing. York was important only for the greater glory of Woodeville.

"He makes fair proposals," Lady Grey was saying, leaning forward, an angel of melancholy, her marble face framed in a nun's wimple. She was robed in sable. Mourning for Edward the King? For her vanished sons? Ah, mourning for her life!

He was meagre Henry Tudor, who had begun to send messages again. He offered himself, the jolly wooer and bridegroom; he promised Elizabeth a crown. Only one difficulty with Henry's proposals—he was but a penniless exile living on the charity of the King of France.

"I shall never have that Welshman," Elizabeth said. She wore a gown of silvery blue, a gown that appeared to be laved in moonlight as she moved about the small barren chamber.

Lady Grey's tongue clicked against her teeth. She was not used to revolt. "You shall do what is best for you, Elizabeth," she said. "This Tudor may become a king."

"Were he lord of the world, I should not want him!" the girl vowed.

"You are a child," Lady Grey observed. "You shall marry where it please your family. I have written to my brother, Sir Edward Woodeville."

Elizabeth hovered near the high casement, the rectangles of golden light that lay upon the plaited straw. Straw for the ruined line of Edward! No Gobelin tapestry, no rich Flemish carpet, no silver plate. The credenza beside the wall was not dark magnificent Italian carving, but a cheap one of English make that held Lady Grey's few vessels. The treasure of Edward . . . where was the treasure of Edward? Seized by Richard or taken to France by Sir Edward Woodeville and Grey, Marquess of Dorset, in their flight to Tudor. Dorset was the only son of Lady Grey upon whom King Richard had been unable to lay hands.

Elizabeth knew that her mother was negotiating with both parties, Tudor and the King. Duplicity, thy name is Woodeville! "You wrote to Dorset, too," she reminded Lady Grey. "You told him to return to England, to Richard. Why did you do that, madame?"

Lady Grey frowned. She resented being questioned. "The King gave me his promise—" She hesitated. Sitting in her uncushioned chair, she looked up at her daughter. "We made a bargain, Richard and I. He said if I wrote to Dorset, I should see my boys in the Tower."

Elizabeth was moving slowly about the room, in the rectangles of gold, in the barred light. She stopped short. "Why, that is wonderful!" she cried. "Wonderful! When shall we see them? Now? Tomorrow?"

Lady Grey shook her head. Her voice was old; old and weighted. "He meant not a word of it," she said. "He only wanted Dorset back. He spoke of a dukedom for Dorset." She stared at Elizabeth. "My last son," she said.

"Of course Richard meant it," Elizabeth assured her mother. "I know him. If he has given you his promise, you shall see the Princes."

Lady Grey glanced down at her slim hands; ringless now and forever. Her jewels had gone with her marriage. "Promises," she said, infinitely bitter. "I've heard too many promises of Richard. Did I not allow Richard to take from me out of sanctuary your little brother of York, because that ancient imbecile Archbishop Rotherham swore in the King's name that no harm would come to my son? In the King's name! Where is my boy now?"

"Yet you wrote to Dorset," the girl said. "You must still keep some faith in Richard."

"Yes, I wrote to him," Lady Grey acknowledged. "Were I a soul burning in Hell, I would write to him—if by that means I might gain one hour with my sweet boys."

Elizabeth said nothing. She sensed the hysteria building in her mother. Whenever Richard's name was mentioned, her mother became like one possessed. "There was always a chance," Lady Grey went on, staring into the April light.

"But that chance is not gone," Elizabeth said. "I'll vow you'll see the boys before April is out."

Lady Grey turned to her daughter. Her voice was hushed. "It was April that Edward died. The ninth, a Saturday. And Richard's son. The son that was to be King after him. Didn't he shiver to death on April the ninth—one year to the day after my Edward? You tell me, I presume, that it was merely chance, a stroke of fate. God had nothing to do with it; God didn't take this boy of Richard's on that dread day. I know, Elizabeth. I know!"

She was beginning to quiver and there was a light in her eyes like the light of Hell. Elizabeth grew cold and frightened. She rushed to her mother, seizing her icy hands. "Please don't," she said. "Please don't." Her mother's hysteria had a deadly quality. Lady Grey had been more than a queen: she had been called enchantress, sorceress, witch. She was the Morgan-le-Fay of York. She had put a spell upon Edward, to gain his love.

Lady Grey shook off her daughter. She rose to black majestic height. Her voice was full of night. "He shall pay for what he has done," she said. "He will wish he had never been born."

Elizabeth shivered. She knew Lady Grey spoke of Richard. "What are you going to do?" she asked.

Lady Grey was walking in the gold and shadow, the bright portcullis of sun. "He shall pay," she repeated. "He will be hated and despised. His name—" And suddenly she paused,

as if struck by a thought. "He will go down in Time's charterbook," she said, in a slow marvelling voice. "The worst
King; the worst villain; the worst man—of all. The worst—
the worst—the worst. And I—I shall see to it. . . ." She
smiled at her daughter.

Elizabeth swallowed, her throat closed and dry. Blessed
Edmund, how she feared her mother! So strong and terrible
was the effect of Lady Grey that Elizabeth never doubted
for one moment that her mother would do exactly what she
threatened. "But if you see the boys?" she said faintly. "If
he keeps his promise?"

Lady Grey turned to her daughter. "You believe in this
man, don't you?"

"Yes," Elizabeth managed to say. It was as if her mother
said: was she troth-plight to the Devil?

"You fool!" Lady Grey said. "You young fool!"

But this was so unjust. Elizabeth turned away, with flaming face. Lady Grey herself had encouraged Richard's interest in her daughter. In the beginning, more than a year ago,
Lady Grey had even instructed the girl on how to impress
the King. What had happened?

"I did not dream but that my boys were alive," Lady Grey
said. "That even Richard must have kept them safe as a
sacred trust to his brother Edward. I was a fool. Now I know
this man. And I shall reveal him to the world. Everyone
shall know him. Oh, his bishops and his Masses! His books
and his talk of knighthood! His coming to do good; to change
our evil ways! Lies; all lies. Do you want to know what he is
really like?"

"He is kingly and brave," Elizabeth stammered.

Her mother gave the girl a pale terrible smile. "Blood
—cruelty—night," she said. "That is your Richard. That is
what he really is. All this time you were deceived. His
charm; his shrewdness. His princely giving of gifts. Only to
mask his evil; only to bind you to him. He has murder in
his soul."

"Listen to me!" the girl cried. Her spirit was all splintered into tortured fragments. "You won't listen to anyone but yourself. You have never answered me. What if Richard keeps his promise to you? I shall ask him. Will you make no reply to Tudor until I have asked Richard?"

Lady Grey was silent a long moment. Her cold, queenly face was cut from Norman stone. Her spirit was mortal and unforgiving. And all at once it occurred to the girl how much alike were those of the Roses. Alike in their sense of vengeance, their nervous craving for blood. White Rose or Red Rose: York or Lancaster. They were one in the passion of death. The infection of a generation. A generation of death.

"I make no promises," Lady Grey said.

❀✦❖✦❖✦❖✦❀

WESTMINSTER was an island. Secluded by wall and river, the whole thrust of buildings that formed the royal enclave of Westminster was like a vast fortress; a stronghold sheltering thousands. Especially was this apect true in the sunset days of His Sovereign Majesty, King Richard the Third, whose personal standard of the White Boar Passant fluttered in an April wind above the Clock Tower.

Wherever one looked, soldiers appeared. A double cordon stood watch about the ancient Palace, built by Henry the Third; guards patrolled the walls, the Gate Houses, the Water Stairs. Recruits, fresh from the North with a shilling a day and all the ale they could hold—the best soldiers' pay in Christendom—made practice of push-of-pike or of the archery butts, under dour Tyrell. To the glance, York's monarchy was stoutly defended. No shabby adventurer from over the seas, in the moneybook of the King of France, was like to topple the Banner of the Boar.

But what was not perceived outwardly, not yet, in the swarming buckram jackets and glinting partizans, in the officers with new steel breast armour, in the flurry of horse-

men with despatches, was the spiritual blight of the monarchy. Evil rumour was a plague that steel and guns could
not cure; that rusted the heart; that poisoned the atmosphere.

Sometimes it seemed to Elizabeth Plantagenet that she
alone kept a faith in Richard. Now as she went about Westminster, penetrating great chambers with stiff silent guards,
walking in the armed and bustling court, sitting in the privy
garden, she was ever alert, wondering. Was the King in good
humour? Had the day's reports been welcome? What was
now the immediate point of danger?

She had scarcely a moment with Richard in these haunted
April days. He was with his officers; he was riding out to survey coastal defenses; he was reinforcing the Tower. Yet, such
as she was, gliding on tiptoe through rumour and doubt, she
knew that he was aware of her loyalty and her love. She signalled to him from afar, at chance encounters in the Palace
or in tense hurried meetings between one council and the
next.

Always she heard within her a voice whispering: Elizabeth, Elizabeth, he has no one but you. He cannot do without you. Life has withered from him. His iron father; his
three brothers; his wife; his son—all vanished. Only he in
this lonely echoing Westminster, in this final fortress, still
survives. This ringed and harried kingship you only can re-
store. In the hour of challenge he will turn to you, to his
love.

And by night, in the great dark that descended with the
sentry's desolate call, she told herself: the King is good.
Richard is good. Not a quiet humble goodness. But good as
the proud are good, in strength and noble disdain. As the
Falcon is good, in solitary and dauntless heart. As the
Anointed of the Sword are good, in the consecration of
blood. As God's incorruptible Keepers are good, sent on this
earth to uphold the divine wrath.

In lesser men such goodness would be frightening. In him,

it becomes the cloak and belt of his royalty. He wears a blazing diadem.

When she cannot sleep, turning on her narrow bed, night furling a shroud about her, she rises and creeps on naked feet to the casement. In her thin white shift, her bright hair flowing down, she gazes out. About her loom Westminster's towers, coldly gleaming. High above huddled London these spires and battlements flourish. She stands at an angle of Whitehall, on the river side. She can glimpse the giant grandeur of Westminster Hall, the square turrets of the Star Chamber, the slim graceful leads of St. Stephen's Chapel.

And at her back, in the small moon-stained room, she can hear the quiet breathing of her sisters Cecily and Anne; while through a connecting door sleep the younger girls Katherine and Bridget. They are in bed by nine of the clock, obedient to Lady Grey. Only Elizabeth is wakeful, musing, aware of night. She looks down at the lost and dreaming river, the river that goes by forever. And now all the times of her wonderful life come back to her and she leans upon the moonlight, she listens to the magical lap and whisper of the river.

The little princess of a gorgeous Court; the darling of a royal father; a child dancing. Gold silk and pearls for the Dolphin of France, to whom she is betrothed. Laughing, merry and brighthaired—remembering her brothers Edward and Richard, her cousin Edward of Warwick, her cousin Edward of York-Gloucester. York had been such a flowering House!

Oh God and Mary, the golden halls of her childhood! The royalty of time! She is like a flame: redgold, warm and evening-born. Breathless, she dances. Her shining hair and milkwhite cheek appear amid the bickering barons like a herald of immortal York. She plays the lute and sings, a tender contralto. She has such a lively air. Men fall in love with her; she conquers without knowing. She has eyes for her father only: the laughing drunken giant, who is always hovering or sprawling in the fiery light, in his silk and purple, his hands upon her, caressing her, and his proud drunken voice full of wine and joy, calling her his pretty Bess, his darling dere, his leman—and somewhere, while this is going on, she glimpses far-off and lovely her pale-haired mother, hard and gleaming and cold as one of her own pale jewels and watching, without seeming to do so, little Bess, marking every movement, as if fearful of too much love between father and daughter.

So Bess learns that in this Court no rivals of her mother flourish. Even the King's own brother, even George, Duke of Clarence. Too bad, they say one day. Too bad about Clarence. What is too bad? Bess wants to know. *He got his in the Tower last night!* Lips behind hands, the shadowy frightened whisper. Last night in the Tower. The poor fellow drank; he talked too much. Drank and talked.

What did he talk about?

It was about the Queen, your mother. He was talking about your mother. She never liked Clarence. She said he was no good; she said he was a traitor to York. York would be better off without Clarence. He couldn't keep his mouth shut. Especially after a bottle or two of malmsey. Paid for his talking, he did. The Queen saw to that!

In these firelit murmurs, these patches of flickering terror, Bess understands that the handsome and elegant uncle of Clarence, and the shouting sobbing lonely drinker—oh, he will never come back again! And afterward that laughing giant her father is sober and silent, staring wet-lashed into the blazing evening, drawing back in horror when a Woodeville offers a drink, and never knowing that his little Bess is near. Lips move, hands twitch—prayers or curses? And the shuddering, useless regret: oh bitter blood of Christ!— they sued by day and by night for the pardon of scurvy rogues, of clerks and lackeys, but not one voice lifted for the King's own brother. Not one prayer for the unhappy Prince of York.

He got his last night in the Tower . . . Disgraced, the dead man's children, Edward and Margaret. Disgraced and hidden away. Bess will see these little cousins no more.

But there is always her lovely, lovely mother, calm and ice-blonde and with the frozen gleam of moonlight. Her mother walking amid the silence and horror of the Court, walking with enchanted grace toward the rigid staring King, and never looking backward, never seeing the appalled faces, the shadows creeping from the walls, never hearing the whispers. . . .

From the river, thirty feet below, Elizabeth catches the muffled stroke of oars. She thinks of some poor wretch on his way to the Tower. Since that trouble in the streets with Clifford, the King has commanded that suspects be removed to the Tower by water. The girl peers into the night, but the barge is just beyond her vision. But, she knows, somewhere on the river's lonely glimmer a boat freighted with doom is moving toward Traitors' Gate, the manacled prisoner sitting upright and gazing into the immense dark, and the tillerman standing hooded in the stern, and the sad slow wash of the tiller, and the eight shadowy oarsmen pulling. . . .

Elizabeth sighs.

At her back comes the gentle breathing of Cecily and Anne; and she recalls how they were all together in sanctuary, fatherless and without money—and how their mother warned them of mortal danger, of Richard. But Elizabeth knew why her mother feared Richard then. The Duke of Gloucester had, after the death of Clarence, edged the Woodevilles in Edward's favour. And by Edward's testament, Richard had been made Lord Protector of England— in the event of the King's untimely death. But Queen Elizabeth Woodeville mistrusted Richard most of all: more than Clarence, more than Duchess Cecily of York, more than the intriguing Jane Shore. Richard knew the Queen's secret— her unlawful marriage: the knowledge of which had brought Clarence to the Tower and sealed his lips forever. And further: Richard was England's greatest captain. Never defeated; never caught unaware.

Elizabeth Woodeville felt secure only as long as Edward lived.

But for York the clock has struck; the hour is at hand; it is the fragrant dying time, the time of April. . . .

Oh Bess! Bess! Yes, she remembers: her father speaks of York and tells them that they must be one. Even in his sickness, the grey face, the sweating and torment of the great decaying body once the handsomest in England, he still thinks of York. He wants to call the Princes of York together, the Queen and her brothers and sons on one hand, Richard and his friends on the other. He wants them to clasp hands, to swear to York. For, he prophesies, they and York will perish else. . . .

But it is too late for vows, for blood troths.

Bess, is that you, sweet darling? Are you come, my Bess?

She is standing in the twilight of her father's bedchamber, in the odour of sickness and creeping death, and in the bed she sees the huge crumpled body. A trembling hand beckons; slowly she moves through the April dusk, horrified by she knows not what, as if she herself were dying upon the gilded bed where her father lies. April tears upon her cheeks, she tried to think of a prayer, any prayer, and she can remember nothing but *Dirige, Domine, et Placebo!*— Direct, O God, and I shall supplicate!—the opening words of the Invocation for the Dead.

His hand hot and shaking touches her face; Bess kneels; the room is like a chapel, with small bright candles like altar lights, crimson draperies, and a smell of herbs like incense. Far off she hears the muttering of the dying man her father; what is he telling her?—she cannot understand, she will never know. Ah—love? Yes, love for her; for York. His eyes glow; he smiles desperately. She strains toward him—but then he is not thinking of her at all, nor of death, but is speaking of his lost brother Edmund, the same that was slain at Wakefield twenty-five years past, perhaps even speaking to him, for it seems that Edmund is there, is not dead at all—and they are boys again in Ireland. . . .

Edmund, Edmund, the gillie is come with word from our father!

Just that. As if death be not an end, but a going away in time, a breaking of time's fences. . . .

Elizabeth hovers beside the bed, her hand in his; looking down at the grey bloated face, that once had stirred so many hearts, and at the swollen body, shapeless, racked with corruption, once so mighty and perfect—ah, she is filled with terror! She is carried beyond the altar lights and crimson draperies and the sick wandering. She stands at some high naked windswept place of the soul. She shivers, cannot endure that her father is dying; no, no—he cannot die, she is dying too! She clings to his hand, wild and pleading—but he does not see her, he is thinking of Edmund, they are boys again, and she is begging, begging, for one look, for one instant of light between darkness and darkness. . . .

Oh Bess! Bess!

Below her the river flows past the memories and the shining towers; she bends toward the night, wondering if Richard is awake. Is he thinking of her? Is he listening for her cry?

The night is silent; the heart's cry falls into glimmering depths. Only the river surges darkly; freighted with death, with life. . . .

❂✦❈✦❂✦❈✦❂✦❈✦❂

A MAN who murders not for personal gain but in the way of duty must have a frightening detachment toward life. . . .

The soldiers were sitting in the White Lyon, it was Tuesday, the day they had their pay, and jokes and friendly insults flew about. Everyone was in a jolly buttock-pinching mood, making the serving girls prance and skip. Everyone, save young Miles of Kent. He teetered at one end of the table. He had drunk a great deal and his eyes were glazed.

Lucy hovered over Master Martin. She was wearing a scarlet kirtle; on her breast was pinned a white marguerite. "D'ye like my flower?" she asked. "It's a marguerite."

"I see that," Martin said.

"You like the marguerite, do you not, Master Martin?"

He looked sharply at the girl. Lucy had a knowing air. He moved uneasily. Never had he spoken here of Marguerite d'Anjou, Lancaster's haunted Queen. She was dead and her time was dead and Lancaster, the real Lancaster, was a handful of shrivelled memories.

"I said nothing of marguerites," he reproved her.

"A gentleman," she said. "A gentleman that fancies marguerites. Is that not right, Master Martin?"

"It is not right," he said. He wondered if Miles had been talking. Or was he becoming edgy again? Imagining things? He had to stop it. The surest way of becoming suspect was to act as if he possessed a guilty secret.

Lucy lingered at Martin's elbow, looking down in the winelight. "Have you seen that Jack o' Ninepence?" she said.

Master Martin took a sip of ale. "No," he replied.

"He didn't pay his score the other night," the girl said. "I saw him go out with you and the boy here."

Master Martin shrugged. "We parted in the street. I know no more about him."

"I asked one or two of the others," Lucy remarked, "but no one has seen him since that night."

Martin touched her wrist. "Did anyone else see him leave?" he murmured.

She shook her head. "They were all merry and blind. He went out just like a candle puff in the night."

"Don't mention that he went with us, lass," he said, putting a shilling into her hand.

"Never a word," she promised. She hesitated and said: "Excuse me, master. Was it bad? Anything bad?"

He reassured her softly. "It's all right, Lucy. He was drunk and may have had an accident. It might have happened to anyone."

She pocketed the shilling and picked up his ale cup. "Another noggin, Master Martin?"

He watched her pass amid evening's red flare. At his side Miles said thickly, "She knows. The wench knows." Martin frowned. "What 'ave you done with the letter?" the boy demanded.

"It's where it will do good," Martin said.

"God grant it be so," the lad said. "The thing were dear enow!" He looked down at his hands.

"You are young for this work," Martin remarked.

Scraps of conversation floated past, on the roiling current of oaths and laughter. "I sez to 'im, I sez, ye fought at Towton, me ass! The likes o' you never set foot on a battlefield. Ye may cuckold Ratcliffe, but ye can't cuckold me!"

"An wot did 'ee siye to that?"

"Wot could 'ee say, the fewterin' knave? Ee knows 'ee don't cozen old blades. Too many o' that sort coming in now. Where be the old fighters, tell me?"

"Rusting their joints. We ain't had a real whack at anyone for nigh on fourteen year. Edward that was king aforetime weren't keen to crawl out of a doxy's snug nest to clap on armour. The army went to hell under Edward!"

Martin glanced at Red Hugh O'Rourke and a West Countryman with a well-malted nose. Red Hugh had an eye on Martin, was watching Miles and Martin without seeming to. The soldier looked away.

Lucy came back with the ale. She leaned over Martin. "Someone asked me just now about Jack," she whispered. "Wanted to know who he was with that night."

"Who asked you?" Martin said in a low voice.

She glanced meaningfully at Red Hugh. "Him," she replied.

Martin nodded. "Thank you, lass. Keep your ears open."

Lucy hurried on. Martin sighed. A man had to do many unpleasant things in the course of a lifetime. He didn't think about it any more. If someone knew too much, that someone had to be put to silence. But death had a way of accumulating. One had to economize, when possible, on death.

Miles said: "I wish I'd never touched that letter. I wish I'd stayed in Kent."

Martin gave him an iron look. "Don't talk about it," he said.

The lad swayed. A lock of hair straggled over one eye. "Three gold nobles," he muttered.

Martin gazed about the room. The clamour seemed to lessen. Red Hugh was speaking in a murmur to a fellow with a black patch over one eye. Martin felt a covert hostility rising in the room. He knew that he and Miles should get out. The lad was too drunk for safety.

Red Hugh's voice came up, like fog upon the night, unfurling from a dense peatbog of surly humour. "Himself was floatin' by Wapping Old Stairs, where pirates be hung in chains for washing over of three tides. Black, 'ee was. Black and that swollen his own mither wouldn't 'ave sworn to 'im."

"Where did yer 'ear this, Hugh?" someone said.

"Didn't I get it from a wherryman at Garlick Stairs? And 'im just back from viewin' poor Jack."

"Sure it's Jack, be they?"

"Eh, and who else? Wouldn't the little Ninepence 'ave come back to us if the breath was in his body? Aye, 'ee were no skulker."

Miles was pale as a corpse. One hand clutched a great cup of ale. Suddenly he called to Red Hugh: "You didn't see him, did you?"

Red Hugh turned, thrusting an Irish face toward the boy. "See 'im? I know what I say, lad. That poor drowned sod, that were Jack."

Miles leaned forward, sweat beading his brow. "He was drowned, was he?"

Red Hugh drew his dagger. He touched his throat with the whetted edge of steel. "They gave him this," he said. "Slit his gullet. Then threw him in the river."

Martin put a restraining hand on the boy. He must make the young fool stop talking. Miles shook off the soldier's hand. "Jack was drunk, was he not?" he said to Red Hugh. "Don't you know he was drunk? He's likely in a stewhouse at this moment."

Martin felt the eyes of every man in the room upon the two of them; a deadly knife-screeching regard. We've got to get out, he thought. At once, before they decide to act.

The soldier in Martin took command. He surveyed the redshadowed room as he would a battlefield. The other Boarsmen were ten in number. They sat across from each other at a trestle table along one wall, a table opposite the door. Martin and the lad sat at one end, a little apart from the others. The door was perhaps half a dozen paces from their end of the table. And near the door a small rush lamp, a tallow wick floating in a basin of oil, smoked and flickered.

His plan must have two elements: surprise and speed. There was also a third element: Lucy. He beckoned to the girl. "Ale for the company—and be quick!" She hurried off.

A murmur of wonder went around. The tension relaxed a little. Martin was praying for a thimble measure of time. But Red Hugh was not done. He leaned toward Martin. "What do the two of yez know about Jack?" he demanded.

Martin shook his head. He had a perplexed look. "I cannot fathom your meaning," he said.

"Cannot fathom me meaning! Sweet tits of Cormac's daughter, now ain't that queer?" His eyes narrowed; his voice pierced the room. "What happened to Jack, ye York-shire barebones? Quick; no blarney!"

"I don't know," Martin said.

"Don't know, sez he. Don't know—when 'tis a man him-self we have to swear by Christ and Mary he saw yez with Jack, the last night anyone saw Jack alive. Is it not so, Bar-ton Quorn?"

The man with the black patch said: "I seen him round about ten o' the clock, him and the boy, and the two of them dragging poor Jack along."

"Where saw you this?" Martin queried.

"Not a score of paces from here. Drunk, Jack was. As the lad says. Drunk and staggering. I heard the clock strike not long after."

"What say ye now?" Red Hugh barked.

So this was what had happened! Their bitter luck—to escape notice within the tavern, only to be glimpsed just as they were making off in the night! Quorn had happened by at the moment they had thought themselves safe. "The man is mistaken," Martin said coolly. "He has but one eye."

One or two of the company laughed, but were silenced by a look from Red Hugh. "I've had me eye on you, Master Barebones," the Irishman said, "and it's two eyes I have. I don't fancy you. Not from the day you joined the Company."

"I'm sorry for that," Martin said. "I've done nothing to you that I know."

Lucy rushed in with a large crock of ale. She leaned past Martin to place the stone jug on the table. "Unbolt the door when I rise," he whispered to her.

The ale went around the table. Martin poured a foaming cup for himself and the lad. Miles had become rigid and speechless, sensing the peril they were in. Under the table Martin's hand gripped the lad's knee. "We're leaving in one minute!" he whispered.

Once more the soldier's gaze swept the smoky flare; evening's old red chamber. Beneath torn banners and dented shields, up and down the table, muttering grew. The dead were calling to the dead. And he was Edmund Beaufort on the field of Tewkesbury, staking all on one desperate throw.

Someone handed Red Hugh a cup of ale. The Irishman dashed it to the floor. It was like a pre-arranged signal. "I'll take no ale of murderers!" he bellowed.

Martin was on his feet, pulling the lad with him. And at once the room was in an uproar. The table went over with a crash, pinning two or three Boarsmen beneath the heavy oak top. Everyone began shouting and steel glinted. Martin had calculated precisely his move. He was at the door two steps ahead of Red Hugh and Barton Quorn. Lucy's trembling hands slid back the heavy iron bar across the door.

The soldier paused, turned and in the same movement seized the rush lamp. For an instant snarling faces loomed out of grease and rush smoke; then Martin flung the lamp. Blazing oil spattered Red Hugh and Quorn. They shrieked with pain, tearing at their clothes and hair. It was the moment of furious surprise that Martin had counted on. It was Edmund Beaufort's hammer stroke on the exposed left flank of Edward's army.

As they hurtled through the doorway Martin saw Lucy's horrified eyes, and a dagger flashed out of the hell about them, raking his shoulder. They were in the street, in the night; and a gusty wind was blowing and they were whisking down a black lane, like history's rats. Martin's shoulder was a fire of pain and he could feel blood trickling down his jacket. He had a bad gash.

They twisted around corners and presently the clamour behind died away and they came to a shuddering halt. Miles stared into the dark. "We've done it!" he exulted.

Martin leaned against a low stone wall. He was losing blood rapidly, feeling faint. The boy glanced at him. "You're all blood!" he cried. Martin sank to the ground. He hardly knew where he was. He seemed to see the inflamed

eye of Barton Quorn gazing from the shadows. The boy
was tearing his shirt into strips.

What an end, the soldier dimly thought. Death in a
drunken tavern brawl. What an end—for knighthood, for
the dream squandered in the bloody marigold of Tewkesbury. Miles was binding the torn shoulder, binding tight to
compress the artery. Martin shut his eyes. The night was
whirling. . . .

❂↦⁎↤❂↦⁎↤❂↦⁎↤❂

IN these times there were certain houses scattered about
London that were used as refuges by the Tudor conspiracy.
These houses were located in out-of-the-way little streets
beyond the city gates. Here came and went Tudor spies and
couriers, preparing the Day of the Dragon when the red standard of their Prince would be boldly unfurled upon English
ground. King Richard knew of the existence of such houses,
but so well served was Henry Tudor that betrayals seldom
occurred. Oddly, Richard was credited by his foes with possessing an efficient secret organization of his own; but the
truth was that the King had been caught completely by surprise in the Buckingham Rebellion of eighteen months previous and even after that lesson he now seemed unaware of
the extent to which his power had been infiltrated by
Tudor's men.

The Tudor leaders maintained, without troubling over-
much about logic, that Richard's reputation had grown so
bad he was unable to get honest men to serve him. Hence,
despite his known generosity, he was betrayed on all sides.
As one tale of terror came huddling upon the next, plain
God-fearing Englishmen fell away from the King. A full
reckoning of his crimes had not even been made. The Tudor
leaders hinted at terrible deeds yet unknown.

However, what was known or publicly imputed to Richard was sufficiently grim to chill the stoutest English heart.

King Henry the Sixth, fond foolish old man, saintly and

harmless—bludgeoned to death in the Tower. Prince Edward of the Red Rose, a youth of wondrous promise—stabbed in cold blood at Tewkesbury. Sir Anthony Woodeville, the most gallant knight in England—beheaded at Pontefract. Lord William Hastings, brave soldier and royal councillor—beheaded in the Tower. King Edward the Fifth and his brother Richard, Duke of York, innocent and gifted boys—done to death in some unknown manner within the Tower. And others of lesser import, such as Richard Grey and Thomas Vaughan, companions of the ill-fated little Princes.

Part of this terrible charge was incontrovertible: Henry the Sixth; Anthony Woodeville; Hastings; Grey and Vaughan. Part was at least arguable: Prince Edward. And part, the worst deed of all, was shrouded in doubt: the boys in the Tower.

The Tudor leaders proceeded on the familiar line that if a man was guilty of five deaths and quite possibly a sixth, it was not difficult to persuade the common jury of the English people of a seventh and an eighth killing.

And so it proved. . . .

To a small house in Fetter Lane, near St. Dunstan's in the West, came a tall, stooped man in a clerical gown. He knocked thrice and was quickly admitted. He entered a dim, sparse chamber where another man sat before a red hearth. Glances met. The two men, the visitor and the fellow with bandaged shoulder, appraised one another. The wounded man got to his feet. "Urswicke!" he exclaimed.

The visitor stared. "You look in bad case, John Flory."

The wounded man swayed. He had lost much blood and his face was haggard. "An accident," he said. "Hazards of the trade."

Urswicke rubbed thumb and forefinger together. "No ~eed to pretend with me. I know about your brawling." His ~ice had a cold intelligent quality.

John Flory sat down. He huddled near the fire. Neither man spoke for a moment, while the twilight grew and silvered in the room. Master Urswicke paced softly up and down. Once or twice he gave the wounded man a quick frown.

Flory looked at him, the look of one accustomed to dealing in all conditions of human being. "What is your business, Master Urswicke?" he inquired.

Christopher Urswicke paused. He uttered a small sigh. "I have heard about you, Flory," he said. "Rioting in a Southwark alehouse. That is not what we expect of our men."

John Flory stretched out his hands to the glowing hearth. The small leaping flame; evening's tender gold. "Had I not acted first, I should have been slain," he commented.

Master Urswicke padded to the fire. Cavernous, he stared down at the huddled soldier. "John Flory, you must learn humility," he warned. "You must learn to be quiet; to accept insult; even blows. But never to betray that which you are. You are a pair of eyes and a pair of ears, John Flory. You must cease thinking of yourself as a gentleman, as a squire of Prince Edward. You are a spy."

Flory swallowed. He looked up at the cleric. "I am a spy," he repeated. "An abominable kind of creature, Master Urswicke."

"A most useful creature," Christopher Urswicke said. "If it will learn its tricks properly."

The soldier nodded. He had a bitter smile. "I shall have to take my tricks elsewhere for the moment."

"Indeed you shall," Master Urswicke agreed. "I am charged to command you to France forthwith."

Flory listened to the crackle of the burning log. Little golden flames spurted up. Around them the room was buried in dusk. "Calais," he said. "Why not Calais?" His voice became suddenly strange. "Did you ever think, Master Urswicke, of what curious company a man might meet with in Calais? Men long vanished from England. Men with secrets. Men wishing to live undisturbed. Oh, you might find many answers in Calais, Master Urswicke."

"There is nothing for you in Calais," the cleric said. "You are to go to Paris."

"Pity, isn't it?" Flory shook his head. "When there is a man in Calais I long to meet."

"And who might that be, Master Flory?"

Flory turned. Urswicke's drooping left eyelid gave him the air of a sinister warlock. "Did you ever hear of a man named John Dighton?" the soldier asked.

Urswicke's face took on a sudden masklike aspect. "What do you know of Dighton?" he said.

"Not nearly what I wish to know," Flory replied. "Dighton is a priest. One of your cloth, Master Urswicke. He vanished from England eighteen months ago. Just at the time of the Buckingham Rebellion. I have heard he's now in Calais."

"And why are you concerned with this Dighton, this priest?" Master Urswicke asked softly.

Flory exclaimed: "Come, Master Urswicke! You have a poor memory for so excellent a servant of the Dragon. Not Canon Dick Fox and the Bishop of Ely are accounted more informed than Christopher Urswicke! Who was John Dighton? Come!"

"Well, I have heard the name," Urswicke said cautiously.

Flory laughed dryly. "I am certain you have," he said. "The Chaplain of the Tower at the time of the Buckingham rising. When the sons of Edward disappeared. It was Dighton, the chaplain, who shrived the souls of those slain within the Tower."

"The sons of Edward disappeared in July," Urswicke corrected him.

The soldier gazed about. He could barely make out the room, all soft and blurred in twilight. April twilight. "Fetch a candle, will you?" he said.

Urswicke rummaged greyly in a cupboard. He found a

candle stump, which he kindled. He appeared increasingly gaunt and magical as the little flame illumined his face.

"I've talked with men who glimpsed the boys in the Tower garden as late as September," Flory remarked.

"They are mistaken," Master Urswicke replied. "The boys were dead."

Flory rubbed his jaw. "That notion doesn't make sense," he observed. "Richard was crowned on July the sixth and went on a triumphal progress almost directly afterward. He had no reason to kill the boys. It was not until the Buckingham rising in October—" He broke off, frowning.

"In your position, Master Flory, I would not concern myself with this matter," Christopher Urswicke said.

"Why should I not?" Flory demanded. "Isn't that what Henry Tudor desires more than anything—to fix the death of the boys on their uncle, King Richard? To achieve that is worth an army division to the Earl of Richmond."

"Do not pry into this matter, John Flory!"

Flory stared into the fire. Urswicke was Morton's jackal. And when he spoke, he gave the view of his master. That meant Morton had forbidden speculation concerning the sons of Edward. Morton had decreed that his men accept this absurd tale of a July murder by King Richard. Why?

Urswicke stood before the hearth, smiling his thin complacent smile, the fanatic instrument of the Dragon. "Put out of your mind John Dighton," he advised Flory. "You'll learn nothing from him."

Flory turned. "Don't you believe even Richard gave his royal nephews Christian burial?" he asked.

"I've warned you against this talk," Master Urswicke said.

"Answer me," Flory insisted.

"I know nothing of the manner of the boys' murder," Urswicke replied.

"But you take the most farfetched explanation possible as to the time of the murder," Flory pointed out.

"It is not my explanation, Flory," Urswicke said with cold

clerical anger, "but that of Henry Tudor, Earl of Richmond, and Bishop Morton. Dare you cross your leaders?"

"I would like to know the truth," Flory said.

"Henry Tudor has given you the truth," Urswicke told him. "What an overweening meddlesome fellow you be!"

Flory chuckled. He did not fear Christopher Urswicke. Nor indeed did he quail before Bishop Morton and Canon Fox. A veteran of Tewkesbury, he had seen too much death to be impressed by this priestly crew that had seized control of the remnant of Lancaster.

"Such levity is dangerous in one of your condition," Master Urswicke glowered. "What will the Bishop say to this matter? A drunken brawl. A wench gossiping."

Flory sat up. "What d'ye mean—a wench?"

"We talked to the boy Miles," Urswicke informed him. "He told us of the serving wench. She knew about this miserable fellow Ninepence. And she has guessed what you are. She is not safe."

"I told Lucy nothing!"

"You were careless, Master Flory," Urswicke said. "You know the Bishop cannot abide that any woman suspect the least morsel of his plans. You talked to this girl. You aroused her interest. For anything you know, she might be paid by Richard."

Flory said quietly, "That's impossible. She risked her neck to unbolt the door so that we might escape. And as for women, the Bishop and your mistress Lady Margaret Beaufort are thick as lovers—to say nothing of his dallyings with Lady Elizabeth Grey!"

"Dare you compare holy Lady Margaret to a tavern drab?" Urswicke choked. He took a turn about the room, a tall rustling figure with black sleeves flaring like batwings.

Flory watched him moving up and down, the strange jerky step and the flourish of the batwing sleeves. Morton; the soldier was thinking of Morton's ice-blue, calculating eyes.

The eyes of a man who had known such vast and terrible betrayal that nothing would ever be safe again. Nothing, that
is, except death. One could still count on death.

"Don't trouble about this girl Lucy," Flory said. "She can
do no harm. She's just an ordinary decent girl."

Urswicke jerked about to confront Flory. "Ordinary?" he
exclaimed. "No one is ordinary, Master Flory. Some nameless quiet person may help lose a battle or betray a kingdom.
If you knew the truth behind the campaign of Barnet and
Tewkesbury—"

"Richard's genius," Flory said.

Urswicke shrugged. "Richard and how many unknown
traitors who prepared the way for York? A masterful display
of treachery. We have studied that campaign, Flory. Much
can be learned of York."

Flory saw him caught up in the inexorable demands of his
trade, the eyes gleaming with guile, the whole vulturous
figure tensely poised. "I will answer for Lucy," he vowed.

"She is not safe. . . ." Urswicke said.

Flory felt a touch of cold; a winter wind blowing from this
black hovering clerk. "She is quite safe," he said.

"We do not think so," Master Urswicke replied softly.

We? Who was *we?* Each member of the priestly band
spoke that way, each one forever unwilling to avow his
own part, forever hiding behind the collective inhuman *we.*
Unpleasant decisions, the necessity of putting someone to
silence—Bishop Morton would say that Canon Fox was
looking into the matter; and Canon Fox would refer questions to Master Urswicke; and Master Urswicke, of course,
was only carrying out orders from a Higher Source.

"I will answer for her," the soldier repeated.

Urswicke nodded. He seemed about to say further, but
checked himself. He went toward the door. Flory stared
after the clerk, his heart growing colder and colder.

Urswicke turned at the door. "A ship will anchor off

Gravesend tomorrow evening," he said, "flying the Burgundian colours and called the *Great Duke of the West*. You will take that ship, Master Flory."

"Agreed, Master Urswicke," the soldier said. He rose painfully to his feet, a fiery ache in his wounded shoulder. The candle stump had guttered and the room receded into purple dusk.

John Flory stood at the kitchen door of the White Lyon. He knocked sharply and heard the quick beat of footsteps within. The door opened and Lucy looked out. She peered at him uncertainly. "Oh, it's you!" she exclaimed. "What do you want? It's after closing time."

"I want to speak with you," he said.

"Not here," she said, a catch in her breath. "You shouldn't come here."

"We'll go along the river," he suggested.

She looked doubtful. "The hostess won't like it," she said. "I'm cleaning up."

"To the Devil with the hostess!" He caught her wrist, pulled her into the moonless night. They were in a small close, a pocket formed by the low backs of several spice shops, their product famous in Long Southwark. Nearby appeared the dim bulk of the King's prison of the Clinke. Over the close hung a reek of garbage.

Lucy glanced up at Flory. "You are a queer 'un!" she said.

They went out of the close and toward the bankside. Church spires glimmered and Pepper Alley straggled toward the Bridge. Near the river were more inns: the Queen's Head, the Tabard, the George. Bridge Ward Without was a haunt of travellers.

She noticed the bulge of Flory's bandaged shoulder beneath the russet cloak. "What happened to your shoulder?" she asked.

"Caught a dagger in it," he replied. He was still feeling weak from loss of blood.

"They've been watching for you," she said, "Red Hugh and the others. They're going to kill you. Red Hugh was burned bad about the face."

"It won't improve his looks," he remarked grimly.

She was silent, and they walked on. They came in sight of the stews which groped along the river bank all the way to the Bridge. It was near midnight and the city was very quiet. Lucy had a worried look. She turned nervously to Flory from time to time.

"You must get away from the White Lyon," he said abruptly. "Go to some unfrequented place in the country."

She stopped short. "What d'ye mean?"

"You're in danger," he told her. "It's my fault. I should never have spoken with you."

"What danger?" she exclaimed. "Who would want to bother me? I've never harmed a soul."

Innocence, he thought, was no refuge. There were no sanctuaries left in the world. "I can't tell you any more. Believe me, I know or I would not have come."

She had a small rosebud mouth. Her young face was framed in whorls of spun gold. So might Jane Shore have appeared when first she came from Cheape to dance at Court and fascinate the dashing King Edward. "I knew you were not of the Boar Company," she said. "I saw you were different—a gentleman."

For the first time he noticed she was wearing a marguerite flower, as on the previous night. He had a moment of unbearable regret. Her words, the white marguerite, recalled to him as never before the image of what he was, of what he had been. No nameless and wandering crepuscule of war— but Messire John Flory, squire of the body to Prince Edward Plantagenet, and banner bearer to Edmund Beaufort, Duke of Somerset. They had been young; war took them on a far journey. And they grew old, they died—all in the space of a fortnight. . . .

"You can trust me," she whispered.

He looked away, angry with himself, with her. She had
called up Queen Margaret; she had made him remember.
But he was Morton's man now. He had put away knighthood, as one put away childish things. "Will you go away?"
he asked curtly.

"Tell me why," she insisted. "What have I done?"

He swung to her, took her hands in his. "A deadly fight
is going on in England," he said to her. "You, without wanting to, without knowing it, have become a part of that fight.
You have called attention to yourself. Through me this has
happened. You must disappear; you must get out of *their*
sight."

Lucy trembled. They were standing on the river bank, on
the opposite shore the twinkling lights of Westminster. The
embattled turrets rode proudly above the dark water. Here
in this citadel of monarchy watched and prowled the defiant
Captain of England. Murderer or gallant Defender of the
Realm?

"When must I go?" the girl said.

"Tomorrow," he replied. "Before anyone is abroad."

"I shall go south, to Dorset," she mused. "My aunt is living there."

He nodded, pleased. She would be safe—safe from he
knew not whom. In this struggle, neither side spared the
knife. She would be unknown again; no one would trouble
about her.

"Was it Richard's men you feared?" she whispered. "Did
you think they would discover I had helped you?"

"It is Richard—and others," he said.

She looked at him with wonder and he had a moment of
tenderness for her. She was so young and alone and gallant.
She asked, it seemed, so little. He stooped and kissed her.

"Ah," she said, "why did you do that?"

He glanced at her yellow scarf, faintly gleaming in the
night. "I wanted to," he said.

"Good reason!" she laughed. "D'ye like me, master?"

"Yes," he replied. He liked her. Perhaps one day he would go to Dorset. She waited for him to kiss her again. He did; and suddenly he wanted her, her fragrance, her fresh young body, her kindness and joy. She folded into his arms.

But it was no use. He was obsessed by Morton, by the necessity of getting away. He could not surrender himself, even for an hour. The Rose was his mistress, the cruel blood-red Rose. Sometimes he hated the Rose; yet could no longer live without Her. Besides, he was coming back. There would be time for Lucy.

He released her. "I'll take you back," he said.

Her eyes were puzzled and hurt. "It's better you don't," she said. "The house is watched. I wonder they did not seize you before."

"I'll come to Dorset," he promised. "It will be better then. Another day for us both."

But was there another day?

"God keep you, master!" Lucy said. She kissed him; and suddenly fled. He was left standing at Time's last corner, about him the climbing steeples of Southwark high and lonely in the starlight. . . .

Lucy heard the sound of buskins ringing on the dark. Her buskins. She moved in night; intense, palpable, depth on depth. Going down, ever descending—a crooked stair into infinity. It seemed to the girl that she had never come this way before. Times fivescore she might have passed here, but never glimpsing, never suspecting what crouched below the wall.

About the girl echoes danced. Other steps mingled with her steps, stealthy pursuing feet. She hurried on. From the close, a shadow leaned; a hand plucked her sleeve. "What d'ye want?" she faltered.

"You. . . ."

Lucy quailed. "Who are you?" she whispered.

"Never mind, Lucy," a quiet voice said.

"Let me pass," she implored. "I've done nothing. Truly I never harmed a soul."

The shadow was shaped into a man, cloaked and hooded. She could not see his face. One bony hand curled about her yellow scarf. She shrank. "God's pity, master!" she cried.

"You've been a fool, Lucy," the voice said. "But you shall be a fool no more."

She felt the scarf tighten about her neck. She struggled. The night about her seemed to press down upon her face. A black terrible weight. She flung up her arms, turning and twisting—and the scarf tightened.

"Goodnight, Lucy. Goodnight, my dear."

❋✦✤❋✦✤❋✦✤❋

ELIZABETH stood on the landing stairs of Norfolk House, the river swirling at her feet and a rainwet wind blowing. She felt cool drops upon her face and breast, a christening of the night. She longed to shed her clothes and plunge into the dark water, to give her body to the rushing tide. She had a sense of dark forces within and without her, a fierce power driving her along strange paths.

She had been a girl; now she entered womanhood. Yet her state was not complete, sealed by love. She waked alone, her body a bright cup never drunk from. Often she would become tense, she would spring up to pace about the room, thinking of Richard. She would behold his long sunken face and piercing eyes, his iron body. His body that was like a sword to cleave . . .

She told no one of her longings. Understand?—how could they understand, these aging schemers about her? Their lives were squandered in the worst of all passions—the passion of money and power. Her desire they would despise. Her love, the unburnt dream of nineteen, was foolish and unprofitable.

And as none of them understood her, no more did any of them understand Richard. Not one of them was worthy of his greatness, his splendour. With pity and contempt, Elizabeth called up the memory of her dead mistress, Lady Anne —a being too frail for a love worthy of Richard. Sweating and feeble, coughing—how could her Richard have endured this woman for ten years? Shamelessly, the girl thought of poor pale Anne entombed and out of the way at last. Of that icy sleep, that endless regal freeze in the vaults of the Abbey —while her own body tingled with blood.

A few feet below Elizabeth, the eyes of the boatman gleamed. He was watching her, wondering about her. She had bribed him well to slip her away from Westminster; bribed him with money stolen from Lady Grey's purse. She had never stolen before; now in the grip of her vision, she did not hesitate. She could always pay back her mother when she became a queen. Besides, it was really Richard's money. Richard was giving Lady Grey seven hundred marks a year to live on.

Occasionally Elizabeth wondered: would this dream of hers be punished? Would they suffer, Richard and she? Even if she knew that suffering would follow, she could not help herself. What she longed for was a mortal sin: incest, incest in the highest degree but one. An incest of soul as well as body. She dared to give herself utterly; to mingle her spirit with Richard's, to become one with him.

Elizabeth groped along the landing, wrapped in a green hunting cloak. Ahead of her loomed the rambling Norfolk House. Should she be glimpsed now, it might be suspected she was a woman of the stews—that cluster of evil dwellings leaning riverward where wretched Clarence had been wont to go. Stew women were women of all nations, instructed in every lewdness, nightly trafficking in their bodies. Elizabeth hastened up the landing.

A man came out of the shadows, carrying a lanthorn. He stopped short; the girl shrank into her cloak. His jacket glistened with rain and he wore a flat black cap. He was young, no more than a lad. He stared at Elizabeth; for an instant his fresh-coloured face was oddly familiar. He drew aside, allowing her to pass. It seemed to Elizabeth that the lad's eyes knew her; but it might have been only the sudden glow of the lanthorn, coming out of the night.

She went on to the postern door of Norfolk House.

The bell tinkled, fading in cavernous depths. Presently the girl heard footsteps. A shutter in the door slid back and a man's face peered out. "I must see Norfolk," she said. His look was doubtful. She plucked a silver half-angel from her cloak. The forbidding face quickly changed. A skinny hand reached out and snatched the coin. "Take me to Norfolk," she requested.

The door groaned inward; and Elizabeth was standing in the small draughty passage leading into the manor. Norfolk's man beckoned with a fluttering rushlight. Together they went down into the cold silence.

As soon as she came into the presence chamber, came out of green dusk into light, she saw how matters were. Norfolk had prepared for her. He was sitting with Francis Viscount Lovell. She hesitated, her eyes blinking, little dancing lights across her vision. The room before her was brightly lit by rush lamps and red candles set in iron sockets along the wall. She might have turned then—departed. Spared herself the humiliation of this moment. But she had dared so much. She could not give up at once.

Nor would it have suited the two lords of York to let her go like that. They had other intentions regarding her. Neither one rose as Elizabeth entered; neither one spoke. They were allowing her to begin. Her words flew silently away, like frightened moths. She gazed about the room, noting how well John Howard, son of Margaret Mowbray, did himself now that he had risen from the bluff squire of East Anglia to Norfolk's dukedom. Tapestries flaring on the walls, chairs with crimson velvet cushions, a tall credenza shining with silver vessels. And everywhere the rampant

White Lyon of Mowbray and Norfolk, on the gorgeous tapestries, on the velvet cushions, on the blue livery of the steward. She wondered, did John Howard have his White Lyon sewed on his underclothing. He was a very recent duke.

Lovell nodded at the girl. He had the more friendly manner of the two. Perhaps it was because he was bred to *courtoisie*. Though he was but a viscount, his blood was among the best in England; and he wore his silver lupus badge—his Wolf Dog—more easily than did Norfolk his Lyon. "Sit down, Bess," Lovell said at length. "Tell us why you have come here."

She sank into a crimson cushion. She felt on the edge of collapse. She had built to such knife-cruel tension for this visit; and abruptly her plans had shattered about her. Norfolk had set the stage. He had confronted her with the man she most distrusted, of Richard's councillors. The man who had been closest to the dead Queen. Francis Viscount Lovell.

Elizabeth swallowed and said: "I did not think to find you here, Lord Lovell. I came to see the Duke."

Lovell smiled. He had a certain handsomeness, a dark ironic face and a lean body. He was Richard's nearest friend, if the King could be said to have any friends in the true meaning of the term. "His Grace of Norfolk has dined me well," he remarked.

The lords had small crystal bowls of brandy before them. During this interval, Norfolk had uttered no word; he continued to fix his heavy gaze upon the girl. She grew nervous and angry beneath this scrutiny, recalling how in the time of her father the King this bulky Essex farmer had been barely noticed. He was always hovering on the rim of royalty, just out of conversation range, grateful when some minion tossed him a remark. Oh, John Howard had bounded to his feet as Bess, his King's eldest child, had swept into the room! A would-be courtier, falling over rustic feet; an Essex grog drinker, square, awkward, the colour of old weathered brick.

"Rash, rash," Norfolk suddenly found his tongue. "I never saw the like." He rubbed his jaw.

It was no use losing her temper. No doubt the lords expected her to throw a girl's tantrum; tears and ranting. But she must be cunning. She must be Woodeville. "My business is privy for you, Your Grace," she said to Norfolk.

He shrugged. "If you mean, lass, that foolish letter of yours, you can cease troubling about it. Viscount Lovell knows."

This news startled her. She had not dreamed Norfolk would go so far. How could she ever have confided in such a thick fellow? She had been desperate, that was it; and John Howard had always been eager to oblige in her father's time. She had forgot that whatever favour she might have shown plain John Howard, she could no longer do anything for the great Duke of Norfolk, the Earl Marshal of England. "Lord Lovell saw my letter?" she exclaimed. "I had not thought it of Your Grace. The letter was writ to you alone."

Lovell spoke up. "His Grace did not give me the letter, Bess."

She turned, frowning. "How did it come to you, then?"

Lovell put his head back, glancing up at the scrolled walnut beams of the ceiling. He seemed to be counting the gilt nail pegs. "How did you send the letter, Bess?" he asked casually.

She tried to remember; every detail was important. She was standing in her chamber, it was dusk—and in the court they were changing the guard. Yes, she recalled all of it, even to the sudden clarion of the Clock Tower bell. She had the letter in her hand, sealed with her own seal of the Rose that her father had given her, and in that instant she glimpsed the thin bright face of Jean of Gloucester passing in the twilight. Richard's only living son, by a woman the King never spoke of, never acknowledged. Elizabeth called to Jean. She hastened with the letter. The boy would do anything for her. They were two outcasts of royal lineage;

he, bastard by reason of his birth; she, made bastard by Act of Parliament.

Every detail was important . . . and Lovell, she could sense Lovell covertly watching her, while seeming to count the nail pegs. The worst was Lovell knowing. Anyone else would have been less dangerous to her hope. She thought back to that moment in the courtyard, Jean of Gloucester beside her in the dusk, torches flaring, soldiers striding about, a mounted patrol jingling in from Surrey. She had given the letter to Jean. . . .

"I am sure of my bearer," the girl said to Lovell.

He shrugged. Evidently he did not intend to tell her how he knew; what he wanted to talk about was the sentiment of the letter. "What you wrote was mad and perilous," he said. "King Richard is your uncle by blood, own brother to your father Edward. You know he can never marry you. You must give up this wild dream."

Elizabeth perceived that under their confident air both men were alarmed by her. Norfolk more so than Lovell. The Duke had come up so rapidly that he might go down equally fast. She was a dangerous unknown element in their masculine equation of power. "I meant what I wrote to His Grace of Norfolk," she avowed to Lovell.

He sighed. "I am certain you did, Bess. That is the worst of it."

"Ye be like to unhorse us all with your larking," Norfolk said roughly. "Lady Grey should set you to some honest task. Braid stitching or quilting. Your place is beside your mother!"

This was so despairingly humorous to Elizabeth that she almost burst into an hysterical laugh. For she was aware—a situation that might never penetrate that Essex pate—that now, perhaps at this very moment, her mother was receiving secretly the envoy of Margaret Beaufort, mother of Henry Tudor; the tall spare jackram Christopher Urswicke, a clerk

in holy orders, with a drooping eyelid and a vast appetite for
intrigue.

"Excuse me," she said, her face flushed with suppressed
laughter.

"This is no laughing matter," the Duke growled. "You
don't know the devilish muddle you are getting us in."

"I'm sorry, Your Grace," she returned. "But it's you who
will not understand. I came to speak honestly with you and
you have done nothing but rate me."

Norfolk didn't like this at all. The girl was being what he
called in his downright Essex, "froward." And John Howard
couldn't abide a "froward" woman.

Lovell intervened. He knew Elizabeth could not be
bullied. "We want your help, Bess," he said smoothly. "Only
you may put matters right." He poured dark-gold armagnac
into a crystal voide and offered the cup to the girl.

She sipped, allowing the armagnac to melt upon her
tongue, a few drops at a time—as her uncle Anthony Lord
Rivers, the poet and chevalier of the Woodevilles, had
taught her to drink French brandy. The tingling flavour of
the armagnac recalled Anthony's ruthless execution at Pontefract, beheaded by order of Richard. A bloody wraith in
Richard's march to the Throne. "What d'ye want me to do?"
she asked Lovell, her tone flat.

"We want you to deny any intent of marriage, except with
some proper person chosen by the Council," Lovell informed
her. "This rash letter of yours may reach Tudor. And you
must deny that you have ever written such a letter. No one
in England must be able to say that you have been encouraged to commit the sin of marrying your uncle and protector."

She listened to him, leaning into the light, the dark-gold
armagnac glistening. She thought how many had already
died for this monarchy; how many more must die. Of
the torment and cruelty of the Rose. And these men were a
part of that. Just as Henry Tudor was, and the heirs

of vengeance, those inspired by the curses and the frenzy of the dead despoiled Queen, Marguerite d'Anjou. And Richard himself. Sins against life, beside which her sin was white. But she could never make these men understand her.

"What is your answer?" Norfolk demanded impatiently.

"Why do you ask me?" she countered. "Isn't this a matter for the King to decide?"

Lovell gave her a furrowed glance. Quietly he explained to her that her letter had made it impossible to overlook her own position. "If the letter falls into Tudor's hands, we must act—and quickly," he said. "We are giving you the chance to deny the letter. If you refuse, there is but one other way."

"And what is that other way?" Elizabeth wondered.

"We're not here to bargain, lass," Norfolk broke in. "Give us your answer."

She hesitated. Not because she was unsure of her reply, but because in the room's warm gold of evening, the ducal glint of silver, the rich shadow on the velvet, she caught a cold grey light . . . the light that falls on all passions, all grandeur and pride. She had a moment of awe. In her was all the pride and terror of the past; the unbidden secret memory that came to her out of all the dark years and storm of dying that she had never known—the blood-memory of her House.

"I shall speak to Richard!" she told the lords.

They were silent. Norfolk had an angry flush. Lovell gazed at her, fingers cradling his brandy cup. Elizabeth turned uneasily, listening to a hollow booming sound—the wind about the walls of the manor. The wind from the river.

"You will not see Richard, Bess." It was Lovell's voice, hard and final.

☙✦↯☙✦↯☙✦↯☙

UPON the King's left wrist perched a silver falcon. A gold chain encircled its stiff short leg, a chain that terminated in

a tiny gold lock. Lock and chain were fast to the royal wrist
by a stout leather band. The hawk was young, a fledgling
on its first hunt. Later, after a number of kills, the bird
might go unfettered. Now it was tense and nervous, the keen
cruel eyes peering at the morning wood, the steel trap of the
beak opening and closing.

The King spoke to the falcon, stroking its pale plumage,
calling it *Flèche d'argent,* which is to say, "silver arrow."
The bird regarded the King. Yellow gleaming eyes met un-
winking the hazel eyes of the man. They gazed silently at
one another. King and falcon: on some naked crag of the
spirit they seemed to meet.

Richard turned. "What d'ye think of Flèche, Lovell?" he
inquired. "Will he be a prize bird, say you?"

Viscount Lovell rested his gloved right hand, reins firmly
in his fist, on the saddle bow. "The first kill is the important
one," he replied.

The King listened. He could hear the beaters hallooing
as they roused the brush. Thank God, Richard thought, for
birds and not dogs today. Birds that are quiet and deadly.
Birds that break the sky in long beautiful arcs. He wondered
what kind of hunter Flèche might prove. Never could you
tell about *argent* hawks.

Lovell's bird was a peregrine, glossy blue-black feathers
and a white triangular patch on the breast. A good hunter,
the peregrine. A bird well-fleshed in killing aforehand. But
this morning Francis Lovell was not bent on the chase.

They rode deeper into Sherwood Forest. Both men wore
buff jackets and long crumpling boots of doeskin. The only
princely accoutrement Richard displayed was a gold chain
of York Sunnes about his neck.

"April mornings remind me of Warwick, when we were
lads together," Lovell remarked.

The King glanced at his Lord Chamberlain and friend.
He hoped Lovell did not intend to begin again on the dead
woman, to invoke sentimentally the image of Anne. It had

been embarrassing, to say the least, when Lovell had burst into sobs at the Abbey funeral service, and the King controlling himself so well.

"You look tired, Lovell," Richard said.

Lovell's cheek twitched. He was pale under his natural swarthy colour. "I never sleep well at Nottingham Castle," he said.

Neither did Richard. Nottingham was his "Castle of Care," where the boy Edward had died in torment the April before. But Lovell was not thinking of the unhappy Prince of Wales. The Chamberlain had suggested the falcon hunt, just he and Richard. He wanted to talk. Richard wondered.

"Grey, Lord Dorset, is about to break from Tydder," the King declared. "What will John Morton make of that, eh?— his Woodeville ally giving him the slip, going back to the old loyalty."

"I wanted to ask about that matter," Lovell said. "It's a bold stroke for you, Richard. What about the price?"

"The price?" Richard turned with wrinkled brow. He was disappointed that Lovell did not show more enthusiasm for this success of his.

"When did the Woodevilles give something for nothing?" Lord Lovell wondered. "Elizabeth Woodeville has never forgot that for twenty years she was Queen."

Richard shrugged. He no longer feared the Woodevilles. Elizabeth Plantagenet had changed all that. Now he tolerated a family once odious to him; now he was even willing to make common cause with this family against Henry Tydder, calling himself Tudor, Earl of Richmond.

"Lady Grey knows she will never be a queen again," he commented.

Lovell looked thoughtful. A whirring came from the wood, a short bowshot away. The two falconers pointed their horses toward the sound. Likely the beaters had flushed woodcock, the common bird of these parts. The hunters had hoped for more exciting game.

Down a little sunlit way, a green and russet cloister barred with gold, the horsemen went. It was quiet in Sherwood Forest, old overarching oak and beech, a cluster of yellow loosestrife, the white St. John's wort, and the bright ghosts of Robin Hood and his merry men walking in the green and morning light.

The King stroked his falcon. He was content, they were both content. Flêche would have his kill.

"Lady Grey isn't scheming to become Queen herself," Lovell said after a moment. "It will be enough for her purpose if her bastard Elizabeth wears a crown. The old witch will have made another Woodeville Queen of England!"

Richard frowned. He didn't like the twist Lovell gave to his words. Besides, who was the Chamberlain talking of? Henry Tydder? Tydder was not like to marry anyone until he had gained an estate, which he was far from achieving. John, Earl of Lincoln and the heir to the throne? Near Princess Elizabeth in years, Lincoln was the son of Richard's eldest sister Elizabeth, Duchess of Suffolk. He had been made Richard's heir on the death of the Prince of Wales.

Though the possibility of Lincoln and Elizabeth had indeed crossed the King's mind, he had found sound reasons for rejecting such a marriage. The bar of bastardy on Elizabeth. The near blood kinship of these two first cousins. Where the possibility of Elizabeth marrying a young popular Plantagenet was concerned, Richard became very strict on the canonical rules.

"I don't understand you," the King said to Lovell.

Lovell was removing the hood from his black peregrine. They were close to the quarry. They could hear the beaters calling to one another and the rustle of wings and the scamper of some small animal, perhaps a hare, through the brush —while sunlight fell in glistening sprays. Lovell jerked his head. "I think you understand me well, Richard," he retorted.

The King's hand, cased in a white gauntlet, caught

Lovell's bridle. "What are you saying, Francis?" he demanded.

Lovell turned, the peregrine fluttering on his wrist. For a moment he stared silently at the King. Then he smiled faintly. "Don't let the prey escape, Richard," he said, breaking the tension between them.

A capless boy with a brown face and lithe body came running down the path. At almost the same instant the hunters glimpsed the stately arc of a cock pheasant. It was a bird sweet to look upon, gorgeous in the morning: plumes of gold, bronze, blue and green; a lordly tail; a white and dark mask.

Richard slipped the chain from the silver falcon's leg. Flêche quivered. Aye, the hawk knew. The hawk knew, though it had never killed before. Lovell held back his peregrine. "Take the beauty, Richard," he said.

The lithe brown boy was driving the pheasant toward the riders. Though royally arrayed, the bird was ill-provided for woodland life. It could not hide, as could its small brown cousin; it could not fly swiftly; it could not, with its awkward train, even run very well. It was a flash of glory; glory that must die.

Richard thrust out his left arm. Flêche bolted into the sunlight. The pheasant glimpsed the silver killer winging. The bird plunged away. Richard followed the pursuit, delightedly noting the instinctive checking of the hawk as it drove the pheasant in an ever-diminishing pattern of choice.

The King laughed. Flêche would do. Flêche would do very well. Nothing in the world so fine as the checking and daring of a keen hawk, this taut and mortal mastery of air, dazzling down, soaring upward, a glint of death in the sun. . . .

"Dorset, her own son," Lovell was saying. "The witch would cast her own son in the scales against a crown for the bastard daughter."

"Nothing was said of crowns," Richard replied sharply.

He did not care to mention to Lovell what had been discussed: the boys in the Tower. "Lady Grey's true interest lies with the old blood of York. Not with a beggarly Welshman."

Lovell smoothed the peregrine's jet feathers. "Next time, next time," he murmured to the hawk.

"Lady Grey is a woman of sense," Richard went on. "She has the political shrewdness of a man."

Lovell had a crooked smile. "Indeed she has," he agreed. "But can you trust her least word?"

The King watched the twisting pursuit. Skimming the treetops, surging into the blue—and ever the silver death, the shining terror of the falcon. Did the hunted bird already know the end? The steel talons gorging the beautiful breast; the fierce beak hammering the helpless brain. As in battle soldiers hammered with mace and axe upon the helm of a fallen knight. Richard felt for a moment numb and horrified. . . .

"That witch might swear to me on the Crown of Thorns entire and I would take measures for the morrow," Lovell vowed.

The King put a hand to his face. The moment passed. It was like trumpets ringing and the flash of an old, haunting country.

Lovell gazed at the doom wheeling overhead. But the compulsions of the royal councillor matched the huntsman's ardour. "Lady Grey tells her daughter that she is royal," the Chamberlain said. "She whispers that the bar of bastardy shall be broke. She leads the girl to dream of golden robes and a crown. Whence came these notions, Richard?"

The King sensed Lovell's drift. His hand clenched. He felt bright anger. Was he, Richard, King by God's Grace, to be questioned by any subject? Francis Lovell was his friend, the only friend remaining from that fierce testing time of youth. But kingship set limits to the presumptions of old friends.

"I don't know where Lady Grey's notions come from," Richard said in a cold flat tone. "She has written to Dorset, but I have promised only fair treatment for her son. The woman has many hours to spin her fancies."

"Is it fancy, then, that this bastard girl—?" Lovell began.

"Must you repeat at every turn her disinheritance?" Richard interrupted. "I am aware of it."

Lovell glanced at the King. The black hawk looked at Richard, too. Each glance was curious and veiled. "This Elizabeth," Lovell said. "Is it fancy that she has written a secret letter to Norfolk—a letter concerning her hope of marriage?"

Richard swung around in the saddle. White Surrey, the noble stallion, started and tossed his Arab head. "Marriage?" the King cried. "Marriage with whom?"

"With you, Richard," Lovell said.

The King turned rigid. For several moments he said nothing. Then he asked in a choked voice: "Do you have this letter?" The Chamberlain handed him a crumpled parchment with a broken seal of the Rose. Richard knew it as the seal of Elizabeth. His heart quickened. He scanned the letter.

Richard looked up; looked away, into the woodland. He stared into the green heart of noon. His fingers trembled on the parchment. Words rang in his mind. *The King is my only joy and maker in this world* . . . that was an old way of speaking, he knew. The way of the North. Maker: the poet, the fire bearer, the bringer of song.

Many had feared the King; some had admired him; a few had called him friend. But no one before had ever cried to him as life's joy and maker!

And the girl Elizabeth had written: *I am his in heart and thought* . . . words stained upon the King's soul for all time. And the rash pen rushing on—love's arrogance and bitter longing—*the better part of February is past and it seems as if the Queen will never die.* . . .

Richard breathed deep. He looked hard at Lovell. "Who knows of this letter?" he demanded.

"Copies are about," Lovell replied. "One may come to Tudor and Morton. They may publish this letter to the world."

Publish his letter! Elizabeth's shining cry . . . Richard went white. His eyes burned in their deep sockets. "If Tudor does that, I will shut his mother in the Tower!" he burst out in a fury. "Lady Margaret shall answer for Tudor's treachery and her own!"

"It will be too late then," Lovell reminded him. "The harm will be done. England will know about this girl."

"I must speak to Elizabeth . . ." Richard said desperately. "She must retract; withdraw. . . ."

Lovell shook his head. "No use, Richard," he said in a sombre tone. "There is but one thing to do now."

The King glanced quizzically at his friend, his companion-in-arms and liegeman. "And what is that, Lovell?"

"You must swear an oath before Lords and Commons," Lovell told him. "An oath on holy relics that never had you considered marriage with your niece Elizabeth."

An oath on holy relics denying Elizabeth. A public oath. Richard revolted. "There must be another way," he said. "This was a private letter writ to Norfolk."

Lovell's tone was earnest, warning. "A copy came into my hands. The girl used a messenger; she has no sense of caution. A letter like that is precious largesse to John Morton. You know the rumours that have been about since Twelfth Night when the Woodeville girl danced at Court in a gown exactly like that worn by Anne, your wife. That affair was bad enough. Morton may have something much worse—a letter from Elizabeth herself that Morton will claim you inspired. This letter will shake your kingdom!"

Lovell put a hand on Richard's arm. "For the love of God, heed me. If you don't act at once, your throne is in peril. Your captains cannot answer for their men."

The King was silent. In the glinting noon overhead, death was near. The pheasant tired, flailing . . . while Flèche hovered with talons unsheathed. The huntsman in the King noted that a more practised hawk would have swooped. Flèche was young, still learning to kill.

Richard turned. "Do Catesby and Ratcliffe know of this letter?"

"They do," Lovell replied.

"Are they of your thinking?"

"In this matter, we are one," Lovell said.

The King nodded, tight-lipped. It was unlike Lovell to turn to these two for support. He had determined to force Richard's hand. The King was stubborn. Did they think, any of them, that they could manage the realm better? As Buckingham had thought. . . .

"I shall weigh your proposal," he said to Lovell.

"We have no time," Lovell asserted. He played a trump. "Lady Grey is behind her daughter. This letter comes from her. The witch has you friendly disposed by means of Dorset. Now she reveals her real intention."

"Have you any proof of this?" Richard demanded.

Lovell shrugged. "The proof of Lady Grey's whole life," he said. "She has been behind every Woodeville scheme for money and power. For twenty years! It's not likely she's changed."

Richard was taken by a flurry in the sky. Death, laggard cruising death, now swooped; a bolt of brightness winging downward, a shock of steel and feathers at treetop level—and killer and prey abruptly disappeared.

Lovell pressed his attack. "Don't you see what the witch is after?" he exclaimed. "She wants the bar of bastardy on her children removed. She will go to any lengths to accomplish that. And once she has got that, Richard, she has got you!"

Richard gazed at the wood, the light, the trees, the shadows that receded into oak-sheltered centuries of English time. Robin Hood, the beloved outlaw . . . why did Richard the Third think of Robin Hood now? Was it because he himself felt a kind of outlaw, a man cut off from the flashing fountains of life? "The woman's friendship is worth something, Lovell," he said. "I know what she is like, I have always known; but I need Lady Grey now."

"Do you think she can ever be your friend, Richard?" Lovell said in a pale voice.

Richard turned, met the eyes of his councillor and friend. He wanted to ask Lovell a question and did not dare. It was a question that could never be asked. He had to learn to live silently and desperately with the fact of the boys, Edward's sons, as a man might learn to live with a disease gnawing at his vitals. The disease might be mortal, it might be destroying him in slow terrible ways, but meantime life went on, hours had to be passed, days got through, the game of kingship played. . . .

"Elizabeth is my friend," he said. "And I hoped—in time—that Lady Grey . . ."

Lovell shook his head. Both men were sombre in the glowing hush of noon, in the green-burning gold of the wood about them. The King remained fixed in his saddle, held fast by some invisible force. His lean jaw was set; his sunken eyes stared into the golden wood. He was a man so unquenchable and timeless that he seemed a riven part of these ancient shadows, of this glistening play and sparkle of Druid light.

"You must give up this girl," Lovell said. "God's Death, Richard! Know your enemies!"

Richard lifted a hand to his face. His cheek was cold; cold as October.

And here came Flêche, hurrying with his kill, exultant as only a falcon can be that has blooded for the first time. He came on a crest of shining air, bearing in his claws the dead pheasant. Richard dismounted. Flêche circled over the King and then, as the hawks in the royal mews had been taught, dropped the prize at Richard's feet.

Richard stooped, picked up the warm punctured body. The gold and bronze, the blue and green were blazoned with blood. Death oozed and trickled from the proud bird.

The King turned to Lovell, in his hand the pheasant's broken splendour. The blood gleamed in the sun. "A royal kill . . ." he said.

❋✧✦❋✦✧❋✦❋✦✧❋

HE glimpsed her, as it seemed, running toward him down a Norman cloister, in a moment of grey-gold light. His heart turned, as on that falcon morning when he had beheld her seal of the Rose. He forgot their blood and destiny, the speech in his mind, the bar of shame upon her. They were alone in grey-gold light; it was April and something had begun and ended for them both. . . .

"I know where you're going!" she burst out. "Don't try to deny it."

He looked at her. She wore a violet cape with a flaring bow of black velvet. She was angry and lovely. Though they were almost of the same height, she appeared at this instant to dominate. She stared back at him.

"I haven't denied it," he said.

She laughed and her laugh was not pleasant. "What are you afraid of?" she demanded. "You an anointed king! A Plantagenet! Why have you refused to see me for three days?"

He breathed quickly, hands fidgeting. "I'm sorry, Bess. The decision is made."

Her gaze was bright scorn. She looked up and down the empty cloister. "Why, you're afraid now," she said. "Trembling lest someone, Lovell or Ratcliffe, should see us together."

"That's not true," he said—and realized it was but too

true. He cared for his kingship as one might care for Heaven.

"All this for a girl's careless letter!" she cried. "That stupid Norfolk. In my father's time—"

"We are not now in your father's time," he reminded her.

"Aye," she said. "He wore his crown twenty-three years and had seven children."

For an instant he hated her. She was taunting him, Richard Plantagenet; telling him that he was not good enough; that his reign would be brief and his stock barren. Was she staring at his shoulder—his high twisted shoulder concealed beneath the murrey cape furred with ermine?

"What do you want, Bess?" he said. "I have little time."

She set her face proudly. Her bronze-coloured hair shone in the old gentle light. "I warn you," she replied, "if you go to St. John's at Clerkenwell, it is finished between us. You and I—we shall be done!"

"You are still my ward, Bess," he said.

She grimaced. "You think you can marry me off, where it pleases you. To some country clod, harmless and smelling of oats. To some lesser Norfolk!"

"You may not marry against my wish," he declared. He found himself growing tense and baffled, as if he were unable to break from this girl. Anne, gentle desolate Anne, had never made him feel this way. Mastering his inner turmoil, he added: "I have sworn to find you a proper husband and to dower you. And equally your four sisters."

"I'll find my own husband," she said smartly. "For some, I may now be well dowered."

He frowned at her. "What d'ye mean? Well dowered? You have nothing."

She shrugged. "If you cast me off, others will not."

He understood. It seemed that whatever he did he was shut in a circular chamber, a chamber with several doors each perfectly alike. And whichever he opened, there grinned the grey mask of Henry Tydder. "You wouldn't be-tray—?" he said to her.

"Oh, what do you wish?" she exclaimed. "Isn't it what you're doing to me? Do you think you can treat me how you please, and I will always be there?"

In a sense that was what he did think. He had to believe in someone; believe that one person always existed who could not be made to betray him. First, there had been his mother, Duchess Cecily of York. Then, his wife Anne. Now Elizabeth. . . .

"I will do anything for you," he promised. "Any-thing. . . ."

Her lip curled. "Anything but give up this absurd mum-mery of an oath on holy relics at St. John's Priory. That is what you can do for me."

He saw that she was amazingly angry and amazingly hard. He had not dreamed it of her. How could he have known her all these years and never discovered what she was really like?

"You have no right—" he began, and broke off. Her eyes, ever a pure azure, had now a greenish tint. She had the right of her faith. It was immense and unanswerable that she should appear to love him. A kind of banner lifted against his foes.

"I want no largesse," she said. "Dowery; money; gowns. Never did I ask for such. My mother bargained with you; but she is not Plantagenet. You have taken away my blood right; my right as King Edward's eldest child. What can you give to replace that?"

And again he felt as if he were bound to her in life and in death. That she was his luck and his talisman; and his doom as well. What he felt for her was beyond love; beyond hope.

"I cannot give you what you did not possess before," he told her.

"I had all—before!" she retorted. "Do I not know what my life has been? Would you take my memory too?"

"Have done with the past," he advised. "You will have another life."

"I shall have the life you give me," she said bitterly.

Her eyes were upon him, her young merciless glance. Suddenly he was conscious of his body. Was she, this royal girl, this radiant daughter of York, was she thinking how meagre he was, how twisted and small? Could she really love him? Was not Lovell right? Lady Grey had been behind the whole affair.

"Why do you not speak?" she demanded.

He bit his lip, a habit of his. Like the trick he had of plucking his dagger up and down in the gold-embossed sheath. A trick that caused his enemies to whisper he was always thinking of murdering someone. But it was only a nervous way he had.

He burned, remembering her avowals. Words taught to her by her mother. And how defiant the girl had shown herself. She deserved a correction. Her pride needed bleeding. For the first time he began to understand that no matter what he had done, or had not done, the Woodevilles would never change toward him. And was not Bess a Woodeville?

"The escort is waiting," he said. Trumpets in the afternoon. The Royal Guard marshalled, glittering at the Gate. Plumed Captains; Heralds in stiff gold and crimson brocade; men-at-arms with the red George Cross; Yeomen of the Crown in blue and murrey.

The glories of blood and state . . .

She said quietly, "Lady Grey told me what you promised her."

He started and his voice rose: "Promised?"

She nodded. "That we should see Edward and Richard, my brothers in the Tower. . . ."

"Lady Grey told you that?" He was stunned. And yet, he

realized, he might have foreseen it. This was the result of trusting Woodevilles! The witch, as Lovell called her, was using her daughter to embarrass and confound him. He felt the girl staring at him again. Perhaps she was thinking of her handsome brother Edward, the gallant well-formed youth that had been Edward the Fifth. Thinking of Edward her brother and of this man with the twisted shoulder, the limp, this man that had never been young. . . .

"When will you let us go to the Tower?" she asked, quivering. "Shall it be tomorrow? Or shall it be the day after?"

He turned aside, so that she might not glimpse his face. "Not at once, Bess," he said. "Later . . ."

"But why not at once?" she cried. "Oh, why not? After almost two years without a glimpse!"

"Well," he said, drawing up and down the opal ring on his right middle finger, "the truth is that young Edward has been ill. We are having a doctor in. You had best not see the boy until we have the doctor's report."

"Is it serious?" she said, imploring. "Something serious?"

He shook his head. "I don't think so. An infection in the mouth. His teeth. It's painful but not, I trust, serious."

"Oh, the poor lad!"

He was looking at her and not looking at her; breathing harshly in the grey-gold Norman light, in the old gentle afternoon. He was aware of black hoods passing and nodding together along the cloister; the black monks of Westminster. And at his feet the timeless glow of light on worn stone slabs, beneath which lay the bones of other monks, centuries of monks, passing, murmuring their beads, the stone hollowed by endless sandals. . . .

"When shall I see my brothers?" she broke in. "Tell me when."

"When I give you leave!" he blazed. "This is not the moment!"

They stood in the hushed cloister, while the ancient coldness seeped about them and in her glance grew a sudden terror. "Is that all you can say, Richard?" Her voice was crushed, hardly heard.

"They are waiting for me." He turned on his boot heel.

Trumpets flared . . .

III. THE DRAGON

Commend me unto Edward my sonne,
The Warden and he together bee
And byd them byrnge Seaven sad yeomen
And all in grene lett them bee,
Changinge their inne in everie towne
Before where they were wont to be;
Lett their backes be from the bench,
Leaste any man shoulde them see,
And by the thirde daye of May
Byd them come and speak with me.

—Song of the Lady Bessy

*W*ANDERING . . . and the terror of twilight, the grey evil sky with black rags of clouds and on ancient stone boot steps ringing. Flory came down the Street of the Temple, the square four-towered donjon of the Temple thrusting into the sky—walls that had sheltered prayers and torture during three centuries, the bastion of the Military Order of the Knights of the Temple. It was the lean and hungry time of twilight; it was the grey grackle light of old stones and old skies dying along the Street of the Temple in the Quarter of the Red Children. It was the mist of tears about crumbling walls, about eyeless raven-haunted turrets, about iron shining blackly from ruined portes.

Wandering . . . it was the sound of voices crying and whispering; the old proud dead. The Rose of tears and blood. It was the little flame of memories, flickering bloodily into the dusk like those desolate red fires around which beggars huddled.

And now the old royal time, the kingly time of pride and dying, came back once more, and he staggered in quietness and in horror down the broken street. Beggars whined; the echo of a drunken song slid along the pointed roofs; a woman's voice shrilled. And listening closely, a kind of dry stealthy counterpoint, a continual rustling—rat's feet.

Death; he might meet Death at any corner, with a thin dark smile and a consecrated knife. *They* were looking for him. *They* were waiting; choosing the moment. It might be *they* would appear at any lonely instant, leaning from the twilight. And always with him, wherever he was, whatever he did, the sound of rat's feet along the shutters of evening.

Fear had no face . . . or fear had a thousand faces.

And at his back the military spires of the Temple thrusting into the leprous sky. Centuries of torment; and with a wrench of unbelief the worst guilt of all came back. The Tower that now seemed a Tower of fancy, like the haunted vision of the Temple riding into the old stained twilight. The Tower, where on such an evening—grey and dim and whispering—had passed the murderers. And you might still hear—oh yes, forever in this twilight!—the young gentle voices, the whispers falling fast and falling faster. Still catch the creaking of a door, the mute incredible visitor, the moment of recognition. And again whispers that were like screams; and the Norman door bolted; and the scratching of panic fingers upon stone. . . .

John Flory turned into a lane leading off the Street of Four Sons, just beyond the Hotel de Clisson. He passed under a fire-scarred eroded arch, gaping like a hideous mouth. Ahead in the apparitional light the Swan came out of the evening, the Swan of Lancaster with a gold chain about its neck.

In the night a shriek rang.

The soldier halted, his heart frozen, his knees turned to water. Someone was dying, around the corner, behind the arch, in the shadow of the Temple. Someone crumpling into the last unending twilight—a huddled form, a trail of blood. And a smile slinking away. It happened every night.

Flory went on.

From the Swan a vein of yellow light glowed; a door rasped. Two guardsmen with the red George Cross on their buff coats clanked toward the Englishman. Tudor's mercenaries. Flory shrank into the shadows. They strode by, and he heard them cursing in Breton down the lane end.

He found the wicket and the door. It was like a magic door opening into a lost and fortunate land. The narrow passage, the girl with the rushlight—and coming out of dusk into the broad pleasant room with rows of gleaming vessels along the wall and the red-gleaming fire brass and the clean bright tiles of the hearth. Oh, the pleasant, pleasant room!

The girl was bending toward Flory, her face a point of light. Her hair was a soft brown colour and brushed back from her forehead. She wore a willow-green kirtle and a white bodice. Her lips were slightly parted and she gazed at him with the steadfast remembered look of old.

He drew her close, kissed her lips. She gave him a radiant embrace. He had left her a child, the year before; now he found her budding into womanhood. "Perrette," he said. Her name shining like music. Her name in the hollow places of the night.

"Why did you stay away?" she exclaimed. "All these months . . ."

There was a country of time; and that country was the true adventure, the last discovery. For now—when he had entered the luminous room, the old white kingdom of the heart—he had entered the monarchy of time. And all this: glinting fire brass; blue and white Delft tile; rows of bronze; and the girl herself, Perrette, in her willow-green kirtle, evening in her eyes . . . all this was as he had known it, as forever he had come back to it. The years changed; now time itself glowed with the burnish of fire brass—and Flory was young again, he was a squire of Lancaster, he heard the trumpets and the singing banners—the cry of bridles in the afternoon!

"Learning tricks," he said. "Useful tricks. Would you like to spy for Tudor, my dear?"

She noticed the torn jacket, the dried blood on the bandage. "You're wounded!" she exclaimed.

"A souvenir from Richard," he said. It was all long ago now. That was the magic of time. For this that had happened only brief days before was older by far than the memories of this room—the memories of this day fifteen years ago.

Perrette bustled about, setting a place at the trestle table, fetching cold roast veal and larks in a pie with a flagon of mulled claret. Before she would let him eat, she insisted on dressing his wound. He felt a fire of pain as she cut away the bandage. She looked up anxiously. Was she hurting him? He reassured her.

He remembered the red George Cross. "Why were Tudor's men here?"

"Oh, you saw them?"

He glanced at her. She seemed uneasy. "What were they doing here?" he repeated.

"They were seeking you," she replied. She hesitated. "There was something about a marriage offer. A man named Betson."

His mouth tightened. Betson! Perrette was in Flory's governance, the daughter of a Lorraine soldier, now dead. Piers Valcoeur had sallied for Marguerite d'Anjou, under de Brezé; later, Flory and Valcoeur had fought stirrup to stirrup in the Household of Burdundy. Valcoeur had perished at Nancy in 1477, with Duke Charles the Rash. Old Tom Betson, merchant of the Woollen Staple at Calais, wanted the daughter of Flory's comrade-in-arms. Betson was a man of fifty. A mere thirty-three years difference in their ages. A real love match.

"Did you have a summons to the Tournelles?" Flory asked her.

"Yes," she said; and wrapped a clean linen bandage about the fragrant herb ointment she had been rubbing on his wound. "It doesn't mean anything serious, does it?"

He frowned, knowing Tudor. "Betson is wealthy," he remarked. "He can do Tudor much good."

"Henry Tudor would give me to Betson to obtain money?" She was youthfully horrified. "Would sell me?"

He swung round to the table. "Great traders like Betson and Tudor don't talk like that," he said, pouring a cup of wine. "It's a question of easing terms, don't you see? You treat me kindly—and I'll see you have generous conditions for your loan. Quite simple, my dear."

She was pale. "You don't really mean that, Messire Flory."

He dipped into the lark pie. He noted approvingly that Guillaume of Lyons had amended his cooking during the past months. The crust, always a tricky matter in lark pies, was just right. "I'm afraid I do mean it," he replied. "Or Henry Tudor means it."

"You won't let them!" she burst out.

He was silent. Increasingly, he fell from this clerical conspiracy masquerading under the noble Rose of Lancaster. Since that talk with Urswicke he had known his way divergent. He did not trust them; and they did not trust him. But he must move carefully. He could not afford to arouse them. He knew too much.

"I will go to the Tournelles," he said.

She looked at him, full of faith. "They cannot take me without your consent," she said. "You stand in my father's stead."

He drank a cup of wine. "John Morton will find a way out of that," he remarked. "I shall be asked to release you from my charge."

"But you will not agree!"

He rose, walked slowly about the room, his thoughts walking with him. He saw the glint of silver, the play of light upon shining brass, and around the hearth the delicate white and blue tiling. "No, I will not," he said.

"Then I shall be safe," she sighed. He swung round to stare at her. How much—and how little—she knew!

"You will not be safe at all," he returned. "There are other ways."

"What ways?" she wondered.

He didn't like to tell her. She believed in him; she could not know how precarious was his life. They could lock him up, seize Perrette. Naturally, being men of the robe, they preferred genteel methods. Flory should resign his right, gracefully; Perrette should be auctioned off to an old lecher thirty-three years her senior under all due forms and sacraments of the Church.

What did *he* believe in? Not Morton's God. . . .

"You were entrusted to me," he said. "I shall keep that trust." He thought of rat-infested years in an oubliette. Better far, death by war.

"Why don't we go away?" she suggested.

A wild hope seized him. To slip away; to flee to Burgundy, to bountiful Duchess Margaret. She who for her own excellent reasons was neutral in the quarrel between her brother Richard and the Welshman.

But in the next instant he knew it was useless. How would they live, Perrette and he? An ex-Tudor spy, he could expect no preferment from Margaret of York. He might end up in chains. As for the King of France—or rather his sister Madame Anne de Beaujeu, the Regent—Henry Tudor was the darling of French policy, a French-backed candidate to the throne of England. All Henry Tudor's ships and soldiers, all the Welshman's money, came from France. Madame Anne would not think twice to clap in a dungeon any Englishman in her domains who abandoned Tudor.

Flory had sealed his destiny long before. . . .

Perrette perceived by his face that this hope was closed to them. Still she kept perfect confidence in his ability, single-handed, to frustrate those who would barter her for a loan on generous terms.

"We shall not part. . . ." Perrette said.

He gazed at her a long time, remembering the kiss she had given him. Another notion occurred to him. He might marry Perrette himself. That would embarrass Tudor and Morton! And then he heard—or fancied he could hear—the drip of sand in the green hourglass upon the wall. The sand that went on pouring. He was thirty-five and she was seventeen. It was better than Betson, but not a great deal better. Twenty years . . .

"Well," she said, after waiting in vain for Flory to speak, "it cannot go so very ill with me. They are men in Holy Orders about Henry Tudor."

He swallowed hard. He thought of Christopher Urswicke and how Urswicke had jumped at Dighton's name. A name that recalled ancient muted twilight; frantic whispers; a chalice of blood . . . an unspeakable sacrament . . . a priest that shrived the tender and the damned . . .

"What are you thinking of?" Perrette said.

"I am thinking of a man in Calais," he replied. "A man that I should much like to meet."

"Do I know him?"

"No, praise God!"

"He is not a good man?" The question came out softly, dying into red dusk.

"He is beyond goodness." Flory turned away. He had an almost reverent feeling for the ruined priest. Ordinary men had the power to redeem themselves. John Dighton was in a state of grace absolute.

Perrette expected him to say something more; but he had said all there was to say.

She was troubled, wondering. She sensed that the room in which they stood was a frame of the past, evoking the magic of their intimate glory. For she herself was a child of that torn dream; of the Rose all bloody amid the marigold. In her was this terrible and beautiful memory.

"Do you know what day this is?" she said to him.

He smiled. As if he could ever not know! "This is the day of Tewkesbury," he replied. "The fourth day of May . . ."

"I was certain you would come back on that day," she said. She was closest to him amid the bright imploring images of the dead.

He took her hands; she drew near. "Tewkesbury . . ." he said, his soul pierced. The name was like a solemn bell, calling him back to all that he had left behind forever. Once more he saw the majestic sun-coloured tower of the Norman abbey; the green meadows dipped in gold; the silver torrent of the Severn Bore. And knighthood: dismounted, the last rally. He heard a blaze of trumpets.

She leaned tensely toward him. Suddenly it was a morning in May; it was the time of Lancaster. . . .

"We were camped three miles outside the town on rising ground, the river at our backs and York's array facing us. I was with the Company of the Swan, Prince Edward's Company, in the centre. Wenlock was in command. On our right lay the ward of Edmund Beaufort, Duke of Somerset; on our left lay the ward of Courtenay, Earl of Devon. Seven thousand men in all. Worn with marching and hunger; desperate. And against us the whole might of York—twelve thousand fresh soldiers under the three brothers: Edward; Richard; George."

He paused, stood immobile in the cloak of light, the red-flickering borrowed evening. Memories crying and shrieking; memories like a sound of great birds. Wings flaring across the sun.

"Men think of Tewkesbury as a time of dying. The end; the doom; the execution. But I saw Tewkesbury when night shattered into day upon our Lancastrian steel and we heard York's cannon like a great beast roaring. We were ready.

There were no cowards left among us; they had deserted long before. We were a band of mudstained final heroes. This was the last Kingdom of Lancaster, this green triangle between the river and the town. We were young; we had not learned to despair.

"The noblest vision in all the world . . . the standards of Lancaster unfurling in the sun. The White Swan of the Prince; the Golden Portcullis of Somerset; the Dolphin of Devon; the Leopards of Anjou. These banners that flaunted in the English air, that immortal morning . . ."

His eyes gleamed at Perrette. She was hushed beside the hearth, her head on one side, her hands clasped. What old deaths, what glistening blood the firelight shed!

"York's young Dickon—that is now King Richard the Third—struck at Somerset's line. Our lads threw back Dickon, with a rare lot of his Company dying on the bloody brambles. Three times did the fanged Boar come snarling at Somerset and three times the Duke bloodied the beast's muzzle. God, it was a sight!

"It was getting on for nine of the clock, York had been smashing at our line for nigh two hours and still they had not broken us. That was the moment. Somerset's moment. The glorious stroke that was to win the fight, make our Edward King, and Anne his gentle wife Queen. Blazon Lancaster's Red Rose upon the Arms of England!"

His voice surged. He stared with deep-set haunted eyes. The marshalling dead; the proud silent banners. Lancaster . . .

"Somerset led his men by hidden ways around Dickon's unguarded flank," he went on. "He broke like a lightning bolt on York. Two thousand men with famished blades. Dickon's ward splintered, began to panic. Now was the instant for Wenlock to smite Dickon in front with the Company of the Prince. We had York between the grinder and the stone.

"Betrayed . . ." He clenched a fist. "Betrayed! Wenlock

had been bought. He never stirred, but sat his horse like a
graven executioner, and Piers Gower that was Sword Bearer
to Prince Edward called Wenlock 'Traitor!' before the Company. Wenlock broke Gower's face with his iron glove. We
must look on, doing nothing, while York's Edward with five
thousand of York's best came to Dickon's aid. Somerset had
no chance. Two thousand odd against seven thousand! And
the rest of our Army sitting on the slope."

He broke off, his gaunt face twitching. This moment, the
most terrible moment of his life, blazed before him. He saw
the great dying in the noon; men writhing on the razored
hedges; the rich glisten of fresh blood; York's furious
thrusts. And amid the cruellest death raged the Banner of
the Boar.

"Somerset came back to our Company," Flory said, "a
battle-axe in his hand, the light of Hell in his eyes. Pepper-
hot, the Beauforts. They had Gascon blood. Somerset went
straight for Wenlock with the axe. Cut down the traitor,
like the Devil's liegeman he was. Bashed out Wenlock's
brains and left him for the flies."

Flory was silent. His face was haggard. He slumped beside the fire. Perrette looked anxiously at him. She beheld
a man full of anger and darkness. Her white hand touched
his arm. He trembled. Remembering; remembering . . .

"The rest . . ." His voice fell to a hoarse mutter of hate.
"Murder; broken faith; execution. To the last knight of
Lancaster. York gave no quarter. Edward had ordered his
men to kill the golden spurs, the knights. The Prince, too.
He was eighteen, a marvellous well-favoured lad with chestnut hair. Clarence stabbed him, they say. The only deed
that George of Clarence ever performed on a battlefield.

"Some ran to the abbey; some to the town; and some to
the river." He glanced about, the crimson hood of firelight,
the shadows huge and crippled on the wall. His eyes were
old. "Some ran to the abbey. . . ." he repeated. "That was
Somerset, the battle commander. He fled to sanctuary, while

his Prince was butchered. Somerset had ripped honour's blue gage. He could only die; wait for Edward and Richard to violate holy sanctuary and drag him to the block."

He stared into the golden flames, wrapped in the terror and splendour of the past.

Presently she rose, went softly about the room, blew out the lights one by one. They had only the fire's last red heart. And the man, the soldier, watching beside the flickering dead, knew that he was on leave from time. He brushed away tears. . . . "What is the hour?" he said.

"Past midnight," she replied.

"It is very late," he said.

She smiled. "Your room is ready. I keep it always so. Will you go now?"

"I shall stay awhile here," he answered her—and heard the bronze stroke of Tewkesbury. . . .

❀➤✻➤❀➤✻➤❀➤✻➤❀

THERE was fire in his walk and a rustle of black skirts; a jingle of silver. He wore no meagre coat and shovel-brim hat with leaden images of saints like that great dead wickedness, the Universal Spider. He liked fine silk, woven in the craft factories of Lyons; he had a silver rosary and a heavy silver crucifix on a silver chain about his neck. His boots were supple Spanish leather, of Cordoba. His black billowing sleeves were the most costly lawn, purple-striped with the bands of a bishop. Upon his head perched a boxlike biretta.

His dearest longing was to behold his black biretta a bright cardinal red.

Not the making and unmaking of kings, though that were splendid sport; not the destruction of rivals; not the weaving of mighty snares; nothing in all the arsenal of statecraft so beguiled his inveterate ego as that vision of cardinal red.

He was one of those who took naturally to power, as other men take to fighting or drink or women. Ever since he had been a young clerk in orders at Baliol, Oxford, years and years back, just after the coming of Queen Marguerite d'Anjou, he had been giving advice and arranging other men's lives for them. His most enjoyable duty had been that of Master of the Rolls; that is, the King's Tax Collector. He had been Master of the Rolls under both Red Rose and White. He loved the experience of serving a king; of breaking the greed and arrogance of the Norman-English barons. His most admired image of the Prince had been Lewis the Eleventh of France, he whom Jean Molinet, the Burgundian chronicler, had termed "the Universal Spider." Lewis had already carried out in his realm what John Morton, Bishop of Ely, proposed to achieve in England.

Bishop Morton felt the eyes of his three clerical scribes covertly watching him, his tall stateliness passing black-robed about the spacious decaying room. He moved lightly, for all that he was a big man, near fourteen stone, and in his sunshot pacing scarce disturbed the labours of the three black-gowned clerks sitting together on a bench like three crows on a branch. He liked to hear the scratching of their pens, reminding him of his incessant and skillful correspondence with the rulers of Christendom: Dom John the Second of Portugal (himself of direct Lancastrian descent from John of Gaunt); wily Ferdinand of Aragon; James the Third of Scotland; Margaret, duchess widow of Burgundy (her Rose was white, but she was no lover of Richard); Madame Anne de Beaujeu of France; and the Council of State of the Republic of Venice.

His chief backer was the Regent of France, Madame Anne, who ruled in the name of her ten-year-old brother, King Charles the Eighth. Madame Anne was the talented daughter of that master of governance, Lewis the Eleventh. In backing Tudor, she did exactly what her father would have done had he lived.

The room where Morton paced was in a dim state. The tapestries were filthy; the casements unleaded; the stone carvings chipped and worn. But the Bishop liked the room, for it had once been the audience chamber of that Lancastrian Prince John of Bedford—who had commanded the English Army of Occupation fifty years before and governed France in the name of Henry the Sixth.

In Bedford's chamber, using Bedford's high scrolled chair of state and Bedford's reading lectern and a table of black oak that might or might not have been his, Bishop Morton felt linked to Lancastrian greatness, to the old marvellous pride of the Rose. Henry Tudor, he knew, would never inspire men as had Bedford or noble Bedford's brother, Henry, Hero-King of Agincourt, or as the shining Marguerite d'Anjou. The lost bright legend, the Rose, the burning tears . . .

But Henry Tudor—or rather Henry's subtle craftsman, John Morton, Bishop of Ely—would perform a glorious service to England. He would make an end of the thirty years war that had desolated the land, filled vast grave pits, made to course fountains of blood. Morton's culminating stroke would be the union of White Rose and Red through the mating of Elizabeth Plantagenet and Henry Tudor. It did not bother the Bishop that neither party to the project was in the least desirous of passing a life with the other. Their mating was essential.

His policy was peace. . . .

He had seen enough of war and the ruin of war to know that no honour, no wisdom, no labour, made up for the losses of war. His first and still most revered patron had been Marguerite d'Anjou, Queen of Henry the Sixth. Heaven knows what they might not have accomplished together, Morton and this radiant daughter of Anjou, had it not been for the fighting that spoiled all. The barons of England had destroyed Marguerite d'Anjou; the barons Red and White. Marguerite's barons of the Red with quarrelling and greed and cruelty; her enemies of the White, equally ruthless and deathbent.

It was a lesson Morton was never to forget. Norman passion of war. . . .

He himself traced his lineage to a Scottish squire, who had come south to Dorset in the days of Joanna, wife of Alexander the Second. He had little cause to love these Norman English. Having, due to the fortune of war, no longer French or Scots to slaughter, the barons had begun butchering one another and the members of the Royal House. Morton could not regret their passing; only the trouble they had created. Violent, spoiled, stuffed with childish arrogance, they had raged redly through decades of murder.

Another time was coming. A time for shrewd thinkers; for planners and for statesmen. A time for Morton.

He gazed levelly at the steel-corseted soldier who had just burst in upon him. In that nimble mind a card was docketed: Cheyney, Sir John. Knt. Banneret, of Falleston, Berks. Yorkist and sometime Master of Horse under Edward the Fourth. One of Tewkesbury's butchers. Went over to Buckingham in October rising. Escaped to France. Made Captain of Tudor's House Guard. Dull and useful.

That was how the score stood. . . .

"You are urgent this morning, Sir John." It was a reminder of the system of protocol that Morton vainly tried to enforce. The Bishop was a busy man; appointments for interviews were made through Canon Fox. It was a system too oft violated by these soldiers, who came thrusting in at every hour of the day with petty complaints and visionary projects.

"My news will not wait, Your Reverence." Cheyney's huge bulk obscured the glistening lance of light. He had removed his helmet, a salade of Italian make. His beefy face crinkled at the Bishop. The blue, oddly boyish eyes were veined with drink. "I came directly I had word of the devilment."

The Bishop said: "Well, what is it?"

"Dorset's gone!"

Morton took a half-turn about the sunpierced room. The scratching of the pens abruptly ceased. "What was that, Sir John?"

"Dorset's gone, Your Reverence. Slipped away between nine and ten o' the clock with a party of horse. Six or seven in all."

The walls of the Tournelles seemed to fold in upon John Morton. He felt an angry incomprehension, as if he had just heard of a miscalculation in Heaven. As if God had grossly blundered.

"What do you mean? Gone—where?"

"He's riding for the coast," Cheyney replied. "Like as not, he's got a sail spread to fetch him to England."

In the game of chess, which Morton played extremely well, the lowly pawn creeping obscurely across the board might in a moment of carelessness flash into a deadly queen, upsetting a man's whole attack. This was the case with Dorset. Thomas Grey, Marquess of Dorset. And again a card slipped into place. Elder son of Lady Grey, by a previous marriage. About twenty-six. Made Marquess by Edward the Fourth. The Governor of the Tower under Edward the Fifth. Fled with royal treasure after murder of brother and uncle by the Usurper. A vain and foolish young man.

But by this totally unlooked-for flight, which might or might not have been engineered by Richard, Dorset had flashed from a pawn to the status of a game destroyer.

"Dorset was our hostage for the good will of Lady Grey and the other Woodevilles," the Bishop exclaimed. "He was the guarantee of the marriage between Henry Tudor and Elizabeth Plantagenet, Lady Grey's daughter. Now—"

He left the sentence unfinished. The danger to their cause was plain. They could not invade England without the assurance of Woodeville backing.

"I will take a party of horse," Cheyney said. "I will bring in Dorset—alive or dead."

"No!"

The command burst from Morton. When would these scraggle-headed fellows learn elementary statecraft? "Dorset must not be harmed, Sir John. He is worth everything to us alive. Dorset dead, we lose our hold on Lady Grey and the Woodevilles. Do you understand me?"

Underneath the greying head, the ale-soaked brain labouring painfully. When so many good men had died, why this fuss about Dorset? "I'd like to gut Dorset," the huge fellow said.

The Bishop gave him a steady look. "Hear me, Sir John. You will answer for Dorset's life."

Cheyney shifted on his heavy boots. His sword clanked. "This is soldier's work, Your Reverence. Dorset and his men are armed. They may fight."

Morton shrugged. He knew Cheyney itched to kill. Blood and bluster. That was the way of the Norman English. He would give much to be able to get along without them. But of course that was not possible. Not yet, anyhow.

"Dorset must not be harmed," the Bishop repeated.

"I don't like it, Your Reverence!"

All right, you don't like it. You and Brandon, the Standard Bearer, and Wingfield and Giles Dawbeney and Thomas de la Mare and Old Oxford and the rest—you grumble about clerks and priests running a man's war. It's action you want. You're perishing for blood. Unleashed oh dogs to flaming war!

But all of you together could not stand against His Hunched Majesty—that twisted creature—toadlike upon England's throne. For victory, you need my brain, my patience, my immense knowledge of men and affairs.

He said none of this. . . .

"I'll send another captain," he remarked to Cheyney.

"Oh, no!" The knight was hurt. "I'll do Your Reverence's bidding. Trust Jack Cheyney. I'll bring in yon Dorset like any trussed goat."

"Make haste, then!"

He took Cheyney to the door. Outside, around the circular anteroom, stone-naked and always cold, roved guardsmen of the House of France, wearing the White Cross of St. Andrew, and soldiers of Tudor's corps, mostly Norman wearing the Red Cross of St. George. The Tudor mercenaries were tough, dark, stocky men speaking a thick Norman patois. Although Bishop Morton knew Parisian French he could make little of this Norman talk. Anyway, they looked like bonny fighters.

Morton noticed a fellow in a worn leather jacket with a cock feather in his cap, sitting apart from the greasy Normans. An Englishman, by his jib. A vague recognition stirred in the Bishop.

Leather-jacket looked up, saw Morton. He got to his feet slowly. Under his shirt one shoulder was bandaged. Ah! Morton knew him. This was Master Urswicke's man, the same that had got into that nasty scrape with Richard's Company. The Bishop frowned.

"What do you want, Flory?"

"I'd like a word with Your Reverence." His face was curiously dark, like any Cornish wight's. Dark and gaunt, with piercing eyes. He seemed older than his thirty-five years.

"No time now," the Bishop said shortly. "Come back tomorrow." He was about to pass on when a thought struck him. He ought to send some English with Cheyney. Blessed Christopher, if Cheyney had only Normans and a fight began! The Normans would as soon kill a man as spit.

He spoke more graciously. "How's that shoulder?"

"Coming on, Your Reverence."

"Can you sit a horse?"

"Certainly."

"I want you to go with Sir John." His voice rose. "Oh, Sir John!" Cheyney was halfway to the portal. He halted. "I've a man for you, Sir John," the Bishop said.

Cheyney peered at Flory. "This rogue?"

"That's right," Morton replied. "He has no duty here and

he is well-fleshed in broils." He shot Flory a cold blue glance. "There's to be no killing, Flory. Sir John will explain."

Flory nodded. "I'll be ready in an hour."

"You're ready now!" Morton said. "You leave at once."

"But—"

"Never mind. Sir John—"

"Your Reverence?"

"Take Wingfield and Latimer, too. Look to it your Normans don't get out of hand."

"I'll do my best for Your Reverence."

He swung back to his study, a picture of energy and craft. His voice came to them. "I'll look for you in three days, Sir John. Bring me a guest!"

☸☀☙☸☀☙☸☀☙☸

THROUGH blazing noon, by the Porte Saint Antoine, they galloped, bucketing over the cobbles of Paris, scattering pigs and urchins. Flory caught a beggar's cracked shriek, oath-scrambling against a wall as the horsemen hurtled by. They were soon beyond the enormous curtain of the Bastille, with its eight round and glowering towers, where the guests of Madame Anne rotted piecemeal in their shackling; past the thirty-foot city wall and Gatehouse of Charles the Wise, with the Tour de Billy on the right; and they were frothing toward the Chateau de Vincennes, in one of the vast upper rooms of which the Lancastrian Hero-King had perished miserably of dysentery.

They were in open country. Oh the land, the land of the Ile de France! In radiant June, in the Araby of life; and the neat cottages with their red tiles and pointed chimneys, the gardens like chessboards, the sleek roan cows, the sturdy dogs. Everything looked fresh, new-mown. The earth was lavish and great-breasted, rising up in songs of plenty. Past war and English envy, past old ruined kings, past all dishonour, the land of France was rich and generous; June-gleaming.

Flory glimpsed the approval on the grim Norman faces hard behind. Peasant stock, these fellows. From dour scrabbed rocks of Normandy, they had adventured in hungry thousands. These were the veterans of Piers de Brezé, Seneschal of Normandy and dauntless captain of Marguerite d'Anjou. They could be counted on to strike a blow against their Norman kin of England; for above all they loved fighting and the *gestes* of war. They were simply accoutred, in chain corselet with a belted surcoat and the red George Cross on the breast. They wore the round pointed Norman helm with the broad nosepiece—the same headgear that had blunted Saxon arrows at Hastings and taken the roughest knocks of Saxon axes. Now, under Henry Tudor, they were about to repeat the exploit of their ancestors under Duke William. This was to be the Second Norman Conquest of England.

With Flory rode John Wingfield and Nicholas Latimer, squires of the Tudor Household. They were young men, in modest circumstances, and they expected much of this Tudor connection: the four ermine bars of a duke slashed horizontal on the right shoulder of the mantle of court.

And Flory thought how very like they were to those other young men who had blazed forth in joyous May, the men of Marguerite d'Anjou. They too had come seeking greatness and they had found death. Piers Gower, the sword bearer; Robin Haleson; Tom Tresham; Arthur Adair; Sir Hugh Courteney; John Beaufort; Henry Vaus.

Soldiers of the Rose!

Gower, missing after Tewkesbury and presumably dead. Haleson, killed on the gruelling march from Gloucester. Tresham and Beaufort, slain at Tewkesbury. Courteney and Vaus, beheaded after Tewkesbury. Adair, lost at sea.

But in some far pavilion, in some gilded meadow, ride

the gallant of the Rose . . . down vast Lancastrian lanes of
blue and white, down the sun of Marguerite. . . .

Remembering then the gold-beaked Bird of Lancaster,
hope blenching in the West and frightened glory in their
eyes . . . Oh Cavaliers!

Passed . . . silent . . . the burnt ash of dreams.

Toward evening of the second day, the fifteen horsemen
entered a rough broken land. They had flogged on unresting, with a change of horses at the post relay station on the
frontier. Madame Anne's seal had brought them the swiftest
beasts. But, though the horses were fresh, the men were not,
and even the hardy Normans drooped in the saddle.

Flory glanced about: at the wooded knolls, the green
sunken parks between, the silent silvery pools. It was like
coming home.

Nicholas Latimer looked up from his gold-braided bridle
rein. He fancied himself, did Nick. He was London's boy.
"Think you Big John knows where Dorset went?" he asked
Flory.

"Madame Anne . . ." said Flory cryptically.

"What of her?"

"She has reports from every toll barrier in the Kingdom
of France. She is not daughter of the Universal Spider for
nothing."

"Madame Spider." Latimer laughed.

"A report came in from a gate near Orléans, not ten minutes before we saddled. Dorset and his party were seen flying by at noon yesterday."

"Dorset has three hours' advantage, then?"

"Roughly that."

Latimer frowned. They were riding toward a clump of
pines and a little watercourse overhung by green willows.
There was a perceptible slope to the land, as if everything
were gradually sliding away. The light was green and cool.

"Orléans . . ." Latimer mused, as if pursuing some private speculation. "But what brings us here? To the Old Country?"

"Well," Flory replied, "I suspect Madame Anne had some information on that score. You know how this Duke Francis played ducks and drakes with Henry Tudor. What more natural for Dorset than to make for the frontier of the Old Country?"

"Why, here a man might—" Latimer flung out his arm— "hide for years," he marvelled.

This was exact, Flory knew. In the Kingdom of France the advantage was theirs. Dorset could not remain long undiscovered. But the Old Country was a different story. Their best chance lay in the fact that the folk of this land had no more liking for English than for French, whatever the Duke's *politique* might be, and would willingly betray Dorset.

They rode two by two along a sunken path, beneath green arches. The footfalls of the horses were muffled on the carpet of pine needles. Through the boughs, Flory glimpsed oriflammes of gold and violet shredding the sky. Night; he thought of night as a great company of hooded horsemen.

They went on for another mile or so and the watercourse widened and Flory perceived an enormous silver shield gleaming between earth and sky. "Grandlieu," he said, half whispering.

The lake was noted for its storms. Already little angry *flots* rippled over the surface and the wind screamed faintly. Wingfield looked back. "There's a village nearby," he said.

The band of horsemen emerged into a broad ragged fen, a sunken land, marshy and silvered by mirrorlike pools. Strange white flowers grew here, beside the willows. The light was the ruinous half-light of ancient granite. The sky was overspread with violet and the wind was from the west.

Wingfield scanned the horizon. His left arm thrust out. "Saint Eloi," he said.

Flory saw cottages break out of the violet evening, shimmering before him like a whole village suddenly painted on the lonely shore of the lake. And he had a moment of doubt. He suspected they were on the wrong track; that they were riding haggardly, uselessly, toward this twilight village.

He had an urge to turn back. And knew that they were all so tired, they must halt. Night . . . it must be a bleak passage here. It seemed to him that the waves were higher, lashing the shore.

They came like shadows into the village. Flory saw a pretty girl in the black kirtle and snowy lace cap of the country. She was standing in a doorway, her face luminous in the dusk. An odd trick of light, Flory thought—for all else was vague and grey. And, so thinking, he found her vanished. She went away suddenly, as if frightened.

A little way off two old codgers in russet cloaks peered at the strangers. Sir John Cheyney reined before the villagers. "Where is your bailiff?" he demanded.

Their seamed leathery faces had no change of expression. Eyes like the agate eyes of birds regarded Cheyney silently. "They don't understand you, Sir John," Wingfield explained. "They speak only the old tongue of the land. Let me try." He put the same question, in a dark quick speech. Curiously, Flory understood every word.

The old men understood. One of them broke into a tense angry declamation. Wingfield leaned from the saddle, straining to catch the meaning. The speaker abruptly halted. Wingfield straightened. "It's something about brigands," he said frowning. "I couldn't follow all of it. He's afraid of brigands, it seems. Thought we might be the same sort."

"Tell him we're English and we come as friends," Sir John directed.

This information produced no visible effect. Cheyney growled: "What's the matter with them? Damn it, Wingfield! Can't you make them understand? We want to bait the horses and we need rest and refreshment for ourselves. And a village boy as guide. We'll pay!"

Wingfield told them this. For an instant the wizened creatures were utterly still. Then one of them cried a single word that Flory recognized as *"Brocéliande!"* The old men rushed into a cottage. The door closed . . . and Flory had a sense of sharp, immensely suspicious eyes peering out from some cranny.

The horsemen went on.

Wingfield nudged Flory. "I passed here last year with the Earl of Richmond," he said. "Saint Eloi, it was—then."

Flory regarded him. He was a lad of twenty-six with chestnut hair and fresh blue eyes. "What do you mean—then?"

Wingfield crinkled his brows. "Why, I have another memory of Saint Eloi," he remarked. "More cottages. People singing in the streets. Every door open. A pack of children about. It's so damned quiet, now. Why, there's not a child to be seen. . . ."

"Things seem different by twilight," Flory said.

Wingfield didn't answer. He looked worried, as if the village of Saint Eloi had played a trick on him. And he seemed to grope for some elusive memory.

"And Brocéliande?" Flory wondered. "Brocéliande?"

"Brocéliande is the most ancient and hugest forest of this land," Wingfield explained. "Folk here believe Brocéliande is the dwelling of warlocks and sorcerers. The great oaks do move and entrap the lone traveller."

"What muck!" Latimer had come up, to overhear the bit about the oaks.

Wingfield looked at him steadily. "Brocéliande . . ." he said. "It's more than a place a few leagues northwest of here. It's more than a forest. It's a name the people give to the powers of Night. Why do you laugh, Nicholas Latimer? You know nothing of this land."

"I know a fool's tale when I hear it," Latimer snorted. "This talk of trees that skip about!"

They came to a grassy square, with a small stone church on one side and a long building with a ridged roof and bars across the casements. Cheyney pulled up. "We'll try to stir up a bailiff," he said, swinging heavily down.

The entrance, closed by an oak door, was screened off from the vaulted Hall. Flory noted sacks piled in one corner. The village tithes, he imagined. They passed into the Hall. All was dusty; utterly still. The soldiers were in a broad oak-beamed chamber with a kind of platform at one end upon which were benches and a reading lectern. A grey wizened light crept through the high casements.

"That girl in the doorway . . ." Latimer said. Flory abruptly turned. Latimer too had seen the girl of the twilight. "She was a pretty jennet," Latimer mused. "Her breasts . . . did glimpse her breasts, Flory?"

"Halloo! Halloo!" Cheyney called. Flory noted that the captain was fingering his swordhilt and sweating. Was he nervous? Silence shrouded the English. Flory made out two or three stone niches along the walls. Tombs?

"What I could do to that doxy!" Latimer exulted.

"Don't talk like that, Latimer," Wingfield said.

"Loved be God, Jack Wingfield, you like a ripe wench as well as any man!" Latimer came back in surprise.

"Will you let the matter be?"

Wingfield's voice rose. Latimer stared at him. Wingfield moved toward Sir John Cheyney, hovering uncertainly in the middle of the Hall. Latimer nudged Flory. "Did you hear him, Flory? I never knew him like that. You'd vow that village girl was his sister."

"Wingfield was here before," Flory remarked. "There's something bothers him."

"He's nervous, that's what. God pity him! How will he be against cannon?"

They could hear Wingfield talking to Cheyney, his voice tight and urgent. "Name of God, Sir John, why do we tarry here? To horse! To horse!"

And Cheyney rumbling in the gloom: "We've got to make a halt, Wingfield. We need rest and refreshing."

"Not here! Not here, Sir John!"

Cheyney buffed his shoulder. "Frightened of something, boy?"

Wingfield made no reply. The Norman troopers moved softly about, like great cats. They muttered in their harsh military speech. This was the speech, Flory mused, that had made the old dreaming poetic tongue of England into the language of war. Saxon and Celt had failed and gone down before these invaders.

And himself? Had the first John Flory, that Jehan Flore, had he come out of Brittany, out of the dark land, two centuries ago, as family legend had it? Out of Brittany and over the sea to Devon. Forest-haunted . . . his spirit, his memory.

It was like coming home again.

He was staring down a well of darkness, as it were, shot with faint silvery streaks, and the Hall was quiet as a sepulchre when he noted on the edge of his vision a little pointed light like a steady candle. He stiffened, watching. Beside him, Latimer breathed tensely. Latimer, he sensed, was watching the light, too. Mute and taut, they gazed into an immense shadow.

The light hovered about twenty feet away. It had a small amber glow and Flory surmised that he was looking at, not a candle, but one side of a hooded lanthorn. He heard Wingfield's whisper and knew that he also had seen the glow.

It must have been some moments before Flory was able to make out the delicate hand above the lanthorn. Perhaps because the light itself was at a level three or four feet higher than the watchers. The hand was pale and slim, like the hand of a woman, and on the mid finger was a large gold band.

"Halloo!" Sir John Cheyney's voice crashed into the dusk.

They looked for a face to emerge, but none appeared. Flory was staring intently at the hand. He noted a red line and then abrupt darkness at the wrist. The soldier hazarded a fantastic guess. The hand had been severed.

Cheyney's sword rattled from its sheath. In that defiant sound echoed all the challenge of the blunt Englishman; the intrepid refusal to admit the alien to his ken. Echoed as well a kind of ingrained denseness of spirit. For this, Flory knew, was no matter for sword and bludgeon.

"Come on, lads," Cheyney roared, waving his sword like Harry at Agincourt. It was a gesture dear to the Norman heart. The troopers clanked after their captain. Only Wingfield hung back.

"Funk," said Latimer. "Sheer funk."

But Flory knew better. Wingfield was afraid of something that would give any man pause—*if he understood it.*

"Damn you, sirrah!" Cheyney trumpeted. "Come forth like a man!"

Oh, it was all English knighthood, the Black Prince at Poitiers, John of Gaunt in Spain, Bedford . . . and it had nothing to do with this Breton night. It was all the silly wild antic of a boy pretending at something utterly beyond him.

Flory understood. He dared not give the feeling a name—not yet; but he understood. It was deep-sunk in his own sombre spirit, his own memory. And he too was afraid. "Take care, Sir John," he burst out. *Let the night be, Sir John . . . don't play with the night. . . .*

But he was English; an English captain. He had no truck with such fancies. What the night needed was a whack with good steel. He lunged; there was a flare of ragged light and a flutter of wind—and thick shadow.

Now—nothing. No light; no hand. A cannon-burst of oaths from Cheyney and the hoarse mutter of the Normans. Flory heard the wind crying at the casement. Suddenly he felt exultant—and terrified.

Latimer stumbled against him. "Can you find the door? We must out of here. . . ."

A confused roaring in his ears; the haunt of the wind and the lost memories beneath the wind. The name he dared not utter echoed in the cave of his heart and he waited like a dead man for what must happen. The door blew open with a sharp crack. Flory's gaze was rigid. Dimly—far off, it seemed—he heard young Wingfield groping; groping and sobbing. . . .

Nothing these young Englishmen had experienced before had prepared them for this. Flory alone knew. Old memories roved; once he had been a young man in this land. A young man with morning in his eyes and a strange desire.

But silver-haired upon the threshold the stranger stood. And torchlight flickered redly upon his beaked nose, his sunken jaws, his burning eyes. "Oh gentlemen!" he cried. "Come this way. . . ."

❀✦↦❀✦❀↦❀✦❀↦❀

THEY were standing in the grassy square, a million leagues of starlight shimmered, and they heard remotely the cannonade of wind upon the lake. . . .

He was explaining to the English that he was the Steward of the Lord of Saint Eloi. His voice had a soft chanting note. He wore a long blue robe, unbelted; in his right hand he carried an ivory staff tipped with a gold ball. His starlit silky hair flowed to his shoulders.

"Regrettably, messires," he said, "my lord is not here to welcome you. He has been called away, to the Court of the Great Duke. But I shall do all for you in his absence."

Flory felt a shiver at these words. An attendant brought a silver cup, a flask of wine, a round loaf of bread. The Steward poured wine into the cup. He uttered a few words, rapidly, in the Celtic tongue and turned down the silver cup. The wine plashed upon the earth. The Steward took the

round manchet loaf, broke it in two, sprinkled a little salt
on each half, and handed one piece to Sir John Cheyney
with a graceful bow and a flourish of the gold-tipped staff.

The libation of wine; the offer of bread and salt—the
Breton ceremony of welcome. . . .

Wingfield seized Cheyney's arm. "We have leagues to
ride," he urged.

"The horses at least are fresh, Sir John," broke in Flory,
pointing to the grazing picket.

The silver-haired man glanced at Wingfield and Flory. A
cold bright look came on those glinting eyes. "No need to
haste, messires. You are in Saint Eloi."

Flory saw the great munching shadows of the horses, while
about the little company fell the silver rain of starlight and
in the village a gigantic darkness lay upon the huddled roofs.
Not a splinter of light gleamed. Everywhere, silence surged.
Not even a bird called.

"Come with me, Sir Captain," the Steward was saying.
"You shall have rest and good refreshing. Wine aplenty and
meat newly blooded."

"A tender joint," Sir John said avidly. "A joint, with the
red blood running." His eyes glistened.

At this mention of blood and fresh joints Flory felt a thrill
of horror. They must get away. He saw Wingfield go pale
as rupert-gloss, that limpid flower of the dead.

But before Flory could speak or move, there burst upon
the night a glorious music, like the very tongues of angels,
rising in a flood of tenderness toward the starlight, the sen-
tinelling dark, the Breton heaven. . . .

The Steward gestured toward the small stone church
where, as if by sorcery, light now flared in every casement.
"The Seigneur of Saint Eloi is a lover of music," he
explained. "His choir is the finest in Brittany. We search
constantly for boys!"

The marvellous voices soared and it was God Himself
weeping, His heart broken by unbearable innocence, His

hands wet with blood, His divine pity echoing to the bright wild adoration. . . .

They rode through the mantling night and Flory glimpsed the Steward's silver hair gleaming like frost at the head of their column. And night, raven-winged, swept down upon them and they heard the lonely cry of wind and the invisible broken murmuring of little streams. . . .

And somewhere, he thought, men were praying to Saint Anne and to Saint Hervé and to Saint Gilles. Saint Gilles!

Praying in loneliness and terror, on their rigid knees, with old cracked voices and cracked hearts. The memory that lay below the memory, the old haunted time ancestral and dark . . . the young man with morning in his gaze and in his soul a strange desire. . . .

"You heard what he said, Flory?" It was Wingfield beside him, hoarse and trembling.

Flory shot him a sidelong glance. "What—that fellow?" he said, biting off his words. He didn't want to be worried by Wingfield.

"You heard what he said, didn't you?" Wingfield repeated, twisting in his saddle. "That he is the Steward of the Lord of Saint Eloi!"

"I heard him," Flory said. He kicked the flank of his dappled mare. Quickly, quickly. Time—oh, he felt time as a force, intense, palpable, swirling. . . .

"You know who was the Lord of Saint Eloi, Flory?"

"Yes." A dread brief syllable, brushed into the dark.

"And us—? Name of God, Flory, what is happening?"

He wouldn't keep quiet. He was just a lad, out of Tarrant Crawford, in Berkshire, and this was too much for him, for his English nerves. It was too old, too terrible; a world of fire and night. Was he crying? Flory didn't know.

"I tried to stop Sir John. I begged him. He wouldn't listen. None of you . . ."

Babbling . . . Flory felt pity, as for a bewildered child.

He recalled that this was the youth who had set his cap for a duke. A duke! "Don't give way, lad," he said.

"I passed two years in this accursèd land," Wingfield gabbled on. "When Richmond was guest of Duke Francis. I hate it! I hate it!"

Flory said nothing. He wanted the ride to be done; to happen what was intended to happen. Oh, from the first he had suspected it! But it could not be explained to the English.

The band of horsemen swung down a ragged escarpment of moorland—stunted trees, furze, bald rock . . . Flory's heart began to pound. He listened to the moaning of the wind and the sad small clip-clop of the horses . . . nearer; nearer. . . .

An intolerable excitement gripped him. Hate this land? Yes; fools and English. Those barred forever from the old dark memories, the fire in the brain.

Flory laughed.

Wingfield twisted to stare at him. "God's Banner, Flory! Did you laugh?"

"You would not understand, lad."

"Ah, no. Never! Thank God for English common sense."

Flory himself hardly understood. Their plight was terrible enough, in all conscience. But he embraced the experience, as if a demon danced in his soul. The riders now plunged onto a broad tableau of rock swept by a torrent of wind. And dead to their gaze reared a strong square donjon with six crenellated towers.

"Machecoul," a voice said.

Flory felt a shiver of awe.

Light blazed in lofty casements. From the barbican gatehouse shrilled a trumpet. The great portcullis slowly raised and the drawbridge creaked down.

Wingfield clutched Flory's arm. "The Breton girl!" he exclaimed. Flory peered into the gaunt night. He glimpsed the pretty Bretonne that they had seen in the doorway at

Saint Eloi. What was she doing here? And clad in white from head to foot. She was a melody of white in the evening. White, it came to him, meant two things: purity and death.

Latimer came up softly. "Do you see her?" he whispered. "Fit for a lord's bed."

Wingfield swung away. His voice came filtering through the dark. "What do you know of it?"

"But of course," Latimer said. "Mark how she be arrayed. A bride to the marriage couch."

Just then the girl turned and they saw her gleaming in the starlight. Her face had a young cool loveliness, black arching brows and a tender mouth. She wore a fillet of gold about her black curls.

"She's going to Machecoul?" Wingfield wondered.

Latimer nodded. "Her fortune, isn't it? A village girl!"

"Her fortune!" Wingfield glanced greenly at him.

And Flory seemed to hear once more the marvellous voices rising and pouring out in the Breton night. The innocence that could not be borne; the angels that must die. This wild ecstasy flung upon a weeping God . . . and the girl, the bride, the stainless heart. . . .

❋➷❋➷❋➷❋➷❋➷❋

NIGHT shrank about them and they huddled in a dank court. They were hungry and weary. Angry suspicions pricked their nerves. The young Englishmen blamed their captain for leading them into a trap—they had heard the portcullis clang!—while the Normans seemed to muster some final Norman defiance to Night.

Worst of all was the sense of horror that grew on Flory. He did not fear steel; arms were his trade. But it was this evil without face or shape, skulking in the cold fathomless light that rained upon the Château Machecoul. Horror that could paralyze a man; cut off his breath; reduce his will to water. It was all Flory could do to keep from shouting.

Wingfield fingered his swordhilt. His voice quivered: "It's bad here. Rotten bad. I tried to warn Sir John. . . ."

"Let's move back, lad," Flory suggested. "If they rush us, the Gatehouse is our only chance."

They crept toward the shadowy bulk of the Gatehouse about a hundred feet away. This was the sole entrance to the inner ward, where the English were. The porte was ajar and Flory and Wingfield glimpsed within two swarthy rogues dicing. They wore helmets and full battle gear. Flory noted that the windlass was evidently in an upper chamber. "Pray Christ they don't have men above," he murmured.

The English crouched against the Gatehouse wall. Starlight gleamed. Machecoul thrust hugely upward, ruined eyeless turrets that might have hid regiments of cutthroats. From the green stagnant moat sounded a frog's rasping horn. A little way off, a clump of horses like a cluster of chessboard knights stirred nervously, great sculptural heads tossing in the gloom. Horses know the smell of danger.

A cry split the dark, a wild red wail that pierced the air above the black turrets. The voice of a young girl, a voice drenched in terror.

The Englishmen gazed upward. Rage and horror rushed upon Flory. He burned to storm this fortress, tear stone from stone. The shriek faded; and now there was only the starlight and the crouching dark and the uneasy horses.

Flory heard one of the Breton gamesters laugh and the other remarked in crude French: "The Sieur de Rais at his sport again. Wish he'd leave us in peace one night!"

Flory dug his nails into the dirt. "Gilles de Rais," he whispered. "Seigneur of Machecoul." It was the name they had been listening for; the dread name. All that strange night. From the first Flory had suspected it: sooner or later they must encounter the ravisher; the devourer of the innocent; night's bloodsick brother—Gilles de Rais, Seigneur and Maréchal, Chamberlain of the King of France, Knight-Companion of the Order of the Ermine. . . .

Wingfield was shaking. "Murder—murder. . . ." he gasped, lunging to his feet.

"God's Wounds—keep down!" Flory dragged him into the shadows at the base of the Gatehouse. "Don't you understand? She is an echo; she is the fearful memory of the dead. Her bones are mouldering in the moat."

"Did you not glimpse her?" young Wingfield said. "Oh, Flory—she was in white!"

"The knave within talked of Gilles de Rais," Flory said softly. "Strangled and burned, he was. Dead these fifty years." He tried to keep the sick hollowness out of his voice.

"Saint Edmund, you don't mean—?"

"That's what I mean," Flory nodded. "Evil cannot be burned. It's in the donjon walls of Machecoul."

They stiffened. Again the dark was riven by that cry . . . freezing . . . shrivelling . . . rending the spirit. Wingfield retched.

A Breton shuffled to the porte. "By that black soul burning in Hell!" he exclaimed. "Why don't the devil kill the jade and make an end?"

The second Breton poured brandy from a goose-necked flagon. "Don't you know, Yves? Sieur Gilles liked to play with the girls a bit, before. Eh, Yves? A little cut here; and a little cut there."

Wingfield was greenish-pale. One hand clutched a dagger. The Breton's glance swept the court, just passing above the Englishmen crouching at the wall. He grunted and spat. "We'll have a slice of fun ourselves this night," he vowed.

"They say," Wingfield whispered, "that he drank the blood of a thousand children."

Flory made no reply. All this—five decades past. The bones: yesterday's blood and agony. But evil; evil could not be burned. Evil that is absolute, that is pure. These sweating stones, this stagnant air, the echo of shrieking—infected, infected the very rock. . . .

"He was a Marshal of France," Wingfield recalled incredulously. "The comrade-in-arms of Jehanne the Maid. He carried the consecrated oil at the coronation of Charles at Reims."

Flory gripped the lad's arm. "Listen . . ." he said.

Death comes on cat's feet. A softly prowling visitor, Death. His claws scratch faintly and he is a lonely shape in the starlight. *We'll have a slice of fun ourselves.* . . .

"They're coming," Flory said. He was sweating; his sword was heavy in his hand. Damn his shoulder!

"What do they want with us?" Wingfield wondered. "Who are they?"

"The old man of Saint Eloi spoke of brigands," Flory said. "We've walked into a nest of the knaves! They want our horses and our money."

"What of the Steward—?"

"A steward—once," Flory muttered. "A half century before. A long time this silver Merlin has been waiting for his lord. His lord!"

He gave a sharp cry. A crossbolt cut the dark, hissing across the court. On every side killers rose. Torchlight streamed on naked steel.

The brigands made a rush. . . .

Flory and Wingfield plunged into the Gatehouse. The Bretons' jaws dropped; and they came up cursing. Flory faced a tall rogue in salade helmet and leather jack. This fighting had little in common with fancy Milanese swordplay. Hand-to-hand—the basic stroke was a slash, not a thrust. Some men used both hands. Only three positions of attack: the head; the great neck vein; the belly—any lucky hit on one of these would end the fray.

They were limited in the play of their strokes by the small circular chamber. Table and chairs crashed, the brandy bubbled away over the greasy rushes.

The tall Breton lunged at Flory's head. The parry only partly blocked the stroke and the broad blade rang on Flory's helm. He staggered, fell back—and the other yelled and drove hard. For a moment he felt Death's leprous breath, but *grace à Dieu!* the Breton tripped. Flory righted himself and threw a shrewd stroke. The two were well matched, hammering away with furious cuts, any one of which might have been mortal.

It was work stubborn and cruel; and Normans and Bretons loved it. The brigand's eyes fired as he slashed at Flory. A massive cut at the neck—clash and disengage—a belly stroke—the shock of the parry—again disengage. The whish-whish of a blade broad as the hand and keen as the devil's tooth. Flory's shoulder blazed. He couldn't keep up the pace much longer.

The Breton felt Flory's stroke slacken. He hurled to the attack. Blades clashed, spitting fire. Flory gave the parry all his remaining strength. The brigand lurched and Flory dropped to one knee, a trick acquired from an ensign of Burgundian cavalry. He hesitated for a twinkle; he had only one thrust and he must be certain. He let the Breton have it, thrusting high and hard, bellyward. He felt the blade bite in at the groin, just at the thigh-bone, sinking in the flesh like a knife in lard. The man howled; purple blood fountained; and he broke against the wall, nails screaming on stone. . . .

Flory shivered. He swung about, blade crimson. Wingfield was pinioned against the wall opposite, gasping—blood pouring from a ragged cheek. Flory cleared the intervening space at a bound, cleft the Breton's skull and saw him crumple.

"Get up! Get up!" he shouted to the sagging Wingfield. "I'll grind the portcullis and do you cut the lashings of the bridge."

He bounded up the narrow stone stair—blood dripping from his blade. His mind worked fiercely and he ignored the burning clamp of pain in his shoulder. The windlass room was small and dark; and he stumbled about, cursing. Suddenly he bumped against the heavy crank. The portcullis was a dead mass of iron; and he groaned and panted against the crank, raising the steel daggers inch by inch.

Outside, savage yells filled the court. Flory toiled on, immersed in pain and frenzy. He could hear the agonizing creak of iron in the grooves as the gate ground upward. He paused, sweat rilling from him, his doublet soaked beneath the steel brigandine. A fresh burst of fury from the court—and he seized the crank. Gasping and sweating like a slave in the hellish dark of a decked galley, he forced the gate slowly up. . . .

Back to back, the Normans fought in a ring of red-flaring light. Eight still stood; but one of these was hideously slashed about the face and neck. Ten bodies strewed the court: six Bretons and four Normans. Cheyney wielded a ferocious double axe, swinging from left to right and bellowing. Beside him, Latimer fought shoulder to shoulder, his deft strokes flashing in and out of the night.

A thunderous crash echoed above the brazen din. Wingfield had cut the guardropes of the drawbridge. Sir John Cheyney heard—and understood. "The bridge, lads! Christ Jesus, the way is clear!"

Step by desperate step, they fought toward the Gatehouse and freedom. And now Flory and Wingfield, coming on the double to the horse picket, cutting the halter ropes, leaping into the saddle . . . they rode down the astonished Bretons, giving the Normans a chance to swing onto their mounts.

Exhausted and bleeding, the little company flogged through the open gate and across the drawbridge. Behind them towered Machecoul, huge and evil, a shriek of stone in the starlight. . . .

❂✦✚❂✦✸✚❂✦✸✚❂

FOUR men were dead and another dying. Flory leaned against a ruined wall, sun-splayed and mossy. It was morning, a quicksilver Breton morning. The light came misted from the sea, glistening across green wet fields.

The Normans were cooking breakfast: fried eels and thick ropy soup. Latimer and Wingfield were talking with Cheyney. Machecoul was a fathomless time away; Gilles de Rais, ashes. Now the English had but one dream: Dorset. That gilded butterfly might appear at any corner of a sunny morning; oh, there had been Breton whisperings, rumours of a passage in the night—but mostly the questioned were dumb and staring, comprehending or pretending to comprehend only the old haunted language of the dead. Door-slamming, secret, strange. . . .

The little company was somewhere about Pornic. From the rise yonder, they had glimpsed the grey Atlantic. Awaiting word from Duke Francis in Nantes. Francis, mad, sick, desperately living on, clinging to life and Brittany amid the prayers and incense of his people; and his fragile daughter Anne, the last of her House—small, ugly, pious, hiding in her splendid chateau . . . the Duke could help the searchers, if he would. . . .

The dying Norman groaned. He had lost blood, much blood. His face was chalk-white and his fingers plucked invisible strings. He muttered, but the other Normans gave no heed. He was dying; Norman and dying, he was going out in the iron tradition. Flory looked down: the matted hair; the blood-streaked face; the fingers forever plucking . . . "Can I help you?" The man stared unseeing. He was beyond anything Flory might do. His lips quivered. Words, thick Norman patois. Tears, strange in that face. He caught Flory's hand in a fierce clasp.

And suddenly: Death with hammering hoofs!

The Normans looked up; Cheyney loosened his great blade. Across the green and broken morning flogged a horseman. He dashed toward the company; reined sharply and flung from his horse. He wore crimson and silver; and on his shoulder the Ermine badge of Brittany.

Cheyney took the man's arm and they moved apart in earnest talk. The others began to saddle. Flory felt the Norman's hand stiffen. He glanced down. The man's eyes were open and white; his mouth slack. He was dead.

They rode through the Celtic morning, Brittany's crimson and silver messenger with them. They headed for the Loire, the noble, bright and dreaming river that divided the dukedom of Brittany from the Kingdom of France. The dead Norman had been spaded into a hasty grave. Now the company mustered twelve: seven Normans, four English, and the Duke's messenger.

"It's like Ireland," young Wingfield said, surveying the misted countryside.

"It is Ireland," Flory replied. "The Ireland of the First Age, before the plague of English." He gave Wingfield a crooked smile.

The lad that dreamed of a ducal coronet gazed at Flory, puzzled. "Where do you belong, John Flory?"

Flory shrugged. He wondered himself. You belonged where lay your heart. He was mixed up with the schemes of this greedy little Welshman and his clerical friends. But that was not his heart. He longed to see Perrette. Perrette . . . an image of brightness on his spirit.

They passed enclaves of green between silver rotting pools and ditches of stagnant water. The country grew ever more flat and the trees thinned out. Here and there a painted wooden Christ agonized on his Cross. Flory noted small neat piles of what looked like mud.

"Dung," said Wingfield, who had passed here before. "Dung for winter hearths. They mix it with straw."

The peasants standing in their bogs with rude wooden hoes were small and dark, stunted-looking. They stared impassively at the little cavalcade. The messenger, tall, bright-haired, magnificent bone formation in his face—a Celtic Hero—was like a being from another race. And this may well have been the case. For in Brittany, as in Ireland, there had been tribes of dark earth-dwelling people before the invasion of the fair-haired Celts.

"He's useful," Wingfield remarked, nodding toward the messenger. "Madame Anne's seal would get us nothing here."

"Nor would young Dorset fare better," Flory added. Thomas Grey, Marquess of Dorset, would stand out in this country like a belled unicorne. But there were still hiding places. They had to trust to the Duke's messenger.

Flory wiped sweat. The sun was a shield of glowing white directly overhead. Hard riding had brought them to noon and the sparkling river; now they followed a course upstream.

"Another hour," Latimer said.

They looked at him wonderingly. The thought haunting all their minds: could they trust Duke Francis?

"Why not?" Latimer demanded. "King Richard has already offered the Duke a bribe last year to send Henry Tudor to England, but Francis refused the money. He bears no love for Richard."

"We're lucky Landais is done for," Latimer observed. "That knave would not delay to take King Richard's gold."

Pierre Landais, Flory thought . . . the son of a tailor of Vitré and all-powerful minister of Francis the Second. A short flame-coloured robe and a tunic of Indian yellow beneath. He wore a green feather in his bonnet. He had just been hanged, to the joy of Brittany, for his thefts and extortions.

The river began to narrow and branch off. They saw several little fishing boats or pirogues standing out to midstream. The fishermen carried nets and long poles with a fine-mesh basket on one end. The land became ever more silent, green and marshy—the horses squelched mud with every step.

"Soon, now . . ." It was Latimer's voice, filtering back

from the head of the column where he had gone to join Cheyney.

Flory felt a sadness in the air, a feeling compounded of the antiquity of the land, the greenness and the silence, the pale misted light. He recalled the dead Norman, a man whose name he did not even know, who had gripped Flory's hand and gone to some bleak Norman heaven.

The Duke's messenger was staring at the wooded shore. He had turned off the main bed of the river and was leading them along a winding reed-haunted stream. Once or twice he reined, examined carefully the lay of the land.

None of them knew where the company was going, what precise spot the young Breton sought. They were riding, as it seemed, forever into green silence, into mist and loneliness. . . .

Suddenly the day turned old. They had been following the watercourse for what seemed hours; and all on an instant the sun was red and dying before their eyes and a little breeze came whisking across the drowned fields.

The messenger held up his hand. He reined and swung down from the saddle. He began to explore the shore.

"I see no track here," Latimer complained. "We've been duped again. It's going to be Machecoul and blood. . . ."

"Wait, Latimer," Wingfield advised.

Cheyney glowered. The seven Normans hovered darkly. Flory felt his scalp prickle. The land was haunted, he was convinced. God's Wounds! what new mischief?

The messenger found what he wanted. He came up to the horsemen with excitement and satisfaction. He indicated they were to dismount.

"Dismount, I'll be damned!" Latimer swore. "That was the mistake at Machecoul. I'm staying astride, ready to make off."

Cheyney hesitated. The young Breton importuned. They could not go where he wished to lead them if they did not dismount. Cheyney assented. "We'll chance it," he said in his growling English way. "But God help ye d'ye play us false!"

The Breton understood—and was content. He smiled, aloof and shining; accepted the gage.

They were seeking a boat, it presently appeared. Not one of the small pirogues, but a craft large enough to float their baker's dozen. The messenger prowled along the shore, the others following cautiously.

"We're like rats," Latimer grumbled. "Rats, Wingfield! We could be cut to pieces."

Flory glanced about. The stream before them, one of the arteries of the Loire, lay gleaming and still. Across the green lost silence rose a plume of smoke. A strange expectant hush: the pause between day and dark. Ducks, in a thin brooding trail, wound whitely through the reeds.

Now they went hunter-wise, clambering over the rocks that crusted the shore and the exposed roots like nerves of giant oaks and beeches. They glimpsed an occasional fisherman, dark and mute. And from time to time invisible things flashed away up the bank; snakes perhaps, or leverets.

Latimer was cursing. "Devil take this bloody Brittany! We're dirked for sure."

Nerves . . .

He was still under the spell of Machecoul and Gilles de Rais. But their Breton guide knew what he wished to do. He led them into a shallow estuary, a half-moon of water, where a large flat-bottomed boat with oars was moored.

A dwelling stood on the rude and broken shore; slate-grey and thatched, a high pointed roof above a single storey. Over the doorway was painted the customary white cross to ward off the evil spirit. The Duke's messenger strode up to the door. His fist hammered the oak.

They stood in a ring, watching. Abruptly, the door swung inward and a huge bearlike creature emerged. Flory held his breath. The man was so little like what he had expected from his glimpses of the Breton. Wild hair above a puckered florid face; inflamed protruding eyes and immense fists. He stared at the intruders.

The messenger spoke to him in the lilting tongue of the Guerande, the Breton district where now they stood. The others knew that he had inquired the hire of the boat. The puckered stare passed over the company, calculating the wealth represented. The boatman considered; and unexpectedly shook his head and made as if to retreat within his thatched fortress.

But this was all a game, as between Breton and Breton, and well understood. The messenger plucked the man's filthy smock, sauced with a thousand meals; took out a gold-embroidered purse. The boatman hesitated, appeared to reconsider; he named a price that seemed to stagger even the messenger, accustomed to ducal spending.

"The pirate!" Latimer exclaimed. But Flory knew the price would come down, with a little bargaining.

So it proved. They reached an agreement in silver sols, considerably less than the original quotation. The money was clinked out of the messenger's purse into the huge waiting palm and they all rushed down to the boat.

The six Normans—one had been left to manage the horses—manned the oars, while the boatman took the tiller. They headed out into midstream, as the light dimmed and evening came down grey and brimming over the land.

Latimer shook his head. "Pray God Big John knows what we're doing," he said. They were sitting in the stern sheets, huddled together and peering at the misty shore, bound by willows and brooding poplar trees. And higher up, tall conical pines sentinelled the twilight.

Flory was eager; he had shaken off the blind anxiety of the ride. At last they neared the end of their quest. As the shore slid by, left behind by stout Norman shoulders, he had a sudden thrust of excitement. "We'll sup with Dorset—or the Devil!" he cried.

Wingfield laughed nervously; Latimer chewed his lip.

The boat moved steadily through the darkening water and here and there, on the low wooded shore, they glimpsed the yellow squares of cottage windows. Flory felt for his sword and dagger; but just then he had no thought of killing. He had the old irreparable wonder of coming home again. The land, this land, with its magical light and shore, its long dense line of mighty trees, the reeds and catkins waving in the quiet water, and the strange dark faces of the Bretons, all this was as he had known it forever—as it had come to him through two hundred years of haunted memory.

And now they neared some high islanded bulk, protruding in midstream; the young man with the face of a Celtic legend stood in the prow, gazing at the approaching island. And instinctively they all knew that this was what they had been seeking, through weary and bloody days.

"How many gentlemen does Dorset have?" Wingfield asked.

"Ten or a dozen—if they all stuck with him," Latimer replied. "Some of them may have funked. I'll bet they didn't bargain for this sort of life!"

The messenger motioned to them to keep quiet; they were coming in to the rocky wedge-shaped shore of the island. The others could perceive nowhere to land the boat and they had no notion of the river's depth. But their guide took them through a narrow neck of water into a concealed inlet, where they found a shallow beach.

The boat grated on the ledge of rock; the messenger leaped out and beckoned. The island was utterly still. Acacias and willows shrouded the shore. A column of ash trees marched up a broken rise into the moonlight. The searchers stepped off into the shadows, single file behind the messenger.

The way was rough; now and then a man slipped and a stone went hurtling into the dark. They seemed to be going through a wood with open patches of moonlight, their general direction toward the island's center. One of the Normans suddenly stumbled and cursed. He called the others. They gathered about, scrutinizing. The Norman pointed; Flory saw the outline of a human body, completely naked. One leg was twisted under the other; an arm was flung across the face. Flory stooped—and abruptly drew back. Something slithered away. . . .

Latimer straightened, his face hard and angry. "One of Dorset's gentlemen," he said.

They stared at one another. The unvoiced question: *who or what had done this?* The Duke's messenger stood bright and watching; and the boatman had suddenly disappeared. Cheyney swore softly, "Love of God!"

After a few minutes of creeping through the giant wood, entangled in prickly vines that fought and tore them like Broceliande itself, they emerged into a clearing. Four or five shadowy forms huddled near a fallen log, sleeping.

The company picked a way carefully. Every man had his sword and dagger out. They formed a ring about the dim forms. The sleepers lay so still, so mute and slack, that Flory had a sudden horrible suspicion: they too were dead. But now one of the forms stirred; a face lifted inches from the ground. A cry of terror split the night. The Normans moved in with hot steel.

"Hold! Hold!" Cheyney's voice barked. He collared a Norman, shoved him back. For they were not waiting this time; they were killing first and asking questions afterward.

A tall fair-haired gentleman faced Cheyney with drawn sword. With a shock, Flory recognized Thomas Grey, Marquess of Dorset. "Who are you? Are you come to murder us?"

"Peace, Master Marquess," Cheyney growled. "We've come to take you back to Paris."

The young man wavered; he was utterly spent, days and nights of fear and hiding. Mismanaged this flight, as all his life had been mismanaged. The rich doublet was shredded and filthy; upon the hollow face a yellow stubble. "Are you

Cheyney?" he asked in a slow marvelling tone. "Sir John Cheyney?"

"None other," Cheyney replied heartily. "Now yield, sir. We mean you no ill."

Dorset rendered up his sword. "I yield me right willingly, Sir John," he said. He staggered; put a hand before his eyes. "Let us away from here!" he cried—to the night, the oaks and Druid moonlight that gleamed about them. "You don't know—don't know—"

Flory remembered the dead man, the rigid torment of the limbs, the half-eaten face. How many others had Dorset lost? Night closed about the English. Dorset was sobbing.

The Duke's messenger desired them to make haste. He knew the peril; they could only guess at it. The place was old: old and gleaming and oak-circled. They helped Dorset to his feet. He was quivering; he had seen the beast of night. . . .

And so they went down, in silence and in dread, as they had come; through the Breton night, the dark wind, the rustling shore, the river of memory that flowed forever through the secret country of Guerande. . . .

☼↗✳↘☼↗✳↘☼↗✳↘☼

EVENING again . . . the bright chamber of the Swan. He sat with her, with Perrette, and there were no words to say or they had said all the words; suddenly shy and forgiving, hands touching in the candle flare.

They were free; all threat of marriage past. Bishop Morton had been delighted over the capture of Dorset. Flory's request for wardship of Perrette had been genially granted, with a shrewd twinkle and an episcopal handshake.

"Gentle Mary be praised!" she cried, when he told her the news.

So there was a moment when he might have kissed her— she was wearing watchet blue, a pale heavenblue, her young face and body clear and womanly in the kirtle—and didn't to his shame, but deliberately drew apart and forced himself to speak of matters alien to them both.

"We shall find you a young lad," he said. "No worthless soldier, but a sturdy lot with a trade."

He meant it. He had grown old in anger and in betrayal. She needed joy, or so he thought; love that was innocent and without shame. They were leagues apart in sense of life.

She gazed at her hands. A flush spread over her neck and cheek. She had a quality of radiance. "Perrette is young and simple, isn't she, Messire Flory?"

He did think that. The unspoilt wilderness of the heart. Like Richard himself, he had been born disbelieving and lonely.

"You know little of me, Messire Flory," she informed him.

"You are seventeen," he said. An irreparable age. But perhaps it was something else as well. Perhaps after all these years of tears and blood—the heart's ruined monarchy—had occurred the last doom, the most terrible of all: the failure of love. Not only Perrette and he. In Westminster, too. Anne—Elizabeth—Richard. But it was a matter dimly understood, if at all. Love, the power to communicate love, is taken so much for granted that hardly anyone realizes this power may be lost.

She came to him, her hair dark gold above the blue kirtle. She suspected that he had not noticed her sufficiently as a woman. "I'll dress that shoulder," she said.

She deftly removed his jacket and shirt; cut away the filthy bandage. The shoulder was really on the mend, despite the last strenuous days. He had a tough frame. She exclaimed at the dried blood. "Lucky this wound didn't go bad," she said to him.

He nodded, watching her bright eyes and young deft hands. Her touch was cool and gentle. He imagined her taking care of him, as old Betson had doubtless imagined her; the warming pan on frosty evenings, the steaming plates, the wine poured out, the fire crackling . . . a wife, she longed to be a wife.

His hand rested on dark gold hair and white neck. She gave him a swift upturned glance. "Perrette . . ." he murmured. "Little Perrette . . ." His voice was strange. He felt like a cheat. He hated to appear false to her; she would be quick in detecting the clipped coin of his heart.

"Why are you frowning so?" she demanded. "How many churlish soldiers have a gentle young girl at their beck, think you?"

"Oh, none. None!" he assured her.

"Smile a little more," she admonished. "You were kinder when the Bishop intended to marry me off. Regret it, do you?"

He squeezed the nape of her neck, the flesh white as milk. Her face, bent through the golden evening, was absorbed and lovely. She had told him—ah yes, he remembered!—that in her country of Lorraine she loved the forests and the mountains, the blue-hung solitary ways.

She finished bathing the shoulder; bound a fresh linen bandage about it. "Ready for the next war," she said.

He sat up; not looking at her, but feeling the intolerable joy and desire of her. For an instant she crouched beside him and he said nothing; and she fled to her feet, but his hands took her back. . . .

"Tell me about Brittany," she said softly, sitting on a small three-legged stool.

He was mute. Brittany: how could he make her know the magic? He groped, while she waited, tense and eager. And then all at once he saw again the dark and marvellous land, memory kindled—and he was telling her: of the silver-haired assassin, the Steward of Saint Eloi; of Machecoul and Gilles de Rais; of the girl that was a shadow, an angel, a moment of terror and light; of the fight with the brigands; of the man that died beside the sea, gripping Flory's hand;

of the coming of the Duke's messenger; of the long pursuit
upstream and the green wonder of the riverside; of rowing
to the island and of the dead man in the brush; of finding
Dorset. . . .

She listened, fire in her eyes. She had not known him to
be a man like this. The memories that lay below the memories. He paused. He had not spoken so much in years. In
telling her about Brittany, he had somehow revealed himself. Loneliness; and the heart forever a stranger. . . .

But then, just as she was sure she had found a way to him,
he fell again into brooding.

"What is it now?" she said.

"What is what?" He peered at her.

"Some new perplexity," she replied. " 'Tis plain in your
look."

"I swore an oath to your father, to Piers," he said. "He
loved you very much."

She regarded him; oh, she might have said, there be more
than one way of keeping such an oath!

Did he dare to think he could avoid the meaning of his
time? Swing back the pitiless door? But every man secretly
dreams of being an excepted angel, singled out for salva-
tion. . . .

She sat utterly still, hands folded; virgin of blue un-
fathomable solitudes. Her dark-gold head was inclined forward. He caught her in his arms. She looked up, eyes questioning. She had had more experience than John Flory suspected with the kind of man who wanted her and would pay
well for his wanting—but she had accepted none. A slight
smile crossed her pretty mouth. "Now, Messire Flory, promise you will learn to laugh!" she said.

He drew back, suddenly himself. He could not promise
what he had not. He had not joy. And if he had not joy, he
was nothing for her. He brought regret. And that was worse
than age. To lay hold on someone out of regret. He shook
his head. Was this the last—the very last instant of love?

But this was the only man, of the hunters and the hunted, that she had ever recognized with the blood-signs of love. She couldn't have told why; he was brooding and strange— she knew well he was a being perfect in loneliness, as well as he himself. That made no difference.

She kissed him. And this time, the first time, the kiss of love. He held her close. Aye, every man must dream of becoming an angel excepted. . . .

She broke away, her voice full. "I am very happy, Messire Flory," she said.

He looked about in the golden-flickering room. This candled moment . . . the fire brass, the ranked pewter, the old green hourglass upon the wall . . . and it was as if he might be healed of his time; and know again the power of love.

They gazed at one another, trying to reach some high noon-shining hill that only they might know. Go back; but they could never go back. It was only the habit of doubt, the plague-sickness of betrayal that had got into his very bones. . . . He smiled at her.

"I forgot," she said. "A letter came for you." She went to the sideboard.

He turned over the grimy paper, folded square. A spidery fussy hand that meant nothing to him. "Did you read it?" he asked.

She shook her head, hurt. "Your letter? Read your letter? I would not do that, Messire Flory."

Warned by he knew not what, he thrust the letter from him. Perplexed, she said: "Why don't you read it?"

"It will keep," he remarked. He went toward her. She had tears in her brown eyes. He knew her; how ever since she was a child she had been moved by sudden storms of feeling. Weeping, he recalled, for days over a slain deer, or the death of a favourite bird. It was a part of her unique solitary self that loved the forests of Lorraine.

But there is news that will not keep, that flies upward,

clamouring. . . . She took the letter. Never would she say
whether or no she knew. She gave it to Flory again.

Doomed and caught, he tore open the letter, held it to
the light. At first he could make nothing whatever of it.
Some female of whom he had never heard and, please God!
never wished to hear, rambling from her cottage in Kent:
the war and the high cost of living and the fearful uncer-
tainties of the times. Why, damn his soul to Hell! why was
the hag writing to him?

And then he saw far down the page—while Perrette
hovered gold-quiet in the evening—mention of a nephew,
of Miles. The lad was sick, it seemed; not right in the head.
London had unhinged his mind. Raved of murder, he did.
Especially of men strangled and black. He had got worse
since the news of—

Flory flung down the letter and would not read another
word. For, he knew, it was come out of Hell, as surely as any
letter ever came out of Hell, to destroy his last moment of
love. . . .

"What is it?" Perrette cried, picking up the letter. "What
does it say, Messire Flory?"

He looked up, old in the candlelight. "Oh, it speaks of
war and death and madness; murder, too. Yes, quite a bit
about murder. Our time, my dearest Perrette."

She was silent before the bright grief of his face. Something had struck at them from the night. Their precarious
turret of hope trembled. "Who was Lucy?" she asked, softly.

He turned to her, bitter and remembering. "A servingmaid," he said.

"She was young?"

"Aye—young." He heaved from his seat, surging about
the room, seeing now the black street and the cold quiet
killer—and himself striding away. Himself, tearless and
striding; and through crooked streets the rat's foot of death.
. . . "Why should it have been her?" he said. "She did no
harm to anyone."

Perrette was watching, pale, wondering, shuttered from him. "Did you love her, Messire Flory?"

He swung about, as if she had accused him. Him! Glimpsed blood on his hands. "I scarcely knew her," he replied.

She perceived that this was not the truth, or rather that there was a kind of easy exterior truth with a lie underneath. He was linked in some mortal way with the murdered girl. "What does it mean?" she cried. "Why this madness and death?"

He gazed steadily at her. "This was decided long ago," he said. "Before ever you were born. Or Lucy."

"But she was innocent!" Perrette said.

"Of course," he agreed. "She died of innocence." He breathed harshly, fist-clenching. The question: *who? who?* Which badge: White Boar or Red Dragon?

She came to him, dark-gold and longing. "This Lucy—this servingmaid—she's dead. Lucy's dead. You can do nothing for her."

He kissed her, her fresh lips and milkwhite throat, Lorraine in her eyes. He lifted his head. "I want to know," he said. "I've got to know!" Lucy had died because of him. Miles, sick and haunted. The touch of Flory was the touch of his time. He must not destroy Perrette.

"You go to London?" she asked.

"Not London," he said. "I'll not find an answer in London."

"Where, then?"

"Calais . . ."

"Calais!"

He nodded, slowly, while time's great wounds bled afresh and they heard an echo of boots scraping the night. . . .

BUT first: Master Urswicke. . . .

A summons to the Tournelles at the hour of prime, the

shuttered August-heavy Paris morning, offal smoking in the court and crows circling in a silvery sky. And Bedford: Flory thought of John Plantagenet, Duke of Bedford, here amid this black oak and mildewed tapestry, the grey gaping arches, a tomb-breath of chill air stagnant in the chamber . . . and sick Bedford, the wifeless bitter governor, the last warrior, dying and signing warrants, Lancaster going out in curses and in shadows, the Paris of the damned slavering for bread and at the gates wolves . . .

Bedford. . . .

But all that was fifty years ago and here was a new Lancaster, black-gowned, clerical, the joyless skull of statecraft.

"Fate is marching, Master Flory. We return to England." Urswicke was walking up and down, gown-flapping in the style of Morton, rubbing his hands.

"The fleet is ready?" Flory asked.

Urswicke nodded. "Provisioning at Harfleur. A matter of days only—and a following wind."

It had come. What they had laboured for since Tewkesbury, fourteen years before; but Flory could feel no triumph, no exaltation. Bought; the bought bright Rose of Lancaster.

What was this foul-breathed clerk saying?

"Our thrusts against Richard have scored. His soldiers are laggard to come in. And of them that do—" Urswicke paused, a pale light in his gaunt grey face. "Many shall do faint service."

Flory was not sure. He had heard that Richard was in process of assembling a fine army. And these "thrusts" that Urswicke spoke of: what were they but backstairs brut, painted tongues, gutter rumours? He reminded Urswicke that there had been no open accusation.

"Not so, Flory!" Christopher Urswicke retorted quickly. "Have you forgot that in January of last year Messire Guillaume de Rochefort, Chancellor of France, spoke thus to the Estates at Tours: *Regardez, je vous en prie, les événements qui après la mort du Roi Edouard sont arrivés dans ce pays. Contemplez ses enfants, déjà grands et braves, massacrés impunément, et la couronne transportée a l'assassin par la faveur des peuples!"*

. . . Consider, I beg you, the happenings which after the death of King Edward took place in this country. Think of his children, already grown and sturdy, murdered with impunity, and the crown bestowed upon the assassin by favour of the people! . . .

Urswicke quoted the words of Guillaume de Rochefort with solemn delight. The speech at Tours had been Morton's masterstroke; and had gone unanswered in England. Still, Flory reflected, that did not mean no answer was possible. Caught in a web, King Richard had only one convincing reply: display of the boys. The one reply, it seemed plain, that Bishop John Morton knew could never be made.

Yet other men might ponder that this appalling charge came from England's ancient enemy, only too eager to dishonour the whole English nation. . . .

"De Rochefort makes the English people Richard's accomplices," Flory pointed out. "The purport is plain: to stain the nation as much as Richard!"

Urswicke frowned; his voice grated. "The purport, Master Flory, is to proclaim this venomous spider a devourer of his own blood. Has any like charge ever been laid against a King of England, without proof?"

Flory shrugged. As always, talks with Urswicke came to an impasse: his own thoughts, his own perception denied him; and a set of Tournelles fetters clamped on his soul. He resented this effort to shackle freeborn untonsured English in the iron brace of clerical conformity. "I am an Englishman," he said. "I know the temper of the French."

Urswicke snapped his fingers. "We are not to consider what you know, Master Flory. It would be well that you should give assurance of your loyalty. There have been rumours, Flory. Rumours that do you small credit."

He broke off; gave Flory a sunken glance. The soldier felt

a shiver of alarm. Urswicke had sharpened a knife for him
since Flory had spoke of John Dighton. He had hit on a secret frightening to Tudor and Morton.

But why frightening?

"We are giving you a final chance," Urswicke was saying,
in a dry confessorial tone, as he might to an unregenerate
sinner thrice backslid. "We are sending you to England.
Every man is needed."

"With Milord Oxford's army?" Flory exclaimed, his voice
suddenly warm.

Urswicke shook his head. "No, Master Flory. Not with
Oxford. We are sending you back to Richard."

"To Richard?" Flory stared.

The cleric said softly, "To the Boar. You will sow doubt
amongst the soldiers. Speak of lies, treachery—and murder.
But come not at the matter directly. Sound each man's loyalty far off, as it were; drop a word here, a word there. . . ."

He paused; his tongue darted out, licking thin bloodless
lips. "Do understand, Master Flory?"

The soldier choked with disgust. He had his fill of carrion hunting; of scavenging rotten souls. What right had
these gowned vultures to force their leprous schemes on
him? He had not sworn to Lancaster to turn into a monger
of treachery and dishonour. . . .

"A nasty business, Master Urswicke," he said. "Let me
take an honourable place in Oxford's army, at Harfleur. Let
me fight without deceit for Lancaster. I was at Tewkesbury,
Master Urswicke."

"No!" Urswicke flared toward him, sunlight webbing his
black gown. For an instant he seemed himself a monstrous
spider. "I care not where you were. You are all alike, you
men of Margaret. Dwelling in the past—sick with dreams!
Guzzlers and potwallopers. Your sort never did anything
for Lancaster save suffer defeat. No one listens to you any
more. Your day is dead!"

John Flory became very white; very still. He felt sweat

on the palms of his clenched hands, rilling down his body inside his doublet. He wanted a drink.

Urswicke stood over him, hectoring, enjoying the destruction. "We are different," he rasped. "We intend to win!"

Flory turned away, terrified at the torrent of hate within him; another instant and he would have throttled Urswicke. He sensed the vulture glance upon him as he groped amid the battered oak and sad tapestry, the gaping arches like ruined mouths from which the torturer has torn the teeth, one by one . . . Bedford . . . Bedford. . . .

He was sweating and trembling. He had to have a drink.

"What is the matter with you?" Urswicke demanded. "Are you ill?"

"A touch of sun, Master Urswicke." He was looking from the casement into the court below. A spotted dog sprawled in the morning glaze, like one of Tudor's curs. "Have you a bit of brandy?" Flory asked.

Urswicke retreated, shaking his head. "I never drink," he said. He put a black sleeve to his mouth and nose. "By the Mass, Flory! Have you caught the sweating sickness?"

Urswicke cowered from that dread infection already ravaging Tudor's horde. The sweating sickness racked its victims with chills and sweats, the onset of icy rigor—and death.

"Frightened, are you?" said Flory, with a withered smile.

"Flory!" Urswicke shrank.

"Take heart, Master Urswicke," he said. "It's not the sweating sickness afflicts me." He was silent, gazing into the court: the sun, the spotted dog broken-backed in sleep, the brightarmed listening August. . . .

"Master Urswicke." His voice came quietly. "Tell me, if we should win England—what then? Will there not remain men who remember Richard in the time of his monarchy? Men who may scruple to accept French tales of an anointed English king?"

Urswicke shot a glance at Flory. Brows furrowed above

the bony ridges, the blue hollows of the eye sockets. "We have thought of all that, Flory," he replied. "Some simple wights may not understand at first. But in time, Flory. In time. . . ." His gaze shifted; raven-mantled, he mused. "This will be a victory not only of arms. It will be a victory of mind. Now is the day of books and printing. A mighty power. Oh—mighty!" He lifted his arms, black batwinged sleeves triumphantly spread. "History shall be written. The history of the Rose. Our new books shall correct errors; they will be remembered."

Flory nodded. A fly droned through the pause. A buzzing in his brain, the wasp of Time with mortal sting. "I see," he said slowly. "But who shall write these books, Master Urswicke?"

"In Italy they know how to set down history that men may read and profit," Urswicke explained. "Dominic Mancini of Rome has already done good service for our own day."

Mancini, reputed the protégé of Guillaume de Rochefort, had written a tale in Latin, *The Usurpation of Richard the Third*; and it was upon this work that de Rochefort had based his Tours speech. Mancini had departed England in July of 1483; he knew of after events only by hearsay. Yet he had forecast Richard's murder of the York Princes by a skillful plucking on strings of rumour, suspicion, presumption—especially the views of a certain "Strasbourg doctor," an attendant of the deposed Edward and the last friend to see the lads alive.

As other witnesses in this dark horror, the Strasbourg doctor had conveniently disappeared; and though Master Dominic seemed intimately courant of the doctor's private opinions in a most clouded matter, he neglected to furnish his readers with the doctor's name.

However, as Urswicke said, Master Dominic knew how to tell a good story. . . .

Flory pondered Urswicke's words. He perceived that Tudor and Morton were contriving another murder—a crime beside which the slaughter of the Princes, terrible as that had been, was of small import: they were plotting to murder truth itself; they were setting about to slay the past.

For suddenly Flory realized that Tudor, Morton, Urswicke were far more formidable than ever he had dreamed. He had thought that they had merely usurped the name of Lancaster—out of greed for power.

How mistaken he had been!

Now he knew that these black-gowned conspirators intended to destroy Lancaster, as well as York; to destroy the vision; to destroy knighthood and the legend of the Rose; to destroy honour and pity; destroy, destroy.

All that Lancaster had stood for was doomed more surely by Tudor and Morton than ever it had been by the iron wreck of Tewkesbury. For York had not slain the vision. . . .

Urswicke was watching him, with that vulturous hooded gaze. "Have you decided, Master Flory?"

He was shaken by interior laughter. He saw this unsavoury mission in a new light. Were the conspirators not offering Flory the means to ruin them? He could go without suspicion to Calais; track Dighton, pry out the truth about the Princes. . . . Afterward: England and Richard. So that even if the Tournelles found out Flory, he was for the time out of reach. And whichever side won, ultimately, he believed, the truth must prevail; this festering corruption of lies would cease. . . .

He did not suspect that truth might prove a looking glass, magically to reflect therein the wish of the beholder.

"I have decided, Master Urswicke."

"And what do you do?"

"I go to England."

Urswicke rubbed his hands together. "Now you prove sensible, Flory. It will bring reward. We never forget particular service."

Flory's glance flickered about the room. *We never forget*

particular service! Perhaps, then, he might not be put to silence: living on, aging and dishonoured, obscure pensioner —already he could see the dim back room, cavelike, the mouldering half-eaten cheese, the spiders and the memories. . . .

Christopher Urswicke was hovering near, a grey waxlike smile, yellow teeth, carrion breath—avuncular, he dropped a hand on Flory's shoulder. "You have chosen the future, my friend."

Flory looked at him. Death peering through the gaunt mask: death the watching familiar, *rigor mortis* of the spirit . . . "You have no doubt of victory, Master Urswicke?"

He stooped; a tainted whisper in Flory's ear. "Crouchback is doomed. The savage bloodsupper shall be thrown down. We have come to terms with Elizabeth Woodeville. It means the union of the Roses!"

Urswicke lifted clasped hands, eyes roving upward, a prayer to a lean bone-hungry God. . . .

⊕→✳→⊕→✳→⊕→✳→⊕

"DIGHTON? Dighton? I don't know the name, messire. A priest, you say? Precious few priests come here."

The black-cloaked visitor glanced about. The Cat's Head was grimy and ill-lit; a smell of cooking fat in the air. On one wall a frowsy green perroquet muttered in a cage. A room for a murderer to hide out. Oh, but you wouldn't call John Dighton a murderer . . . he had only done his duty to shrive. . . .

"Bring me a cup of Portugal wine," the visitor said; and stretched upon a bench.

The wine drawer's bristling face bent toward him in the half-light. "Pasty, too?"

John Flory shook his head. He had dined in the saddle and he was bone weary; ridden like a herald of Hell the fifty odd leagues between Paris and Calais. Calais! the focal point of the last English foothold in the Kingdom of France.

Three strong points: the castles of Hammes and Guisnes and the port of Calais itself. Oxford, the Silver Molet of Barnet field, had been pent up for years in Hammes—captive of York.

The drawer's footsteps clattered over the rough boards. Flory heard a noise from the kitchen. They were dragging a heavy object—like a limp body—across the kitchen floor. It was doubtless a wine cask that they broached. He sighed into the shadows. The night was warm; August on the Manche. Twenty miles away rose the embattled cliffs of York's last monarchy.

Flory had tracked Dighton from one wretched haunt to another; and now the Cat's Head, at the broken fosse beside the barbican gate. The drawer came with the wine. He plopped it down, spilling a little. Flory cocked an eye at him. The fellow had a sullen night face, dredged with discontent. He would betray—had he anyone to sell. "You've not much custom," Flory remarked.

The fellow grunted. Surly, he turned away. Flory drank. The wine was heavy and dark. He thought of the Lancastrians, of those who had usurped the great name of Lancaster: the young squires like Wingfield and Latimer, lusting for titles and manors; Sir John Cheyney, renegade Yorkist; Sir William Brandon, the Standard Bearer, another renegade; Morton and Tudor, the brains and the blood, both consumed by the fierce dazzle of kingship.

And Harfleur: the curving caravels and nefs anchored beak to beak, the long lines of Normans with great casks, the crude winches hoisting on board the bombards and culverins, the mercenaries in battle gear with white surcoat and red George Cross—and Morton standing by, his mighty moment, the last throw, the beginning and the end for John Morton, Bishop of Ely.

The door of the Cat's Head was abruptly flung open. Two soldiers burst in. Flory looked up and nodded. "Good welcome, masters," he said.

Warily, they approached; lean hard-muscled fellows in ragged jacks. They wore no badge; wise, when badges altered from day to day. "Will you drink?" Flory invited.

They stared at him, like two stray mongrels confronting a third. "I don't know you," one said.

Flory shrugged. "I deal in hides," he replied. Indeed he did, he thought with bitter amusement. They sat down, still cautious. Flory summoned the drawer. "More wine," he ordered.

"You are lately from England?" the first man said.

Flory nodded. "I came with a cargo on the *Mary of the Lea.*" This was an English ship that Flory had glimpsed in the harbour.

The second fellow leaned forward. "What is it like in England?" he said softly. "Are the lads coming in? Will the King be ready?"

"They are coming in," Flory assured. "The North is mustering. King Richard will have a mighty power."

They had gap-toothed smiles. "I'm Grantley," the first said. "And this is Kilcullen. We're Tyrell's lads."

"I'd guessed as much," said Flory.

"You heard about Jamie Blount?" Kilcullen remarked. "That were the precious Governor of Hammes? Turned his coat, he did. Went piss-hot to Henry Tudor and that swine of a Bishop. And took Oxford with him. An oath of fealty! Sweet tits of Magdalene!"

"A lord's fealty, Kilcullen," Grantley said. "Jamie Blount is own brother to Lord Montjoy, that be Governor of Guisnes. Lords are different from you and me, laddie."

"Tyrell is true," Kilcullen said. "A man can say nary a word against Sir James Tyrell."

"He's holding Guisnes, is he not?" Flory commented. "In the absence of Montjoy?"

Kilcullen nodded. "Aye, that he is. But 'tis rumoured that he will take us to England to fight for the King. We be five hundred-odd and may do good service in the field."

Grantley shook his head. "Don't you believe it. Tyrell knows when he's safe."

Flory shot a glance at him. That last remark had homed on the target. Safe! Tyrell remained above the conflict. Where did Sir James fit in this skein of treachery and conniving entangling them all? Think back . . . eighteen months past—to October, 1483 and the Duke of Buckingham. Where was Tyrell then? Not with the King, not with Richard. In London, presumably. Doing what?

"He's close and deep is Sir James," Kilcullen said. "You'll never catch him out."

And wasn't Knight Banneret Sir James Tyrell, Master of the Henchmen, under the direct command of the High Constable of England—he of accursed and mortal fame: Henry Stafford, Duke of Buckingham? Was he not bound to carry out the orders of the Duke? Then the King to whom they both owed everything had been many miles distant from London, on his royal progress. But in this time of dread October the King had possessed perfect confidence in his High Constable and in the officers of his Household.

Flory came to a decision. He took a draught of wine and wiped his lips. "Do you know a man named Dighton?" he said. "John Dighton?"

They gazed at him. A shoulder of spitted veal hissed on the hearth. The candles dripped a wan gold. In its little cage the perroquet fluttered.

"Dighton?" Grantley repeated. "Who might that be?"

"A priest," Flory replied. "He is said to live in Calais."

Grantley frowned, black-browed above his twisted nose that had taken a knock from a holy water sprinkler. "Oh," he said, "a priest." He hesitated. "There be a clerkly fellow comes in here of an evening. Never says a word. Has his supper and goes right out. I never knew his name."

"He's the wight that lives in the Street of Two Archers," Kilcullen added. "You know the place, Grantley. At the bread seller's, Madame Celeste."

"Where is this bread seller's?" Flory asked casually.

"Not far from here," Grantley said. "Down the lane, turn left and follow the ditch until ye fetch up at Warwick Gate. The Street of Two Archers leads off the Gate. What d'ye want of this Dighton fellow?"

John Flory shrugged. "Just a bit of talk. I was one of Dighton's parish not long since. More wine, masters? Drawer!"

"What are you seeking, messire?" The woman's crafty eyes explored Flory's face.

"You have a man living here named John Dighton?"

She was abruptly dumb. She leaned into the close, fragrant with a smell of fresh bread. Her handsome bosom rested upon the ledge of the open serving door. Behind her loomed long round loaves of newly baked *batards* and *baguettes.* Flory fumbled for his purse. He clinked two half-royals into her palm.

Her face invited beneath the jet-dark hair. She had a long nose and thin sensual lips. When she smiled, she seemed to take you to bed. "Come in, messire," she said.

He entered, stooping. Everything was quiet as a ghost. The room appeared to recede down infinite aisles of darkness, broken by the red flicker of the ovens. Madame Celeste handed him a warm manchet or quarter-loaf and a cup of rich Burgundy.

"You are a friend of Messire Dighton?" she said softly, her mouth close to his face.

"Messire Dighton is known to me from England," he told her. "Is he here?"

She continued to smile, with her dark eyes, her wide lewd mouth, the merry crinkles at the corners. Catlike, she was playing with him. "I do not know, messire," she said.

He felt certain that she was lying. That somewhere in the little *boulangerie* on the crooked way of Two Archers the priest John Dighton lay hid.

"Where is the stair?" he asked. She beckoned. They went past the glowing ovens and down a narrow pavement that led into a closed court. A circular stairway wound upward. Madame Celeste clutched Flory's leather sleeve. "The stair is broken," she warned.

He went up, clambering into the black. He felt the stair sag and splinter beneath his boot. The night was pitch, the air dense and warm. He came to a small landing that protruded into the court. He stood for a moment at the door, listening. Not a sound . . .

The echo of Flory's rap died into the night. He waited, but no one came. He put his shoulder to the door, heaved. The latch, a bit of rotten leather, burst, and Flory fell into the room. He righted himself amid a cluttered gloom, pieces of shadowy furniture, the iron brackets of extinct rushlights; in one corner a pile of books mouldered.

He turned, assailed by a sudden dread. As if the room concealed an appalling memory.

A little glimmering light waked from the gloom. Flory peered rigidly. He glimpsed a round wrinkled face and a patch of grey hair. Dighton . . .

"Who are you?" a voice creaked.

"John Dighton?" Flory demanded.

Dighton thrust his candle before Flory's face. "I do not know you," he said, staring. "How came you here?"

"But I know you, Reverend Dighton," Flory said. "I am late of your parish."

"My parish!" He lit a rushlight. The rush wick flared in the basin of oil and the room leaped up in fiery brightness. Flory's glance swung about the barren chamber . . . rushes on the floor, greasy and infested by vermin; a battered chair and table; a narrow bed with a straw pallet; dirt everywhere . . . *O Brakenbury, I have done those things that now give evidence against my soul for Henry's sake; and see how he requites me!*

Dighton set his candle on the scarred table, where the remains of a dreary meal festered. He had once been plump, but now the flesh hung slack beneath the frayed cassock. His face that might have been full and florid was now wrinkled as a withered apple. He had been in the uncountable long ago a country parson; roses in the dooryard; a robin on the grass; children laughing at the gate.

Children . . .

"I've not the honour, master—" he said.

Flory said: "In the service of the Dragon, reverend sir. The name matters not."

Dighton's frightened eyes roved the room. "What do you want with me?"

It was a cruel jest that this country parson should have become damnation's witness. His soul floundered in night. To do his duty as a Christian priest—and to become seared for eternity. Flory took a long breath.

"You shall have the appointment of a profitable living, when our Prince has triumphed," the soldier said. "A living in England."

"Then I may go back to England?" he asked eagerly.

Flory shook his head. "Oh no, Reverend Dighton," he replied. "You may never go back to England. You shall live here and have the fees of the living."

Dighton's face sagged. He coughed. A single night intervened between him and England. A night of all nights the worst, the most terrible. Murder; murder slavering like a wolf bitch. "I so wanted to go home," was all he said.

But—never. Flory knew he was right in telling him, never. "Have you seen Tyrell?" he said softly.

Dighton jerked up his head. "Sir James Tyrell?"

Flory nodded. "Sir James Tyrell—also of your parish."

The priest stepped back. "How do I know you come from Henry Tudor?" he cried. "What warranty do you have?"

Flory handed him the broken gold angel of King Henry the Sixth, minted at the Tower, that every emissary of Tudor carried in his wallet as a credence. Dighton turned the coin between his fingers. Flory noticed that he appeared to recognize the angel for what it was—a Tudor credence.

"Well?" Dighton said at last.

"Tyrell?" Flory reminded.

He clutched the sleeves of his cassock. "No," he said, "I know nothing."

Flory was silent. He remembered Lucy and how all she wanted of life was a smile and a kiss. Instead she had been given—he felt sweat on his hands. "In England they tell of a priest named John Dighton that died of pestilence some twenty-two months past," Flory remarked. "A few days after two lads disappeared and were seen no more."

Dighton was grey-faced. A nerve fluttered in his cheek. "Two lads?" he said.

"Aye," Flory replied. "Two tender babes. Mewed up, they were. In the parish of this John Dighton."

Dighton swallowed. "What do you mean, master?" he said hoarsely.

Flory gave him a long look. "The Chapel Royal of the Tower," he said.

Silence rippled out to the edges of night . . . Dighton plucked at his cassock. Shreds of holy ordination clung to him; the consecrating hands, sallow and liver-spotted, that had substantiated the wine and the bread . . . *this is My blood shed for thee . . . this is My body broken that ye may live. . . .*

But no man should be required to bear the divine guilt, the horror that lies coiled at the root of life. . . .

"I know nothing," Dighton repeated. Clearly, he had been saying this for months. Trying to mew up in some attic of his soul the ghosts that cried and echoed.

"The Chapel Royal in the Tower," Flory said. "Your parish, reverend sir. For a single night." He paused; gathered himself. "It was October, before Saint Edward's Day. You were called to a secret shriving. A shriving of the dead."

Dighton performed a complicated manoeuvre with his hands, a washing motion. This too he must have been doing for months. He was all unconscious of it. He stopped hastily when Flory's glance reminded him. "What affair of yours is this tale?" he said.

Oh, but it was the affair of all. Of poor gentle Lucy that had died of it. Of young Miles that had gone mad through too much reality. Of Master Flory himself, that had squandered his life questing a vision, a country of the gallant and the young. When the truth for all might be unstoned in this miserable back room of bartered Calais.

He leaned forward. "I know ye," he said.

Dighton turned away. He was always in some sort of movement, fussing amid the desolation. Now he straightened a rush bracket that leaned to one side, and cast a nervous eye on a scraping sound from one corner. Vermin . . .

"You saw the lads buried, did you not?" Flory went on. "In some hole within the Tower?" He must act as if he too were privy to the secret—or to a part of it. What he knew had been pieced together: stray whisperings among the Company of the Boar; the brut of Tudor squires and York renegades; the suspicious response of Urswicke to Dighton's name, the angry insistence on a July murder.

The priest breathed heavily; his glance darted about. Upon the table lay a large bread knife. He moved toward it. Flory caught the intent—and felt old with the pursuit of terror. Once evil had begun, there was no end and no limit.

Soldierlike, Flory acted. The bread knife, wrung from Dighton's grip, rang upon the floor.

"I only wanted to cut myself some cheese," he said, with weak bitterness.

Flory looked at him. "You have already dined."

Dighton rocked gently on the balls of his feet. "Why do you torment me?" he whispered. "Are you a devil out of Hell?"

In this last broken world, this sweating sickness of the soul, no one escaped. Love: would love ever return again? "You have a duty, Reverend Dighton," Flory said. "One remaining duty. . . ."

Dighton came back to him; back from some private reverie that Flory was thankful he could not share. "What duty might that be?" the priest wondered.

"The truth," Flory said.

"The truth!" The word exploded. *The truth!* Again he performed the hand-washing ritual.

"For that horror in your soul, there will be lies, treachery and death—" Flory said. Evil, pure evil, was a stone dropped into Time's enormous pool, the ripples spreading out to uncounted years, unborn generations of guiltless. . . .

"I do not know your name," the wrinkled priest said, gaining force from his very dread. "No matter. You seem to me either a very clever knave or a fool. Whatever you are, I have nothing to tell you."

Flory moved into the ruddy light. He opened his cloak, his arms spread like great wings. "Do you know this badge?"

The priest stood mute.

"What—from Hell, then?" Flory said. "You yourself have vowed it."

"A Stafford knot," Dighton's voice quivered.

"A gold Stafford knot," Flory repeated. "The badge of Henry Stafford, Duke of Buckingham."

"Buckingham is dead," Dighton said tonelessly.

"Dead—and in Hell," Flory added. "If ever man went to Hell. It was murder, was it not? The Princes of York stood between Buckingham and a throne. He threw the blame on Richard. Was not that the way of it?"

"Why does Henry Tudor come to me?" Dighton burst out, a high ravaged hysterical note. "He knows. Tudor knows!" He shuddered into silence.

Tudor knows! This was what Flory had come for.

Dighton, shoved into this black hole of Calais, had been a link between Buckingham and the party of Tudor. Buckingham, directing the murder in England; Tudor and Morton, silent accomplices in Brittany . . . the hideous deed a political necessity to set the stage for the Buckingham-Tudor Rebellion of October, 1483. A deed to rally to the rebels disaffected Yorkists who believed in Richard's guilt; a deed to remove two claimants to the throne with titles infinitely superior to the titles of Buckingham or Tudor. . . .

"Oh, reverend sir," Flory asked gently, "Tudor knows what?"

Dighton's face shut. "Nothing—go away . . . go away, God a' mercy!"

The room was flooded in silence. The priest struggled to a rotten chair and fell into it. He rested his head upon his arms. His shoulders heaved; a gasping sound escaped him.

"Shall I tell you a tale?" Flory said cruelly. He served a harsh and haughty mistress—he served truth. "You were a priest of the Chapel Royal in October, twenty-two months before. One night near Saint Edward's Day you were summoned—in haste—to perform the rites of the dead. You went. They brought you to the White Tower, to the donjon vault; showed to you the naked bodies of two boys upon the earthen floor. . . ."

Flory glanced down at the greasy rushes, as if the young dead might yet be glimpsed before them. "Two dead boys. You never heard the names. You didn't need to. All England had been ringing with these names for months. You knew. You always knew."

Dighton lifted his head. Now he sat immobilized, coffin-yellow, his face in rags. The tranquillity of a rotting soul . . .

"Of course you can't by canonical rule shrive the dead," Flory noted. "Yet there was something special about this. Death by violence—the lads had been pressed to death between two mattresses—royal death, the strict command of an exalted lord, who might not endure that his tender victims should be spaded into earth without a holy murmur or two. That was where you came in, Dighton."

Dighton groped to his feet. "Lies," he croaked. "All lies. I'm a man of Holy Kirk. Look upon my cassock and my beads."

Flory resisted pity. Had one of these men displayed pity? October pity? "If you were true man of Holy Kirk, you would have refused. But you were a coward, John Dighton. Besides, they offered you money. They are still offering you money. I did not lie to you about a fat living in England."

"England . . ." The name hung dying in the room; an image remembered beyond time, an incredible dream.

"There was another reason for your presence, reverend sir," Flory said, "in addition to offering the consolations of faith, the murderer's pious kiss upon the cold bodies of the butchered. Aye; another reason . . ."

No sound from Dighton. Perhaps this, like so much of his life in these last months, had become a moment so strange and unmeasurable that he was stunned into acceptance. For —as in any ancient devotion—the murderer and the murderer's creatures are beings of habit. The pursuit of terror can become a way of life as any other.

Even for victims and casualties. . . .

"To bear witness. . . ." Flory continued. "To carry to your masters in Brittany the frozen greeting of the dead."

"You are a devil," Dighton whispered. "Straight from Hell."

Flory stood in the rushflare's ruddy gold. About him an obscure cluttered decay; life's broken toys, the accidents of murder. Flory understood—as much as he was ever to understand. He tore the Stafford knot from his breast, flung it on the rushes. "Be easy, Reverend Dighton," he said, "I've not ridden from Hell." He paused, exclaimed: "For this be Hell, Reverend Dighton; nor are we out of it!"

Dighton's eyes opened wide in the curling golden light, stared; a gleam of horror amid the ruin. Memories clung to him; memories like frantic birds crying and fluttering.

Flory groped into the night. . . .

IV. THE WHYTE BOAR

*Well beloved friend, I commend me to you, letting
you to understand that the King's enemies be a land,
and that the King would have set forth as upon Mon-
day, but only for our Lady Day, but for certain he
goeth forward as upon Tuesday, for a servant of mine
brought to me the certainty.*

*Wherefore I pray you that ye meet with me at Bury,
for by the grace of God I purpose to lie at Bury as
upon Tuesday night, and that ye bring with you such
company of tall men, as ye may goodly make at my
cost and charge, besides that ye have promised the
King, and I pray you ordain them jackets of my livery,
and I shall content you at your meeting with me.*

—John, Duke of Norfolk

*R*ICHARD'S privy closet was lit by two tall white candles
at either end of a walnut writing table. Between the candles parchment documents piled, awaiting signature. The
air was heavy and still. Murrey curtains labelled with White
Roses were drawn tightly across the casements.

It was much after the hour of sleep. . . .

The King had long since given up regular hours. He took
but little rest of nights and though he did not, as some reported, rise and run about his bedchamber dagger in hand,
looking for assassins, he did often wander into the great galleries of Westminster, musing on past the flaring torches
and badges of the White Boar. He was indeed at such moments searching for something or someone; but exactly what
this something was even he could not have told. Perhaps it

was the lost talisman of his blazing youth, the touchstone of his early glory. He had taken life by storm, ridden like War's godchild at fame and victory. He had never known defeat. Nor ever before the weary night companion, the blind and speechless brother, Doom. . . .

Or perhaps he was seeking the promise of love. Now this was an odd treasure for him to quest. He had always been scornful of love. Love; and matters like charity and grace. He had got on well without them. They weakened a man, prevented him from achievement.

Only lately, in the last few months, had he begun to sense the power of love. What love had done for others, might love not do for Richard? He was not aware—and nobody in his life had ever explained or made clear to him—that he would never find love, companioned as he was by vengeance, war and death. Nor why when he had been offered the gift of love by two women, his own wife Anne, and his niece Elizabeth Plantagenet, he had been able to do nothing whatever with it.

He knew that—though Anne had been mortally ill—he, the King, had aided in the death of this woman who loved him. He had ceased wanting her to live, that was all he had done—but it was enough. He had felt no frenzy of grief at her passing, no intolerable sorrow such as crushed young Richard the Second at the death of his Anne. He had mustered a few tears at the Abbey service; and immediately afterward he had summoned workmen to do over the dead Queen's rooms. For fear, he had explained, of infection.

Curiously, now that she was dead, he thought about her more than he had ever done. For the first time, he realized that he had cheated her of life. He had, in a fashion, consumed her whole life and had given her in return only this ceremonial dream of kingship—something she didn't want. And their ten years of marriage in the North amid flying winds and steel sunlight of Wensleydale had been years of castle-haunting on her part, years of intense driving ambition on his part.

Yet—Anne had loved him. That was the great fact confronting him at the swift autumn of his life. That made him suspect he had passed by a strange and even terrible force. He had been obsessed with outward forms of power. An interior power, capable of transforming utterly the soul— what could be more dread, more fascinating? Anne's love, to be sure—like Anne herself—had lacked force and clarity. Love about his neck like a sad tremulous kitten. Still, how in the beginning she had feared and scorned him! Accused him in her soul of murder. And she, even her sad and pleading love, was not that wonderful to have come by? Now that Anne was gone, he realized that her love had possessed a secret grace for him, a grace without his even knowing—that in some fabulous manner it had been more than a little responsible for his triumphs.

There remained Elizabeth Plantagenet, his niece. Proud passionate blood-devoted Elizabeth. . . .

The King got up from his imported Venetian couch, with its cover of gold and red damask with the three gold guardant Leopards, and limped to a tall pier glass. He stared at himself in the room's flickering dusk, in the little blazing eyes of the candles. His long sunken face; his lank red-brown hair hanging to his shoulders; his cruel eyes, deep-set, that seemed to change from hazel to green in the fluttering light. He studied his figure, in the long loose maroon robe, furred with ermine and belted with a gold chain of York Sunnes. A slight figure, with left shoulder high and left arm short. And the leg that was ever so short and dragged.

No, he was not handsome. Not as so many of his tawny magnificent House, sprung from the mating of Anjou and Aquitaine. Whenever he considered Elizabeth, he remembered. He dreamed a young man's dream of royal limbs, of shining hair. Like that Prince Edward of Anjou fallen at

Tewkesbury. Fallen? Say, rather: put to the sword. His blood—red as the doomed and beautiful Rose of Lancaster. Vengeance for Edmund, for the lost splendid brother, murdered at Wakefield. . . .

Turning from the pier glass, he thought of his forty changes of raiment, his baths every two or three days, his fine-smelling herbs—none of this made him into a romantic cavalier. But he could do better than poet-knights of Old Provence. He was the last Plantagenet; the last rightful King of England. And he had schooled himself in war, so that he was as fit for a girl's adoration as Harry Hotspur of old.

And he had received that kind of adoration from Elizabeth; mixed with the love she bore for her father, for her Plantagenet descent. Oh yes, he had been certain of the girl. But this was before he had publicly rejected her; torn up the document of their love like outworn parchment. Since that bitter day, she had made him aware of his body. Her blue glance upon his lameness, his crooked shoulder. She was proud and she was a woman and she knew how to hurt.

This love, too, had availed him nothing. . . .

He sat down again on his couch, stared into shadows. He felt once more the old ruinous questions creeping like gaunt spiders on him. He had begun with so much. He was as fit for kingship as any who had sat upon the Leopard throne. What had happened? By the Nails and Blood! what had gone wrong with his life?

There were several possible answers to that question, but the true answer, the only one that really mattered, lay in the granite silence of the Tower; silence abrupt and shattering as the burst of bombards. His nephews, Edward and Richard. They stood forever between Elizabeth and him. Peevish brats. He had never liked them. Woodeville, Woodeville.

But in death, as others about him, they were stronger than in life. The persons he touched with his passion, his terrible lust—who in a sense had died of him—Marguerite d'Anjou, Anne, Edward and Richard; why, these went on existing after death, more alive than ever, companions to his every act, shaping his fate for him—as never in the body could they do. Death bestowed a marvellous strength on these companions of his, these slain.

Elizabeth would find out about her brothers one day. Her love would turn to hate; hate by night and hate by day; hate in dreams (for such is by no means impossible) and hate awake. It was no use, he knew now, accusing Henry of Buckingham. He had been offered such a chance on All Souls' Day, eighteen months before, and he had thrown it away. He had doomed Buckingham, unheard. His pride, his wanton pride, that would not let him confront his great betrayer. Now no one would believe for a moment that he had not known all about Buckingham and those boys in the Tower; even inspired the Duke to kill them.

And Henry Stafford, Duke of Buckingham, young Buckingham, witty and irreparable, he was another of those busy and perilous dead that would not halt in the grave so lovingly prepared. No, he must be up and about, his lies and deeds worth God knows how many gold florins and troops of cavalry to Henry Tudor, his smile mocking Richard as in the days of their common glory it had mocked Woodevilles.

Had it not been for these unresting dead, Richard might have lived out his reign full of years and honours—gone down as one of England's just and mighty kings, worthy of the last Plantagenet. . . .

As it was . . .

And suddenly, huddling the dead in their unspeakable night, he remembered the living. He thought of Henry Tudor and was swept by a torrent of hatred. He became once more the falcon. He knew what he was going to do. *He was going to kill Henry Tudor.* He, the King, would cut down Tudor on the field of battle. Never had he felt such passion for blood. This creature, this worm, this bastard upstart—he would crush Tudor as he would any vile thing.

Tudor had lied about him. Tudor had spread the blackest

tales: that Richard had done to death his nephews in the Tower; that he had poisoned his wife Anne; that he had threatened to first ravish and then murder his niece Elizabeth unless she yielded to him—and had been only restrained from this project by the intervention of his war captains. Between him and that Welsh toad lay nothing but violent death. For one or the other; for both.

For if Richard did what he intended, what no English King since the first Richard, the Lion-Hearted, had done, to lead an assault in person into the centre of his enemies' battle line, he might well doom himself. Oh—he was prepared for that! If Michael, the Avenging Angel, did but grant to his Richard the mongrel Tudor, the King was ready to pay Michael with his own life.

Watching the shadows, the lions crouching, the gold and murrey tomb. And rage, rage, hot and choking in his narrow breast. He wanted to get his steel in Tudor's flesh, to see his falchion smoking in Tudor blood. His fury was the greater because—despite all—he knew that these lies had some small grain of verity, however villainously altered. He had wished his wife Anne through eternity's ravenous door; he had coveted his niece Elizabeth; he had locked his nephews in the Tower and given the key to Buckingham. Buckingham that hated the boys. It was as good as putting a knife in the Duke's hand.

Hadn't he been guilty of all this? And wherefore, O my lords, this talk of pity? Of love?

He sprang up and went shambling up and down, shadowhuge and projected on the murrey shroud, his face old and twisted. Images formed in his mind, images of terror and splendour. The blaze of trumpets; the war glare of great horses; the way blood glistened in May; dead faces bottlegreen and crawling. . . .

Images, marvellous images . . . the shining boy crumpled on the bank beside the Severn, the roiling river, the crash of the tidal Bore . . . Somerset on the scaffold that golden bell-haunted morning . . . the triumphal entry into London . . . trumpets and tabors, the cry of the Heralds, Clarenceux, Marchmont, York and Windsor, the shouts and waving coloured silks . . . and ruined Margaret, mad with grief, drawn in a char at the fore of all the Army . . . behold! this is she, the witch-enemy—come to make a York holiday. . . .

And midnight, the old man, old Harry, the grey trembling head and filthy robe, the rook's glitter—and the way the bent, swollen fingers uncurled . . .

He paused starkly before the murrey curtains labelled with his White Rose. These deaths—necessary. Killings for York; for his brother Edward. He tore aside a fold, peered out. The night was thick and hushed. Only the flames of torches in the base court roared redly upward. The guards were living statues.

What is the hour? he wondered. *Where is everyone?*

And in the King's mind marshalled the bright host that he would captain against Tudor. Forty thousand gleaming lads. But—he had not the money for such. Nor for twenty thousand. Nor for twelve. And ten? Oh, let him have but three thousand staunch hearts, Yorkshire oak, and he would trample Tudor and his hired scoundrels!

The armoured dream receded . . . and he was alone in surging dark, the red banners of light flaring upward . . . listening, now—the lost and haunting sound of his wife's name, his dead wife. *Anne, Anne* . . . his lips formed the name. An echo ringing far off, in tears and shadows.

Walled and lampless; listening at the lock. Was this to be Hell and Heaven? And again, the dead woman—forever on some torn coast of suffering; some Land's End of the soul. But what would Richard know of that? Pity had never been his line.

He turned from the night; the great murrey shroud with its Pale Roses fell across the casement. He gazed at his rings, small flashing fires in the candleglow. Opal, sorcery; ruby, blood; ~~emerald, kingship.~~ He murmured hoarsely, *Rich-ard the King—King Richard—the most excellent Prince and dread Lord, Ricardus Tertius, by the Grace of God, King. . . .*

❀✧☀✧❀✧☀✧❀✧☀✧❀

RICHARD passed somberly before the casement, glancing into the Swan Park below. He had recently stocked the lake with a fresh marke of birds purchased from the Duke of Norfolk. Norfolk's steward cultivated swans.

The black-robed woman in the chair was waiting for him to begin. Glancing about her meagre room, he remarked: "You might do yourself better, Lady Grey. I give you seven hundreds a year. You've not even a fit carpet."

Her voice flashed: "Think yourself generous, Richard?"

"I am generous!" he said, resenting not only the remark, but the omission of any sign of respect for his royal rank. And he had dressed richly that morning: a purple satin doublet lined with holland, white cloth-of-gold hose. From his shoulders swung a vermilion velvet cape wrought with golden garters. "Had you to deal with Henry Tudor," the King continued, "you'd find out how generous. With him, you'd be lucky with fifty pounds a year."

Lady Grey got up from her chair. She was taller than Richard; ice-cold and regal, like a visionary Queen of Winter. Her pale hair gleamed like sun on a frozen morning. She walked toward the King. The thought came to Richard, just whipping foxlike across the moor of his imagination, that she was capable of killing him. He stiffened, feeling the cuirass beneath his doublet.

Perhaps the same notion occurred to the woman, for she paused and smiled with a deadly smile at the King. He recalled accusations concerning her powers of witchcraft.

"Why have you come here?" she demanded. "Not, surely, to talk over my household accounts?"

He stared, anxious not to miss a move or gesture. You

never knew what might be significant with Lady Grey. It was best to take no chances. Clarence had been careless, had treated this woman lightly. And Clarence had been strangled.

"I want you to tell me if you've been writing to Lady Margaret Beaufort," he replied. It was a formal question. He knew how Lady Grey had been betraying him these past weeks. He wanted her to realize that he was aware of everything.

She put back her head, the long black veil of the coned headdress fluttering. A sharp laugh. "What thrust that into your mind, Richard? What reason have I to write to Lady Margaret Beaufort?"

"I know you, madame," he broke out, his voice angry in the room. "You've been dealing with my enemies behind my back. Writing to Tudor's mother, Lady Beaufort, about Tudor and Elizabeth, your daughter."

"Nonsense!" Lady Grey said. "You're imagining things." She looked at him carefully, winter eyes exploring his anxiety. "They tell me, Richard, that you cannot sleep. They say you wear a steel corselet constantly." She glanced at the bulge of his doublet. "You are wearing it now. Why?"

And under her gaze, the hate congealing, darkening in her eyes, the King felt her cold rage. All his soldiers might avail him little against a witch.

"Threats have been made against my life," Richard said.

Her eyes widened. "Say you so?" she exclaimed. "Ah, Richard, how bad the world has grown! That anyone should wish to kill an anointed king."

Mocked. Little recked she of his anointing, of his kingship. For there had been another—a youth anointed, if at all, in Heaven.

"Oh, to be sure," Lady Grey went on, "ill examples have been set of late in England. Sacred oaths, the highest charges of duty, have been broke."

"Speak plainly, madame," the King said.

"Who took an oath to protect and serve his brother's son?"
She swung away, trembling.

Edward the Fifth. That child followed Richard everywhere. Bastard-born; insolent; head stuffed with books. Not
the kind of lad to strike a warrior's fancy. But how was it
this peevish boy grew more real in death than in life?

"A king born of unlawful marriage is no king," Richard
said.

Her lips moved; but no sound came. He wondered if she
could be cursing him. "You must cease writing to Lady
Beaufort," he said. "I am a patient man, but I cannot suffer
that you betray me with my enemies while living here in
my palace and on the means I give you from my privy
purse."

She lifted her head. Her face, even he had to admit, possessed a marble beauty. "I know why you want me here,"
she replied.

She lived in Westminster because he did not know what
else to do with her and he could keep one eye on her. Also,
her residence in his palace was a kind of standing denial of
the rumours that her sons had been made away with. But
little did they ken Lady Grey, who believed that! She was
capable of dissembling even to a man she suspected of murdering her boys. Dissembling for the purpose of her own
vengeance. Richard was not fooled. "I shall place a guard
over you," he warned.

"The King fears—women?" she said, erect and scornful.

He feared women! That was exactly what he did fear.
Just as he was unable to understand or make use of a
woman's gift of love, so was he unable to prevent women
combining to destroy him. Had he known what to do about
women, he might have been a great King.

He had been the twelfth of thirteen children; weak, puny,
despaired of, smothered in female care. He had to achieve
himself, to climb out of the pit of motherhood, as it were.

Never was he quite able to get rid of the power of his mother, Duchess Cecily, but with other women he kept the hard integral diamond of his being.

A man troubled and haunted by such various conditions of women as jolly Jane Shore, the image (to Richard) of ruinous lust; the red war-Queen, Marguerite d'Anjou; the golden Duchess, Margaret of Burgundy, his own sister, she who had abandoned him in his hour of need. And this black-draped deadly Elizabeth before him, her intolerable queenliness that clung to her despite all he could do.

"Pledge me, Lady Grey, to write no more to Margaret Beaufort."

She looked at him for a moment, her hard gleaming look, and unspeaking she flared about the room, moving amid sparse shabby furnishings and gold-chequered sunlight. Presently she said: "You gave me a pledge, did you not?"

He plucked his dagger up and down in the silver sheath. "Yes," he replied.

"I wait that pledge," she said.

And he had only the answer he had given Elizabeth, her daughter. "Edward has an infection of the mouth. We are having a doctor to care for him."

She was not looking at him, but standing in a shaft of sun, her black against the gold—one pale veined hand resting on an old credenza. "I don't believe you, Richard," she said.

"You shall see your lads," he vowed. "My faith as a knight."

She was silent; her hand went to her breast.

He limped toward her, bitterly aware of having to woo Lady Grey. He was prepared, nay eager, to dispute his crown on the battlefield; but this sort of contest angered and shamed him. He had willed his life to the direct fierce way of the soldier; and he had somehow become involved in a gigantic deception. A deception he was powerless to control, whose end he could not foresee.

Now he was playing for a few days' respite until Dorset—
that gilded darling of his mother, Lady Grey—should reach
England. . . .

"I shall prepare an order tomorrow for Brakenbury to
admit you to the Tower, when the lad Edward is fit and free
of infection."

"Another day," she said. "Always another day. A day that
never comes." She looked at him with her terrible eyes. "Do
but one thing for me, Richard."

"What is that?" he asked.

"Tell me how my boys died," she whispered, her lips moving carefully, as with a speech long pent, the fine dry
wrinkles at the corners of her mouth.

He felt her curse, as years before he had felt the curse of
Queen Marguerite d'Anjou. She had cursed the House of
York, root and branch. And him especially. The two
Queens, Red Rose and White Rose. The red witch and the
white witch. The red witch was dead, the white witch here
with him.

She rustled toward him. He felt her hand, cold, cold as
the hate in her eyes. Her voice, quiet, merciless, "It's not
much to ask, Richard."

He gripped his daggerhilt. "Nothing to tell you, Lady
Grey. Nothing's happened to the lads!"

Her fingers pressing his arm, her pale witch-fingers. "You
can't refuse me. Only to know—at last. I can bear anything,
if I know. Richard—"

He tore away. She kindled a fury in him. His whole life
had been a war with this Elizabeth Woodeville and her
Woodeville family. At moments he would like to doom
every Woodeville in England. Could a witch be killed? By
fire, they say. He tried to think of that blonde adored body
amid blood-red flames.

"Not much," she was saying. "Everything else—you have
taken everything else. You could leave me that, could you
not? What can it matter to you?"

The slim blade of his dagger. She must be made to keep silent. They had a score to reckon, he and Elizabeth Woodeville. She had done to death his brothers. Clarence, by midnight ropes of terror. Edward, by sorcery and lust. Now she meant to finish off Richard.

No Plantagenet, of the great Leopard House of England, had stained his hands with woman's blood. Richard breathed hard. He did not assassinate women. He was a soldier and a knight. His belted Garter, the Order of English honour. *Loyaultie me lie . . .* loyalty binds me! The device above his garter stall at Windsor.

Yet—if the woman were a witch? Was it not his bounden duty as King to protect himself and his realm from sorcery? And he was persuaded that the woman before him was a witch. . . .

Lady Grey turned toward an inner doorway. Richard remembered: *if a dagger pricked a woman and she did not bleed, she was a witch* . . . His steel shone.

She was gazing at the arras—a Unicorne with gold hoofs upon an azure field. The shrewd woman had Richard under her eye. She knew what was happening. As he drew near, she gave a quick sign and the arras was lifted.

Elizabeth Plantagenet stood before them. . . .

Richard fell back.

"Come, Elizabeth," Lady Grey said. Her eyes fixed on her mother, the girl moved into the room. She was wearing turquoise, a gown sea-coloured and glimmering.

"Richard brings sweet news," the chill voice said.

He looked at Lady Grey in astonishment. Had she decided to accept his assurances? Or was this another Woodeville manoeuvre? Confused, he came back to the girl and was startled at the change in her. Elizabeth was moon-pale; her eyes were ringed. All verve had vanished. "What is your news, sire?"

Sire! She had never called him sire. It was always Richard and Bess with them. She appeared, it suddenly came to him, as if she were her own funeral effigy borne through London's streets. He swallowed and plucked at his opal.

"Tell her, Richard," Lady Grey urged. "It would mean much to their sister to hear the news from your lips."

He frowned at her. A witch—a witch burning in Hell! No one but Lady Grey could have so wrecked hope and all his monarchy. What was she saying, thin parchment lips working, whispers in the sunlight? . . . *where is your brother's blood, Richard?*

"We spoke—" his voice crackled—"of the lads in the Tower. I shall give an order on Sir Robert Brakenbury to admit Lady Grey." He broke off; sweat on his palms, rilling down his body crammed within the padded doublet and iron shirt.

Elizabeth gave a cry of joy; she knelt and kissed the King's hand. "I knew—I knew you would!" she repeated again and again, in a half-sobbing, half-strangled voice. "Oh, Richard!"

And Lady Grey, Lady Grey gleaming in the room like February sun, tall, gilt-haired, intolerably regal. "Will you take an oath?" she demanded softly.

"An oath?" He stared at her, lank brown hair hanging about the velvet gorget of his cape. "My word as a knight!"

"A holy oath," she explained. She turned. "Fetch my reliquary, Elizabeth." The girl went to the old credenza, that might have come up from Padua when York was young, old leagues and leagues of time dead; she opened a small door and took out a silver case.

"Do you know this, Richard?" Lady Grey picked from the reliquary case an ivory and silver crucifix. She watched him.

Know it? Aye, did he not! "It was Edward's. . . ."

She nodded, coming close. "He died, Edward died—it was clasped in his hands. And before him, Edmund carried it at Wakefield. The crucifix was found on his body. It's old; no one knows how old. It came down from the Duchess."

She held out the crucifix to Richard. . . .

Wordlessly, he accepted it, his lean strong fingers closing like talons about the blessed relic of his House. He gazed down at the little silver Christ on the ivory cross. He felt the eyes of both women on him. If Margaret Beaufort had asked such a thing—but Elizabeth Woodeville! She had only one faith: the glory and the power of Woodeville. Was not this oath to requite Lady Grey for the public affront of Saint John's Priory?

But he could swear; and he could unswear. Dorset, he remembered Dorset—and lifted his hand, the crucifix held between thumb and forefinger. "I swear by God and all the Blessed Saints that you shall see your lads. . . ." His voice dying away in the sun, the utter silence of June.

Elizabeth's eyes filled with tears. She looked at him with happy anguish—and once more a fluttering candle flame of love. Love . . .

What when this demand note he had just given fell due? This sacred note. Perjury . . . perjury in the highest degree. But he must think of his throne. Richard saw with sudden alarm that he was still holding the silver crucifix. He thrust it from him.

Elizabeth said: "Now I vow never to doubt King Richard. Nor ever to marry, but where the King would I did. . . ."

He glimpsed the cry in her eyes. For an instant it was Bess and Richard again. He remembered her in yellow.

He heard the bright moment break, as if it were a moment of glass. Lady Grey rustled between them. "No one has ever suggested you should marry out of the King's consent," she said. She flashed a look at Richard.

She could lie as smoothly as Buckingham. More so, even— for she was not a witty person like the Duke and therefore she was a more effective liar. The more solemn the deceit,

the more likely to persuade. Richard thought how Buckingham had hated Lady Grey and had wished to destroy her.
Yet—there was not so much difference between them.

Lady Grey carefully restored the crucifix to the reliquary
case. She carried it to the credenza; and the King mused
how anyone, glimpsing her in raven robe, carrying a reliquary, would ever dare dream that this woman had had men
strangled and beheaded; that she had bewitched a king with
her body.

She closed the small cabinet. The black walnut doors
were carved in beautiful scrolls and the inside was lined
with balsam. She turned back to the room. Elizabeth
laughed. She laughed with sudden gasps. Her mother
walked toward the girl. "Why are you laughing, Elizabeth?"

"It's all right now," she gasped. "All right . . . Our Edward and our Richard . . . all right . . . oh, *misericorde*
of the Cross!"

The King stood in Westminster Court, on the great paving near the Hall of Richard the Second. Westminster Hall:
oh rock of doom and glory! The lion-magnificence of the
past. Four hundred years of coronations. His own, two years
before . . . the Sword of Mercy and the Sword of State,
borne by Northumberland and by Surrey . . . the royal
sceptre, borne by Suffolk . . . the ball and cross, borne by
Lincoln . . . the Sword of Justice, borne by Lovell . . .
the Sword of God, borne by Kent . . . the royal train,
borne by Henry Stafford, Duke of Buckingham, in black and
crimson velvet and blue cloth of gold.

The full throated roar: *Long live the King! May the King
live forever!*

The Coronation Banquet . . . the King's Champion, Sir
Robert Dymoke, on a black destrier . . . the challenge to
fight *anyone whatsoever of high or low degree that doth dispute the right of Our Dread Lord Richard. . . .*

Buckingham, oh Buckingham! The red exploding glare of Hell about that ducal brow!

The King stood gazing at the stone whorls of Westminster and the great granite stare of Edmund the Martyr, looking down from the West Portal. It was a strange moment. He was alone. He was just like anyone else now. Like a shilling-a-day trooper of the guard.

A yeoman in blue and murrey came out of the Clock Tower to peer at the solitary King. Others about the Court paused to frown and wonder. Richard sensed uneasiness. Their King, who gilded each public moment, was naked in the afternoon.

An important-seeming fellow bustled up. Richard turned. Catesby, of Ashby-de-la-Zouch, Leicestershire, in lawyer's black and violet. Catesby, that had sold Hastings his master to follow the glittering star of Richard Plantagenet, Duke of Gloucester.

"Good morrow, Catesby," was what he could think of to say.

"I've been looking everywhere, sire," the lawyer puffed. "I've news."

"Good news, Catesby?"

"I fear not."

Well, good news was scarce as strawberries in winter. He was used to it. "Say on, Catesby."

"Dorset was caught," Catesby said, hoarsely and quickly. "Sent in irons to Paris and locked up by the French. He'll never get away now."

Dorset! Richard felt himself grow tired and hollow. The vain, empty young man that was King Richard's last card. The means to break the deadly union twixt Woodeville and Tudor. At worst, a means of compelling precious delay in the cementing of Richard's foes—a delay that might enable the King to draw the poison of the plot.

Dorset! gaming idle fool, a prey to every wind and every current—and so ruinously irredeemable.

Richard seized Catesby by the shoulders. "Are you certain of this, Catesby?"

Catesby flushed and blew. "Messenger from Guisnes, just rode in," he sputtered. "No doubt of it. Let me go, sire!"

His voice ended in a yelp. Richard released him. The King's Leopard ancestor, gold-maned Edward, would have had the bearer of such tidings flogged. Times had gone soft.

By God and Michael! . . . and he glanced up, eyes on Blessed Edmund the Martyr. Blessed Edmund seemed to be looking at Richard, with gentle eternal gaze. Ah, it were no light matter to perjure by the saints! See how they had punished him—and in the same ill day.

He said: "No word of this, Catesby. Keep fast the messenger. We must gain a few days. Time! . . . Time! . . .

His voice rose. He was shouting; into a stone waste, a catastrophic silence. . . .

۞✦✳✤۞✦✳✤۞✦✳✤۞

AWAY from Lady Grey, from the white witch, he put on proud monarchy. Immured within the Tower, his gold-crimson Leopard flaunting from the pinnacled White Tower, his Yeomen of the Crown in blue and murrey, axes shining, his mounted sentries in full war armour visored at the gates, his burnished bombards, truculent mouths gaping at Tower casements, the trumpet's brazen cry as cavalry patrols clattered in and out . . . these sights and sounds of his power, of his visible angry might, the fang and claw of the Boar, comforted the King.

And now: the fascinating business of gunning an army for war. They had given Richard his five thousand men; the Stanleys, Tom and Will, were to bring another four or five thousand to the field. True, there were certain conditions. Henry Percy, fourth Earl of Northumberland, had insisted on leading his own contingent of border ruffians, though Richard had desired to give a divisional command to Lord

Lovell. But Northumberland must have the command. A risk. The Percy earls were notorious for blowing hot and cold. This same Henry Percy the fourth had betrayed Warwick in Seventy-one. And Henry Percy the third, the father of this nobleman, had betrayed Edward, brother to Richard.

The King scanned the parchment roll, inscribed with the war materiel of the Tower Armoury. Twenty-five hundred glaives, partizans, and pikes; one thousand helmets; five hundred German breastplates; eight hundred pairs of steel gauntlets; three hundred broadswords; one hundred double-bladed axes; one hundred maces; four score "holy water sprinklers" or spiked steel balls atop short shafts; fifty steel targets or round shields; fifty sets of rowelled spurs.

"Fifty steel targets," Richard commented. "Fifty! We should have five hundred."

He was standing on Tower Green with the Master of the King's Ordnance and John Kendall. A little way off hovered Sir Richard Ratcliffe, Captain of the Guard in succession to Sir James Tyrell, transferred to Guisnes in Calais.

"Buckingham plundered the armoury, sire," the Master of Ordnance reminded Richard.

The King gnawed his lip. Buckingham confronting him at every turn. Made Constable, the Duke had used his high office to steal from the Tower in order to equip his mutiny. The missing targets were no doubt now hanging in Welsh huts.

"And maces," Richard said. "We had more maces. And more holy water sprinklers."

The Master nodded. "Buckingham's work."

Richard threw down the list. "Not enough arms," he broke out. "Not nearly enough. Five thousand men!"

"Some of the lads will have arms furnished by their Standards," the Master of Ordnance suggested.

Aye, some would. But the King wanted this to be a royal army, with royal equipment. He longed to take these recruits, raw-boned lads from the North and West, sturdy Essex crofters, lean apprentices from Holbourne, and weld them into a beautiful company.

"Kendall," he said to his Secretary, "set down what we require and send it to the shire lieutenants. Let them collect weapons, as well as men. There are certainly five thousand targets in the realm, if we can but lay hands on them!"

He unfurled another roll: the inventory of guns. This was more satisfactory. Even the Duke had been unable to filch the royal bombards. As Richard examined the items, the names of the great guns blazoned York triumphs in his mind. "Edward" and "Richard Bombartell": Barnet and Tewkesbury. "Newcastle" and "Dijon": Bamborough and Alnwick, Lancastrian strongholds in the North. "Roaring Alice": a giant serpentine: Tom o' Falconbridge and the Kentish rebels.

And other pieces, in addition to these 10,000-pound fifteen-foot bombards: breechloading fowlers, eight feet long; muzzle-loading falcons and culverins, six feet long; toads, four feet long; down to the falconets, the smallest type of cast gun, that could be carried about and set up by a single man.

The July sun glittered like a thousand needles on the King's breast armour. The mirrored and polished steel, gold-crested, gave off a dancing light, like the flashing harness of a sun god.

Richard nodded approval at the roll. Guns might not win battles, but they had their uses. Terrorizing the enemy's horses, protecting an entrenchment against assault. And if the foe was blasting away with guns, it gave stomach to one's own men to hear an answering roar.

But guns required waggons to haul them. Not yet had the English adopted the latest Swiss models, guns mounted on a carriage and wheels, permitting the much more practical method of hitching directly to horses.

"An additional fifty waggons for the guns," Richard estimated. "Kendall, write an order on London for fifty waggons."

A further aspect troubled the King: bombardiers, gunners, men trained in fire-power. He had no such band of men, nor had any English monarch before him possessed such men. For gunners, Lancaster had gone to the French. But no French whoremongers for York!

"Burgundy had bombardiers aplenty," Sir Richard Ratcliffe said. "Martin Schwarz, the German, and his company."

Richard shook his head. Burgundy had helped with gunners in the miraculous return of Seventy-one; but today he would get no men from Duchess Margaret. Incredibly, another woman—his own sister—had turned against him. Believing, it seemed, the filth spewed by Morton.

"No hired scoundrels from abroad," he replied, falling into his Council style. "We'll fortify with English oak. Do you, Ratcliffe, inquire among your men for bombardiers."

Ratcliffe looked doubtful, but replied: "I shall try, sire."

The King gazed about Tower Green. Engrossed in preparations for battle, he had been oblivious to the July morning —the parquet of golden light upon the greensward, the stately sycamores, the ravens strutting on the grass. An atmosphere of peace; yet surcharged with ancient violence, as if this tender gold of July were but a pause, a breathing space, between acts of terror and vengeance. It was here, where Richard now stood, that Hastings' head had been hacked off; here, that his nephews, the little sons of Edward, had practised archery before being mewed up forever; here, that the bloodstained corse of Henry of Lancaster had been borne from the Wakefield Tower to St. John's Chapel in the White Tower. . . .

And he wondered if it might not be near here that the dead boys had been hid. He had been tempted to search; but then he knew that no good would come to him from finding the bodies. It would be said that of course he had found them, since it was he that had them spaded away. The secret was safe in Hell—with Buckingham.

"Here is the horse roll, sire," the Master of Ordnance said.

Horses, battle mounts, to ride down Tudor and his cowardly crew. And noble White Surrey, Richard's gelding, at the fore. He took the roll from the Master. A trumpet blazed. Richard's head jerked up. Sudden uneasiness assailed the King. He turned toward the Garden Tower, where the lost boys had been walled. Hoofbeats thudded; the portcullis grated upward. A party of horse came thrashing into the Inner Ward. Lovell. . . .

But a Francis Lovell bereft of courtliness. A Lovell muddy and distraught, black with rage. He swept up to Richard, flung from his lathered horse. "A mob in Cheape," he gasped. "Drunk and killing-mad. They'd have unhorsed us, but we set spurs to our mounts."

The King heard this as he might have any routine report. He noted with regret that his Lord Chamberlain seemed to have lost his control. "What do they want?"

"Who knows what a mob wants?" Lovell exclaimed. "A pack of cutpurses and drunkards leading them. They cried—" He broke off, turned from them in the glistening light.

"What did they cry?" Richard asked gently.

"Murder . . ." The word came out old and quiet, a stone dropped into a silent pool.

Murder? It was as if he had been waiting for the word. He had been living with murder these many months. Now at last it was out. "You ran away, Francis," was what he said, after a pause.

"Ran away—!" Lovell choked, scarlet. He stooped to brush his orange velvet jacket and fawn-coloured boots that crumpled about his thighs. Behind the Chamberlain, a man slumped across the saddle horn. Blood welled from a jagged cut over one eye.

"Take the fellow to the White Tower guardroom," Richard directed. He turned again to Lovell. "What's happened to you? You allow London scum to drive you from the streets."

Lovell straightened. He glanced about, drawing assurance from the massive granite. Majesty's unshakable fortress. "I'm not afraid of such," he muttered.

"Why did you leave the field, then?" the King demanded.

Lovell drew close, his words intended for Richard's ears only. "We're hated!" he burst out. "It's not Tudor's hired rabble; not the bought curses of drunkards. Not only them. It's decent men and women. Boys in the streets. Their faces, the way they look at us. . . ."

Richard's mouth was tight and harsh. His gaze pierced the man before him. Never like this. Always shrewd and ready, arrayed in confidence. Well, if the Wolf had turned faint, the Falcon remained—the Falcon. "What have I ever done to these fools, save give them the best rule they ever knew?" he flared.

"It's not enough," Lovell said. "It's not enough."

"Christ's Blood, Francis! What is enough?"

"Belief in the King," Lovell replied.

Richard knew what the Chamberlain meant. In this Leopard House of Plantagenet, three hundred years of fire and gold, but one monarch had lost this vital magic: King John. Despised, driven from his throne, hunted like a beast about the land, he had died alone and writhing. . . .

What had John done? He had blinded and strangled his nephew, the young Arthur of Brittany, the son of John's elder brother. Arthur that was Arthur the First of England, by direct blood, just as young Edward of York had been Edward the Fifth, by elder right.

But Richard the Third was no John of Anjou. He would not allow that those vile perjurers and traitors, Elizabeth Grey, John Morton, Henry Tudor, should brand him a King John, should destroy his name. What his foes dreamed of was just such an outburst of guilt and grief—appalled, staring.

He turned to Ratcliffe. "Take a score of lances, Ratcliffe," he commanded. "We ride to Westminster on the hour."

"Don't, Richard," Lovell said. "Stay this night within the Tower."

"I'm with Milord Lovell," Ratcliffe said.

He looked at them. Lovell lean, dark, wire-taut. Ratcliffe sly and sniffing. How unlike mortal Tyrell! "Am I to be served by women?" Richard cried. "When the King may not ride through his city, then is he King no more. Saddle White Surrey!"

Lovell stood proud and still. They had travelled a long way, from Warwick's green lost hunting land and the dazzling light of fourteen. . . .

"I'm riding, Richard," he said.

❁⤙❀⤙❁⤙❀⤙❁⤙❀⤙❁

THROUGH the Inner Ward's Byward Tower Gate, across the Outer Ward's two bridges of the Middle Tower and the Lyon Gate rode Richard and his visored band. The day was sunny, with a few clouds leafing an immense azure. They passed with lance tips flashing, swords ready; the upright frowning King, then Lovell, then Ratcliffe and the twenty guardsmen of the White Boar.

Down Tower Hill and along Woodruff Lane, a narrow way from the Hill into Harte Street, the royal party cantered. Now, emerging on an expanse by Aldgate and the Nine Gardens, they came to Leadenhall. So far they had encountered no riot. Certain resolves had formed in the King's mind. He blamed Lady Grey for this outbreak; she was paying off his perjury concerning the boys; she was labouring ceaselessly against him. It had become essential to separate Elizabeth from her mother; to convey the girl northward, to the fortress of Sheriff Hutton. Richard himself intended to set up military headquarters outside the city—but after he had taught London that the King was not afraid.

Down Leadenhall, street of markets, wool, corn, wine, and past Bishopsgate, where loomed Crosby Hall, Richard's town house and the scene of intense nights during that brief bloody Protectorate. And now to High Cheape, another and greater mart, Cheape being Danewird for trading place; but in that broad way the shutters were on the stalls and small surly knots stood about whispering. The Londoners gazed sideways at Richard, but no one stirred. The company passed with bridles ringing. . . .

Lombard Street: haunt of goldsmiths and drapers, of Florentine merchant strangers, "licking the fat from their beards"—and of the notorious Mistress Shore. Jane Shore, merry Jane, with melon breast and eager thigh, wife to William Shore, goldsmith. Jane that under the Protector had done penance for a wanton life by walking barefooted in her shift and with lighted candle past the Lombard Street house that she had dishonoured.

The King's company rode by the Old Jewry, Jewless now and for many decades past, to the High Cross, the Eleanor Cross. This: one of the twelve resting stations of the funeral cortege of Queen Eleanor, wife to Edward the First, on its journey from Lincoln to Westminster. And before this homage to a gentle Queen, the great gilded Cross, the Resurrection images of Christ and the apostles, surged a lewd tumult, a compost of cordwainers in leather aprons from Bowe Lane, fishmongers in boots and stinking smocks from Friday Street, bakers encrusted with flour from Bread Street, pimps, beggars and strumpets, not a few drunk, clamourous, spitting.

The soldiers closed up, horses slowed to a walk. The King surveyed his subjects. He estimated three or four hundred barring the way to the Palace of Westminster. And quite enough, though armed only with bricks and paving blocks, to massacre the royal band. Richard gazed at dirty grimacing faces, sullen and deprived; and they stared back. It was the moment when both he and they discovered his right to kingship.

Richard lifted his visor. "What do you want?" he shouted.

The rioters fell back. A sudden silence struck them. Here was the King before them, he whom they had been reviling; and now he had come to parley with them. Or was that his intention? About Richard the horsemen froze, grim statues, lance tips bright.

"Can't any of you speak?" Richard demanded. "Why are you breaking my peace?"

By the great conduit from which prilled fresh water for London a voice cried: *Where be the lads, Dickon? where be the lads?* About the King an assenting murmur took up the question.

Richard heard; the cry smote his ears. He glanced at Lovell, pale in the sun. "Dare you speak so to your King?" he rated them. "Insolent rogues!"

Show us the lads, Dickon!

It was another voice, faceless as before. On the fringe of the crowd a tart jigged, skirts lifted to brown naked thighs. A fellow in a shovel hat and greasy cloak took a great gulp of ale. He spat—as Tyler had spat before the young Richard the Second.

Cat—Rat—Dog; all under the Hog!

Richard recognized a rude version of Will Collingbourne's libel, for which that traitor had been torn to pieces on Tower Hill. But he had no blood lust against these foolish Londoners; he wanted no killing in his streets. He felt desolation. Desolation for the lies that encompassed him.

"You are law breakers and rioters, every one," the King said in a hard cold gleaming voice. "I command you: make way!"

The crowd faltered into silence, awed not so much by the fact of royalty—for London had terrorized kings ere this—as by the spirit of the man. The decisive moment had come. Richard shut his visor. He turned to his escort with a swift downward movement of his arm, steel gauntlet a fist. Lances flashed down, at the ready.

The horsemen moved off, toward Old St. Paul's and Paternoster Row; slowly, maintaining a tight formation, steel tips on the long ash shafts levelled at the mob. Defiance began to melt, as the rioters realized that the King meant business. The most had come to curse and drink; not to run afoul of steel. Only a hard core of riot stood firm.

The horsemen broke into a trot. Bricks sailed through the air. A voice blared: *Murder! Murder!*

Richard saw through the armoured slit in his basinet a section of sun-dappled street and a wavering clump of old cloaks and wild drunken faces. He uttered a prayer and spurred directly on them, sword in his strong right arm. As the lances struck, the clump burst—fragmentized. Men were flung beneath plunging hoofs; others rolled like casks along the High Cheape. One or two lay huddled with split heads. In a hot instant the company was through and pounding toward the Fleet and Temple Bar.

❋⤙❋⤙❋⤙❋⤙❋

"WELL, Francis," the King said, "your fears were groundless, were they not? A taste of steel—and that's an end to riot."

Lovell looked up from the damask couch where he sat. They were in Richard's privy closet at Westminster. "It was a risk," he replied. "If the knaves had stood their ground—"

Richard shrugged. "Every act of my life is a risk," he said. "Always has been. I was born for risk. Were it not for that, we should not have triumphed in Seventy-one and the House of Neville would be today upon the throne of England. Warwick, of course, was aiming at the Crown. And you, Milord Lovell, would be a simple country squire of Northumberland and not High Chamberlain and the possessor of the fiefs of the Earldom of Essex."

The King was in rare good spirits. The brush with the rioters had taken the edge off his continual tension; and he had produced a musty claret for Lovell and himself.

"I wonder if that might not have been a better fate," Lovell said.

Richard laughed. "Come, Francis. You don't mean that. Why, you're as ambitious as the next. You'd be wretched if you were left out of power."

He poured wine into tall, marvellously clear glasses, spun of green light and sea crystal; and passed one to Lovell. "Look you," he said, "the King himself acts as your cup-bearer. Are you not a surly fellow to complain?"

A thin smile broke Lovell's taut dark face. "I admire you, Richard," he acknowledged. He hesitated; and remarked: "You are splendid in war."

"Why not splendid in peace?" Richard returned quickly. "I want peace, God is my witness. If only they would allow it to me!"

He was right, Lovell mused. He was a just and shrewd governor of his realm; yet the essential secret of his nature was expressed in acts of war. His spirit flamed out like an avenging angel. He had won a reputation for deeds of battle that had eclipsed other aspects of his monarchy.

Richard began to pace up and down, glass in hand. "I am setting up military headquarters at Nottingham," he said. "The army rendezvous will be in the heart of England. We shall be in a position to strike at an enemy landing at any point on the coast."

Lovell nodded. "Excellent. You don't mind Nottingham now?" Nottingham, Richard's "Castle of Care," where his only son and England's heir agonized into darkness one April day.

Richard went up and down with tilted shoulder, glancing at himself in the pier glass. "Of course I mind," he replied. "That's naught to do with it. If Nottingham is our best rendezvous, I must put aside feelings."

If the boy had lived, Lovell wondered—would anything have been changed? Would Richard have become calmer, less tense and harried, less frantic for hand-to-hand combat with his foes? Less tormented by the lies and plotting about him? Lovell suspected that the King had never quite overcome the notion that Lady Grey had been at the bottom of his son's abrupt death.

"I've been thinking over the divisional commands," Richard said. "Norfolk, as Earl Marshal, will have the van. I shall keep the centre. I had intended to give you and Ashton the rear." He frowned and drank. "But Percy of Northumberland is coming to the field and insists on a command. I had hoped Percy would fester at home and send me money and men. If he comes, I've no choice because his is the largest rally of Northerners."

"I've small taste for service under Northumberland," Lovell remarked dryly.

Richard stroked his long jaw. "There's the fleet at Southampton," he said. "Six vessels: *Nicholas; Governor; Falcon; Mary of the Tower; Grace à Dieu; Martin Garcia.* I need a trusty admiral."

Lovell lifted a hand. "I want to remain with the army," he protested. "Besides, I'm not a Tom o' Falconbridge to pirate the seas."

The King's eyes glinted at the name of their old enemy, that had cost York a bloody campaign in Kent. "You're not Falconbridge," he agreed. "But no more is Henry Tudor. Could Tudor's fleet be scattered, that would be valiant service."

"Command my post, Richard," Lovell said, "but I beg you to consider the army will have need of every loyal captain."

Richard stared from under reddish brows. He said nothing, but Lovell knew they had the same thought. The war loan had aroused angry protest among the gentry; collections were slow in coming in and some persons had evaded payment altogether. Richard had made a tactical error by his promise of perpetual relief from the arbitrary war taxation of his brother Edward. This measure had gained the

King much approval at the time, but at the heavy cost—how plain now!—of mortgaging his own future in an hour of peril.

He resumed his restless arc about the room. Suddenly he paused. "Was anyone killed on Cheape?"

"Two drunken rogues," Lovell replied. "One, a baker's apprentice. A man of ours was wounded."

"How was that?" the King demanded.

"Knocked from his horse by a flying brick," Lovell explained. "It happened at the Eleanor Cross in West Cheape. Ratcliffe rode out to fetch him with archers of the Household."

Richard lowered. "Did they find the fellow?"

"Aye, they found him." Lovell shook his head. "A nasty business. Ratcliffe was pale as parchment when he reported."

"What do you mean?" the King exclaimed. "What happened?"

"Filthy trulls had been at the man with knives," Lovell said.

"Did they geld him?"

Lovell nodded slowly. Richard was silent. Grim, he tightened one hand about his daggerhilt. "Damn their souls!" he cried softly. "I'll rack every one of them. To use one of my men so."

"Oh, they ran away," Lovell said. "You'll not catch them."

The King swung away abruptly. He drank, and refilled his glass. For a long time, it seemed, they were silent, while July dusk silvered the room. And they were two forms now, one seated and one standing, rich in velvet and gold. Outside the sentries called the evening guard and the clank of swordchains came faintly up the summer pause.

Lovell heard the King speaking, musing, the voice sharp-timbred with infinite days and nights. "Why should they insult my badge like that? Why?"

And then, with a shiver, Lord Lovell perceived that another person had just entered the room. A man tall, handsome as a god, with thick curling black hair and a flashing smile. A man radiantly clad in coronation doublet of black and crimson, with a mantle of blue cloth of gold. He saw them, saw Lovell and the King; and his face glowed with terrible joy.

The man in whose fell and wondrous brain had hatched the whole monarchy of the Boar. Who had persuaded Richard of the need to get rid of Rivers and Grey; who had suborned Will Catesby to betray his master, Lord Hastings; who, with Catesby, had borrowed two hundred gold pounds on the decisive Council morning of Friday, June the thirteenth, and had used this money to equip a few score brawling bullies and to untie by bribery the loyalty of Hastings' men; who by subtle argument had cozened Rotherham, Archbishop of Canterbury, to surrender out of sanctuary into the Protector's clutch the little Duke of York; who had pronounced the great Guildhall plea for the enthroning of Richard Plantagenet, Duke of Gloucester. . . .

And all this—oh princely Buckingham!—but the entrance-way to the mind's privy chamber, the steps going downward. . . .

Lovell saw the King watching, too. In the silver dusk, in the summer shadow. "I could not know that he would kill the lads," Richard said. "I did not dream that he was aiming at the throne." He hungered for reassurance. Buckingham was guilty, but that did not make Richard innocent. And moreover he could never prove what Buckingham had done.

"You could not foresee what manner of man he would show himself," Lovell replied.

Richard studied him narrowly, wondering if Lovell had surrendered all doubt. Had there not been a time when Lovell had suspected Richard? They looked at each other . . . and again were aware of that soundless terrible exulting, that cry frozen in the summer eve. Blood and sable for a gorgeous Duke; the smile on the mobile mouth, the mad brilliant eyes. And the whisper: *What fools—both of you!*

Steps going downward, into the dungeon of a man's mind. Doors opening into granite dark, the smell of horror . . . the great strangling hands of October . . . the creatures that from the night adventure forth to execute this smiling demoniac will . . .

Lovell stirred tensely, for a moment shutting out dread October. A voice within him clamoured: Richard had been right! And the men about Richard, save traitorous Buckingham, had sought justice only: to see upon the Leopard seat England's rightful heir. Did it not say in Holy Writ *Bastard slips shall not take deep root*? That text on which Ralph Shaw, doctor of divinity and brother of Edmund Shaw, Lord Mayor of London, had preached to the city at Paul's Cross. Doctor Shaw—another of Buckingham's dazzled instruments. Who then but his Grace of Gloucester, of old undoubted lineage, had true right?

Justice . . . and that June day when Robert Stillington, the Bishop of Bath and Wells, had sobbed out in Council the secret of Edward's unlawful marriage. But a secret that the House of York, to its shame and anger, already knew. *Bastard slips shall not take deep root.* . . .

"There was some foolish business over the Earldom of Hereford," Richard said, his slight form against the heavy murrey folds, the White heraldic Roses of York. "He claimed the title and movables of Hereford, in right of Eleanor de Bohun, wife to Thomas of Woodstock. But that claim had been taken by Henry the Fourth, who married Mary de Bohun. I said to him—this was just after the Coronation—'will you, Milord of Buckingham, claim to be heir to Henry the Fourth? You may then haply assume his spirits and lay claim to the crown by the same title.'"

Richard gazed out from a murrey shroud. "I spoke in jest," he said. "But he looked at me, never speaking, not a word—and suddenly he went away. I should have known, then."

"Oh, he was deep!" Lovell said. "He kissed most where he would kill."

Their voices hushed. Lovell could barely see the King; old torn shadows and a silver lamp flickering out. . . .

From the dark door the Duke still smiled. He would always be with them; in life and in death. Lies, deceit, treason, rebellion—all had been sloughed off like the gay trappings of his body. Now a pure gleam of terror: the inner jewel.

Lovell sprang up. "Let us have a light, Richard!"

The King advanced into the room. "A candle here, beside the table."

He struck a light; a little yellow flame spurted. His face, gaunt and narrow, the long nose, the cruel mouth, the fierce reddish brows—stamped in that small cupped flame. He seemed incredibly old; perhaps the wasting effect of his boyhood illness. He seemed already to have lived beyond the span of most men.

As Richard leaned toward the candle, the room flared into life. Lovell turned. Gold and crimson damask and three gold guardant Leopards blazoned the evening.

He listened.

. . . a scratching, rat's feet in granite night . . . a faint shriek . . . laughter. . . .

❀✛❁✛❀✛❁✛❀

IN the blue and crystal kingdom, the lost monarchy, the country of the twilight . . . melting into August sun. This blazing talisman of York; and the glow and terror of the past. And old shrieking battles, a sound of weeping long ago. . . .

Names, marvellous names: Wakefield, Second St. Alban's, Towton, Barnet, Tewkesbury . . . the bannered and mouldering dead, the bone-whitened grandeur of the fallen . . .

Rutland, that sweet murdered Rose, the best-disposed lord that was in the land; Warwick, mighty Bear and Ragged Staff; Salisbury and Old York, the grey dripping head paper-crowned atop Mickle Bar; Edmund Beaufort, that might have been a king, the betrayed and doomed Duke of Somerset; Wenlock and Clarence, a pair of coat-changers, iron captain and fond foolish drunkard; Courtenay, the Dolphin Earl of Devon; James Butler, Earl of Ormonde, red-crested Irishman and lover of Queen Marguerite; young gallant-springing Edward of the Red Rose.

Voices . . . shadows . . . trumpets glittering . . . the armed and bloody dead. And the last . . . what last? Why, the last voice; the last shadow; the last of the ruined Leopard. This House, this wondrous Blood, out of Aquitaine in Old Provence, out of Anjou and Normandy, out of Castile . . . fire and the proud heart. Victorious and doomed. This was the requiem of Plantagenet: a fiery and most suitable requiem. The King: redgold and companioned by the dead, the candled evening memories of York glory.

Richard . . . Richard . . . a name haunting the wind, gleaming and August-moted in the sun of Nottingham.

They were stretched in the bright courtyard, old soldiers in their buff and leather, sitting broken-legged in the soft warm morning. . . .

"Old Dick's ahunting in Sherwood Forest," one said. "You'd swear he'd be too pressed for harrying of birds."

"Always was a huntsman, Dickon," the second fellow said. "Some men drink and others wench. Dickon hunts. Where's the harm?"

"Oh, none. None." The soldier belched reflectively and scratched his haunch. "They say the City is sending more men. A regular troop. They'd better hurry, damn their eyes!"

"Who told you that?"

"Cousin of mine in York. He sent word by the last post. A

real trumpet muster did they make for Dickon. Paying the lads a shilling a day, too. Think on that! A shilling a day plus keep for common push-of-pike fellows."

"In York they'll do anything for Dickon," the first man said.

They were silent, meditating into the sun; old torn memories of war and of the flashing falcon they served. Like most of Richard's army, they were warriors for the working day: well-paid, well-kept, well-captained. They were confident in their ability to beat the little Welsh milksop straggling up from Wales with a crew of hired Frenchmen and renegade English.

But . . .

Were this all, there would scarcely be a battle. Tudor might well dissolve, as Buckingham had dissolved, in cowardice and desertion. Creep out of England in final shame. It was not all.

"Look at 'im, in his plumes and German armour. Never guess he's no better than a bird in a cage."

The soldier nodded toward a tall young man crossing the donjon court of Nottingham between two strapping sergeants of the guard. The young man walked with head erect, frowning; his gorgeous ostrich plume a flame in the sun. But he was no coxcomb. He was a brave and troubled young man who at any moment might be hailed, tapped on the shoulder by Death.

"Lord Strange," Will Grantley said. Grantley, late of Calais and Castle Guisnes. "It's Stanley's son."

"How pale he looks!"

"You would too, laddie boy, were you on your way to Dickon and your own father a lying turncoat."

"Oh, but no man knows what Stanley will do. He's in the West, mustering. The King's Commission of Array for Derby, he bears."

Will Grantley's laugh was a scornful bark. "He'd muster anyway. Commission or no. Dickon canna prescribe 'im.

Where's the profit in that? But Dickon's got 'Auld Eagle's' son. He's got Lord Strange."

"Do you think Stanley will come to the field?"

Grantley nodded, staring after Strange, as that young lord passed through the glinting jaws of a massive portcullis into Nottingham Keep. Strange walked as if to the dead march of a drum.

"He'll come," he growled. "But God help us all. It's worse than if he had unfurled his true colours, his Welsh white and green; openly proclaimed Tudor."

"God's Death, Grantley! What d'ye mean—worse?"

Grantley spat into the dirt. "It's no difficult, man. Even you, Dick Kilcullen, can grasp it. Look: ye have, by God's favour, a battle position and an army to hold that position. Where ye stand, the risks ye take, to attack or to hold—all that, man, depends on what ye know about the foe." He paused, drew a line with his keen-edged dagger. "You're here, man. And the foe, devil take them! be here." He drew another line in the earth. "Now—" He bristled, his blue cold eye on Kilcullen—"Now, laddie, ye have another array here. But what array? Not with you? Not with the foe? You don't know. But—how manoeuvre? How order the battle? That's what I mean. Such a thing can destroy the best position; the finest plan; the best-captained host."

Kilcullen stared at the rude drawing in the earth. He wet his lips with his tongue. "Jesus God!" he whispered.

Grantley nodded. "D'ye think Tom Stanley intends that Dickon shall know Stanley's true purpose? Why did he send 'im Lord Strange? Send the Boar his own son and heir? Because Stanley never means to show his colours—until the end."

Kilcullen plucked his dagger up and down in its sheath, as Dickon himself was wont to do. "Why not fall on the traitors now?" he rasped. "Slit their gullets whilst Tudor is yet in Wales."

A good question. So good there was no answer to it. Or rather—

"It ain't only Stanley," Grantley said.

Kilcullen looked at him with horror. The very ground beneath their feet was shaking. "Not only Stanley—" His voice broke in the sun. It seemed they heard the beat of great wings, a rush of darkness in the sky. The crows of Cressy . . .

For a time they were mute, breathing harshly. Kilcullen wet his thumb and drew it along the edge of his dagger. Once or twice he shook his head.

"He pays men well," Kilcullen said softly.

"Aye."

"He's a blazing captain."

"Aye."

"He has never lost a battle."

"Aye."

Kilcullen screwed an eye at his friend. "Name of Christ, Will! what is it? What has happened to his luck?"

Grantley turned away. He drew a net of lines upon the earth that appeared like a mesh—or a fishing weir. His mouth tightened; he cocked an ear. "There it is again," he exclaimed.

"What's that, Will?"

"Listen!"

Kilcullen frowned, listening. "That song, Will?"

Grantley nodded. "Aye—that song . . ."

Kilcullen stared. "Why, it's 'Merry Lincoln,' Will. 'Down, oh down in merry Lincoln . . .'"

The words came crying into the sun: *Down oh down in merry Lincoln . . . it rains, it rains in merry Lincoln . . . it rains both great and small . . . when all the boys come out to play . . . to play and toss the ball. . . .*

The hunters jingled into the brown deep oak light of

Nottingham Hall. Sweat gleamed on their faces and leather jackets were powdered from the ride. Richard was accompanied by Francis Lovell, and two broad-shouldered Northern men, Sir Robert Percy and Sir Robert Brakenbury. Percy of Knaresborough was an officer of the Guard and Brakenbury was the King's Lieutenant of the Tower.

John Kendall awaited them at a table thick with documents. Beside Kendall stood a fellow in the crimson and silver of York City. The Principal Secretary got to his feet. "John Sponer, Sergeant to the Mace of York, sire," he said to Richard.

Richard thrust forward, hand outstretched. "Welcome! Thrice welcome, John Sponer. Thank God for York and for Yorkshiremen!"

John Sponer took the King's hand. "I bring good news, sire," he said. "The Corporation has voted a troop of soldiers under the captaincy of John Hastings, Gentleman to the Mace, to your royal service. I am sent to discover your pleasure as to the disposing of this troop."

Richard smiled at his gentlemen. "Now Northerners, stand up for Plantagenet! Percy, Brakenbury, and you Francis Lovell: here's proof, if proof be wanting! Richard is not forgot amongst the old English. Would God he were King of Northern men only!"

Percy addressed the messenger. "We need the men at once," he said. "Send them to Nottingham."

"I'll remind you, Sir Robert," Lovell said, "that this be Lady Day, the fifteenth of August. On the morrow we march."

"Where shall the troop be sent?" Sponer queried.

Richard was pacing up and down. He wore long crumpling doeskin boots and silver spurs. About his neck was a collar of York: Sunnes-in-Splendour of beaten gold alternating with enamelled White Roses. He was immensely alert, sleepless, joyful; his eyes ringed, his gaunt face paler than ever. "We go to hunt the Welsh ferret!" he exclaimed. "Let the men of York follow our track."

Sponer looked puzzled. "But where shall we rendezvous, sire?" he wondered.

Richard gazed at him, eyes glowing. "Follow the track," he repeated. "This Welsh vermin gives off such a stink, it may be like a bitch in rut, smoking a trail through the land." He laughed, a quick sharp sound; and walked to the oak table in the midst of the Great Hall, under the eleventh-century louvre. The light, drained and old, fell on the King's face. He picked up a parchment scroll, glanced at it, tossed it aside. Abruptly he turned back to the messenger of York. "How many men is the Corporation sending me?"

"Four score, and it please Your Highness."

"It pleases me. Oh, it pleases me much!"

Lovell spoke. "Rendezvous about Leicester town," he said to Sponer. "Let the men have provender for a fortnight. They shall serve with Sir Robert here."

Percy nodded. "Aye, give me an army of such fellows!"

Richard's hands played nervously through the documents. "Where is my proclamation to the army and people of England?" he demanded of John Kendall.

The Secretary fumbled amongst the parchment, extracting a roll bearing the red-wax imprimateur of the Great Seal of England. Richard snatched the parchment, unfurling it. He scanned the proclamation, lips moving . . .

"Forasmuch as the King, our Sovereign Lord, hath certain knowledge that Piers, Bishop of Exeter, Jasper Tydder, son of Owen Tydder, calling himself Earl of Pembroke, John, late Earl of Oxford, and Sir Edward Woodeville, with others diverse, his Rebels and Traitors, disabled and attainted by authority of the High Court of Parliament, of whom many be known for open Murderers, Adulterers, and Extortioners, contrary to the pleasure of God and against all truth, honour and nature . . ."

This was the true ring of the King's style, this fierce exaltation, this blazing scorn . . . on everything he wrote was this crimson stain of eloquence, so pure and terrible it could never be mistook.

> ". . . have chosen to be their Captain one Henry Tydder, son of Edmund Tydder, son of Owen Tydder, which of his ambitious and insatiable covetise encroacheth and usurpeth upon him the name and title of Royal Estate of this realm of England; whereunto he hath no manner of interest, right, title, or colour, as every man well knoweth; for he is descended of bastard blood, both of his father's side and of his mother's side; for the said Owen the Grandfather was bastard-born; and his mother was daughter unto John, Earl of Somerset, son unto Dame Katherine Swynford, and of double adultery gotten. . . ."

He read fiercely, his voice rising, echoing through the donjon light, the worn tragic light that fell through stone embrasures. This was his word, his testament to the English people; that they should prefer an ignoble creature like Tudor to a prince of the ancient Blood was a thing unbelievable to the King.

> ". . . the said Henry Tydder and others have intended at their coming, if they may be of power, to do the most cruel murders, slaughters, and robberies, and disherisons, that were ever seen in any Christian realm. . . ."

He broke off, his breast heaving. His eye roved. Suddenly he stiffened. "Strange!" he exclaimed tensely.

The young Lord Strange had been standing beside the oak screens of the Hall, mute between his warders. Richard advanced toward the son of Stanley. "You—Strange!" he repeated.

Stanley bowed. "Sire . . ." he said.

Richard gloomed at him; the fingers of his right hand bent like talons about his embossed daggerhilt. "Where is your father?" he demanded. "Where is Lord Stanley? I sent for him to come to us in defensible array."

The young man hesitated. "My father has the sweating sickness," he replied.

Richard's lip curled. "More like the sweating treachery," he corrected. "Why, they say that traitors do sweat great cold drops. He has sent you, his son, in his stead. Do you know what message I shall return Lord Stanley?"

George Stanley swallowed. He had a fair fresh cheek, blue eyes and nut-brown hair. "No, sire," he said.

Richard gripped his dagger. "Why, George, I shall tell him only that your handsome head shall answer for a father's loyalty. George, ye are but young to die. I pray God give you a long life. A loyal life."

Stanley looked at the King. His hand twitched to his smooth cheek. "I have been loyal, sire."

Richard stood frowning. "Oh—loyal," he said. "How do I know what is in your heart, George Stanley?"

"We were out against Buckingham in Eighty-three," Stanley reminded the King.

Richard shrugged. "Certes, ye were out," he said. "But ye did no fighting. The storm . . . the Duke of Buckingham's Great Water. Ye were not tested."

He swung away; toward the listening gentlemen and York's messenger. A halted absolute moment, leather jackets and crimson and silver mingling in time's brown lonely light. He turned back. "Your uncle, Will Stanley, is already a proclaimed traitor," he remarked. "They say your father is out raising soldiers. Hardy pastime for a sick man."

Young Stanley breathed quickly. "My father is confined, sire. He hath not left his chamber this fortnight."

Richard rubbed the knuckles of one hand against the palm of the other. He looked at the young man. "Ye are young to die, George," he said.

George Stanley knelt; gasped a plea . . .

Richard shook his head. God's Wounds! . . . they forced death on him. The young man before him, he was little older than Edmund of York when struck down at Wakefield. Or Prince Edward Plantagenet, that had been martyred at Tewkesbury. Was it so bitter to die young? He himself had done well to have vanished in his glory.

"Rise, George Stanley," the King said. "The matter rests not with me nor with you. It rests with Lord Stanley, with him that sent you."

He glanced at Kendall. "See that Milord Strange has all for his well-being," he directed. "Set a guard continually about him. He is precious to us." He strode to the table, picked up again the parchment with the red-wax imprimateur of England.

"You have heard my proclamation, Stanley's son?" he asked.

"Aye, noble sire."

Richard's eye flashed down the scroll, found the concluding avowal:

. . . "And our said Sovereign Lord, as a well-willed, diligent, and ever courageous Prince, will put his most royal person to all labour and pain necessary in this behalf, for the resistance and subduing of his said enemies, rebels, traitors, to the comfort, weal, and surety of all his true and faithful liegemen and subjects."

His voice rang proudly. There was an instant of utter silence. Richard flung down the parchment. "Let him come!" he cried. "Let Tudor come!"

He turned; cocked his head. He frowned. "What is that? Some minstrel lad?"

A voice that cried and echoed in time's brown remembering light; in the donjon, in the great hushed well of the Hall . . . a young sweet voice singing of Lincoln, of merry Lincoln. . . .

❀➤✳↩❀➤✳↩❀➤✳↩❀

KING RICHARD flared out of Leicester on the Sunday, in the bell-bright August morning. Shutters were wide, with maids in mobcaps leaning out. Down High Cross Street, across Bow Bridge over the River Soar, and along Kirkby Mallory Road shrilled the war-trumpet; and a cloud of small boys hurrahed after.

Leicester had never seen a king ride forth to war. The casements were crowded, the doorways were filled as Duke John of Norfolk passed with the Standard of the White Lyon. In the wake of Norfolk's snorting bay horse marched four thousand valourous lads in Norfolk blue, five abreast, stepping to the wild sweet clamour of drums.

A pause . . . then a gasp, an "oh-oh!" and a "God save us!" as the splendour of the army reached full noon.

First trotted five Heralds in magnificent tabards bearing the Royal Arms, a trumpeter beside each: Gloucester, Norroy, Clarenceux, Garter; and the Pursuivant *Blaunche Senglier*. Then broke into view Sir William Parker with the Royal Banner, the Lilies d'Or on azure and the Golden Leopards on crimson. After rode the famed Standard-bearers of York: Sunne-in-Splendour, Falcon Unfettered, White Boar—great silken standards that streamed in the August gold.

And now, Richard; now, the King. On his gelding White Surrey he came, cased in the victorious armour of Tewkesbury with a golden circlet about his helm. The King's visor was up so that all might look upon him: his sleepless glory, the terror and beauty in his face, the war gaze of old England, cruel and proud and lonely, that now went forth to the final battle, the last shock of arms. . . .

And with the King rode his gentlemen of the Household:

Lovell, Percy, Brakenbury, Ratcliffe, Kendall, Catesby. And on either wing trotted six trumpeters on coal-black horses, their gold sarcenet trumpet-banners blazoned with crimson guardant Leopards.

Then the five thousand of the Royal main ward: the mounted Guard, steel-clad men-at-arms and the special corps of black archers in helmet and breastplate; liveried foot-soldiers in murrey and blue laced in quilted jacks and carrying pikes and partizans; then a detachment of Yeomen, also in livery, but wearing steel corselets and armed with halberds.

The King disappeared into the sun; the day burned white —now Northumberland's rear ward, three thousand black-and-white mosstroopers of the North and quilted archers of the Scottish March. Their badges were the Silver Crescent and Gold Shacklebolt of Percy. Henry Percy, fourth Earl of Northumberland, who had borne the Sword of Mercy in Richard's Coronation Procession. . . .

And was not this panoply more akin to a coronation than a fierce battle? Or was this moment to be Richard's true anointing—that of fire and blood?

In the wake of this gilded array laboured the gun-bearing waggons, crunching through the dust, accompanied by the yells and curses of the drovers. Culverins, serpentines, toads, bombards: snout-gleaming "Edward" and "Richard Bombartell," that had bathed the Lancastrians in hot chainshot at Tewkesbury; "Dijon" and "Newcastle," brazen veterans of many a Northern siege; "Iron Mary" and "Roaring Alice," that had fragmented Falconbridge at London's Bishopsgate.

Richard's army blazed down the Kirkby road. On Bow Bridge the King grazed his spur against the stone coping and a small gilt prong broke off. No one save a boy standing nearby noticed the mishap. The army pointed toward the village of Sutton Cheyney, on the edge of Redmore Plain.

The sun was brilliant; the day, burnished noon. It was York weather. . . .

John Flory had neared the end of his quest, one piece still missing, he believed, in the intricate coloured glass. But he had a notion what that piece might be. . . .

He had glimpsed Stanley's messenger, the badge of the Gold Griffin Claw on the crimson jacket, sliding through the royal camp. Flory had followed the man to the flap of Will Catesby's tent. Now he lingered outside, as a murmur of voices floated from the secret parley within.

In Richard's battle company, Flory mused, rode his friends and staunch captains. All save one: Sir James Tyrell. Tyrell had remained out of the fight, on the other side of the Channel. Had he been summoned? It was most likely. Why, then, had Tyrell held aloof?

Flory had a suspicion why.

Tyrell was playing "best man win"; as he had seemed to do when Buckingham had broke out his Standard at Brecknock. In reality, however, Tyrell of the secret gaze and shuttered heart had been beholden to Buckingham and Buckingham to Tyrell far more than anyone had dreamed.

Murder shrieks out . . . blood flies upward and bedews the Heavens.

The dread killer of Edward's sons, the Princes of York, had been Buckingham. Out of mad, insatiable ambition. Flory was sure of it, now. The killer had to be someone leagued with Tudor, someone that the clerical conspirators at the Tournelles were avid to shield. And someone with an opportunity to perform the deed; a high officer with ready access to the Tower.

Who but Buckingham? Who but Richard's High Constable had both the motive and the opportunity? Who but he had concerted with Morton to ruin Richard; to murder the boys and throw the blame on Richard?

He knows . . . Tudor knows!

But such a deed could not be carried out alone. Accomplices were necessary. Tyrell, for the chief. Black Will Slaughter, jailor of the Tower, for another. Dighton, the stained priest, to shrive the royal dead and to bear witness. And then a go-between, to convey instructions from Buckingham at Brecknock to Tyrell in London. Someone sheet-fellow to both Buckingham and Richard. The missing piece, in fact.

Flory hovered near the tent, the sun going down in a huge stain of crimson, Redmore heath burning bronze; and beyond Ambien Hill the thin blue campsmoke of Henry Tudor's sick and mangy horde. Southeast of Richard, about three miles off, lay the red-jacketed force of Lord Tom Stanley. No one knew the colour of his mind.

Little Catesby had always played a double game, Flory reflected. First, he had played Richard against Hastings; then, Buckingham against Richard; and now, Stanley against Richard. But this was Catesby's last throw. Not even the velvet-stepping little lawyer might continue such a course indefinitely. And the irony of it was, Catesby genuinely liked and admired King Richard. But the passion of double-dealing was too strong.

About Flory the soldiers of the Boar squatted over their cook fires. The glowing forge of summer eve burned dull red. Helmets and breastplates, thigh tassets, gleamed in the old red light of ecstasy and death.

Flory knew it well!

An occasional murmuring arose from the men around the fires, a few sad jokes dying into the sunset, the immense sky like dried blood. But for the most part the soldiers were quiet; only a rattle of cups and soup bowls, the glug-glug of wine pouring. . . .

A fine army, Flory mused; such as Richard could be depended on to array. Fantastic, when that pitiful band across the hill was compared. Washed up from Wales on a tide of ever-increasing horror, the sweating sickness carried from France by Henry's curs. A pestilence that struck with sudden fever and delirium; then, shivering and a coffin-cold rigor; then, a foetid perspiration; then, death. All in the space of a few hours. The simple country folk fled from their Welsh "liberator" and his fatal crew, as from some great terror.

To flog out of England these shivering curs could scarcely be called a battle.

Yet, what of the Stanleys? There, Flory considered, lay the battle. Sir William Stanley had two thousand sturdy lads camped northwest of Richard; Lord Tom Stanley had three thousand girded and stalwart southeast of the King. The last Plantagenet was neatly boxed.

The tent flap parted. Stanley's red-jacketed envoy loomed beside small eloquent Catesby. Flory withdrew a few paces. For an instant the messenger hung at the flap in the glowing hush, the little lawyer gabbling at his ear. He nodded, curtly; Catesby seized an arm, the mouth working, working, pouring out treacle—praises and promises.

The man broke away. Catesby stood alone for a moment, twitching. A kind of horror slanted over his face; he stared into the huge red sky, lips moving, whispering. . . .

Flory turned, leaving Master Catesby at evening's mighty door. He pursued Stanley's man. He paced amid the white gorse and small purple buttons of the heath; down a treeless slope, with great raw stones like carbuncles; running now, Stanley's man running too, both pelting across the red dying light and the broken caul of the slope.

Flory gained; and suddenly his man gasped to a halt and flung around, steel in hand. Flory unbladed; and with a deft flat stroke slapped the poignard to the ground. He jumped the knave; wrestled him down and wrenched from his grasp a vial. Flory dashed the glass upon a rock; it broke, and shimmering moonstuff ate into the earth.

Quicksilver: a few drops caused instant blindness.

He held a dagger to the fellow's throat. "What was your message to Catesby? Quick!"

The man had a sullen frightened look. "You won't kill me, will you?"

Flory said: "Not if you talk. The message!"

"His Lordship said as how Master Catesby warn't to worry. His Lordship ud look to him, however things befell." He glanced up. "Will you let me go now?"

"Give me the rest of it," Flory demanded, moving the point of the dagger gently up and down against the great vein in the throat.

"Master Catesby was to see to Lord Strange. See he took no harm for his father, when the time come—" He broke off, frightened eyes clutching at Flory.

"Go on," Flory said softly.

"When his Lordship might strike—" and he froze into terrified silence.

Flory released him. "That's all," he said. "Get away from here!"

The man scrambled to his feet, dodged through the nettled brush. Flory could hear him hammering down the slope, stones flying. Well, Flory had what he wanted to know. Master Will Catesby was the missing piece.

He walked slowly back to the camp. . . .

⊗⤙⁎⤛⊗⤙⁎⤛⊗⤛⁎⤛⊗

THE ROYAL Army lay at Sutton Cheyney, ten miles from Leicester, encamped at the base of Ambien Hill, One Tree Hill, from the original Saxon name. With the aid of his scurryers' reports, Richard was able to piece together the general aspect of the field and the position of each of the other three forces. Just at cockshut time, he had gone about the camp in company with Norfolk and Surrey, to cheer the men and to inspect the posting of the guard.

Now in the last thinning light, Richard made a final survey of the field. Due south, at Gamble's Close, arrayed three thousand Derbyshire lads with the Griffin Claw badge of Lord Thomas Stanley; while across Ambien and northwest of Richard hovered the bloodcoated cavalry of Sir William Stanley. Henry Tudor and his Welsh and French marshalled below Ambien, three miles west of Richard.

The King considered that the four armies lay roughly in the form of a rectangle, enclosing an area of about fifteen hundred acres. . . .

Richard realized that this was a battle position unique on an English field, and perhaps on any field. It had come about, he knew, because of the Stanleys. William Stanley was an attainted rebel and his Cheshire cavalry was operating as an independent unit with the invaders. Thomas Stanley, on the other hand, was ostensibly leading a loyal corps in support of the King. He had therefore pitched down on Richard's side of the hill, in a position from which he might move swiftly to the King's aid. Stanley might also—a fact which did not escape Richard—move swiftly to an attack on the King's rear.

Richard went to his tent, a little distance from Norfolk's advance position. His armour unbuckled and readied for the morrow by Squires of the Body, the King threw himself on his camp bed. But sleep, that wayward jade long banished from his side, refused him. As night's forlorn candle burned on, he fell to thinking; and suddenly all the moments of his marvellous life came back. His mother, Proud Cis, and boyhood at Fotheringay; the last farewell to his father the Duke and to his elder brother Edmund before their December ride north to mortal Wakefield . . . his youth at Warwick Castle, and Anne whom he had loved—as much as he could conceive of loving anyone . . . the flight to Burgundy when Warwick had turned on the House of York and had tempted weak arrogant Clarence into a Judas betrayal of his own blood. . . .

And then, for Richard—the beginning, the glorious adventure!

Constable of England at nineteen; Duke of Gloucester and High Admiral; victor of Barnet and Tewkesbury; saviour of London from the pirates of Falconbridge . . . the right hand of his brother, King Edward. And afterward, Anne. Anne, his dream. Anne, whom he had found beaten by life and hiding as a scullery maid. But no more did she take note of his raised shoulder, his chained step; he had taught her and all England the kind of man he was. He had hammered with fists at destiny's door. That door had cracked open, like the miracle of the reliquary of Blessed Anne at Daventry, on the dazzling road of Seventy-one.

Nothing he could not do, by his will, intelligence and courage . . .

Outside the tent, the King heard the sentry pacing, a faint clink of harness, the skirl of wind upon the heath. Out there lay his army, his splendid army that he had gathered from every corner of England—the best he had ever commanded. But now in the King's mind, in the mirk of night, glowed doubt. His talisman that somehow, somewhere, he had lost. Did the soldiers know? Did they sense, simple bright-hearted lads, the agony of their Captain? The loss of the Midas glory of his youth?

For this—and he knew it now, but how bitter to know it so late when he might no longer do anything with the perception!—was the quality that made the difference in men; not gold, not arms, not physical might, not even shrewdness alone. None of these. But some inner magic of well-being and joy, a sense of conquering life. He had possessed that once: his touch.

Richard clambered from his camp bed and lit a candle. In a corner of the tent lay his helmet, his white Tewkesbury armour, his two-edged sword, his axe. Aye, he might still do execution on his foes; on the whoreson knaves of Tudor and, if fate were kind, on Tudor himself. But—and this was

the thought that rang in the night—other Buckinghams,
other Tudors might arise. He could never trust anyone
again. Henceforth he must rule alone and by terror. . . .

Richard wandered about the tent, picked up a bowl of
wine, took a long swallow. He gazed at the candle's fiery eye.
Burning, it came to him, the term of his life. He was not
goose-livered for death. Why, Death and he had lived on
familiar conditions for a long time.

Only . . .

There was his work, his unfinished kingship; there were
the friends who trusted and admired him; there were the
people of England in their humble thousands that he, Richard Plantagenet, had ruled wisely and who did not deserve
a wretched milksop such as Henry Tudor; there were his
mother and Elizabeth. . . .

At the thought of Elizabeth, Richard halted. She, least of
all, deserved Henry Tudor. The King put a hand to his face.
His brow was cold, glistening with sweat.

"Bess!" he said softly, "Bess!" Her name dying in the corners of the night.

A vision—Elizabeth and Richard. It could never have
been. Ah, but this vision had the quality of his life: magical,
haunted, irreparable. He had not willed his life. He had but
followed the secret track within, never pausing, never looking back—until these last months.

Marvellous triumph had been his; and grievous failure.
Edward's sons. . . .

Yet have I with strict penance and salt tears expiated the
same offense, which abominable crime I require you of
friendship as clearly to forget, as I do daily remember to
deplore and lament the same. . . .

He was speaking to his army; confessing to the Image of
the Sword . . . as if some late absolution of war might yet
bring back the lucky past. But—a confession to Night only,
to the shroud of sleeping silence that wrapped tomorrow's
field. A confession that failed into darkness.

For the army, he must be bold; lionlike; unchained of doubt . . . he had prepared something of this kind.

Richard limped to the tent flap, listened for a moment to the dark mutter of the camp. Joy and dread shook his soul. Now the last trumpet, the final Company of the Sunne. And now the Coronation that all this while he had been waiting for. A coronation of fire, upon a blood-bright morning. . . .

Richard turned. He drained the bowl of wine. Suddenly warm, the King looked toward his bed. He blew out the candle. . . .

Light silvered the King's tent. From without came a bustle, the hiss of cook fires, a rattle of harness. The clarion shouts of Standards of Horse mingled with the bark of Foot Lieutenants. Richard stirred and, as was his wont, awoke abruptly. He got up and threw off his nightrobe.

Two Squires of the Body entered.

"Array me," Richard commanded. He turned to the armour. The Squires laid out steel back and breast; gorget; brassards; tassets; greaves; sollerets.

The royal tent was suddenly filled with clanking knights: Lovell, Percy, Clifton, Ferrers, Ratcliffe, Brakenbury. Tudor, it seemed, was not yet alive; but Stanley was stirring and his scurryers were out. If only they could be sure of Stanley, Richard's officers were ready to fall on Tudor like a thunderbolt.

"Where is Norfolk?" the King inquired.

"On his way hither," Lovell replied.

Richard nodded. "Chain mail," he said to the Squire. The youth held out a coat of mail, formed from the linkage of hundreds of tiny iron rings. This had been the principal defense of the warrior for centuries. The coat of mail was worn over a padded nether garment.

"Are the guns up?" Richard wanted to know.

"Some guns have arrived," Ratcliffe reported. "The waggons are still coming in."

"They say Tudor has guns," the King commented. "Stole them at Shrewsbury and Litchfield. Did any of you, by the way, hear the tale of Tom Mytton, Bailey of Shrewsbury? This precious Tom swore an oath the rebels would never enter Shrewsbury, save across his belly."

Richard laughed; a harsh splintered sound. "But Tudor had a talk with Tom. Money clinked. And Tom, for saving of his oath, lay belly-up in the main gate of Shrewsbury for Tudor to walk over!"

No one spoke. They were held by the sudden aspect of Richard's livid face. Norfolk and his son, the Earl of Surrey, shouldered in. They halted at the sight of Richard, staring. . . .

"Do I look poorly?" the King remarked. "I took ill rest this night. Never mind. I'll sleep tonight!" He laughed again. No one stirred. "Something I wish to say to you, messires—" He hesitated, frowning. Involuntarily, the King's hand strayed to his side, to pluck an invisible dagger.

The Squires were buckling the leather straps on back and breastplates. The Captains waited. Still Richard hesitated. "Give me some wine," he said.

A blue and murrey page reached for the bowl on the camp table, beside the guttered candle. "The bowl is empty," the King said impatiently. He tried the jointure between breast and back. "Tighter!" he directed the Squire.

"Milord—" It was a man in Norfolk blue, the White Lyon badge on his shoulder. He clutched a scrap of paper.

Norfolk bent a burly shoulder. His son Tom, smaller and dark-hued, hovered at his side. "Well?" the Duke demanded.

The man thrust the paper at Norfolk. "This was pinned to your tent, milord." Norfolk took the paper, turned it over in his meaty hand. He started; passed the scrap to Richard.

The King read, brow-wrinkled. He looked up. His voice broke high and taut across the listening silence: "*Jocky of*

Norfolk, be not too bold; for Dickon thy master is bought and sold!"

The Captains burst into a clamour. Richard smiled grimly. He stared away for a moment, from their disgust and outrage. A pretty rhyme! the King thought. This doggerel exactly expressed the case. He turned to Sir Robert Percy. "Send out a Pursuivant-at-Arms to Lord Stanley," he directed. "Bid him come up at once with his force, or it will be the worse for his son George!"

The King gleamed in his armour. One Squire was buckling on the greaves, or leg pieces; the other stood by with the long pointed sollerets, the steel foot guards.

"Now," Richard said, "while we wait on His Lordship's pleasure, I shall tell you what I had in mind to say before." He took a draught of wine, set down the bowl carefully.

"However fortune falls," he declared, "the old rule of England must utterly change. If Tudor, by treachery, should prevail, he and all his line will govern as bloody tyrants—merciless. For what claim other than theft have they to kingship? And England will be undone.

"Should I gain the victory—"

He considered them, eyes flaring in his ravaged face. He paused, while the steel gorget was fitted about his throat.

"You all know how I have ruled until this moment. I have forgiven much; allowed my enemies to dwell in peace within my gates." Richard took a sudden breath; an iron first crashed on the table. "No more!" he cried. "By God's Holy Writ, no more! I'll wash out treachery in blood. I will be hard; unforgetting; vengeful. I will learn—" his gaunt cheek twitched—"I will learn to exterminate!"

He broke off; there was a grey appalled silence. The Captains of York looked at one another. . . .

Richard turned. "My sword," he said to the Squire. His voice lifted: "To battle, messires!"

The sun of Bosworth rose at a quarter past five. Almost

three hours were spent in marshalling the army in battle position on the crest of Ambien Hill. By nine o'clock Norfolk's van ward bristled on the ridge, along some six hundred yards of front. Norfolk looked down on the green and white tents of Henry Tudor, the white uniforms of the rebels filtering through the morning haze. Tudor, the scurryers reported, had broke his camp at Atherstone the day before, marched along Fenlane, crossed a little stream called the Tweed, and camped the night at White Moors, a close one mile west of Ambien Hill.

The royal main ward was posted a few yards behind the crest of Ambien, in support of Norfolk. Northumberland, with the rear ward, lay at Sutton Cheyney, presumably to watch Stanley and to keep that doubtful Eagle from turning the King's rear.

As Norfolk dressed his lines, the King's Leopard Banner appeared. Richard rode up, surrounded by his Household. He shook an iron glove at Norfolk. "What is Tudor's strength, milord?"

Norfolk came forward, brows a harsh ragged line. He was having an intense morning. "Towards six thousand, sire."

Tudor's force had swelled on the march from Milford Haven. The original two thousand French mercenaries had bulged into six thousand rebels; with two thousand Shrewsbury men under Sir Gilbert Talbot, the uncle and guardian of the young Earl of Shrewsbury—now ripe vengeance for the insult inflicted on Eleanor Talbot by the House of York twenty years before; with five hundred Cheshire lads under Stanley's nephew, Sir John Savage; and with a band of black Welsh under Rhys ap Thomas, marching under the Red Dragon of Cadwallader.

Richard listened to the report, tight-reined on his noble gelding White Surrey. Tudor's strength was but half the King's; and much of that ill-equipped and mangy. The thing looked easy. But—still no word from Stanley.

The King gazed down the shining Norfolk line: billmen

in the centre, with flanged partizans and glaives, the long cruel billhooks, the curved raven's beaks, to pull a man from the saddle; archers on the wings, bent forward hornwise, to crossfire into an advancing mass; and by the White Lyon Standard a mounted reserve of knights and men-at-arms.

"I'll have a word now," Richard said. He rode uncovered along the line. His redbrown hair, carefully dressed, curled over his gorget. He disdained the common bowl-shaped shearing of battle. The King reined almost exactly in the centre of the line; he raised in his stirrups, so that all might glimpse him.

"Ye know how the devil hath entered into the heart of an unknown Welshman, exciting him to aspire to our realm, crown and dignity. Ye see how a company of traitors, outlaws, and runagates of our own nation be aiders of this enterprize. Ye see also what a number of beggarly Bretons and fainthearted Frenchmen be with him, arrived to destroy us, our wives and children. Which imminent mischiefs if we will withstand, we must live together like brethren, fight together like lions, and fear not to die together like men. . . ."

Richard paused. August morning burned upon a great brazen pool of silence. He felt through the wall of glistening day Time's mighty heartstroke.

"We have manifest causes of triumph. The Captain of this rebellion is a Welsh milksop, a man of small courage and less experience in war, brought up by my brother's means and my own like a captive in a close cage at the Court of Brittany, and never saw army, nor is able of himself to guide one. And for the Frenchmen and Bretons, their valour is such that our noble sires have vanquished them oftener in one month than they at first thought possible to do in one year. . . .

"Dismiss all fear, lads, and like valiant champions advance. Let everyone give but one sure stroke and the day is ours. By God our Father, I will triumph or die!"

The men of East Anglia stared from under their iron salades. The King saw the hardy challenge of proud doomed England. His heart glowed. He raised high in the stirrups and trumpeted: "Saint George, let us forward!"

A cheer rang. Richard rode back to the Standard. He could count on the Essex lads.

About the White Lyon there was a stir. Tudor was forming his line. Norfolk looked at the King. "Strike now!" he exclaimed.

Richard regarded the Earl Marshal. To hit first was an immense temptation. It was the tactic suited to his falcon spirit. But he was also a shrewd field commander. He had noted carefully the ground between the two armies. Directly below, at the foot of the hill, lay a large soggy patch, the result of an overflow from a spring on the southern slope. Now this bog stretched between Tudor's position and Stanley's Horse, the best unit of the rebel army. If Tudor—or rather the Earl of Oxford, his Field General—could be induced to advance up the slope, the rebels would be unable to make effective juncture between Tudor and Stanley. The marsh would nullify Sir William Stanley's threatening cavalry strike.

All this passed with lightning instancy through the King's mind as his practised eye surveyed the terrain below. He longed to hurl his army upon Tudor; but in consideration of the two Stanleys, the wise course was to hold fast to the hill.

Norfolk was regretful. The burly Duke recalled Barnet and Tewkesbury; and how York's Sunne-in-Splendour had blazed to the attack.

Richard shrugged. "Let Oxford come on," he said. "We'll catch him halfway up the slope and smash him. Drive the Blue Boar into the bog!"

Norfolk was about to reply when a thud of hoofs made him turn sharply. *"Blaunche Senglier!"*

The King's Pursuivant-at-Arms coming at the gallop with Lord Stanley's reply. Richard stiffened; his kingship, aye his life, rode on the moment. He glanced at the Household where George Stanley, Lord Strange, hovered in Catesby's charge.

Blaunche Senglier flung from his horse, knelt at the king's stirrup. His breath came in gasps.

"What word from Stanley?" Richard demanded.

The Pursuivant got to his feet. He was young; tall and chestnut-haired, wearing an heraldic surcoat of the Royal Arms and sleeve badges of the White Boar. "Lord Stanley sends greeting to—to—" He faltered.

"Well, well; go on!" Richard said.

"To Richard Plantagenet," the Herald said, looking for forgiveness to his master, "and will come anon. He has other sons."

Not His Dread Lord and Mighty Highness, the King; but plain Richard Plantagenet! The King flushed. He cried: "God curse Stanley—thrice-damned traitor! He shall have need of more sons." He swung in the saddle. "Catesby!"

The little lawyer, having discourse with the Household, broke off and hurried forward. "Prepare George Stanley for death," Richard commanded.

Catesby stepped back, with a startled air. "Now, sire?"

"Now!" Richard blazed.

Catesby hesitated. "How shall he be killed, sire?"

"I care not—so long as he be dead!" Richard replied. Stanley's ruinous treachery had broke the taut nerve of the King's control. He craved blood.

Still the lawyer temporized. "Shall Stanley not be shriven?"

Richard shrugged. "Shrive him, then. But haste!"

"We have no chaplains," Catesby reminded the King.

An odd oversight for one like Richard, so ridden with

scruple that he would not even begin his battle march on Lady Day, but must wait the morrow.

"Shall Stanley die unshriven?" Catesby pressed. "Or shall we send to Leicester for a confessor?"

Richard gave his adroit mouthpiece a quizzical look. Catesby—scrupulous of death? Catesby, that had been hot to doom Rivers and Grey; that had found ready argument why Hastings could not stay alive; that had persuaded the King to refuse Buckingham a final hearing at Salisbury. "Ye be tender of this traitor's whelp, Master Catesby."

Catesby rubbed his hands together, a habit in moments of stress. "Were it not best to abide the victory, sire?" he said.

Walter, Lord Ferrers, who stood by, also urged: "Stay until the issure of battle, Your Highness. George Stanley is clean of his father's double-dealing."

"That is he not!" Richard burst out, "but sweating with treachery, like every Stanley!" He turned away, gnawing his lip.

From the enemy camp a trumpet flared. Richard's head jerked up. A sudden shout: Norfolk's line inched forward, wire-strung. A scurryer dashed up. "Oxford's Standard is advancing, sire!"

Richard swung White Surrey toward the battle line. He rode forward. At the King's back, Catesby exchanged a glance with Lord Ferrers; ever so gently the little lawyer shook his head. . . .

⊛☌❋↴⊛☌❋↴⊛☌❋↴⊛

GUNS cracked. Cadwallader's Red Dragon roared. On the slope of Ambien bounded iron cannonballs, skipping amid the bracken. A shower of arrows fell. This fire, more accurate than the guns, brought down an occasional man in Norfolk's rank.

From the vantage of Ambien crest, Flory saw the rebels advance to the attack. They marched well, he thought. Better than might have been expected. Oxford's Blazing Star led the van; and Flory minded that April dawn when this Star had extinguished Hastings and his whole ward at Barnet. Now John de Vere, thirteenth Earl of Oxford, led some four thousand French, Welsh and English toward Ambien.

Staring down the slope, Flory picked out the silverblue of Oxford's livery; the white hoods of Sir John Savage's men; the Talbot Dog of Shrewsbury; the black and scarlet of the Welsh.

It was ten of the clock. The sun of Bosworth rode steelbright in a gunmetal blue . . . the royal van ward hung taut and watching on the crest. The rebels marched eastward from their camp at White Moors; but when they struck the marsh, the column made a left wheel to pass around the bog. Now Oxford's troops were moving north, with the sun on their right. A steam of dust began to rise over the field.

Flory perceived Richard's strategy: to allow the rebels of the assault column to put the marsh between themselves and Sir William Stanley's supporting cavalry. Now as the column fanned out to advance up the slope, the marsh was at the soldiers' backs and Norfolk could drive them down into it. Thus the shrewd Falcon on Ambien crest had won an enormous tactical advantage right at the start.

Flory glanced along Norfolk's line. Suddenly he exclaimed: "By the Mass!" He glimpsed Grantley and Kilcullen in the front rank. Edging over, he hailed the Calais lads: "Did you bring Tyrell?"

Will Grantley turned. "It's you!" he blurted. "The wight looking for parsons. Did find what ye wanted?"

"I did," Flory said. "Many Calais lads with you?"

Grantley shrugged. "Not many. A few of us took a notion to see England once more." He gazed about, at the iron cloudless day, the ragged heath with brown and green patches—and the reddish clay from which Redmore Plain took its name and not, as some recruits direly asserted, from prophecies that the field should be drenched in blood. "England . . ." he repeated.

Flory knew what he meant. Word has got about that King Richard had foretold the utter undoing of England, as a result of this day. Men felt that in very truth some old gleaming light was going out of the world.

A trumpet flared. Along the row of linked serpentines, snout to snout, bombardiers leaped with lighted matches to their touch-holes.

"Now it's the turn of our guns!" Grantley exulted.

Range was between four and five hundred yards, Flory calculated. At this distance, little accuracy could be expected. However, the guns had a valuable psychological effect. Tongues of orange and crimson flame flashed out; a ragged roar shook the hill. Iron balls and chainshot screamed down the slope. Much of the volley ploughed harmlessly into the heath, but a few hissing fragments of chainshot scored. White and silverblue coats were splotched crimson; shrieks tore the day. The ranks faltered; opened. . . .

Now—Norfolk's archers. The crossbowmen on the wings loosed a volley. Oxford's Company was caught in a crossfire. Steel shafts ripped the rebels; men spun around, clawing at air.

"We've got them!" Kilcullen cried, showing broken teeth.

Flory felt a moment of wonder. It had been no part of his intent to fight for King Richard. His quest was done; and he had his answers. But he could not leave. He had come too far. He had to know the last of it. . . .

And on this betrayed field Richard Plantagenet, refusing to flee, determined to stand or die beside the Royal Leopards, was now mantled in the knightly legend; the dishonoured Rose of Lancaster had become the flowering Sunne of York. At the end, Richard achieved that burning-gold of pity and noble defiance once given to Lancaster.

A trumpet blast split the air. A surf of Norfolk iron

flooded down Ambien. Flory was swept along, with sword and belt axe. The wedge-shaped mass crashed into Oxford's division. About Flory, faces rose up, mad, cursing—he heard a steady animal roar, like wind in a cave. He was trapped in the fury and he laid about, thrusting as fiercely for Richard as ever he did for Lancaster of old.

Oxford's line wavered; wrenched backward. Nowhere to retreat but the marsh and butchery. Flory fleshed his blade with a grim silent lust. He took a crack on the helmet, staggered; nearby, Kilcullen went down, blood gushing from his neck. And dimly, from a far-off flaming shore in the bursting sea, Flory heard trumpets. . . .

The rebels were falling back, gold-sashed officers shouting, "To the Standards! Retire to the Standards!"

Disengaging—no easy matter for the best troops—and pulling back their lines around the Blazing Star and the Talbot Dog. Flory marvelled to see such flea-ridden losels achieve this manoeuvre: a tribute to Lord Oxford, their Captain.

Norfolk's wedge halted too, a sudden involuntary lull, panting, bloody . . . and now came the White Lyon himself, Howard of Norfolk, thundering on his great bay horse. "Why d'ye halt?" Norfolk blared. "On! On! I'll gut the first man to turn!"

The Essex lads hurled forward, following Norfolk and Surrey, his son. Oxford's division had changed position and Flory was suddenly in the thick of the Welsh, their red tunics and black capes. They carried short curved swords and leather targets. Flory thrust, felt the blade bite—and a scream broke past his ear. . . .

A man loomed before Flory out of the furious dust, a giant black and terrible with a dripping mace—the instant of a drunken nightmare. Flory had just time to take the stroke on his steel shoulder-guard. He sagged to one knee, while the Welshman came at him with the mace.

How strange to die here for the betrayed Sunne of York. . . .

But in that infinite dread moment the battle shocked into a new fury; the swart giant was swept aside, howling in Welsh. In danger of being trampled, Flory fought to rise. The focus of the struggle had shifted again. Flory was carried along, flailing, unable to know friend from foe.

Presently, through the steel and dust, he understood. By the Gold Griffin Claw on the breast; by the Eagle Displayed. By the scarlet shout ringing over the field: "À Stanley! à Stanley!"

The traitor Stanley had hit Norfolk's flank with his whole force and crumpled it; three thousand Derbyshire lads thrown in at the crucial turn. That had been the purpose of Oxford's disengaging manoeuvre, to shorten his line and make way for Lord Stanley, coming up on the double. Far from falling into a trap, Oxford had set one for Norfolk. . . .

"À Stanley! à Stanley!" tore at Flory's ears.

The press was now so dense it was impossible to strike a telling blow. The battle swirled about the Standard of the Lyon, where Norfolk and Surrey fought on.

"À Stanley!"

And the mortal answering cry: "À Norfolk!"

The tumult slackened. Men broke apart in gasping truce. Through Death's opening ring thrust John de Vere of Oxford, his Blazing Star banner-bearer beside him. Tudor's battle captain, in silver armour with a round basinet, came straight for the Lyon Standard. For knighthood was not utterly dead. Not yet; though it might perish on this field.

Norfolk, in black armour with a pointed basinet like a dragon's snout, wheeled his bay charger. He carried a sword; Oxford, a battle axe. As if by unspoken agreement, the knights of the Standards left each Captain to combat. In the first shock, Norfolk all but unhorsed his foe with a savage stroke. Oxford was seen to reel: the point of Norfolk's sword glanced off the Earl's basinet and ripped the bridle arm.

Oxford recovered his seat. The two knights made another rush and Oxford dealt a massive blow on Norfolk's visor. The steel helmet shook; the bay horse reared—and when the dust had settled, Norfolk had lost his helm. Oxford's axe glinted. . . .

"God and Michael!" a fellow beside Flory swore.

"Strike, Oxford!" shouted the tense clump about the Blazing Star.

And through the furious haze behind echoed the warcry: "À Stanley! à Stanley!"

But Oxford, Tudor Captain though he might be, was a Soldier of the Rose; Lancastrian, of the golden memory. He forbore to spur on unprotected Norfolk. But as the Duke sat astride his horse, stunned and bloody, a coward arrow came wandering from the molten sky and struck John Howard in the face.

The Essex men saw their leader slump across the bay's withers; then slide slowly to the earth . . . the broken quiet dead. . . .

Uncaptained, the soldiers of the Lyon fought on; under Surrey, under Conyers and Clarendon, under Sir Gervase Clifton, the Sire of the Rose, whose father had died for Lancaster at Tewkesbury. But the Lyon had received a mortal wound; only the King might rally the ruined line.

Flory felt a sudden smoking pain. His hand dropped; blood welled from his thigh. He had taken a lance-thrust. Nor did he ever glimpse the fellow. Like the shaft that slew Norfolk, out of glittering day had flashed a deadly lance. . . .

He went down; the iron wave washed over him, retreating down the edges of death—and in the fog that wrapped his brain, he knew a wrenching loneliness, an unspeakable pity.

From his command post on Ambien, Richard saw the

mortal treachery of Stanley; the breaking of Norfolk's line. Scurryers brought word of the Duke's death; of the capture of Surrey.

When Stanley had hurled himself on Norfolk, the King had despatched *Blaunche Senglier* to Northumberland, at Sutton Cheyney. If Percy and his three thousand moss-troopers came up, all might yet be retrieved. Now Richard's gaze burned ever south, to glimpse the Gold Shacklebolt.

Observing Catesby pass, it occurred to the King that he had given orders for the execution of George Stanley. He called the little lawyer. "And is young Stanley dead?" Richard demanded.

Catesby faltered; "I shall see directly, sire."

Richard seized him by the arm. "Don't you know, Will? Didn't I give you the order?"

"Yes—yes," Catesby stammered. "But we had no priest."

"Priest?" The King laughed savagely. He thrust Catesby from him. "Do as I bid, Will. We must wipe out traitors."

Catesby stumbled away. . . .

Richard sat erect on the noble gelding White Surrey. He stared into iron horizons, smoke blue and vast. In the steam and slaughter a few hundred yards down the slope, where the remnants of Norfolk's ward struggled uselessly; northward, toward Market Bosworth, where Sir William Stanley hovered with his bloodcoated cavalry; west, toward Shenton, where, the scurryers reported, Henry Tudor had established a command post.

If Northumberland failed him . . .

And suddenly Richard was alone on the ridge; dazzling noon sparkled on his armour; and far off he glimpsed a solitary horseman on the horizon. The King gazed and his being was flooded with joy, for he knew who that horseman was.

Below Richard, the line abruptly broke: men scattered— and the troops of Tudor went hacking down the hill. Murder . . . aye; the orders of a new-hatched tyrant. The King became rigid; clenched a fist.

He felt a tug at his stirrup; turned, saw a kneeling frightened page, heard words falling into the white shining loneliness . . . the King looked up. A little way off, he beheld
the Pursuivant *Blaunche Senglier,* dismounted, bridle in
hand. . . .

And instantly he knew that Northumberland had refused;
the last betrayal, the black heart burning in Hell. . . .

"Percy! Lovell!" the King called.

And round the Royal Leopards came the knighthood of
the Sunne, armed and glittering: Percy (Sir Robert, a distant cousin of the noble traitor), Lovell, Ferrers, Ashton,
Brakenbury, Clifton, Ratcliffe. These were the terror and
beauty of the Rose; the men who had followed Richard all
that blazing road from April death to Bosworth morning. . . .

He regarded them, his fierce sunken glance asking what
he, the Falcon, had ever asked: the flame of glory or death.
"Let all true knights attend me, and I will put an end to
this quarrel. But if none follow, I will try the cause alone!"

He shut his visor; gripped his battle axe, turned White
Surrey's head north. West lay the marsh; south the forces of
the traitors Stanley and Northumberland. Only one way to
Shenton and Tudor's command post—northward down the
slope and around the bog, then wheeling sharp west and
striking directly at Shenton.

Richard lifted his arm. A trumpet flared. The Royal
Household readied, some ten score knights and men-at-arms.

But before them lay a dread risk: Stanley's cavalry near
Market Bosworth, guarding Tudor's flank. Yet a risk that
York had ever taken: Duke Richard at Wakefield . . . Edward in the bloody snow of Towton . . . the return from
exile in Seventy-one . . . York had always played for fire
or death.

Again the trumpet flared.

Sir William Parker rode out, the Royal Leopards proud

and high. And now the cavalcade, the Sunne of England and his knights . . . *oh he knew! he knew!* He had seen the horseman on the horizon.

But men would remember: a streak of flame through Time's dark pavilions. . . .

Richard's spur touched Surrey's flank. Through the slit in his basinet, the King glimpsed the gleaming crest of Ambien, the patches of bracken, the yellow gorse, the small blue flowers . . . flowers. . . .

He felt Surrey's sturdy muscles pumping, the long slim legs driving down the slope, the saddle rocking . . . and at his back the thunder of his gentlemen. His heart was singing; all doubt, all bitter anxiety washed away in one fierce instant. He was riding to glory; riding to the Sunne. And all the flame and wonder of his life came round him—and he laughed and shook his axe.

From Ambien crest to Shenton: a distance of some two miles. The two hundred of York surged down the slope and swerved sharp right, to go around the swamp; about them the bleeding wreck of Norfolk's command and the savage yells of French and Welsh as they dirked the maimed and footless.

For any who cared—and despite chivalrous Oxford—this was as much an English defeat as that on any foreign field. . . .

Swinging wide now, Parker with the Royal Leopards beside the King, and hammering through the gorse in an ashy cloak of dust, sweat pouring down inside the eighty-pound armour . . . and somewhere off to the deep right, Richard knew, patrolled Stanley's cavalry, invisible in the dust. But if Stanley was invisible to him, he was not invisible to Stanley.

Tudor was the goal. Tudor and Morton and not far off the bright mocking ghost of Buckingham. It was they had done this to York's monarchy; made this cauldron of lies, treachery and murder. Richard kept his slitted gaze on sun-dappled Shenton. In the glare and dust he made out a bannered clump on a little elevation off to the left.

Tudor!

And the image of the pale grey-eyed schemer burned in the King's brain. Blood . . . Tudor's blood! He spurred toward the glinting Standards; feeling the long stride of White Surrey, the great legs beating out the rhythm of his vengeance. Sweat, Richard was drenched in sweat; the wine he had drunk, the weight of the armour.

And now he could see directly ahead the Red Dragon of Cadwallader and he exulted: for here was the halting place of his chiefest enemy. He glimpsed a flurry in that bannered clump. For they had seen him, blazing on them like Death's dread Angel.

Tudor's Household milled about, without purpose, without command. It was what the King had counted on: the mortal shock of his falcon swoop. He estimated some three hundred in the Household. Outnumbered, three to two . . . he gripped his axe. He would scorn twice the odds for a thrust at Tudor.

Straight for the Dragon, Richard flared—a terrible Saint George with bright avenging axe. Sir William Brandon, the Standard Bearer, sat numb astride his horse, paralyzed, as in some fearful dream. They had come so far, dared so much—and now to be struck down at the very bellchamber of success.

Richard's axe crashed: Brandon reeled, broke to earth. From limp uncurling fingers, the King plucked the Red Dragon. With a shout, he hurled the Standard into the dust. Richard wheeled White Surrey to confront a knight whom he knew at once as the renegade Sir John Cheyney, Master of the Horse under Edward.

Outweighed by far by massive Cheyney, Richard avoided a body clash. He took the pass as in a joust, skillfully turning at the moment of contact, as Warwick had taught him infinite summers ago. His axe rang on Cheyney's steel shoulder. Instantly, Richard swung about and blazed to the kill. With the taut fury of his ancestors, the last Plantagenet struck fiercely at the back of the helm, where it joined the iron neckpiece.

Cheyney sagged; toppled. . . .

Tudor's men were running; running from Richard's steel. But one thing more: to find and kill Henry Tudor.

Richard turned, staring about the field. Tudor? Hell scorch the Welsh sneak! Tudor might be any of a score of visored horsemen. The cowardly milksop had took care to wear no easy badges of his so-called rank. The King must rip off helm after helm to find the hated face.

And, meantime . . .

In the fire and rage, under steelbright noon, time melted and ran in molten drops down the sky. A sudden thunder splintered the day, the pounding beat of that unbannered horseman. . . .

Stanley's two thousand. . . .

Richard knew; knew before he whirled to face the thunder, before out of an iron cloud hurled a bloodcoated cavalry. He had lost . . . and what was begun a long agony ago had now come home to him: the final flame, the last death. Two thousand against two hundred, ten to one.

He was suddenly in the midst of charging troopers, the Silver Buck's Head upon the crimson sleeve. He felled one foe with a slash of his axe; but then seven or eight were hacking at his helmet, smashing at his burnished armour. He was beaten down; exhausted, a broken-winged falcon torn by dogs.

Crumpled to earth, Richard heard shouts: old cruel war-cries, the chant of death and shining blood—his Coronation. And with axe-strokes shivering his basinet, blind and dying, he cried into darkness. . . .

❂✦✲✛❂✦✲✛❂✦✲✛❂

THEY were shaking him and he listened to voices, dis-

embodied voices like faceless whisperings of the dead—and
he came back to them, out of a blood-mist of agony and regret. He was ringed by Tudor green and white and his first
thought was: they are going to kill me. They have come to
put me to silence.

He closed his eyes. . . .

And again they shook him, someone held a cup of water
to his lips; he struggled to sit up and felt a stab of fire in his
thigh. He glimpsed Nicholas Latimer.

"Can you stand, Flory?" Latimer was saying.

He set his teeth against the pain. Why couldn't they leave
him in peace? "Let me be," he groaned.

"You must not miss it!" Latimer declared. "Never such a
sight as this!"

He peered at Latimer.

"We've won!" Latimer cried. "Won, Flory! The Boar is
dead . . ."

Richard dead. Flory glanced down at his bloodstained
badges: the Fanged and Rampant Boar. As in a fantastic
dream, he recalled how he had fought for Dickon and the
Sunne. Caught in the frenzy; refusing at the last to abandon
the man he had hunted, whom he had helped to ruin.

What did Latimer surmise? Flory searched the face of the
young Tudor squire. But Latimer—whatever he suspected
—said nothing to the fact that Flory had fallen on the field,
wearing a White Boar badge.

"A marvellous day for us, Flory," Latimer pronounced.
"And for England!" He stooped, put his arm about Flory's
waist. "Try to rise," he urged.

Flory struggled to his feet. For a moment he hung wavering on the mangled slope. It was, he judged, early afternoon. . . .

"The crowning is to take place at Stoke Golding," Latimer said, "A mile and a half south of here."

"Crowning?" Flory stared.

"The crowning of Henry Tudor," Latimer explained. "The first King of England to be crowned on the field of battle!"

"Henry is to be crowned?"

"Aye—victorious Henry!" Latimer cried. "Jesu, Flory, are you not joyful?"

Flory was silent. Now—Henry's England. Richard was dead and Richard's England had perished with him. About Flory sprawled Norfolk's Essex lads, in stiff contortions, ribboned with black and green flies.

They brought Flory in a horse litter across the field; past red-knifed French and Welsh, murderous with drink. Cursing . . . his ears rang with foul Te Deums of Henry's triumph. Sick, he turned from the cracked voices, the blood-daubed faces of Norfolk wounded. The savages were killing English lads; slaughtering the men that had gone out for their King.

He seized Latimer's arm. "Can't you stop these butchers?"

Latimer swung to him in surprise. "God's Nails, Flory, ye must allow the fellows a death or two. They won the fight, did they not?"

Flory said softly, "Murder . . ."

Latimer turned away. "Never mind, **Master** Flory of the Boar," he said. Flory suddenly realized that Latimer knew the truth: that Flory had fought for Dickon.

And now through terror and burning afternoon they came to a field of marigold, a jewelled field, waist-deep in sun, crying in the young and radiant summer . . . the littermen put down Flory on a little knoll, from which he might overlook Henry's crowning. Drenched in summer gold, Flory gazed at the strange array: the lordly smiling traitors, Thomas and William Stanley, Henry Percy, fourth Earl of Northumberland; the black-robed kingmakers, consecrating the red steel, John Morton, Bishop of Ely and Canon Dick Fox; the English battle captains, John de Vere, thirteenth

Earl of Oxford, Gilbert Talbot of Shrewsbury, Sir John
Savage; the Welsh and French commanders, Rhys ap
Thomas and Philibert de Shaunde.

And in their midst Flory glimpsed the smirking Henry
Tudor, princely in a purple velvet cloak furred with ermine,
on his breast a great Dragon badge worked in crimson silk.
Now would Richard have had little care to identify his rival.
And all was hushed and golden in the radiant English death,
above the blackened listening dead, the marigold and the
blood. . . .

"What are they waiting for?" Flory wondered.

"Why, the crown. The crown!" Latimer said.

The crown? Had Henry Tudor brought a crown in his
baggage? Latimer smiled. "Certes, Flory. Our Henry has
plucked Richard's crown as prize. Look!"

And here came Christopher Urswicke, his black skirts
tucked up and running on his spindly shanks through glistening fields, in his hands the battered golden circlet hewed
from the dead King's helm.

"A soldier found it in a hawthorn bush," Latimer said.
"Near Shenton, where Richard fell."

"Richard died fighting?" Flory exclaimed.

"Fighting? Oh the Devil's Claws! Fighting! He did for
Brandon and Cheyney and three or four sturdy fellows before they brought him down."

Flory said quietly, "The last King of England. . . ."

The Tudor squire turned toward the sunlit hill. "We
have a new king," he said. "A new England. . . ."

And on the hill that henceforth men would know as
Crown Hill, Christopher Urswicke handed Richard's dented
relic to Lord Tom Stanley. Richard's High Steward approached purple-wrapped Henry Tudor, bearing a Plantagenet's battle crown. Henry, obscure, Welsh, ill-favoured
and penniless, stood purple-bright beneath the torn and
dusty Dragon Standard that Richard had hurled to earth.

A moment of angels. . . .

Flory heard an echo of laughter, muted, shining. . . . Beside him, Latimer's face gleamed. "Isn't Henry splendid?" he exulted. "A royal presence!"

Lord Stanley was kneeling, down on old treacherous knees, the crown on a silken cushion between upraised hands . . . now it was Morton's turn. The Bishop of Ely took the crown from Stanley and turned to Henry. A great pause bannered out from Crown Hill. Reverently, the Bishop placed Richard's golden circlet on the sparse locks of Henry Tudor.

A shout broke the day. Henry hovered in his purple glow, perhaps even he but half-believing in his immense fortune, a dry ageless smile on his lips.

Latimer turned to Flory. "Henry the Seventh!" he cried. "Lancaster come home again. . . ."

Flory frowned; remembering the blood and marigold of Tewkesbury, the flaming road . . . and his young self crying for Lancaster, for the lost kingdom. . . . *No, whatever it was, it was not Lancaster, it was not the Rose.* . . .

Smirking in the sun; the new patchwork royalty; the purple lie . . .

Flory looked away. A horse and rider approached slowly from the direction of Shenton. He stared in the August flare, unbelieving. . . . He became rigid; but it could not be possible, *it could not be possible.* . . . Flung across the horse's withers was a naked body, all blood and filth, redbrown hair hanging down. A swarm of drunken soldiers and camp women shrieked after . . . clods of mud; stones; blows rained on the limp body. . . .

Flory recognized the rider: *Blaunche Senglier,* Pursuivant-at-Arms to King Richard the Third. *Blaunche Senglier,* his royal tabard of the Leopards and the Lilies, the Arms of England, stained with mud; dishonoured. *Blaunche Senglier,* compelled to this last hideous duty.

"What is that, Latimer, passing there?"

Latimer glanced from the joyous crowning; uttered a scornful laugh. "It's bloody Richard going to his rest."

Flory saw them spit, hurl mud—the body quivering beneath blows. "Dishonouring the dead . . ." he said. "A noble victor does not dishonor the dead!"

"He was a murderer, Flory," Latimer said. "He deserves no pity. Did he pity Edward's tender babes strangled in the Tower?"

Flory gazed after the appalling rites paid to England's royal dead. Henry's rites. A murderer? . . . And in the haunt and glisten of the August afternoon, in the bright horror of three o'clock, there came back to him the old English song, the lament for a murdered child . . . *Down, oh down in merry Lincoln.* . . .

He burst out: "Richard did not do the murder, Latimer! He did not! It was another. A man he trusted and who betrayed him; sold him to Hell!" He looked Latimer in the face, said slowly, "The murderer was Henry Stafford, Duke of Buckingham."

Latimer was silent for a long glistening moment. Abruptly, he gripped Flory's shoulder. "I am your friend, Flory," he said in a low warning tone. "This talk is nothing but madness. I know what you did on Ambien. I know who you fought for. But I shall keep my peace. Only—you must wipe from your mind this wild notion of Buckingham. Buckingham was our ally, two years before. And now we have the victory."

"But Richard did not slay the boys, I tell you! I have proof!" And his memory swung back to that dingy room in Calais, the grey frightened face, the haunted eyes—Dighton.

Latimer shrugged. "You have no proof, Flory." He pointed to the shining Hill. "Proof is here. In the faith of Henry the Seventh. Your king, Flory."

"Doesn't truth matter?" He stared at Latimer.

"This is truth," the hard empty voice of the new day echoed. "Victory and kingship!"

This was what he had discovered: the end of the quest. The dishonoured broken body passing, like the bloody shame of a perished England. Men would become harder, more cruel; there would be less truth, less love.

The bitter failure of love . . .

Could he learn from Perrette? Not hurt; not spoilt; not plundered—not yet. Perhaps through her he might achieve grace. Lorraine in her brown eyes; the glow and singing of the forest heart.

O ma Perrette, si belle et si douce! Ma Perrette des montagnes; des forêts; des sentiers perdues . . . jamais je t'oublierai!

On Crown Hill, they were still cheering. He turned to Latimer. "Goodbye, Nick," he said.

Latimer stared, astounded. "Goodbye? But we've won! England is ours, you mad fellow!"

Flory shook his head. "No, Nick," he replied. "We've lost. Lancaster is done. And I'm going home."

"Home?" Latimer exclaimed. "Where the devil is home, then?"

"A pure heart," John Flory said.

V. SHERIFF HUTTON

She tooke a booke in hir hande
And there did reede of prophesye,
How she should be Queen in England
But many a guyltles man firste muste dye;
And as she red faster she wepte. . . .

—Song of the Lady Bessy

*E*LIZABETH awakes, drenched in sun, the brief summer of the North. She thinks that Anne too has seen this gentle poignant light, that Anne too has awakened in August dread. Upon Elizabeth's face tears have dried and the pillow is still wet. Her heart has emptied in the night (and this, too, recalls Anne) . . . she is aware of confused dreams of armour and of blood. But is not all this a Plantagenet memory, the heritage of terrors long ago that she can neither understand nor control?

She is a naked young bride, with her ripe breasts, her red-gold hair, her cream-coloured skin. She is like that Ysabeau of Portugal, the first wife of Duke Philip the Good of Burgundy, for whom, it was said, the Duke named his Order of the Golden Fleece, in tribute to his wife. But within Elizabeth, as she lies all desirable in the sun, is a poisoning of the wells of her being. She listens to a cry that goes on and on, blowing from some secret, black and torn heath. Now arising, she walks slowly about, touching objects. Then she stands rigid and intolerably lovely in the sun, in the August brightness that floods her chamber.

Murmuring to herself . . . *he is mine only joy and maker*

in the world, and I am his in heart and thought—had she written these words, long ago in a winter dusk?

And still in that trancelike pose, like a vision of her own effigy upon a funeral char, Elizabeth's eye falls upon a clawed beast woven in gold, white and red—the symbol and colours of the House of the dead woman; that woman whom it is whispered she and the King have made to die. Elizabeth knows the charges against her. Has she not reckoned them up in the infinite hours between midnight and dawn, the hours longer than death?

But this charge concerning the dead woman, the woman of gold, white and red—this charge is not true. . . .

Elizabeth is her own Judge, her Procurator and Defensor —and her own executioner. Never has she wished evil to strike that sick unhappy Queen that lay in her own blood. Never has Elizabeth been other than devoted; constant; cousinly.

Never?

And like a gush of jugular blood comes the memory. Words, crimson words that Norfolk and Lovell have seen and perhaps that small yapping Catesby as well. Words that echo a bitter unused passion . . . *Oh the better part of February is past and it seems as if the Queen will never die!*

Elizabeth is breathing quickly; she is walking again, blanched and alone. The charge is true. Her own words. She has wished Anne dead. She did torment the wasted Queen with her youth, her glow, her power for love. She even wore yellow.

But she is not sorry. No, not really. She knows her fire and beauty; she knows that she would be a shining queen. Anne was never more than half alive, withering in the very radiance that Elizabeth adores. The Sunne of York; the Sunne of Richard; the Sunne of passion and the bannered heart.

She goes to the casement, open to the east. A lattice of ivy falls away in a thick green tapestry. She gazes at blue horizons of Yorkshire, at gold-misted rolling country that flows up to Scotland. Beneath her, purple and white heather surge toward the walls of Sheriff Hutton. A royal carpet for a victorious king. Riding through the summer gold, in war armour with the circlet of majesty gleaming about his helm, his gentlemen about him, his battle standard with the great flapping blazon of the Boar. Trumpets in a sunroyal morning. For this our Prince rides home again!

But what is it that clouds this scene, that now seizes Elizabeth, hands cold and trembling, an icy cold stomach? Ah, she has never been a coward; she will not be a coward now. She has learned from her mother, that pitiless being whom she fears but may never escape. She has learned from Lady Grey how to deal with life. And the Lady Grey in her, the despised part and the hard proud resourceful woman within the golden shell of beauty, holds her up.

She turns, hearing a clatter of buskins, the hiss of newly laid faggots, the faint shrill cries of women . . . Sheriff Hutton, York's final fortress, is astir. Below, liverymen in murrey and blue are readying the morning cup: beakers of ale, thick fresh bread, Wensleydale cheese. And the others, York's few last fledglings: John, Earl of Lincoln, the Heir to England; Edward, Earl of Warwick, the son to the dead attainted Clarence; and the Lord Bastard, that is not the girl's vanished royal brother as some simple folk outside imagine, but the bastard of King Richard, the boy Jean of Gloucester.

Fire and a York morning: Elizabeth listens for a flare of hoofbeats. . . .

Robed in silver blue, Elizabeth descends the winding stone stair. Upon her breasts and shoulders falls a foliage of gold and dark, sunlight piercing high furrowed slits. She remembers the day: Wednesday, the twenty-fourth of August—the Feast Day of Saint Bartholemew. Through branches of light, she passes into shouts and laughter and sudden tense quiet; into the donjon Hall.

They are all seated at the long table before the open

hearth; Lincoln, young Warwick with that vacant heart-wringing smile (him that they say of: "He cannot tell a goose from a capon."), slim dark Jean of Gloucester with that bladelike look, and John Nesfield, King's Squire of the Body and a royal watchdog. Elizabeth joins them.

Beside her lounges twenty-two-year-old Lincoln, sturdy and fair-haired, the son of Elizabeth de la Pole, Duchess of Suffolk and elder sister of Edward the Fourth. Elizabeth Plantagenet takes a cup of hippocras, a spiced sweet wine, with her bread and cheese. The others are drinking ale. She listens. Her cousin Lincoln is running on with some tale of counterfeiting that fell under his eye as President of the Council of the North, the King's principal officer above the Humber.

"Fellow named Stafford," Lincoln remarks. "John Stafford. A sly rogue, if ere I saw one! When York's Council collared him, he had a sackful of gold crowns, new-minted with the Crown and Fleur-de-Lys of France. And yet another sack stuffed with gold of Burgundy, stamped with the cross of St. Andrew. With a value of twenty-five silver sols to the crown, Stafford had money enough to outfit a duke's train."

"Was it true gold?" Nesfield asks. He is a tough, taciturn fellow, appearing constantly in need of a shave. Elizabeth has cause to remember John Nesfield. It was Nesfield and his knucklemen who cordoned Westminster Sanctuary for well nigh a year, while Lady Grey and her five daughters secluded there. And, later, it was Nesfield that doled out the seven hundred marks yearly stipend allotted Lady Grey by the King.

"True Gold? Certainly not!" Lincoln shakes his head. "The knave had scarce two farthings of his own to rub together. He took base metal, coated it with a thin layer of gilt, fired it and let it stand for a year or more. That way, he obtained a passable likeness of gold. The stamping irons he stole from Old Shrewsbury's Winfield Manor in Derbyshire."

"Shrewsbury?" Nesfield wrinkles coarse black brows. "What was Shrewsbury doing with French coining irons?"

Lincoln takes a draught of ale. "He was Deputy in France, back in Fifty-two. He had license to coin."

"License from thieves," Nesfield grunts. He helps himself to ale, swigs a long draught.

A hit at the ruinous governance of Lancaster, under Henry the Sixth. Yet Lincoln, principal heir of York, mislikes the remark. For it is a hit too at his father's family, at his own grandfather William de la Pole, the "Ape-clog on a chain," as the Duke of York, Lincoln's other grandfather, had been wont to call him. The first Duke of Suffolk had been one of the chief ministers of Henry the Sixth in those times.

"License from England," Lincoln snaps. "Any English Deputy would have had the same right." The young de la Pole has not made up his mind whether Nesfield and his band are here as protectors or as jailors.

Nesfield has a dark ironical smile. His manner seems to say: We are in this together. No use rating me. I have my orders from the King.

And Lincoln understands. He knows that Nesfield is one of the instruments of York's nightside. Just as Elizabeth and poor guiltless Warwick and Lincoln himself are York's day-time, so this bristling dog carries the stigmata of murder and ambition that scars the strife of the Roses.

"You've not finished your tale, milord," Nesfield urges.

Lincoln continues: "York's Council sent Stafford to me for a hearing. The knave told me to my face I had no jurisdiction. It seems that counterfeiting foreign coin is no crime in England. He was actually indignant over his arrest."

"You strung him up, of course," Nesfield says.

Lincoln lifts his empty cup. He watches the drawer pour a foaming head. "I did nothing of the sort. This is not the governance of the Grand Turk. Stafford was quite right. There exists no law in England against the counterfeit of foreign coin."

Nesfield shakes his head. Perhaps he is thinking how John Tiptoft, Earl of Worcester, that scholarly and terrible justiciar, would have handled a similar case. "What did you do, milord?"

"Took his irons away and sent him back to York's Council to punish as they would," Lincoln replies. "He had committed no offense against the King."

Nesfield laughs, a bark. "Why take his irons away?" he wonders.

Lincoln disdains the remark; cuts a slice of cheese. Elizabeth looks admiringly at her cousin. How brave and upright he is! How handsome; young! For an instant she regrets Richard's decision against a marriage of the two chief heirs of York. An instant of betrayal of her love, of Richard. For her regret has nothing to do with Lincoln's position as Heir; it is an irreparable nostalgia of youth; of the well-made straight-limbed body of her cousin; of the generous unstained spirit. A betrayal of the man she loved, who is neither young nor straight-limbed nor stainless of heart. . . .

"You are silent, coz," Lincoln says to her.

She shakes her head and turns away. She is thinking of Richard again; now her cousin is little more than a boy and she remembers with longing the wonder and midnight heart of the King.

"Another day of waiting," Elizabeth says, abruptly rising and crossing the Hall. She gives utterance to what they are all thinking: that somewhere two or three hundred miles south the fate of England and of all of them is being fought out.

It is Jean of Gloucester who goes to her, who loves her and who has the sensitive constant wound of the disinherited. He stands beside her in a deep stone bay curtained with Warwick red and white. "He will win, Elizabeth," the bastard son of Richard whispers.

She glances up; to the lofty oak ceiling blazoned with York White Roses set in the Sunne-in-Splendour. Richard's work at Sheriff Hutton. His castle as Captain of the North under Edward the Fourth. She cannot; dare not reply. The moment holds too much.

Nesfield shoves back his chair. He is wearing an old quilted jack and thigh boots. "Are you coming, lad?" he says to Warwick. For oddly, the tough henchman has taken a fancy to the weak-witted lad and Warwick follows him about like a pup.

They go out together. Lincoln rises. "A game of chess?" he remarks to Jean of Gloucester.

It is eight o'clock in the evening. Nesfield is beside the flickering hearth, for there is a tang in these Northern nights even in August. He is teaching young Warwick how to wind a crossbow. The lad is intent, fumbling with the silken cord, all childish smiles and awkwardness.

"Take this steel crosspiece," Nesfield says gruffly. "Plant it point downward. Now grasp the wooden stock with one hand, the left; and with the right, do you crank clockwise."

Warwick's hand slips, the silken cord runs through the notched winding gear. He looks up baffled. Beside him is a handsome crossbow case covered in blue and murrey velvet. The case is crested with Bull and Bear badges and the bow is a gift from the boy's father, Clarence.

"Now, now," Nesfield reproves him. "You don't start right, Ned. Everything is in starting right. In winding crossbows, as in other matters."

Nesfield breaks off; rises catlike to his feet. The Hall is shrunk in shadows and there is a glint of weapons from the wall. He has heard a bell without. It is the watchman's bell at the postern gate. He stands, listening. Again sounds that small insistent clamour in the night.

Nesfield walks slowly toward the doorway; and now appears a red glow of torches bloodying the shadows. A helmeted guard bursts in.

"Lord Stanley without, Captain!"

Nesfield considers. The fingers of one hand twitch; his swordarm. He hesitates over his word. But is not Stanley King Richard's field commander? Abruptly Nesfield nods. "Admit Lord Stanley," he directs.

Beside the hearth, young Warwick still clasps the crossbow. John Nesfield stands erect and waiting.

And here comes valiant Tom Stanley, bulling his way in, hot with riding, helmet dented, boots caked with blood and dust. Stanley the warrior. His shrewd eyes dart about. Behind him crowd two score liveried Derbyshiremen, wearing Stanley crimson beneath their steel jacks. "Nesfield?" Lord Stanley exclaims. His tone is that of an angry, righteous man.

Nesfield's hand falls. "Milord—" he says only.

"Where is the Princess Elizabeth?" Stanley demands.

Nesfield gazes at Stanley, the High Steward of his master, King Richard. Suddenly he blinks and chokes a cry. He has seen something and his heart cracks.

"No, my God!" Nesfield bursts out. "No!"

For about Lord Stanley's swordarm is bound a green and white ribbon. . . .

❂✱✦✱❂✱✦✱❂✱✦✱❂

ELIZABETH has heard the bridles in the court, the champ of horses and the clanking of iron. Hurriedly she rises, slips into a robe of murrey furred with vair. She flees down the dark stair, clutching a candle. She is cold, cold as Anne; the cold within and the cold without, centuried in this winding stone. She bursts into the Hall, where the fire dies in the black hearth, the fond piteous child of York stands with the bright bow, Nesfield stares from his dark, cruel and lonely face—and Stanley like a frowning husband waits at the head of his armour.

"Stanley!" Elizabeth's voice breaks.

Stanley has taken off his dented helmet. His bullet crop gleams faintly and the old white scar of his councilhood. Bloody Friday at the Tower.

"Leave us," Stanley orders. "And take these two."

The Derbyshire lieutenant understands. They have been through much these last hours, he and his master. He escorts Nesfield and Ned of Warwick from the Hall.

Stanley turns. "I've come to take you away, Elizabeth," he informs her. His tone is quite different from that used on Nesfield: a mixture of respect and admonition.

But the battle? Has Stanley forgot the battle? Elizabeth stares, incredulous. He glances away. His men have left a single torch in an iron link upon the wall. The red glow falls on Stanley, his lean dry face, his glinting armour.

"Redmoor Plain," he says to Elizabeth. "We encountered twelve thousand and broke them. A work of two hours."

Twelve thousand! What is Stanley talking about? She knows that Henry Tudor could have mustered no such company.

"The fighting is done," Stanley assures her. "It remains to heal England's wounds. A new time and a monarchy of peace."

All this: Richard could have said this, certainly. No man wanted peace more than Richard. But somehow—

"And is the King safe?" she asks.

"The King is in excellent health, Elizabeth," he replies.

"But did you see him safe?" she insists.

"I come straight from His Majesty's presence," Stanley responds. "His first thought was of you."

She catches her breath. Her heart soars. She knew it; she always knew it! They would go back, she and Richard. Time would return—the winter dusk, the lights of Westminster, the river surging on forever past these Norman stones and great drawbridges of the soul. Elizabeth, sister and niece of kings; daughter of monarchy. . . .

Still he will not look at her, meet her glance. The torchlight flickers on his face, a warglow under the great shadows, the huge silent Hall. "How soon will you be ready?" he asks abruptly.

Ready? But she has promised to wait for Richard at Sheriff Hutton. That was their plan.

"You are to come with me," Stanley tells her. "Such is Milord the King's command."

She stares at him, restless in the torchflare; and suddenly she sees the green and white brassard; she sees the Tudor ribbon. Elizabeth puts a hand to her mouth. . . .

"You come from Tudor?" she whispers.

Stanley lowers at her. "I come from His Majesty, Our Dread Lord Henry the Seventh."

She trembles, the cold seeping into her blood, into her young warm body. "What have you done with the King?" she cries.

"The King, mistress, is in Leicester town. That hellhound Richard is dead."

"You murdered him!" she blazes. "Betrayed and murdered!"

Stanley regards her. Never a woman, no matter her degree, may daunt Tom Stanley. Is not this the Yorkist knight, reeking with Lancastrian blood, that burst on Queen Margaret at Little Malvern Priory one crimson morning in May to roar the butchery of her son?

"You least of any soul living have cause to regret that bloody dog," Stanley says. He does not roar at Elizabeth. She will be his queen one day. "Our glorious Henry has avenged a fearful deed—the slaying of your brothers, Edward and Richard."

"My brothers are alive!" Elizabeth retorts. "How dare you, Stanley? Alive and in the Tower."

He shakes his head. "D'ye believe that, lass? Richard lied to you. Tricked you. Your brothers are dead. They have been dead this twelvemonth; aye, mayhap more."

She gropes, hands fluttering. Red-wavering shadows close on her. "Dead?"

"Our men have possession of the Tower. They have searched every apartment—every vault."

"And what did they find?" Her voice sobbing in the stone silence, in the Norman night.

"Nothing. . . ."

She looks up, tears shining. "Nothing? Then they are not dead. My brothers are not dead. Stanley, you lie!"

He checks an impulse to buffet her. She will be his queen; the union of the Roses—as it is already spoken of. Queens have been deadly ere this. Remember Elizabeth Woodeville.

"Nonsense," he replies contemptuously. "Certes, they are dead. Would not Richard have displayed them, if he could? He is a murderer, the worst of all. A child-killer. The people have cast him out."

She recalls something her mother once said. An appalling thing. "He will go down in Time's charterbook," Lady Grey had vowed. "The worst King; the worst villain; the worst man—of all. The worst—the worst—the worst. And I—I shall see to it." And Lady Grey had smiled at her daughter.

But Elizabeth will not let Lady Grey and the others have their way; these old, these hateworn, these life-spoilers. As long as one person remembers . . . and in her anguish the girl sees again the Falcon, England's flashing captain that had ridden out with gage of battle. "How did Richard die?" she wants to know. "Most valourously, in the midst of his foes? Fighting until all breath was quenched?"

Stanley stares at her, astonished. "How did you know?" he exclaims.

"I know Richard," she answers; and her voice now is quiet. She is pale in the warlight. "He died a king. . . ."

"He died at the foot of his Standard," Stanley says. "He overthrew Brandon and Cheyney before we—" and he glances away.

She is fierce with scorn. "Before you Stanleys destroyed him with treachery!"

He comes back to her, the old evil face, a face of craft and cruelty. "You forget, mistress, that he was the murderer of

your brothers—of those tender babes, Edward and Richard.
Ne'er was such a deed seen in England."

She stands alone, light flickering on her in the midst of an
immense shadow. She will always be alone. Always this Saint
Bartholomew Even of her soul. How is it that she had not
known this—that she too would die with Richard? And she
remembers, she remembers! How torn and haggard he was;
how driven. Night had entered him and he had entered
Night. How little she had been able to help him. . . .

"How soon will you be ready to ride?" Stanley inquires,
once more.

"Henry wishes to marry? He is hot to marry?" She has a
bitter smile.

Stanley swallows hard. "His Mighty Highness, Henry, by
the Grace of God, King . . . may deign to marry Elizabeth
Plantagenet, Princess Royal and Heiress of England. . . ."

Lady Grey will be pleased. This is what she has longed
for: this sonorous moment of queenship. But Elizabeth, ah
Elizabeth knows her value. She has a price. "And my
brothers?" she demands. "Edward and Richard?"

Stanley shrugs. "Dead, I tell you."

"You have not found them," she reminds him. "Nay, I do
not think you will ever find them. But if they be dead, it
was not King Richard killed them."

Stanley lifts his hands.

"Oh, I know you hate him. All of you," she goes on, defiant. "But you don't hate him for my brothers. Nor for my
Uncle Rivers nor my brother Grey. Nor for Hastings. For
none o' these." She pauses, breathing, eyes flaring. "You
hate Richard because he was brave and generous and wise.
Because he had the hearts of the people. Because he was a
king! 'Tis why you hate him, Milord Stanley."

Stanley flushes. One finger taps his helmet. "A murderer,"
he says. "We delivered you, mistress. Snatched you from his
blood-smeared grasp."

She gazes at him, the turncoat, the mercenary of the

Welsh-French Usurper. "Henry must not accuse Richard of my brothers," she gasps.

"Must not! Must not!" Stanley rages—as Norfolk once had raged at Elizabeth. "D'ye wish your head broke, mistress? Who are ye to demand and parley? A disinherited bastard!"

But Stanley goes too far. Morton would not approve. Elizabeth catches him up. "Nay, I cannot be bastard, milord. Or your master would not have me."

Stanley clamps a brake on his choler. "Pardon me, mistress."

She nods. "Richard must not be accused," she repeats. "I'll not marry Richard's defamer."

"Lady Grey will see to that," Stanley retorts.

"Nothing!" she cries. "Nothing that any of you can do! Shut me in a nunnery. But you need me, Stanley. You need me to royal that fire-new crown of Henry's."

She is right. In his heart, Stanley knows. He sighs. "Henry will decide," he replies.

Time; a kingdom is waiting for Elizabeth Plantagenet. She turns, to go into the iron shadow, the Norman dark. Her race, her redgold tragic splendour . . . it is midnight, the midnight of her House. And now! Now! The sound of York time . . . the clock, the trickling sand, the lovely unbearable echoes of great bells . . . six sons. . . .

But if one person remembers what Richard was truly like, one person that loved him, then he will not perish in lies and horror. . . .

She hovers at the azure velvet arras, her murrey against the blue. This is her night: York's final night—the Even of Saint Bartholomew. Time has stopped for her. Time has stopped with hands that point forever to love and death. . . .

Elizabeth glances at Stanley. "I am ready, Lord Stanley," she says.